"YOU SAY YOU WOULD DO ANYTHING FOR ASHBURY. JUST HOW FAR WOULD YOU GO?"

She spoke with the fervency of a prayer. "I would do anything to gain Ashbury, milord, anything. But I have naught to offer you—" her gaze flitted away and her voice caught breathlessly, "—save myself."

His fingers stroked her nape, sending fiery shivers coursing through her veins. "I would understand you, Kathryn. You would give yourself to me, without question, if I relinquish my possession of this humble keep?"

Kathryn closed her eyes, unable to look at him. "Yes," she whispered . . . and knew it for the truth.

My Cherished Enemy

Samantha James

AVON BOOKS ◆ NEW YORK

MY CHERISHED ENEMY is an original publication of Avon Books. This work has never before appeared in book form. This work is a novel. Any similarity to actual persons or events is purely coincidental.

AVON BOOKS
A division of
The Hearst Corporation
1350 Avenue of the Americas
New York, New York 10019

Copyright © 1992 by Sandra Kleinschmit
Inside cover author photograph by Almquist Studios
Published by arrangement with the author
Library of Congress Catalog Card Number: 91-92434
ISBN: 0-380-76692-2

First Avon Books Printing: May 1992

AVON TRADEMARK REG. U.S. PAT. OFF. AND IN OTHER COUNTRIES, MARCA REGISTRADA, HECHO EN U.S.A.

Printed in the U.S.A.

RA   10   9   8   7   6   5   4   3   2   1

Prologue

"I cannot do this, my lady! I—I fear they will find us and we will both be killed, the babe and I!"

The high thin voice belonged to a young girl of no more than fourteen summers. Her body was stout and tall for her age; she came from hearty peasant stock. She knelt in the rushes before the Lady Elaine, the woman she had served as long as she could remember.

"Gerda, you must!" Elaine spoke sharply, in a tone Gerda had heard but rarely. "If my son is to be saved, it is you who must save him. You must flee this keep and take Peter back to Sedgewick." Her eyes briefly sought the sunken gaze of the woman who lay abed, Lady Claire Chandler, but it was Gerda to whom she spoke.

"We are marked, all of us here. You have seen with your own eyes the bloodlust of our attackers. They spare no one—not the farmer in the field, nor women or children. I prayed it would not come to this, but they know not yet of you or Peter."

Outside in the bailey, the skirmish raged anew. The ramparts were filled with the sounds of bat-

1

tle. Harsh guttural sounds tore from men's throats. Sword met sword, the clang of steel against steel ringing through the air. A terrified scream reached a shattering crescendo, then fell eerily silent.

The raiders were sly and cunning. Led by Richard of Ashbury, they had entered the keep as friends, not foes, seeking an alliance with Claire's husband Geoffrey, castellan of Ramsay Keep. They had barely passed through the gates than the unwarranted siege had begun.

For three days, Ramsay Keep's defenders had fought a valiant but losing battle. Claire's husband Geoffrey was left with only one choice. Yet Geoffrey's offer of surrender had been met with treachery. He was struck down from behind and still the raiders stormed the walls; still they maimed and killed.

Elaine's tone grew beseeching. "Please, Gerda! I plead for the life of my son. These raiders take no prisoners. Their horses trample the dead and the dying. I would have Peter spared—and you as well!"

Gerda began to tremble. She had been with the Lady Elaine forever, it seemed to her young heart. Lady Elaine had laughed with her, scolded her, protected her from her father who was wont to wield the stick whenever he was in his cups. Indeed, it was her father's wrath which had caused the injury to her knee when she was but a babe. Others ridiculed her clumsy gait, her awkward progress whenever she tried to hurry. But the Lady Elaine guided gently and praised her care of the little lord Peter. Who would guide her when her lady was gone?

Gerda was immediately ashamed of her selfishness. With eyes like the summer sky and hair as gold and glistening as a radiant halo, her lady was a vision from above, Gerda thought. And she was good and kind and sweet.

She began to weep. " 'Tis so unfair, my lady! If your lord were here, these wretched robber barons would not have dared attack Sir Geoffrey or any of his vassals!"

So be it, Elaine agreed silently. Her heart twisted. Gerda's words rang pure and true indeed. Sir Geoffrey held this keep for her husband, Guy de Marche, Earl of Sedgewick, who was a man of the times. Like all men of his rank, Guy had trained as a warrior throughout his life. His prowess as a knight was known from the mist-shrouded land of Scotland to the rugged coastline of nearby Cornwall. He was a fierce and lethal force in combat, deadly and precise and fearless. But Guy de Marche was also a man of great honor and he ruled his fiefs with a just and noble hand.

But Guy was half a world away. Both he and Sir Hugh Bainbridge, Claire's brother, were on crusade. They had been gone nearly a twelvemonth.

"Please, milady, will you not come?" Gerda begged her mistress. "You say this keep and all who dwell within are doomed. Come with me, I beg of you!"

At this, Claire stirred slightly. She groped for Elaine's hand. "The girl is right, Elaine." What might have passed for a smile crossed lips that were once rosy and full with the sweetness of youth. Russet-brown hair lay matted and drab against the pillow. Her skin was white and colorless, her breathing shallow and raspy. Elaine despised herself for the thought, but she prayed that this ague which had sapped the life breath from her friend these past weeks would soon send her to God's kingdom. Better that than death at the hands of the treacherous butchers who ravaged the village and even now pillaged the keep.

"Nay," Elaine said softly. "I cannot leave you, Claire. Your brother Sir Hugh has served my husband too long and too well for me to forsake those he holds dear. And you, his sister, are my dearest friend in all the land. As there is honor among the living, there is honor among the dead. I ask only that you save the life of my son." She touched the dry parchment-thin cheek of her friend. "I fear there is not much time. The fighting grows close. Quickly now, I bid you tell Gerda the way to the monastery. The monks there will see that they are sent to Sedgewick."

Claire closed her eyes in silent assent. In a voice grown weak from strain and sickness, she told the girl of the secret staircase behind the bedstead. The staircase led to a tunnel that led outside the keep to a hut near the woods. It was but a short distance to the monastery. From there the girl could seek refuge and escort back to Sedgewick.

At last Claire slumped back against the pillows. Elaine lifted the sleeping child from the wooden cradle and gazed down at him. Tears glistened in her eyes.

She touched his cheek gently, marveling that God had given her such a wondrous gift. She buried her face against his unruly dark curls. Peter was the image of Guy, every bit his father's son. He had been conceived on her last night with Guy. This Elaine knew with all her heart. Her one regret was that her beloved husband had yet to see the fruit of their love.

God, how she loved them both! With tears blurring her vision, she drew back to trace the babe's features one by one: winged brows as black as night, tiny nubbin nose, the beautifully shaped mouth that even now held a touch of his father's sternness.

The tears spilled over. She would never see Peter grow sturdy and tall as the oak trees which grew near Sedgewick . . . as tall and proud as his warrior father. But even as she dried her tears, Elaine refused to think of death. She thought only of life . . . her son's life.

Very gently she wrapped him in swaddling cloth and gave him over to Gerda. The child slept on, cuddled against the young girl's breast. Elaine slipped open the hidden panel behind the bed and turned to Gerda.

She clasped her sturdy young shoulders and looked the girl straight in the eye. "I trust you in this, as I have never trusted anyone in my life, Gerda."

Gerda looked ready to cry. "I—I will not fail you, mistress."

Elaine squeezed her shoulders and smiled. "I know," she said simply.

Gerda clutched the babe in one arm, a tallow candle in the other. She stood in the threshold of the secret stairway, frightened for herself, frightened for her lady. Tears streamed down her cheeks. Her shoulders shook with the force of her emotions. "I will pray for you, my lady," she sobbed. "I will pray that what you fear will not come to pass and you will once again grace the hall at Sedgewick."

And she would pray for naught. But Elaine withheld these words; instead she tipped the girl's chin up. "I know you do not understand, Gerda," she said softly. "But I do what I must."

"But you choose to die."

Elaine was already shaking her head, a sad, faintly wistful expression on her face. Her hand came out to rest for an instant on the cloth covering her child's head. "No," she said quietly, "I do not choose to die. I choose for *him* to live." She gave the girl a gentle shove toward the darkened stairway. "Now go, Gerda. Fly as if the devil himself were at your heels and do not stop until you are safely inside the monastery."

They shared one last hasty embrace. Elaine watched until Gerda disappeared from sight and the echo of her shuffling footsteps became faint and distant. At last she closed the heavy door and slid the secret panel back into place.

When she turned she found Claire's eyes upon her, clearer than they had been for days. She crossed to her quickly and sat down on the edge of the bed.

Claire feebly gripped her hand. "Had I known this would happen," she murmured, "I would never have bid you come to me." She tried to smile. "But I wanted to see you and Peter one last time," she whispered. "And I am afraid I am much like Gerda, for I fear I do not understand why this is happening— why Geoffrey was killed. Why Richard of Ashbury covets this humble keep."

" 'Tis not your fault." Elaine soothed her with a tender touch upon her brow. "King Stephen's rule has been naught but a time of lawlessness and greed. 'Tis said that vassals battle one another throughout the land, while Stephen tries vainly to restore order, to tame the pattern of violence. As for why, I cannot say. To war," she said sadly, "is the nature of men. And Richard is an evil man. He seeks that which is not his, for that reason alone." She could not change the course of events and so she must accept them.

Elaine stayed by Claire's side throughout the long day, listening as the battle drew nearer ... ever nearer. Dusk crept through the clouds hovering on the dismal horizon. The shadow of darkness—the veil of death—crept within the chamber. Elaine felt the strength wane from Claire's hand and knew that she slipped into sleep . . . sleep eternal.

Hers was a hurt too deep for tears. Elaine lovingly folded Claire's hands upon her breast, silently praying she would be granted a Christian burial. She was dimly aware that the crush of battle had extended into the great hall below.

She fleetingly thought of following Gerda and saving herself. But the notion had no sooner chased through her mind than fate decreed otherwise.

There was a heavy footfall of steps in the passage outside. The door was flung open.

A great hulk of a man filled the doorway of the chamber, dark and evil-looking. A vile lust gleamed in his eyes. Blood dripped from his sword onto the rushes.

But Elaine drew herself up proudly, quaking inside but determined to show no fear. She was the wife of Lord Guy de Marche, Earl of Sedgewick.

The man stepped forward.

Elaine began to pray. She prayed that Gerda's journey back to Sedgewick would be a safe one. She prayed that the Lord would watch over Guy and keep him safe from the heathens in the Holy Land. She prayed that Guy would soon return home to Sedgewick to love and protect the son he had never seen . . .

May her soul rest in peace.

Chapter 1

Spring 1155

" . . . may her soul rest in peace."

Guy de Marche, Earl of Sedgewick, knelt before the grave of his beloved wife. The words were the closest thing to a prayer he was able to summon, though his countenance was far from prayerlike. For even as he spoke the words, all the curses of hell sprang forth within him, fighting to be free. His mind was consumed by thoughts of but one man.

Richard of Ashbury.

High above, Ramsay Keep squatted on the hilltop. A melancholy veil of fog surrounded its crenelated towers and jagged outline, a reflection of Guy's dark and somber mood. For two long years Richard had laid claim to the keep, but no more . . . *no more*. Guy's battle to regain Ramsay Keep had been satisfying short, yet the taste of victory was like dust in his mouth.

He rose to his feet, a powerful figure garbed in the fiercesome trappings of war, his helmet tucked under his arm. Behind him, atop the rise that guarded the gravesite, a body of mounted men watched somberly, awaiting his command. The silence was broken only by the occasional snort of a stallion and the gurgling rush of the stream, swollen by early-spring rainwater.

Another man walked slowly to his side. Guy stirred only when a rough callused hand clapped against his shoulder. Neither man spoke; yet their very silence was rife with words unspoken.

Sir Hugh Bainbridge gazed solemnly at the other man's profile. His sister Claire was buried but a few paces distant from Lady Elaine, and so he had more than an inkling of the pain Guy felt. He called Guy lord as well as friend. As a boy, Hugh had been page to Guy's squire and served at his side whenever the call to duty arose. Hugh had shared in all his lord's triumphs—both on the battlefield and off—just as he shared this loss as well.

It was Guy who broke the silence. "Why," he murmured in a voice thick with emotions held deep in his heart, "must the Lord see fit to give with one hand and take with the other?"

Hugh gleaned his meaning only too well. Guy's marriage to Elaine was truly nothing short of a miracle. Theirs had been an arranged marriage, and yet the two had fallen madly in love with one another. Hugh and his friends had chided Guy greatly about his adoration of his wife, for no one liked the ladies more than Guy. But lo and behold, Guy found marriage to the lovely Elaine no burden at all and it proved the end of his wenching.

In truth, Hugh had faintly envied Guy's happy contentment and his desire to settle into his estates and concentrate his efforts at building a family. Hugh was a knight bachelor and possessed no holdings of his own; he was certainly not yet sought after as a husband. Indeed, it was only of late that he'd even begun to think of gaining a wife . . .

"I should have been here." Guy's mouth twisted as he sucked in a harsh breath. "God damn it, I should have been here!"

His violence stunned his men-at-arms. They glanced uneasily at each other and wisely moved away, leaving the two knights alone.

Hugh was the only one who was not startled. "Do you think I have not said the same a thousand times since?" he replied unevenly. "We cannot alter the course of our lives—we cannot change the past."

"And I," Guy ground out tightly, "cannot forget!"

"You had no choice but to honor the call to arms."

"The call to arms?" Guy's laugh was bitter. "My friend, you and I have been gone from this land for three harvests! Half of that time was spent in that bloody dungeon in Toulouse!"

And it was there that Guy discovered the existence of his son Peter. It was there he was also told of his wife's murder. Guy had been so shocked— he'd had no idea Elaine was even with child—and then wondrously elated at the news of his heir. From the heights of happiness . . . to the dregs of hell . . . in the blink of an eye.

"Had we not been there," Hugh reminded him, "we might never have run into Henry's forces when we were finally able to escape. And methinks it less than wise to be on the opposite side of our new king."

"True indeed," Guy agreed with a grim smile. "I had no choice but to pledge my sword to Henry."

Hugh's shaggy brownish-gold eyebrows shot up. "You regret it?" he asked in some surprise.

Guy shook his head. "Nay," he replied. "Henry strikes me as a man of many faces. But I think 'tis well that with Stephen's death Henry has reclaimed the throne of England. I suspect 'twill not be long before this land is on the road to recovery." He fell silent for a moment. "And I gained Henry's sanction to recoup that which was taken from me."

"Which you have done."

"Which I have done."

Guy's gaze flitted to the gates of the keep. His tone was harsh, even bitter. Hugh watched as a mask of hardness settled over his handsome features. Seeing it, Hugh suffered a prickly sense of unease. He knew Guy as well as anyone—better than anyone—yet in that moment he felt he knew him not at all.

Guy caught his friend's uncertain expression and gave a twist of his lips. His next words were not what Hugh expected.

"Your brother-in-law Geoffrey served me long and well in holding this keep, my friend. Now he is gone, and your sister as well. 'Tis time you were rewarded for your loyalty, Hugh. Therefore I offer Ramsay Keep to you—though not to hold this manor and lands for me and mine—but as your own, to do with as you will."

For just an instant Hugh was stunned. Ramsay Keep was a fine and wealthy manor—not nearly so grand as Sedgewick, but it was all he had ever dreamed of. And yet . . .

"May I speak plain, my lord? Not as your servant, but as your friend?"

"I would have it no other way, Hugh. You know that."

Hugh smiled slightly, but it was a smile that held no small amount of sadness. "Your generosity overwhelms me, Guy. Would that I could accept it. But mayhap 'tis just as you said. Claire died here, and 'twas here that Geoffrey and the Lady Elaine were slain most cruelly." He hesitated. "I fear I could never forget the evil that was done here."

Guy was silent for a moment. "Then you are with me?" he said finally. "I need you now more than ever, Hugh. But only if you are willing."

There was no further need for talk. Guy turned and strode into the circle of stampeding horses and fully armed men. He paused only for one last glance at Ramsay Keep.

His eyes squeezed shut. Elaine, he thought desperately. So sweet. So gentle and tender . . . *Elaine!* He screamed her name in silent anguish. Pain ripped through him like a sword from throat to groin. He saw her as she had once been, golden and gloriously beautiful, her spun-gold hair spinning about her, laughing in that lilting musical voice of hers. He had always teased her that she had been crafted by the angels in heaven . . . and it was there she now dwelled.

It was terrible, my lord . . . horrible!

The words Gerda sobbed out upon his arrival back at Sedgewick took the form of vivid, horrible images in his mind's eye.

Richard and his men came in the name of peace. Then they raped and killed and butchered . . . They spared no one, not women, not children. They showed no mercy, my lord. No mercy at all!

The vision in his mind shifted and twisted, like a windswept fog . . . He saw Elaine as she must have died, lying bruised and violated in a crimson pool of blood . . .

He felt he'd been catapulted once again into the wild foray of battle, seized by a red mist of rage deeper than anything he could ever remember. His head, his blood pounded with the heat of his wrath.

His eyes opened. His wide unblinking gaze took in the final resting place of his wife and the many others who littered the grassy hillside.

"Your death will be avenged, my love," he murmured aloud. "This I promise. This I vow, by all the saints."

Hugh nudged his destrier beside him. "It does not end here, does it?" he said quietly.

Guy's silver eyes glittered like steel. His face had taken on an expression which would have frightened many a brave man. Guy de Marche was not a man given lightly to revenge; he fought when the need arose, to protect and defend, but he was not a cruel man. Yet Hugh did not pretend to misunderstand the bent of Guy's mind at this moment, the raging storm roiling within him, swirling and growing stronger by the second.

"Nay." Guy stared straight ahead. Never had a single word sounded so ominous and deadly. "It only begins."

He wheeled his mount to face his men-at-arms. "We ride for Ashbury!" he shouted. Sunlight glinted against the steel of his sword as he ripped it from his scabbard and held it high above his head. A raucous cheer went up from the men. With the thunder of hooves shaking the earth, they raced madly after the Earl of Sedgewick.

Thus began his quest for vengeance.

The great hall at Ashbury Keep boiled with life like stew in a kettle, but the ladies' bower was calm and peaceful. Several serving girls sat beneath the window, winding wool into long skeins. Another sat spooling thread onto bobbins. The rhythmic clack of the loom in the corner filled the air, a soothing backdrop to the talk and laughter exchanged between the servants. Another woman, daintily blond and beauteous, smiled and nodded and occasionally joined in the chatter.

From her place near the doorway, Kathryn of Ashbury fixed brilliant green eyes upon her sister, her expression disturbed. How, she wondered silently, would Elizabeth take the news? Would she cry? Pretend she understood and then run into her room and weep silently into her pillow? A feeling of guilt wound through Kathryn. Either way, she wasn't sure she could stand it.

Elizabeth was happy here, happy and content. The bower was a place of privacy, where Elizabeth was able to relax and be herself; she was neither timid nor fearful, or plagued by the memories of a past that seemed to never drift out of reach.

A pang swept through Kathryn. In the four years that had transpired since their parents' death, she had done her best to shield Elizabeth from further hurt. And now, all was well. All was quiet and serene and settled in Elizabeth's small world. But with what she was about to tell her . . .

She stepped into the bower. "Leave us, please," she said briefly to the three serving girls. Two scrambled to their feet immediately. But Helga, the eldest of the three, complied with far less haste.

Kathryn watched as Helga slowly pushed aside her distaff, praying for a patience she had never been blessed with. The girl then began neatly piling the skeins next to her. Kathryn pressed her lips together; she knew better than to believe the girl wished to make herself useful, for she was well acquainted with her laziness. More than likely, Helga's supposed tidiness was meant to irritate.

It was all Kathryn could do to hold her tongue. Helga's grandfather had been the smith at Ashbury even before Kathryn's father Sir Damien had been lord of the manor. The old man had passed on several years ago, and Helga, whose parents were also dead, had been brought into the keep to serve

as ladies' maid. But she had done precious little in
the way of serving the two ladies of the household;
Kathryn and Elizabeth saw to the upkeep of their
clothing and chambers, and Kathryn had quickly
learned she could not speak freely before Helga.
She suspected her of carrying tales to her uncle
Richard—as if her uncle were not already eager
enough to see his niece take the bite of the lash
or the cuff of his hand.

Yet Kathryn could not dismiss the girl either,
though Richard had turned matters of the household over to her. To do so would be tantamount to
admitting defeat. Her uncle would glory in knowing
he had provoked and bested her; Kathryn refused to
give him the satisfaction.

But it also appeared Helga was not above using
her womanly attributes to advance her position.
The girl openly returned the admiring gazes of
her uncle's knights; she laughed when a male
hand trespassed boldly beneath her skirts. And
of late, Helga hinted that she had oft shared
Richard's bed. Kathryn had long since ceased to
be shocked. Richard's wife had died in childbed long ago. Since that time, countless serving
wenches had warmed his bed. If Helga were the
latest, Kathryn feared the girl's insolence would
know no bounds.

Helga continued with the task. The bodice of her
rough woolen gown gaped open but the girl paid
no heed. Kathryn lost her temper at last. "Make
haste, girl," she snapped. "There are no knights
here to ogle your charms and I would speak with
my sister."

The girl withdrew at last, but not without bestow-
ing on her mistress a triumphant smile. Kathryn
ignored it, closed the heavy wooden door, and
prepared to face her sister.

Elizabeth had pushed aside the loom. Kathryn turned and beheld her sister gazing at her with a slight smile curling her lovely mouth. Her sheer veil only enhanced the shining glory of her hair. Like the finest beams of the sun, the shimmering strands sparkled like a pale golden waterfall down her back. Her face was small and heart-shaped, her eyes the color of the sky on a warm spring day.

Seeing her sister thus, Kathryn felt a painful squeeze of her heart. Elizabeth deserved so much more than what she had—spending her days cloistered in this bower for fear of the outside world . . . a world filled with men who knew nothing but war and lust. If only their parents had lived, her sister would have wanted for nothing! There would have been a husband, and children Elizabeth could love and cherish.

But dreams were for naught. Dreams were for children . . . and fools. It was a lesson Kathryn had learned well—within months of the time she and Elizabeth were given over to their uncle's care. Richard was their father's bastard half-brother; King Stephen was so busy trying to restore order to his lawless kingdom he had little time for other affairs. He had wasted no time in granting all of Sir Damien's lands and holdings to Richard. There was little two young maids of fourteen and fifteen could do. Now, both women were subject to the whim and will of a man whose moods grew fouler with each passing day.

Kathryn's shoulders slumped. She was being foolish, she told herself bleakly, foolish and fanciful. It was possible their lot in life would have been little better had their father lived. Had Sir Damien chosen to marry either of them off, it would have been for one reason only—to unite lands and holdings. Not for love, Kathryn thought bitterly, *never* for love.

As women, they had little say in the matter. But at least Ashbury Keep would have been *theirs* . . .

Kathryn did not aspire to happiness. She aspired to freedom, to at least some measure of it, however small. She yearned to live her life as *she* willed— to make her own choices and decisions—and not beneath the domineering hand of her uncle.

Perhaps she could not gain all that she sought, but she was not like Elizabeth, content to gaze out at the world and never really be a part of it. But there was a tiny kernel of hope inside her. It was blighted hope, perhaps. But it was all she had.

And it was this which brought her here.

Kathryn crossed to where her sister still sat upon a low-backed chair. She knew of no easy way to break the news to Elizabeth and so she simply came out with it. "Roderick has asked me to marry him," she said quietly.

Elizabeth stared at her numbly. "Marriage?" she echoed. Her lovely forehead pleated with a frown. "Surely you jest. Why, Uncle seized our dower lands long ago. Even if he approved, what would you bring to the marriage—"

"I would bring naught but myself." The subject of their dower lands still rankled; Kathryn cut her sister off more sharply than she intended, but Elizabeth didn't notice. She still looked rather stunned. Well, better that than tears. "Roderick is willing to take me as I am," she added quietly.

Elizabeth rose from her chair, an odd expression on her face. "Forgive me, sister. But I cannot see you a meek and servile wife."

Meek and servile? The thought made Kathryn smile, a smile that was all too rare these days. "In this I fear you are right," she admitted.

A hint of puzzled hurt crept into Elizabeth's beautiful blue eyes. "I do not understand," she murmured. "I do not understand why you should wish to marry Roderick. You do not love him, surely!"

It was more an accusation than a question. A trickle of shame crept through Kathryn. For all that Elizabeth was younger by only a year, she was remarkably naive. Many times, she saw only the goodness in life; her heart was filled with hope and kindness.

Perhaps it was for the best, for Elizabeth had seen . . . what no woman should ever see.

Kathryn went to her and pulled her down on the cushions before the window. "Nay," she said quietly, "I do not love Roderick. I love no man." *Nor*, she added silently, *will I ever*. Since the death of her mother and father, she had known little of tenderness, save Elizabeth's. The world was a harsh one; it was a man's world, controlled by men. Their needs, their wants, their desires were all that mattered, and women were there only to fulfill those needs. In her heart Kathryn knew she had little choice but to tolerate the unfair treatment of her sex . . . but her rebellious mind refused such passive acceptance.

Elizabeth's lips began to tremble. "Then why? What will happen to me if you marry Roderick? He has a small fief of his own. No doubt you—you will leave here! I—I do not understand, Kathryn! Have I displeased you? Made you angry that you wish to quit this keep and be rid of me?" Her spiraling voice reflected her fears. "If you leave with Roderick, what will I do? I love Ashbury as much as you, but I could not stand it here without you, Kathryn! And Uncle refuses to let me take the veil!"

Kathryn's laugh was tinged with bitterness, but she sought to ease her sister's mind. "I do not seek to leave here, Elizabeth, for this is *our* home. It does not matter that our bastard uncle calls himself lord and master," she said fiercely. "When Father died, King Stephen granted his lands and our wardship to Uncle, but he has done naught but seek more, always more. 'Tis men whose laws say that we as women cannot pay homage; therefore it does little good for a woman to inherit! But in my mind, Ashbury is ours—yours and mine. And I make you a solemn vow here and now, Elizabeth. Someday Ashbury will be ours once again!"

Elizabeth gasped in horror. "How can you make such a sacred vow? Especially one you cannot hope to keep!"

Kathryn leaped to her feet, her eyes blazing. "I cannot go on like this any longer. If the past four years under Richard's thumb have taught me nothing else, I have learned that 'tis the way of men to take what they want. In Uncle's eyes, we are no more than servants. He makes us beg for what little we have—what belongs to us. And 'tis for this reason that I would ally myself with Roderick."

Elizabeth hesitated. She envied her sister, for Kathryn was quick and intelligent and witty—and not afraid of her own shadow as she was.

Kathryn's face softened when she saw her sister's confusion. "You still do not understand, do you?"

Elizabeth shook her head miserably.

"Uncle is driven by greed," Kathryn explained quietly. "He gave away our dower lands for one reason only—he seeks to keep us here with him forever. He fears a husband might challenge his claim on our father's lands."

Kathryn thought of Roderick, chief retainer of her uncle's knights. Many times in the last four years had Kathryn wished that she had been born a man so that she could challenge her uncle sword-to-sword for what was hers by right of birth. But being a woman, she must fight with what weapons were at hand.

And this was one time her womanhood might be a blessing and not a curse. Kathryn knew nothing of women's coquetry, but she was learning. She hadn't mistaken the flare of desire in Roderick's eyes; only this morning he had declared his love for her. With a touch, a word, she hoped to be able to sway him to the bent of her mind. She had prayed long and hard for freedom from her uncle's tyranny and God had led her to this crossroads. She despised the method and the means, but fate left her no other choice.

"There are still those knights who are loyal to us here, despite Uncle's attempts to roust them and replace them with his own." Her voice rang with quiet determination. "I am counting on that loyalty as well as Roderick's position and leadership to help us assume our rightful place here. Roderick has knights of his own loyal to him. With Richard gone and Roderick as my husband and protector, Ashbury will be ours once more."

Elizabeth's eyes grew wide and fearful. "Rebellion? You would dare a revolt against Uncle in his own keep?"

For just an instant Kathryn's eyes flared. Then she glanced quickly around the chamber. "Keep your voice down," she cautioned. " 'Tis the only way. Richard is a harsh and brutal lord. There are many who would gladly see him replaced." Elizabeth said nothing. After a moment, Kathryn shook her head sadly. "Tis not the way I would have it happen. And it may take time, but I see no other way."

"I—I think I understand." Elizabeth drew a long, shaky breath. "But must you *marry* Roderick in order to carry out this plan?"

"It is the only way," Kathryn replied calmly.

"But he stares at you so, when he thinks no one is looking. Methinks he is nearly as greedy as Uncle." Elizabeth shivered, thinking of the tawny-haired Roderick. He was tall and broad-shouldered, broader even than her uncle. And while he was handsome and not ill-mannered as some of the other knights, there was something about him . . .

"I do not like him, Kathryn." Elizabeth shuddered. "How can you even think of marrying him?"

"You like no man," her sister pointed out. And Elizabeth feared *every* man, though she was better at hiding it than she'd once been.

Elizabeth regarded her sister. No two sisters could possibly be more different, either in looks or demeanor. Kathryn was as dark as Elizabeth was fair; Kathryn was firm and unwavering, afraid of nothing, while she cowered here in her bower. Yet never had Elizabeth wished she were more like Kathryn than at this moment!

She wrung her hands. "If only I were more like you. If only I were as brave and strong as you! I am capable of nothing but hiding in this chamber like a child who fears the dark!"

Kathryn felt a wrenching pain in her chest. Her sister had witnessed their mother's violent rape and murder; it had gouged a wound which had never healed. Uncle called Elizabeth's fear of men unreasonable. But Kathryn understood. Countless nights she had held Elizabeth's shuddering body, her mind tortured by dreams in which she lived through that horrible day once again. For Elizabeth, the nightmare had never truly ended.

Warm fingers pressed against Elizabeth's trembling lips. "Hush," Kathryn said softly. "You are good and kind and sweet. I would have my sister no other way." They embraced tightly, but Elizabeth's delicate features were still etched with worry when she drew back.

"I still do not like the thought of you marrying Roderick," she said quietly. "Besides, what makes you think Uncle will permit it? He wishes to keep us under his thumb."

"He believes he controls Roderick," Kathryn reminded her. "Through Roderick, 'tis my hope Uncle will feel he has twice the power over me. But if he balks at granting consent, I plan to tell him I am with child."

Elizabeth gasped. "With child!" Her gaze slid down her sister's slender form.

"I am not. I am as untouched as you." Kathryn laughed. Elizabeth was as shocked as she had expected. They both knew what went on between men and women, especially Elizabeth. As for Kathryn, some of her uncle's knights were crude and lewd. They spared no thought for her tender ears. Kathryn had no doubt that such an act was vile and disgusting. It was but one more way men sought to subjugate women and the thought hardened her heart.

The words she spoke were bitter. "Richard has Ashbury. He has usurped other lands as well." Her soft lips curled with disdain. "And he thinks he has gained honor to his name. But for once, that is well and good. The shame of his niece giving birth to a bastard is one he dare not take. He desires no further stain on his name."

Elizabeth folded her hands in her lap. "And so you think he will grant consent to your marriage to Roderick?"

"Aye."

Her sister regarded her somberly. "I fear men," she said softly, "while you scorn them. You swore that if we were ever free of Uncle, no man would conquer you. No man would claim you. Yet you would give yourself to Roderick." She shook her head. "This is not the time to be reckless and head-strong."

Kathryn lowered her eyes. Elizabeth had lit-tle interest in the outside world, but at times she showed unusual wisdom. Her sister's words pricked her deeply. Kathryn swallowed and went on bravely.

"I have prayed for deliverance, Elizabeth, and this is the course set out for me. Were I a man, I would challenge Uncle in battle for what is right-fully ours. Alas, I have the courage but not the strength. And no matter what the outcome, I will have the satisfaction of knowing the choice was mine. To Roderick, I am not just a mere vessel; I am an equal. It is the only way, Elizabeth, the only way. Marriage seems a small price to pay."

Elizabeth's gaze was troubled. "And when Uncle discovers you are not with child after all?"

"The deed will already be done."

Elizabeth watched her sister depart from the bower, her narrow shoulders stiff with pride. Kathryn possessed the same proud and stubborn spirit as their father. Indeed, he had fought to the death rather than surrender Ashbury to a band of raiders. She flinched at the memory. He'd been badly wounded during the fray, yet still he claimed victory. Two weeks later he'd died from infection.

Elizabeth loved Ashbury as much as Kathryn and their father did; she hated her uncle's presence here. Within these lofty stone walls, she felt secure. But it was love of Ashbury which had robbed her of the lives of both parents, and the knowledge pierced her chest like a knife blade.

Her hand fluttered to her breast. Dread filled her mind and heart, spreading like slow poison. "Kathryn, I fear you are too much like Father," she whispered aloud. "You may well succeed and claim Ashbury as your own. But at what cost to yourself?"

Early that evening Kathryn slipped outside the castle walls. A misty drizzle fell from the sky, but she paid no heed. She merely gathered her thin woolen cloak more tightly about her and draped the concealing hood over the braided coronet atop her head.

She stopped only once, when a waning sliver of sunlight streaked through the cloud blanket. To her right, fat sheep slouched in the pasture. To the left, the pounding waves of the sea crashed against the shore. She loved Cornwall, its wildness and its mystery. She stood for a moment, a still figure crowning a lonely hilltop. Then she hurried on.

She stopped when she reached the secluded covert where she was to meet Roderick. A prickly unease crept up her spine. Just for an instant, she had the strangest sensation she was being watched.

A tall figure stepped out from behind a thicket of spindly trees.

"Roderick!" She pushed back her hood and held out her hands, suddenly ashamed of her fleeting apprehension and reassured by his presence. He grasped her hands and gazed down at her. She did not miss the flare of approval in his eyes.

Aye, she thought, she had chosen well. Roderick was strong and quick-thinking, and, above all, ambitious. She was counting on his ambition to help her regain Ashbury. It was but a boon that he was pleasing to look upon. With his tawny-brown hair, his imposing stature and blazing golden eyes, he reminded her of the majestic lion gracing the silk tapestry her father had brought back from the Holy Land.

"Well?" One thick golden brow hiked upwards. "I can wait no longer for your answer, lady. Do you or do you not seek to be my wife?"

Her eyes lowered demurely. "I do," she said with the tiniest of smiles. She glanced up in time to see an expression of triumph settle on his features. Roderick had, she realized, never doubted her answer.

Kathryn found the notion vaguely disturbing. At times Roderick's behavior bordered on arrogant. But wasn't it true that this, too, might be a blessing in disguise?

She let him lead her beneath the shelter of a tree. His smile contained a rare flash of humor as he grandly spread his cloak upon the mossy ground and pulled her down upon it. She was surprised at his set expression when he turned to her. "I have thought long and hard about what you said earlier—that your uncle may balk at letting us marry."

Kathryn bit her lip. "I, too," she confessed.

"I fail to see how he can say me nay when I take you unto me with no marriage portion."

Her eyes flashed fire. Her chin shot up and her mouth opened, but before she could say a word Roderick chuckled. "You are very proud, my love. I like that, just as I have always admired the way you stand up to your uncle. But there is no need to do battle with me, sweet." The laughter went out of his eyes. "I will not let Richard stand in our way. If I must, I will snatch you from this place and we can be married at the monastery near Boscastle. The abbot there is a distant cousin of my father's and will give us no trouble. Once the deed is done and the marriage consummated, there is naught Richard can do."

His frankness made her flush with embarrassment, but she laid her hand on his arm. "There may be another way." Her skin pinkened further. "I—I thought we might tell him I am with child."

Roderick laughed heartily. "You are a cunning one, aren't you? Well, perhaps you have reason. I've oft thought that Richard has not done right by you and your sister. Mayhap we will change that once we are married."

But Kathryn heard only one word . . . *Cunning.* She felt she'd been dealt a stunning blow to the head. Desperate, mayhap . . . but cunning? The word brought to mind deceit and deception . . . traits that belonged to her uncle.

She wasn't like him. *She wasn't!* She was doing what she had to; it was the only way she could hope to wrench Ashbury from her uncle's greedy hold. She would surely die if she and Elizabeth were forced to live out the rest of their lives with him!

As for Roderick, she reminded herself she had not lied to him; she had never professed to love him, nor had he asked that she love him. Who married for love anyway? Marriage was for expedience and gain.

She swallowed the pangs of guilt and forced a smile. Roderick ran a finger down the tapered line of her jaw. "Come here, love. I crave a sampling of the sweetness soon to be mine."

Kathryn tensed. His gaze had fastened on her mouth. "Roderick," she began, "I do not think that we—"

He reached for her. His words were smothered against the softness of her cheek. " 'Tis only a kiss, love, just a kiss . . . nothing to what we shall share a month from now."

She lifted her hands to push him away, only to find his arms wrapping tightly around her. She saw his eyes, the flame of desire high and bright. His head lowered slowly . . . Startled by the touch of a man's lips against hers, she felt herself go slack in surprise.

His touch was not what she expected. Handsome as Roderick was, in some distant corner of her mind she had thought to be repulsed by such intimacy. But for all his fierce gaze, his kiss was gentle and sweet; her fingers gradually uncurled against his leather gambeson. Indeed, the kiss was scarcely unpleasant. Was it possible, she thought in amazement, that there was pleasure to be found in a man's touch?

Her lips parted softly in surprise, and then suddenly everything changed. She felt his hands in her hair, tugging at her braid, his fingers loosening the silky ebony strands. Deftly he unfastened her cloak and pushed it from her shoulders. She moaned, a tiny sound of protest and distress, but it was smothered against a mouth gone hard and demanding. In rising panic, she struggled against his hold. But he crushed her against him and bore her back against the ground, his body completely covering hers.

Somehow she managed to tear her mouth free. "Roderick," she gasped out. "Roderick, please!"

But it wasn't her voice that stopped him cold; it was the unmistakable sound of steel whispering sleekly against a scabbard . . .

Roderick twisted and bounded to his feet. Kathryn jolted upright. Her heart seemed to freeze in her chest. It spun through her mind that if she were wise, she would leap up and run as if the yawning pits of hell gaped at her feet.

For if the devil were flesh and blood, it was surely Satan who stood before them now.

Chapter 2

In truth, Guy had no patience with these two young lovers. Soon darkness would cloak the earth in its murky shroud. Ashbury Keep lay but a short distance away. The groundwork for his siege was already in place on the far side of the keep. He had only to move his remaining troops into place under cover of night and await the dawn.

And soon . . . soon Richard's soul would rot in hell.

For now, it was necessary to make sure these two did not raise the alarm. He signaled to one of the foot soldiers to disarm the man.

When his sword and dagger had been stripped from him, Guy sat upon his destrier and surveyed them coolly. The man was tall and strong-looking, his body well conditioned; Guy would have been proud to number this man among his own. There was the unmistakable look of a warrior about him, sharp and alert. He stood poised and ready for any sign of provocation, yet he wasn't foolish enough to endanger either himself or the girl. As for the girl, she had yet to move. Indeed, Guy thought with cynical amusement, she looked utterly terrified.

It was the man who spoke first. "This land belongs

to Richard of Ashbury. Who are you and what brings you here?"

Guy's lips smiled. His eyes did not. "I might ask the same of you, sir knight. But 'tis plain you seek the pursuit of love here, not war." The smile dallied about his lips. "But I fear our arrival came too soon for you to fully pluck the fruits of this comely wench."

Wench! Kathryn's fear vanished. She saw the mounted knight through a fiery mist of rage. The scornful tone of his voice was too much to bear. She scrambled to her feet and marched forward.

"You go too far, sir!" she hissed. "I am no serving maid that you may insult at your leisure. And I demand that you honor our request and make known your intentions! You and your men come here armed and ready to do battle. Is that the role you seek—that of conquering invader?"

Amazed at the girl's audacity, a low murmur went up among the men. Guy stared at her in silent speculation. Her woolen dress was worn and thin, little better than a servant's, which he had assumed she was. But now that she was up and on her feet, he saw that she possessed pride and grace. He was both irritated and intrigued by her boldness.

And it seemed he had misjudged her. She had the courage of a man, but the recklessness of youth. He could let neither pass by unnoticed. There was too much challenge in her voice, in her entire stance. *Girl*, he thought, *'tis time you learned just how much you dare.*

"My purpose," he said in a voice that was all the more chilling for its very softness, "remains my own, but I tell you this. I'll not let you or anyone else sway me from my goal."

He nodded again to several of his men, who grabbed her companion and pulled him aside.

He tossed his reins to his squire and dismounted, deliberately taking his time. He walked toward her, never taking his eyes from her. Her gaze faltered only once, but the next instant she confronted him just as boldly. She was nervous, he decided, but determined not to show it.

In truth, Kathryn was wholly unnerved. There was a bloodthirsty air to this entire group of knights—especially their leader. His pennon was altogether fitting—red silk emblazoned with a pair of combatant falcons. The knifelike edge in his voice must have made many a soul cringe in fear, and his features were just as frightening.

His eyes were pale and glittering. They burned with all the fires of hell as he approached. His hair was as black as her own, his skin as dark as a heathen's. Another might have thought him handsome, but Kathryn thought his sculpted features harsh and ruthless. His mouth was thin, almost cruel. His jaw was square and strong, his nose thin and straight and arrogant.

From his place next to Guy, Sir Hugh Bainbridge watched Guy's progress uneasily, unsure of his friend's next move. *He has changed*, Hugh thought. He was unpredictable—as now. He was as hard as steel, as unyielding as stone.

Guy stopped before her. His breadth totally eclipsed her view of his men-at-arms. Kathryn was stunned to see that his eyes were a pale translucent gray, in stark contrast to his swarthy skin. He towered over her, nearly two hands higher than she.

"Shall we settle the issue then?" His voice was soft, almost whimsical. To Kathryn, it was like steel tearing through silk. She shivered in spite of herself.

He placed his hands on his hips and walked round her. "You claim you are no servant," he announced. "Mayhap that is true. But you have moss in your hair, lady." He plucked several fat tendrils from her hair and displayed them with a flourish.

Aware of her hair streaming wildly over her shoulders and down her back, Kathryn shot a fulminating look at Roderick. He looked ready to explode, the guard on each side of him the only thing holding him back. For an instant it was gratifying to see him thus bound.

"Or perhaps—" The dark knight's voice dropped to a silken whisper meant for her ears alone. "—you are no lady at all."

Both his tone and his expression were ripe with taunting mockery. How Kathryn stopped herself from striking him, she didn't know. She sensed he was goading her, toying with her like a cat plays with a mouse before tearing the mouse apart. Well, she wouldn't give him the satisfaction of seeing her cower!

A sudden breeze molded her gown to her body, outlining her form in explicit detail. The dark knight's eyes slid boldly over her. Too late Kathryn remembered her cloak upon the ground behind her. His gaze lingered for long uninterrupted moments on the firm upthrust of her breast. Kathryn flushed painfully, hating the betraying color which rushed to her cheeks.

His lips curved in a challenging smile. "Indeed," he said softly, "methinks it highly unlikely that you are even a maid."

Kathryn couldn't help it. She struck out blindly. Unthinkingly. If she had had a weapon, she would surely have slain him.

But his fingers closed around her wrist, like iron manacles, thwarting her. Those ice-fire eyes never strayed from her form.

"Ah, that was not wise," he murmured. "What if I should be tempted to retaliate?"

"You offend me most cruelly! And I am not afraid of you!"

No, Guy thought slowly, she was not. Their eyes locked in a silent battle of wills. He gazed down at her, and slowly—reluctantly—became aware of something else. Oh, the burning in his veins was still there, but it was not from anger at the girl's insolence.

It was desire, stark and strong and almost painful in its intensity.

"Damn you!" shouted a voice. "Let her go! She is no servant to be handled so roughly—she is Lady Kathryn of Ashbury!"

Kathryn stared helplessly into the hard-featured face above hers. His eyes were piercing and relentless as they stabbed into hers.

The pressure on her wrist tightened so that she nearly cried out. His lips barely moved as he spoke. "Surely you are not Richard's *wife?* His daughter mayhap?"

She bit back a gasp of pain. "Nay! His wife died long ago. I am his niece!"

He released her so suddenly she almost stumbled. "Leave us," he said to his men. He stared at her harshly; Kathryn was only vaguely aware of his men dispersing. She didn't understand the silent accusation which smoldered in his eyes.

She regarded him warily, absently rubbing the place where his fingers had gripped so fiercely. Who was he, she wondered, this dark and fearsome knight? And why was he here? He was not on a mission of mercy, that much was clear. She had seen the way his troop of men was armored and mailed; nor had he come in friendship.

Comprehension dawned with shattering clarity.

"You are here for Richard," she whispered.

"And if I am?" His face was a mask of stone. She could read nothing of his thoughts.

Kathryn hesitated. With the way she hated her uncle, Richard's enemy should have been her staunchest ally. If only it were so simple! But alas, she knew of these male creatures and their will to quarrel. They dealt in lies, giving with one hand and snatching back with the other.

"You will do as you wish," she said quietly. "There is naught I can do to stop you."

Her calm seemed to infuriate him. His eyes blazed with the sizzling heat of a lightning bolt. "Aye," he said grimly. "And I'd best make certain that you don't."

A muscled arm shot out. Kathryn wasn't prepared when he seized her about the waist and lifted her clear off the ground. She gasped and began to twist and flail, struggling to free herself from his grip. His mail felt like hundreds of knife-edged teeth sinking into her back but she paid no heed.

"You stinking knave!" she cried out. "Get your filthy hands off me! Have you no respect for the fairer sex?"

"Not when she's likely as not just as treacherous as her uncle. I've no doubt you'd like to stick a dagger in my belly but I'll not give you the chance."

They hurtled to the ground. Kathryn lay stunned, the breath knocked from her lungs. She couldn't even cry out when he thrust an iron-thewed leg over hers and yanked her hands above her head, anchoring them to the mossy ground with one of his own.

His other hand skimmed lightly—boldly—over her. Arms. Breasts. Belly and hips, brutally thorough in its quest. That accursed hand even trespassed beneath her skirts, sliding up the naked length of her thighs. To Kathryn's horrified mind, he touched her everywhere. It scarcely registered that he was searching for a hidden weapon. She fought wildly against his dispassionate encroachment but he only pinned her more tightly to the ground. At last she closed her eyes against the cool detachment of his features, shocked and shamed by his intimacy. But inside she raged against the very helplessness thrust upon her by virtue of her womanhood. The only indignity spared her was that his search wasn't performed in front of his men. It didn't occur to her until much later that he might have done so on purpose.

The task completed to his satisfaction, he bounded lightly to his feet. God, how she hated his false and knowing smile! A saving anger flowed through her, washing away her humiliation. Kathryn slapped away the hand he offered, muttering every vile curse she could think of as she rose unassisted.

"By God," she said fervently, "you are a bloody bastard!"

"The question of my legitimacy does not arise," he parried smoothly. "I fear you cannot claim the same of your uncle, which reminds me . . . I find I am most eager to make his acquaintance. And I'm sure you'll be happy to know that you have just provided the means."

For the second time in just a few short minutes, he walked round her again, surveying her with the same critical judiciousness. "A pity," he said with a shake of his head when at last he stopped before her. "You have moss in your hair again, lady. I must admit—" His slow-growing smile mocked her. "—it suits you."

Kathryn was speechless with rage. Just then she didn't know who she hated more—her uncle or this nameless arrogant knight!

* * *

She was just as silent on the way back to the keep. Roderick was bound, his hands tied tightly behind his back. Kathryn walked beside him. There was little chance of escape, for they were guarded well by the dark knight's men-at-arms. Kathryn's skin grew icy-cold as they passed row after row of men armed with lance and shield. She saw archers and crossbowmen. Catapults and battering rams.

The dark knight had not lied. He had come prepared for battle; he had come for war.

More, he had come to win.

Roderick edged closer. "You know who he is?" His voice was meant for her ears alone. With a jerk of his head, he indicated the dark knight mounted up before them. Not once had he looked back at them.

Kathryn shook her head.

"He is Lord Guy de Marche, Earl of Sedgewick."

"The Earl of Sedgewick," she murmured. Her brow knitted in concentration. "The name is familiar yet I can recall nothing of him."

Roderick bent his head closer. "Guy de Marche was one of the most powerful lords in Somerset." His gaze was sullen as he glanced at the seemingly endless formation of men and arms. "It seems 'tis still true."

Kathryn stepped over an exposed root, wishing she had her cloak. The damp air seeped through her thin gown clear to her skin. "I did not know he was an enemy of Richard's," she said very quietly. "This is the first I've heard of it."

Roderick hesitated. "I can think of only one reason," he said slowly. "The earl left on crusade more than three years ago. Not long after, Richard heard that he'd been captured in Toulouse. Richard was always careful to stay clear of him but when he heard the news, he captured one of the earl's fiefs just across the border in Somerset—Ramsay Keep."

"He attacked the holdings of an absent crusader!" Kathryn's lips pressed tightly together. This news only confirmed her opinion of her uncle—he was lower than a snake's belly. A simmering rage filled her veins. Her resentment burned deeper yet when her gaze fell upon the ramrod-straight back of the earl, he with his battering rams and troops.

The evening mists swirled all around. Night fell swiftly, like the smothering folds of a cloak being dropped upon the earth. Kathryn saw that they were almost upon the gates of Ashbury, just outside the wooden palisade. She wanted to cry out in despair as she spied only a handful of men clustered around the outer walls.

This was her home, she thought desperately. Hers and Elizabeth's! And the Earl of Sedgewick would see it razed to the ground! God, how she hated her uncle for leading them down this wretched path of destructiveness—and she hated Lord Guy de Marche just as much. He would not be satisfied until he saw her beloved home destroyed!

The earl had dismounted quietly. Kathryn could scarcely see his shadowed form but her eyes conveyed her hatred as he conversed earnestly with one of his men. The others retreated slightly, jerking Roderick along with them. The earl watched them a moment, then turned and beckoned to her. Kathryn briefly entertained the notion of pretending she hadn't seen his gesture. But in the end she complied, deciding it might not be wise to provoke his anger.

His tone brooked no argument. "I need a way into the keep other than through the gatehouse. We will wait until those within are asleep, and then you will show me."

Kathryn was first startled by his daring, then furious at his stealthiness. "What, milord, do you fear a little swordplay?"

Guy's jaw snapped shut. "By God, lady," he said through his teeth, "did your uncle never teach you any manners?"

"What he has taught me, sir, I fear you already know!"

Guy muttered under his breath. He'd never met the likes of a wench like her; she was sorely in need of a strong hand and a will of iron. If he but had the time, he'd have liked nothing more than to instill a little respect in her.

His legs planted wide apart, he eyed her critically. "You refuse to show me then?"

Her chin lifted haughtily. "You are a fool if you believe I will help you throw open our doors and storm within. Ashbury is my home, milord, the only home I have ever known. I'll not help to destroy it."

Her contemptuous calm was infuriating. Guy's reaction might have been entirely different if he hadn't glimpsed the frantic fear in her eyes. "I've no wish to storm these walls, demoiselle. I seek only your uncle."

His words gave her pause. And yet . . . could she trust him? Now there was a question. She stared at him as if to seek an answer. But in the murky gloom he appeared dark and featureless, evil and forbidding.

I can't, she thought in panic. She cared nothing for Richard, but what of the others? What of Elizabeth? What of Aislinn, the cook, and Sir Ralph, her father's chief retainer? There were others who had served her family long before Richard came. Everyone would be caught off guard—indeed, no one would even miss her since she'd told Elizabeth she planned to retire for the night after meeting Roderick.

"I can wait no longer." The sound of steel hissed through the night. Moonlight glinted on the silver blade of a dagger. Kathryn paled when the earl stepped forward. A mocking smile curled his lips when she instinctively stepped backward. He beckoned quickly with the hand that held the dagger and Roderick was led forward once more.

He paused before Roderick. "What say you, Hugh?" he asked of another knight who had joined them. "Shall this brave knight be the first to shed his blood this night?"

Kathryn went white with dread. She couldn't tear her eyes away from the earl's long-fingered hands, absently sliding up and down the length of the dagger.

With a lightning movement he pressed the dagger to Roderick's throat.

The earl's eyes never left the other man's face as he said, " 'Tis up to you, milady, whether your lover lives or dies."

Kathryn's heart leaped to her throat. For the first time, she knew fear as Elizabeth must have known it, watching their mother slowly die.

She cried out sharply. "No! No, please do not!"

Roderick's face was a mask of stone. "Do not listen to him, Kathryn! Would you forfeit the lives of those within the keep?"

The earl's lips twisted. "Noble words for a man about to breathe his last." His eyes flickered to Kathryn. "I say again, lady, I have no more wish for bloodshed than you. I seek no war. I want only your uncle."

Kathryn's hands were shaking. How was she to choose? How could she live with the stain of another's blood upon her hands?

The moon slid out from behind a cloud. The knife pressed harder against Roderick's throat. Dear God! The tip of the blade was crimson with blood.

"It is your choice," the earl repeated.

She jerked when a hand touched her arm. Startled, she looked up at the knight the earl had called Hugh. She was stunned to discover compassion on his face.

"Milady," he said softly, "my lord is a man of his word. 'Tis not his way that others die needlessly."

Kathryn closed her eyes. She had faith in no man's honor . . . in no man. Yet she had no choice— no choice at all.

"Then let him give it," she whispered. "Let him give his sacred vow that there will be no murder at Ashbury."

"Kathryn, no! Do not trust him!"

She opened her eyes and gazed at Roderick. "My sister saw our mother die." She swallowed against the burning threat of tears. "I'll not stand by and watch her die—or you, Roderick."

The earl spoke. "I give my word then."

Her eyes blazed fiercely, yet her voice caught painfully. "Your vow, my lord. I would have your sacred vow!"

Guy's jaw tightened. No meek and biddable woman was this! She should have been born a man!

Kathryn sought his eyes. They were hard and completely unreadable. The silence was deathly.

It seemed an eternity passed before he spoke. "By all that is holy, there will be no murder here. As for your uncle, he will have a fighting chance." His voice was harsh. "I promise no more than that."

For an instant Kathryn went weak with relief. Elizabeth and Roderick would be spared. She watched Roderick being led away once more, then straightened her shoulders proudly. "Supplies are taken in through the postern on the far side of the keep. We can enter there."

Hours later, storm clouds gathered dark and forbidding in the night sky. Thunder raged across the earth. The wind was chill and biting, howling eerily as it lashed the ramparts. Deep inside the keep, those within lay deep in slumber.

Kathryn sagged against the damp stone wall, awaiting the earl's next move. There was a cold tight knot in the pit of her stomach. Weary and bitter, she decided that Lord Guy de Marche had the luck of the devil to whom she had unwittingly compared him. Only a moment ago he had received a signal—the guards on the parapet had been subdued. And now the storm would muffle any sound his troops would make inside the keep. He had already sent his friend Hugh to sneak through the bailey and open the gates for his men.

His eyes found hers through the inky darkness. She stiffened when his arm stretched out and brought her back against him. He bent his head low. "Which way to your uncle's chamber?" he whispered.

Kathryn wanted nothing more than to whirl and claw his arrogant face. Oh, if only she dared! Despising her weakness, she nodded toward the stairway at the other end of the great hall. He nudged her forward.

Her slippers made no sound as she led the way, the earl's arm tight about her waist. A small group of men trailed behind them. They were well trained, she noted scathingly. Indeed, they might have been fairies of old, for they made no sound, weaving quietly and stealthily behind their leader.

At the top of the stairs, she paused. Her mind raced in tempo with her heart. What if she were to lead them to the floor above, where Richard's knights lay deep in sleep?

But alas, *he* had felt the sudden tension in her body. His hated breath fell upon her cheek. "Do not think to deceive me, milady. I could crush the breath from you in an instant." His arm tightened as if to make good his threat.

But he had come too far to risk making his presence known, and Kathryn knew it. She met his gaze fearlessly. Their eyes clashed wordlessly. Realizing the futility of her plan and the helplessness of her position, Kathryn tightened her lips and gave a jerky nod. "Uncle's chamber is at the far end of this floor."

She was taut as a bowstring by the time they arrived outside her uncle's door. The earl's presence beside her was unnerving. She hated the touch of his hand on her body; she suspected he knew it as well. He held her as if he feared she would bolt any moment, yet she was surrounded by his men. Where could she run that he could not find her?

"He is within?" He spoke for her ears alone.

Kathryn nodded. She tried to pull back but he wouldn't let her. His eyes gleamed. "Oh, no, lady. If you betray me now, I would know it." With that he flung open the door of the chamber and pushed her inside.

The knight he called Hugh stepped in as well, carrying a rushlight. The room was illuminated. Kathryn held her breath, unsure of what to expect.

"Damnation!" thundered a booming voice. "Who dares disturb me at this hour!" A meaty hand reached to thrust aside the bed curtains but another was too quick.

"You are Richard of Ashbury?"

Richard, red-faced with fury, fell back against the pillows. His eyes widened at the sight of the earl, towering threateningly above the bed. Beside him, another figure stirred. Helga sat up, rubbing her eyes and blinking sleepily.

The earl spoke but three words to her. "You, girl. Out." Helga took one look at the earl, grabbed her clothes, and fled. Another time, perhaps, and Kathryn might have been amused. She doubted Helga had even noticed her standing near the wall.

The door creaked shut behind her. The knight called Hugh walked over and slid the bolt. The air was suddenly pulsing with tension.

"I ask once more." Guy's voice was deceptively mild. "You are Richard?"

Richard's mouth opened then closed. He hadn't missed the murderous rage in the other man's eyes. His nod was jerky.

Guy stared down at the man he'd sworn would be his. His smile was savage.

"Who are you?" Richard gasped. "I have done you no harm, sir knight. Yet you invade my home. My very chamber!"

Guy's handsome features froze. "I am Guy de Marche, Earl of Sedgewick."

Richard blanched. His gaze darted to the corner. His sword lay propped against the wall, along with his dagger and other trappings of war.

The earl's hand fell to his own sword, still in its scabbard at his side. He caressed the handle with deliberate intent. "You would do us both a favor to go for your weapon," he said softly. "I've a mind to end this quickly."

Kathryn pressed herself against the wall. The earl looked ready to tear Richard apart, limb by limb. God knew she wanted nothing more than to be rid of her uncle, but the menacing intensity of the earl's expression was terrifying. She inhaled sharply. "You can't," she reminded him quickly. "You promised there would be no bloodshed. You promised!"

Richard's eyes lit on her. His face contorted with rage. "You traitorous bitch! You are the one who brought him here! You have conspired with him to see me thrust from my own keep! Bedamned, girl! I'll see you and that spineless sister of yours thrown out on your ears—"

Guy stepped forward. "This girl is guilty of nothing save being caught outside the walls with her lover."

Richard's eyes bulged. "Her lover!"

Kathryn's small chin lifted. "I was with Roderick, Uncle. He and I wish to be married."

"Married!" He cursed lewdly. "By God, who do you think you are to—"

"Enough!" The thunder of the earl's voice shook the rafters. "You forget the matter at hand. You'd best think about your own dilemma instead of the misbegotten ways of your wayward niece."

Kathryn's spine went rigid. Misbegotten ways! Wayward niece! How dare he defend her one moment and slap her in the face the next! But all else was forgotten when the earl seized her uncle and dragged him from the bed.

"Dress yourself! I'll have you face me as a man and not cowering in your bed like a sickly old woman."

Richard scurried to comply. Kathryn averted her head but she heard the rustle of clothing and soon she heard him say, "I tell you again, my lord. I have no quarrel with you and yours."

"No?" The earl's tone was silky-smooth. It sent an eerie chill through Kathryn. "You should have thought of that before you attacked Ramsay Keep

two winters ago, held for me by my vassal Sir
Geoffrey."

There was a taut silence. Kathryn held her breath.
The earl looked like a man possessed; the tension
that gripped his features was frightening. There
was more, she suspected, than Richard attacking
the keep of one of his vassals.

Richard's voice, when it finally came, was scarcely audible. "I did not know, my lord, that Ramsay
Keep was held by you, I swear—"

"Spare me your lies." The earl's voice matched
the fury of the storm that raged outside. "You
knew that land was held by me, just as you
knew I was on crusade then. You knew and still
you attacked!" He pointed at Sir Hugh. "Geoffrey
was Sir Hugh's brother-in-law; he married Hugh's
sister Claire. Geoffrey was murdered during your
siege . . . as was my wife."

Richard went white. He gestured vaguely.

"Do not deny it!" the earl shouted. "It was only
by the mercy of God that my wife's maid escaped,
along with my infant son. 'Twas she told me of
your treachery—how you pretended to come in
friendship and then laid siege to the keep. You
gave orders that no one was to be spared—not
women, not children—*no one!*"

Kathryn's eyes squeezed shut and her stomach
heaved. Her uncle's wickedness knew no bounds.
To kill defenseless women and children but for the
sake of killing . . .

Sweat popped out on Richard's brow. "What do
you seek, milord? I yield Ramsay Keep back to
you . . . I will repay you the rents I have taken . . ."

"A futile gesture," the earl said flatly, "since
Ramsay Keep is once again under my protection.
I recaptured the keep three days past. My men took
the utmost care to make certain your messenger did

not precede me here." His lips formed a twisted parody of a smile. "Even now this keep is being overrun by my troops. Indeed, victory is already mine. You cannot hope to escape and incite your men against me. If you do not believe me, ask your niece."

Richard's gaze slid to Kathryn. "It is true," she said woodenly. "Ashbury is surrounded. He has twice the forces you possess, Uncle."

Richard fell to his knees. "I will give you anything you wish. Silver. Jewels . . ."

Guy's mind screamed with outrage. *You killed my wife, you filthy bastard! The only thing I want is to see you dead at my feet!* Yet even that was denied him . . . because of a damned vow to a mere woman!

His gaze flickered to the girl. Her eyes were huge in her pale face; she was as white as bleached linen. If she had been anyone else—anyone but Richard's niece—he might have found some small scrap of compassion for her.

Damn, he thought savagely. *Damn!* He smote his fist upon his hand, feeling as if he would explode inside. He wanted Richard dead—to pay in kind for his coldhearted murder of Elaine! Only then could his tormented mind find a measure of peace. But he'd given the girl his word. He could not break it . . . at least not here at Ashbury.

"Believe me," he told Richard coldly, "nothing would please me more than to rob you as you have robbed me. To strip you of all that you hold dear—"

"I will do anything you ask, my lord! I beg of you, spare me! I have no wish to die . . . please, milord . . ."

Guy was suddenly furious. There was no triumph in watching Richard grovel, trembling in fear for his life. Did he have no honor? No pride?

"Your lands are mine even now," he said flatly. "You were granted these lands during King Stephen's rule. Now that Henry is on the throne you have been ordered to relinquish your title."

Richard looked stunned. Sir Hugh stepped forward with the king's document. Richard gazed at it numbly.

Guy smiled grimly. "Henry is aware that you dared to attack the vassal of an absent crusader. That is why he has seen fit to forfeit Ashbury and all your other possessions to me."

Kathryn's head began to spin. Ashbury . . . in the hands of this devil-knight. For an instant she thought she would faint. She made a choked sound deep in her throat, dimly aware that the earl spoke once more.

"As for your punishment . . ."

Richard staggered to his feet. "Henry has stripped me of my lands! Is that not enough?"

The earl's jaw tensed. His eyes were cutting; they shone like glittering steel. "Not," he said through clenched teeth, "for what you did. That is why the king has seen fit to leave your fate in my hands."

Richard's shoulders sagged defeatedly. "And what is my punishment to be?"

"I have not yet decided," the earl said coldly. "Until that time you will not leave this chamber. You may content yourself with the knowledge that I allow you to spend your last days in comfort— and not in the dungeon." He spun around and strode from the room. Hugh motioned to Kathryn. She stepped past her uncle without sparing him another glance.

She stopped short out in the hallway. The earl stood there, arms folded across his chest.

Kathryn did not wait for him to speak. "Is there to

be a guard outside my door as well?" She couldn't hide her bitterness, nor did she wish to.

Something flickered across his face, something that made her think she wounded him . . . It was gone in the blink of an eye. In its stead was the cold merciless knight she had seen thus far.

"Not unless you give me reason," he replied coolly. "But bear in mind, lady, that if you do, I'll not hesitate to throw you in the dungeon with your lover." He glanced at his friend. "Hugh, see the lady to her chamber. I'll take the others and meet you where we entered."

Kathryn wasn't sure which infuriated her more—his mocking smile or the fact that he considered her no threat. She marched off in the direction of her chamber, leaving Sir Hugh no choice but to follow behind.

Her temper had cooled by the time she reached her door. She paused and glanced across the passage where Elizabeth slept. "I must—wake my sister and tell her what has happened." She spoke the words with difficulty.

Hugh touched her shoulder gently. This had been a blow to her, he suddenly realized. He had thought to hate her—after all, she was Richard's kin—yet he could not. She had had no part in her uncle's treachery. And now she looked almost . . . beaten.

She looked up at his unexpected touch. "I see in your eyes," he said softly, "that you think Lord Guy has been hard and cruel. Believe me when I say—"

" 'Tis not that," Kathryn said quickly, shaking her head.

"What then?"

"Have you . . . have you ever lost your home, Sir Hugh? Your lands?"

Hugh's smile was crooked. "Nay, for I have never possessed my own lands. My father had a small manor in Sussex, but I am naught but the third son. The manor went to my eldest brother upon his death." He gazed up at the arching stone walls. "Nor was it so grand as this."

She looked away, her expression pained. "I hated it when my father died," she said tonelessly. "Elizabeth and I were born here, as our father and father before him. Richard is my father's bastard brother, but he did not grow to manhood here. When Father died four years ago, Richard ran to King Stephen and pleaded for Ashbury, when it should have gone to me—and Elizabeth. He cared nothing for it! He sought only the rents it would bring. He was here but a fortnight when he sold our dower lands!"

She blinked to hold back the unexpected sting of tears. "When Richard came here, I felt he was an invader, because he did not belong . . . as Elizabeth and I did. I felt as if I had lost everything . . ." Her eyes squeezed shut. "Now Ashbury belongs to your lord. 'Tis not so much for myself that I fear the future, but for my sister . . ."

Hugh patted her shoulder awkwardly. "You need not fear, my lady. Lord Guy is a just man, I swear."

Her eyes opened suddenly, clear and brilliant but shadowed with sadness. "Mayhap," she said quietly, "it would be best if Elizabeth and I packed our chests—"

"To go where?" Hugh said, aghast.

"There is a nunnery not far from here . . ."

"Milady, you presume too much! Lord Guy's quarrel is with your uncle, not you! Nay, I'll not hear another word. Guy is not a heartless beast, no matter what you think . . ."

He was so unlike his lord, Kathryn thought a

few moments later. Sir Hugh was gentle and kind and generous. With a weary sigh she closed the heavy oak door, peering through the gloom toward Elizabeth's bed.

But Elizabeth was already scurrying across the floor. "Kathryn! You are safe! I—I was so frightened . . . I checked your chamber and you were still gone . . . I could not sleep and then I heard strange sounds . . ."

Kathryn gripped her sister's hands. There was so much confusion—so much turmoil and pain inside her that for a moment she was unable to speak. Her lungs burned from trying to hold back her tears.

She led Elizabeth over to the bedside and haltingly told her of all that had happened tonight. Oddly, Elizabeth looked almost relieved when she had finished.

"Why do you look like that?" Kathryn asked quietly.

"Do you not see?" Elizabeth said simply. "Uncle is a wicked, wicked man. No doubt the Earl of Sedgewick will mete out a punishment that is swift and severe." She tipped her head to the side and smiled. "We are free of him, Kathryn. We have what you wanted—we are free of him!"

"But we do not have what we wanted!" It was a cry of outrage, of anguish. "We do not have Ashbury—and I *helped* him wrest it from our grasp!" True, they were no longer at the mercy of Richard, but now they were at the mercy of the Earl of Sedgewick. Kathryn's heart twisted in despair. Her life was still not her own . . . and it never would be.

If only she could be as accepting as Elizabeth, the loss would be so much easier to bear. If only . . .

To her horror, a tear slid down her cheek. Then another and another.

For once it was Kathryn who sought refuge in the arms of her sister, sobbing out her bitter heartache. She cried in fury; she cried in pain. She cried for all she had lost . . .

And all that would never be hers.

Noonday saw a curling fog creeping round the towers. The sky was a depthless gray; a thick layer of clouds smothered the presence of the sun.

Guy turned away from the narrow window, cursing and rubbing his knee. The weather was a melancholy reflection of his mood. Damn, but he hated the chill and misty climate of Cornwall! The damp sea air did naught but make all his old wounds ache.

He was tired, he realized. Tired of war. Weary of war within war. He was suddenly anxious to be back at Sedgewick; to see his son Peter and hold him close . . .

Hugh threw open the door of the counting room. "What! Are you still brooding? Never has victory come easier. Richard's knights are in the dungeon, but I've no doubt they'll swear their loyalty to you when they realize Richard will never command here again. And we lost not a single man!" His voice faded as he beheld his friend's countenance.

Hugh sighed. "It's Richard, isn't it?" He needed no response. He had only to watch Guy's features harden into an implacable mask.

He walked over and laid a hand on Guy's shoulder. "You have Ashbury, Guy. I know you already have lands aplenty, but didn't you see Richard's face last night when you told him Henry had ceded Ashbury to you? You have broken and beaten him. Throw him in prison for the rest of his life and let it be over and done!"

Guy closed his eyes. Gerda's words echoed over

and over in his brain, like a death knell. *They showed no mercy . . . no mercy at all!*

His hands clenched. "But he still lives, Hugh. Richard still lives while Elaine—" There was a rough thread of pain in his voice. "—Elaine is dead." He shook his head. His eyes opened full of anguish. " 'Tis not so easy to let go, when the thought of Richard dead is all that has driven me for the last two years—that and the thought of seeing my son."

Hugh watched him for a long moment. "There is also Lady Kathryn to think of," he reminded him. "I understand there is a sister as well."

Guy snorted. "I'd be wise to throw the lady in prison along with her uncle."

Hugh smiled. "Were it not for her, you wouldn't have taken Ashbury so easily."

"I almost killed an innocent man because of her! And I crave nothing more than to put my fingers round Richard's throat, yet because of her I can't lay a hand on him!"

"At any rate, I assured her you were a just lord who wouldn't dream of casting her out of her home."

"You what! Egad, man, is she a witch who's cast you under her spell? What foolishness is this that you dance to her tune so readily?"

"She has no love for her uncle, Guy. Not because of the taint on his name but because of his treatment of her and her sister. Stephen granted Ashbury to Richard when her parents died, but she feels it would have been hers if Richard hadn't intervened. He also sold their dower lands."

"Is that what she said?"

"Yes."

"And you believed her?"

"Don't you?"

Guy rubbed his chin, pricked by a sudden doubt. His first impulse was to cast aside all her claims as ridiculous. Yet knowing Richard's deceitful nature, it was possible she spoke the truth. Still, instinct told him that she must be watched, that she could be dangerous.

Hugh sighed. "You can't turn them out of their home, Guy. Why, she was ready last night to scurry off to a nunnery—"

Guy gave a shout of laughter. "A nunnery! By God, man, that's rich! Have you forgotten how we found her?" He sobered abruptly and gave his friend a long hard look. "Indeed, she seems to have you well in hand. Mayhap she knows rather well how to bend a man to her every whim."

Hugh denied it, and they soon moved on to other things. But Guy's thoughts returned again and again to Richard, and Hugh's plea to let his vengeance end.

Nay, he thought grimly. A voice within him still cried out for revenge. He could not let go so easily. But he could not lay a hand on Richard—at least not yet. There had to be another way.

He would not pronounce his sentence just yet, he decided. Richard feared for his life, and the thought of Richard stewing—trembling in fear—appeased the storm in his soul . . .

For the moment.

Chapter 3

Richard did indeed fear for his life. But far from stewing, his evil mind was busy searching for a way to save his skin. He sat in the high-backed chair in his chamber and rubbed his hands with glee. When Helga brought his morning meal, he bade her send his niece Kathryn to him as soon as possible.

It was nearly time for the evening meal when the wretched girl got round to showing herself. Richard chafed at the delay but he was feeling immensely proud of himself—and inclined to be lenient with her. And just as he'd thought, the guard at the door thought nothing of the fact that his niece sought him out.

"You sent for me, Uncle?"

She stood before him, haughty and proud. No doubt she was glad to see him held prisoner in his own keep!

He tapped his pudgy fingers on the arm of the chair. "I have a task for you, girl."

Winged black brows shot up. "Indeed?" she said coolly.

Richard longed to slap the insolent smirk from her lips but thought better of it. "Aye." He beckoned her nearer. "Come here. I'll not have the guard at the door hear what I have to say."

Kathryn hesitated, then moved forward a step. "This task," she said slowly. "It concerns the Earl of Sedgewick?"

Richard's eyes gleamed. "Aye. That it does."

Her lovely mouth turned down at the corners. She and Elizabeth had spent most of the day in the bower, both hesitating to move about freely with so many of the earl's men milling about.

But she had watched the earl from the gallery off the great hall this morning while he informed wide-eyed servants that the keep was now under his protection. Later she'd glimpsed him in the bailey with the steward. He was every inch the master in command, she reflected bitterly. The servants went on about their business as if nothing was amiss. The smith pounded horseshoes at the forge; grooms swept out the stables and fed the horses. Indeed, today had been like any other day, except Richard's knights were locked up in the dungeon.

Her eyes flashed as she smoothed the folds of her wimple. "If it concerns the earl," she said shortly, "then I want no part of it."

"Hear me out, girl. I want you to kill him."

The world seemed to tilt alarmingly. Kathryn stared at her uncle uncomprehendingly, convinced she hadn't heard right. She resented the earl, yes. She hated the very thought of him possessing Ashbury . . . but she did not want him dead.

"You cannot be serious," she said faintly.

He leaped to his feet. "I've never been more serious in my life."

Kathryn whirled and bolted for the door. She'd almost reached it when a cruel hand forestalled her flight. Merciless fingers bit into the soft flesh of her arm and spun her around. Her uncle dragged her back across the floor and thrust her into his chair.

She tried to jump up. "No!" Her eyes were dark and wild. "I—I won't do it, I tell you!"

He shoved her into the seat and clamped his hand over her mouth. "I say you will!" he hissed. "By God, girl, if it were not for you, I'd not be locked up here! Now listen and listen well. I know you still have the dagger that belonged to your mother. De Marche is a strong man—likely as not, you'll have only one strike, so aim for the heart."

Kathryn shrank back in the chair. "I cannot!" she cried. The words were muffled but he must have understood for his eyes blazed fiercely.

"You can!" he grated. "You're not a weak spineless idiot like that sister of yours."

Kathryn was too stunned to take notice of his taunt. Her eyes were enormous in her pale face.

"Make sure he is alone and there is no one around—unless you wish to be caught, of course." His eyes gleamed.

Kathryn was faint from lack of air when Richard lifted his hand from her mouth. "You have no influence over me now," she gasped. "You are the earl's prisoner."

"Only for the moment! You say I have no influence but you are wrong. Even now my knights seek a way for me to escape."

"Your knights are imprisoned in the dungeon!"

"Not for long. Indeed, it would only take a handful to help me escape. And make no mistake, girl, their freedom is easily gained—through a number of ways." His laugh was chilling. "I've no doubt if Helga gives her favors to the right guard, a lock or two might be accidentally left open. Or she might lay her hands on the key herself."

Kathryn felt as if a cold wind had blown across her heart. "You forget the king has granted Ashbury's title elsewhere. You risk King Henry's wrath if you do this."

"Bah! Henry is no different than Stephen. He will be most eager to line his coffers with silver, which I shall do willingly when I am free. Guy de Marche is the only one who stands in my way. If he falls, his men will retreat."

She pressed her lips together bravely. "I'll not do it," she said again. "You cannot make me."

Menace raged across his blunt features. For an instant she thought he would strike her. She braced herself for his blow but all at once he grinned slyly. "You think not?" He placed his hands over the arms of the chair so that she was trapped.

Kathryn stared at him. *Oh, God,* she thought, feeling sick, *what now? What evil treachery does he plot now?*

"If you do not slay the earl, when I am free I will see that your sister is given to my knights. Not just one, mind you—" His lips drew back to reveal yellowed teeth. "—but all of them."

Kathryn's mind was racing. What if he should succeed? If he should gain his freedom, she didn't doubt that he would do exactly as he proposed. And poor Elizabeth was so frightened of men! She couldn't even bear the thought of a man touching her in gentleness . . . Kathryn began to tremble. Dear God, it would kill her—it would kill her as surely as a sword driven through her breast.

Her shoulders sagged. It took a tremendous effort to make her lips do her bidding. "The earl's knights swarm within the keep," she said tonelessly. "They are everywhere—"

"They don't sleep with him, do they? And no one will suspect you, a mere girl."

Her eyes widened in shock. She folded her hands together to keep them from shaking. Her voice was unsteady when she spoke. "Surely you cannot be suggesting that I . . ." She turned her head away, unable to finish.

Cruel fingers wrenched her chin and forced her gaze to his. "That you bed the cur?" His voice was as unyielding as his hands. "If that's what it takes to see him slain, then so be it. Indeed—" His laugh was chilling. "—'twould be easy to slip a knife within his breast in the heat of passion."

Kathryn went hot inside, then icy-cold. Unbidden, the memory of the earl's search of her body rose high in her mind. She could feel once again the heated strength of his fingers sliding over her skin. That had been bad enough, she thought with a shiver, yet her untutored mind warned her that his scalding touch was nothing compared to the intimacies carried on between a man and a woman.

Something of her horror must have reflected on her face. Her uncle made a sound of disgust. "You'd have me believe you know nothing of the ways of men, yet you wish to wed Roderick? Your feigned innocence is wasted, girl. Roderick is not a man to be held off for long."

Kathryn flushed, remembering the impatient desire she'd sensed in his arms last eve.

Richard smirked. "Or mayhap you feel bound to be faithful to him, eh? Put the thought out of your mind, girl. One man's blade is the same as any other."

His crudeness made her burn with shame. Kathryn grew desperate. "The earl has no liking for me."

"Hah!" Her uncle's chuckle made her skin crawl. "All the more reason for him to take you to his bed. He need not like you to desire you, girl. Haven't you learned that yet?" His gaze raked over her. "You're a comely wench with that rich dark hair and ivory skin. A trifle thin for some men's taste, but no matter. And your coolness but makes a man burn for you all the more."

Kathryn jerked her head away. Her hands clenched in her lap. Oh, God. To lie with the earl . . . She'd seen the way he looked at her—as if he hated her! He would be like Richard; he would not be gentle. He would delight in hurting her . . .

Richard wrenched her from the chair and gave her a shove. "Begone now! It matters little to me if you play the slut for him. I care not how you go about it, as long as the deed is done."

She moved numbly toward the door.

"Kathryn!"

She half-turned.

"I would see him slain this night!" he warned. "If not, it will go all the worse for Elizabeth."

Kathryn fled, his guttural laughter ringing in her ears. She knew it pleased him mightily to see her cowed, but for once she could not summon the strength to fight him.

The sanctuary she sought was simply not to be. Kathryn had barely shut herself in her chamber than she heard a knock on the door. When she opened it, she found one of the earl's knights there.

"Yes?" Her voice was breathless. She wanted to moan her distress aloud. Was this a summons from the earl? What did he want of her? How could she face him?

"Milady? Sir Hugh most humbly requests your presence—and your sister's as well—in the great hall. To dine, if it pleases you."

Sir Hugh. The relief which flooded her veins was short-lived. If Sir Hugh was there, the earl would be there as well.

More than ever, she dreaded facing him again, yet she knew the time would come eventually. And Richard had said tonight . . . *I would see him slain this night.*

A curious sort of numbness befell her. "Please tell Sir Hugh that my sister and I will be down shortly."

But Elizabeth was reluctant—she preferred to take her meal in her chamber. Kathryn was just as reluctant to face Sir Hugh—and the earl—alone. She needed Elizabeth by her side. She argued and coaxed, and at last Elizabeth agreed. They quickly washed and changed their kirtles.

In the great hall, servants scurried to and fro, setting out platters of roasted meats and breads on three long trestle tables. The sound of laughing, boisterous male voices filled the air. Elizabeth's steps slowed; Kathryn had to tug her forward.

Sir Hugh stood before the huge arched fireplace. He saw them immediately when they reached the bottom of the stairs and came toward them. He wore no mail, but a rich brown velvet tunic. Kathryn felt a rare pang of embarrassment as she thought of the thin woolen kirtle she wore. It was one of her best, but she'd chosen it because she hoped the rich crimson color might lend her a bit of sorely needed courage. Still, there were places where the material had been mended several times over. She glanced quickly at Elizabeth; her sister looked just as dismayed. But Sir Hugh appeared not to notice as he drew nearer. His face was lit with pleasure.

"Lady Kathryn."

"Sir Hugh." She smiled slightly.

He bowed low over the hand she offered, then turned to Elizabeth. "This lovely lady is your sister?"

"Yes," Kathryn replied as Elizabeth, her eyes downcast, bobbed a tiny curtsy. "This is my sister Elizabeth."

"I am Sir Hugh Bainbridge." He clasped Elizabeth's small cold hand warmly between his own. Elizabeth's eyes widened but she did not snatch back her hand, as Kathryn expected.

He glanced between the two of them and smiled. "I must confess, I would hate to say which of you is the younger—or the most beauteous."

Kathryn smiled. "I am older than Elizabeth by a year." There was a small pause. "I trust we did not keep you waiting," she murmured.

"Not at all." Hugh led them toward the wooden dais at the far end of the hall. Unbidden, Kathryn's gaze swept the hall for any sign of a tall black-haired man. But the earl was nowhere in sight; Kathryn was torn between a deep-seated relief and a feeling of helpless frustration. Richard's decree could not be carried out if the earl was not here.

"Lord de Marche does not join us?" She posed the question as Sir Hugh seated her and Elizabeth.

He shook his head. "Nay. He rode out with the bailiff to speak with some of the tenants. He has not yet returned."

Kathryn was barely able to stop her lip from curling in disdain. The conquering hero had gone out to survey his domain and judge its worth. An acrid resentment simmered within her as the servants placed trenchers of bread before then.

There was fresh herring spiced with ginger, an array of breads laced with honey and nuts. Kathryn had little appetite though the evening was less of an ordeal than she expected. Sir Hugh was charming and witty. Elizabeth was nervous as always with so many men milling about; she was quiet and spoke little, yet she smiled several times at something Sir

Hugh said. Indeed, at any other time Kathryn might have relaxed and actually enjoyed herself . . . but thoughts of the night to come hung over her like a death shroud. At every lull in the conversation, Richard's voice spun through her mind.

Even now my knights seek a way for me to escape.

If only Richard were wrong. If only she could be sure he would not escape before the earl pronounced sentence upon him. Then this horrible charade need not be played out at all.

If Helga gives her favors to the right guard, a lock or two might be accidentally left open. Or she might lay her hands on the key herself.

She had to think of Elizabeth. She had to protect her sister, for there was no one else to do so.

The time passed more quickly than she wished. Before she knew it, it was time to retire. Sir Hugh rose and insisted on seeing them to their chambers. Halfway across the hall, another knight waylaid him. He promised he would be only a moment, so Kathryn and Elizabeth moved off to await him near the stairway.

A small group of men had just entered the hall. They had to skirt them in order to get by, and as they passed, one of them fixed greedy eyes on Elizabeth and Kathryn. "Now there's a way to warm a man's behind the night through," he said to his companions. "One on each side! What say you, lads? Shall we roll the dice? We've yet to see the spoils of victory."

Elizabeth went deathly pale. Kathryn whirled on the knave, a scathing denunciation ready to spring from her lips.

"There will be no plunder. There will no booty taken from this keep. Did I not make myself plain, gentlemen?"

Kathryn knew, even before her head whipped around, who stood behind her. That chillingly cold voice was one she'd not soon forget. She thought dimly that the Earl of Sedgewick possessed an uncanny power. He had no need to resort to violence; he could punish and whip with only the sound of his voice . . . the touch of his eyes.

One by one the men fell back beneath his blistering stare.

Something seemed to freeze inside Kathryn. How kind. How noble. Ashbury would not be looted or robbed. The earl was no better than their uncle. He would steal what was theirs—hers and Elizabeth's—and claim it all for himself. Yet such was the nature of life—and such were the ways of men, she thought angrily, hopelessly.

"My lord." Kathryn tipped her chin up and regarded Guy de Marche coolly. She neither curtsied nor offered him her hand. By God, she'd not humble herself before him.

His gaze had settled upon Elizabeth, who was still visibly shaken. She was also clearly anxious to escape the hall—or perhaps the earl's presence. Kathryn fancied it was the latter and slid a protective arm round her sister's shoulders. "You have not yet met my sister, Elizabeth. Elizabeth, Lord de Marche, Earl of Sedgewick."

"Lady Elizabeth. The pleasure is mine, I assure you." He bowed slightly and gave a smile that was almost warm.

Kathryn was suddenly overwhelmed with angry frustration. Why did he bother? Why had Sir Hugh bothered? They played at pretense, both of them, when in truth they were the triumphant heroes and she and Elizabeth naught but the vanquished. Yet a tiny inner voice whispered that their circumstances could have been dire indeed. He could have enslaved them. Worse, they could have been fair game for his men.

Not for the first time that day, Kathryn wondered what plans—if any—the earl had for them. Yet what did it matter, for he would soon be dead . . .

Guy watched her, silently weighing and measuring. He saw many things flit across her lovely features in that moment. Anger, though he knew not why. Defiance. Even the unexpected—a hint of defeat. But haughty pride quickly followed, an expression he was beginning to grow rather familiar with . . . He curbed his irritation and stripped off his gloves, tucking them under his arm.

It was then that Kathryn spied Roderick past his shoulder. Roderick and several more of her uncle's knights. Mother of Christ! Was it true then? Did her uncle's men even now hatch the plot that would set him free?

Too late she saw that Guy's gaze paralleled hers. She wet her lips, suddenly nervous. "Is it not dangerous to let Uncle's knights wander the halls?"

"Your lov—" There was a small pause where he glanced at Elizabeth. "Your betrothed and a few others," he finished, "have sworn fealty to me as their new lord."

Kathryn glared at him. She sensed his scorn, and his mocking half-smile told the tale only too well. If Elizabeth had not been present his words would have been far different.

"You are a trusting man," she told him stiffly, "to free them so quickly."

He fixed those strange crystalline eyes upon her face. "There can be no honor without trust," he murmured. "And Sir Roderick, as your uncle's chief retainer, has some influence over the other knights. You may rest assured these men are being watched, despite my show of good faith. But do not count on seeing the rest of your uncle's knights up and about so quickly. In time, they will be given the choice to accept me as their lord as these others have done."

"And if they do not?" Dimly Kathryn wondered what madness possessed her that she challenged him so.

He shrugged. "They will regret it," he said simply.

A smile that was almost lazy lurked about his lips, but Kathryn was not fooled. She could detect no hint of mercy in his carved features. Did the man have no heart? she raged silently. No compassion? Was he as merciless and cruel as their uncle?

He has spared Roderick, a voice in her mind reminded her. *And he has spared both you and Elizabeth.*

Beside her, Elizabeth edged closer. "Kathryn, I grow tired," she whispered. "Let us retire."

Sir Hugh chose that moment to finally join them. He clapped a hand on the earl's back. "Guy, you missed a most entertaining evening," he proclaimed.

Guy glanced between the two sisters. Kathryn was smiling, as if in total agreement with Hugh. But Elizabeth's face was downcast.

The two were nothing alike, he found himself musing. One was as dark as the other was fair; Kathryn was wind and fire, while her sister was soft summer rain, fragile and breakable.

"I was just about to escort these two ladies to their chambers," Hugh said. "Then I thought I'd return here for a spot of ale. Mayhap you will join me."

Guy shook his head, suddenly conscious of how bone-weary he was. "I think not. I intend to sup in my chamber and then retire for the night."

Hugh nodded. Guy turned to the two women and bowed slightly. "Ladies, I bid you good night."

Moments later, Hugh did the same, raising each of their hands to his lips before murmuring his good night. Kathryn was startled to discover Elizabeth's eyes fixed upon him as his footsteps carried him down the long hall.

"He is not what I expected," she murmured.

"Who? The earl?" Kathryn's voice was almost sharp.

Elizabeth shook her head. "Sir Hugh." She seemed to hesitate. "He was kind and gentle and . . . very gallant."

Kathryn was sorely tempted to laugh in delight. Never in her life had she heard her sister use those words to describe a man. Her expression softened. "Aye," she said gently. "But he is also a knight, Elizabeth, one of the earl's knights. And—we cannot forget why he is here."

Elizabeth shivered. "Do not speak of the earl! Now there is a man who truly frightens me! He has the strangest eyes, almost like—like crystal. And when his gaze chanced to rest on me, it was as if he looked right through me—inside of me!" She shivered again.

The hair on the back of Kathryn's neck prickled. *That he does*, she agreed silently. She had no desire to face him again tonight, but Elizabeth had just unwittingly reminded her that she must. She leaned forward and kissed her sister's cheek. "You look tired, Elizabeth. Let me brush your hair and help you to bed."

So it was that Kathryn left her sister a short time later. She did not step across the passage to her own room, however, but started in the opposite direction.

The earl had taken a chamber overlooking the guardhouse. One of the servants had been tidying up when she visited her uncle earlier. Kathryn approached the earl's chamber with all the enthusiasm of a man going to the hangman's noose. Mercifully the halls were deserted; no one noticed her halt before his door. She marveled that her knock was so firm and sure, for inwardly she was quaking.

The door opened. The earl stood there, bold as a man can be . . . arrogant as only *he* could be.

Those eyes Elizabeth had called strange swept over her; it was almost as if he expected her. A flurry of panic set in. Surely he didn't *know* . . .

She spoke quickly, before she lost her nerve. "My lord, I crave a word with you."

Those devilishly arched eyebrows shot up in silent question, but he said nothing, merely opened the door wider.

She stepped inside. The room was brightly lit by an array of candles on a small table. A fire crackled and roared in the fireplace, casting out its warmth. Yet a chill raced up her spine when the heavy oak portal cracked shut behind her, closing the world out . . . sealing her in.

"You surprise me, Lady Kathryn. I had not thought that you would seek me out for any reason. Indeed, your sister avoided the touch of my eyes as if she feared I would cast a plague upon her. Do you not feel the same?"

Kathryn welcomed his sarcasm, for it swept away her fear and uncertainty. She watched him move to the table where the remains of a meal lay upon a small tray. He did not sit, but turned to await her response.

The bite in her tone was thinly disguised. "Elizabeth is uneasy with so many men about wearing the trappings of war."

"I fear it cannot be helped." His tone, cool and distant, matched hers.

She folded her hands and gazed at him evenly. "She is also unsure of our position in the household, now that you are here. That, my lord, is the reason I am here. I would know your intentions regarding my sister and me."

I would know your intentions. Her choice of words was irksome. She did not ask. She did not plead or gently seek. She demanded, as if it were her due.

His eyes narrowed. "I had not given it much thought."

Her lashes lowered. The merest of smiles curved her sweet lips. "We are yours to command, my lord, yours to claim by right of ownership. I am prepared for anything, be it slave, servant, or scullery maid. I ask only that you take heart and rest easy on Elizabeth. She is much more delicate than I."

Guy was both angry and impressed. God, but she was a cool one, cool and enticing and defiant. He could sense it in her, though her pose suggested she was the humblest of women. The fighting spirit in her could simply not be ignored. It beckoned to him; it challenged and dared.

"There's no need for that." His tone was curt. "You and your sister may remain here. Your position is no different than it was before I came."

A taut silence descended. Kathryn couldn't bring herself to thank him. Her expression held a watchful caution as he half-turned and poured wine into a silver goblet. Watching him, Kathryn experienced a curious pang. He had removed his hauberk and wore only his boots and a light linen tunic. His dark hair was tousled, as if he'd run his fingers through it repeatedly. He looked tired; there were faint lines etched beside his mouth, a mouth that no longer looked quite so hard . . .

The reality of what she was about to do sank in like the talons of a hawk. She thought of the dagger strapped to her arm, hidden deep within the folds of her sleeves. She was to kill this man, who was so tall, so strong, so vitally alive. Soon his heart would be still and silent. His body cold and stiff.

Her mouth grew dry. Her palms felt sweaty and damp.

I cannot do it, she thought in sudden panic. *I cannot* . . .

"You must tell me about your visit to your uncle."

A little shock went through her. Her eyes jerked up to find him regarding her with a knowing expression on his face. Panic raced through her like flames blazing out of control. He couldn't know why she'd come here . . . He couldn't!

"I would not have gone if he had not summoned me." To her horror, there was a slight catch in her voice.

He paused, the goblet halfway to his lips, his fingers curled around the dull silver. They were long and bronzed like his hands, not fleshy like her uncle's, but lean and strong-looking . . .

Silently he approached her. "I have the feeling," he said very softly, "that you hide something from me, Kathryn. I ask again what has brought you to me."

She wet her lips nervously, unaware that Guy's eyes tracked the movement. "I have told you, milord. I came to discover your intentions for my sister and me—" She broke off, for he was shaking his head.

"I think not. You must forgive my suspicious nature but I'm much more inclined to believe your uncle sent you."

Kathryn gritted her teeth, neither confirming nor denying his words. She despised her own transparency.

He stopped before her. The self-satisfied curl of his lips was maddening. His eyes slid leisurely down the length of her body. Kathryn's face flamed. She felt stripped to the bone.

"He seeks to appease me, eh? You are to be the bartering chip, the sacrificial lamb. He would use you to sweeten my soul and thus go easy on him?"

"I think your soul is already black," she said daringly, "and cannot be sweetened."

He laughed as if she'd said something truly amusing. "And you, dutiful niece that you are, would do anything for him."

"Nay! If the truth be known, I would do anything to be *rid* of him. Why else do you think I sought to marry Roderick?"

"Why, indeed?" Guy quirked an eyebrow. "Pray go on. I would know all the petty little intrigue that goes on in your uncle's household."

"Uncle's household!" Kathryn's eyes blazed. "Elizabeth and I were here long before Uncle. He paid a king's ransom to steal Ashbury out from beneath us!"

"So I've heard," Guy murmured. "And you sought to wrest Ashbury from his grasp?"

"Aye!"

Guy frowned. "I do not understand. How, pray tell, could you hope to accomplish this by marrying Sir Roderick?"

Kathryn was too angry to think clearly. What did it matter if he knew? "You said it yourself in the hall. As chief retainer of uncle's knights, Roderick carries considerable influence. If he were to turn against Uncle, many of the knights would follow his lead."

Guy was stunned at her audacity. This—this chit would have used all her considerable charms to influence her husband and incite open rebellion . . . and she might well have succeeded!

But the next second, his jaw hardened. It was just as he'd suspected. The Lady Kathryn was trouble. He no longer doubted that she hated her uncle—he was surprised she hadn't murdered him in his bed! Nor was there any doubt that her uncle's blood flowed swift and strong in her veins, for she was as shrewd and cunning as he.

He set aside his wine and walked slowly around her, hands on his hips.

"I am curious, Kathryn." The pitch of his voice was very low; it drifted over her like the whisper of silk. "You say you would do anything for Ashbury." He paused, directly behind her. "Just how far would you go?"

Kathryn froze, suddenly afraid to even breathe. Her heart lurched. She had the terrifying sensation that if she moved, he would snatch her to him and she would never be free . . .

She spoke unthinkingly, with the fervency of a prayer. "I would do anything to gain Ashbury, milord, anything. But I have nothing. I have naught to offer you—" Her voice caught breathlessly. "—save myself."

All at once his hand was upon her nape, shocking in its warmth, startling in the way his touch suddenly filled her with a slow melting heat.

His fingers stroked her nape, sending fiery sensations coursing through her veins. "I would understand you, Kathryn. You seek to ease my lonely nights while I am here? You would give yourself to me—without question—if I relinquish my possession of this humble keep?"

Kathryn closed her eyes. "Yes," she whispered, and knew it for the truth. She would sacrifice the only thing left to her—her virtue—if only Ashbury could be hers once more—hers and Elizabeth's. It was the one true dream she had yet to shed—that they could live their lives as they chose, free from the tyranny of men.

Guy felt her tense and wondered idly at the cause. The air of innocence which clung to her puzzled him, for he already knew that she was as wild as the wind which blew from the sea. And it was no gentle lover's play he'd caught her in last night with her lover. Was this naught but a game to her?

Slowly he turned her around. His fingers fell away from her nape and slid to her shoulders. God, she was lovely! Her features were dainty and fine, her lips the color of crushed roses. Wide green eyes the color of spring leaves gazed back at him, framed by thick sooty lashes. Desire cut through him, hot and potent.

There had been other women since he'd learned of Elaine's death. Nameless, faceless women who expected nothing of him. Yet he knew instinctively that if he were to take Kathryn, he would not soon forget her. Her exquisite face would be burned into his memory for a long time to come. Nay, there had been no one like this since . . .

Elaine.

Pain ripped through him, like fire in his soul. He did not understand this gut-twisting desire, for Kathryn was willful and proud where Elaine had been sweet and loving; she was aloof and stubborn where Elaine was warm and eager to please. And her hair was like the wings of a raven where Elaine had been as fair as a gossamer moonbeam . . .

Savagely he wrenched his mind from thoughts of his beloved wife. He was here to avenge her death. Yet here was this . . . this scheming temptress who sought to seduce him!

But that was not right. Kathryn was here, yes, but in truth she wanted no part of him. No, it was neither passion nor desire which brought her to him this night.

It was selfishness and greed, pure and simple. She would give of herself . . . thinking only of herself.

But she possessed a dark bewitching beauty, a beauty that lured and enticed him to her . . . and he hated her for it.

Still he wanted her.

But he'd be damned if he'd dance to her tune. Yet he knew that he would have her . . . when the time was right, when the time was of his own choosing.

Kathryn was suddenly trembling. His eyes were like glittering torches of silver, burning through her, inside her. Shaken to the core, she tried to step back but the hand on her shoulder tightened just enough to remind her she wasn't free. Her lashes fell to shut away the sight but hard fingers captured her chin and brought her gaze to his once more.

His lips twisted. Did he smile? Or did he leer?

She stared at him with eyes both pleading and accusing. The air around them was suddenly seething with an unbearable tension.

He was so close . . . too close. She felt his size with all that she possessed. She could feel the heat of his body, the warm rush of his breath on her cheek. He frightened her, not as he had last eve, but in a way that was terrifying and alien to her.

His voice was strangely thick. "You say you would do anything for Ashbury. I find I am most anxious, Kathryn, to test the truth of your claim."

He caught her against him. His head swooped down. His mouth claimed hers with a suddenness that tore the breath from her. Snatching the gauzy wimple from her head he tossed it aside. Lean fingers plunged into the silk of her hair, bringing it tumbling down over his hands. His kiss was raw and hungry and greedy, filled with the thunder of emotions gone wild and rampant.

He pulled her full and tight against him, imprinting the feel of his body against the softness of hers. In some dark and distant corner of his mind, he registered the sweetness of her lips, the slender suppleness of her body.

But Guy was driven by the sudden fury that still claimed him. He wanted her to remember him, to know that he was not a man she could bend and twist to her whim and will. He touched her as if he owned her, acquainting himself with the ripeness of her breast, the slim fullness of her hips.

At last he pushed her away. She trembled still; her lips were damp and swollen. For just an instant, Guy thought he glimpsed a hint of hurt vulnerability in the wide depths of her eyes . . .

Yet he knew it could not be so, and the thought served to harden his heart. He turned his back on her and moved to the table, reaching once more for his goblet, willing away the pulse of desire which beat at him still.

"I fear I shall have to refuse your kind offer." He smiled tightly, picturing her anger. "For you see, I crave no martyr in my bed, but a woman true, warm and willing. You, dear Kathryn, are naught but a cold heartless bitch with ice in her veins."

Kathryn stared at him. Heartless, was she! A reckless anger consumed her, as hot as the flames which blazed in the hearth. She snatched her dagger from its berth and struck out blindly.

Guy turned just in time. The light from the fire caught the glint of shiny metal. He flung up his arm instinctively, deflecting the blow which would have torn through his flesh. His goblet clattered to the floor; his hands closed in a merciless grip about her wrists, forcing her to drop the dagger. It spun and whirled across the chamber, coming to rest in the corner.

Still she fought him, trying desperately to pummel his chest. Guy dragged her close and stared into her outraged face. Her eyes were scorching, her hatred fired as deeply as his own. He had no doubt that she would have gladly robbed him of his life.

He had been right to begin with, he thought furiously. Kathryn was no angel spun in heaven. She carried the same blood as her uncle.

"So," he said coldly. "The truth comes out. You came here to kill me."

"What does it matter?" she cried out in impotent fury. "You are alive and I have failed."

"And Ashbury is still mine, and will remain so." He took immense delight in reminding her. He thrust her back from him. "My patience wears thin. Begone before I throw you in the dungeon where you belong. But be warned, girl, I'll not turn my back on you again."

He watched as she backed from him slowly, then spun for the door. But before she could reach it, his voice rang out.

"Kathryn!"

She stopped, but did not turn to face him.

"I sent a message earlier today to King Henry, requesting guardianship of you and your sister." His voice was mild, his smile pleasant as she whirled, white-faced and stunned.

"I think your wedding to Sir Roderick shall not take place after all. But do not fear you are doomed to maidenhood. If you behave yourself, mayhap I'll marry you off to some wealthy merchant."

Kathryn yanked the door open and stumbled out. She didn't stop running until she'd reached the sanctuary of her chamber. Even there, she couldn't shut out the sound of his mocking voice.

She pressed cool hands upon her burning cheeks, willing her hands not to shake. God, but she hated him! He had humiliated her, shamed and degraded her. She would never forget the ruthless skill with which he had touched her—the blatant intimacy of his tongue in her mouth, the shocking feel of his hand plundering her breast. She drew a deep shuddering breath. Even now, she could still feel the ridged hardness of battle-toughened thighs forged against hers.

And it was all for naught . . . *all for naught.*

With a little cry she flung herself upon the bed. If the earl had his way, he would send her from here. She would never see Elizabeth again . . . never see Ashbury again . . .

Ashbury was lost to her. She knew it as surely as night followed day.

Bitterness choked her. Her heart was empty and cold and hollow. She would never learn, it seemed. She must ever bow to a will greater than her own, for this was the chessboard of England.

And as always . . . as always, she was naught but a pawn.

Chapter 4

Kathryn woke slowly the next morning, feeling peculiarly lethargic. Curled on her side beneath her furs, she closed her eyes, oddly content to keep the fringes of her tardy mind from struggling to awareness, sensing that to wake fully was to remember something awful, something she would rather forget.

It was early. Through the wooden shutters, the first faint fingerlings of dawn began to creep into the room. Belowstairs, the household was rumbling to life. She heard the faint sounds as if from a great distance away.

Down the hall, there was a scream so shrill it could wake the dead.

Kathryn bolted upright. Mother of God! What on earth . . . ? The piercing scream came again, just as she pushed her legs from beneath the furs. Her heart pounding, she threw on her clothes and thrust her feet into her slippers.

She raced down the passage, her heart pounding apace with her feet. The door to her uncle's room had been thrown open. She started to rush inside, only to stop short with a gasp.

Helga sat in the corner, openly weeping. Richard's bed was surrounded by a crush of men—among them Sir Hugh. Kathryn jumped when someone brushed her elbow.

But it was only Elizabeth. Her skin was ashen, her eyes huge in her pale face. "What is it?" she cried. "What is happening?"

Just then one of the men stepped aside; Kathryn had an unobstructed view of her uncle's bed. His body lay open to her gaze; a sticky pool of crimson flowed across his pillow . . .

His throat had been slit.

An icy jolt of shock ripped through her; her head swam giddily. For an instant Kathryn feared she would be sick.

"My God," she said faintly. "He's been murdered . . . Uncle's been murdered!"

Kathryn saw nothing of the earl that morning. She was informed by one of the servants that he'd left the keep shortly after dawn.

Pray God that he never returned . . .

But alas, he did, just after the noonday meal. She saw him with Sir Hugh in the bailey, deep in conversation. Kathryn stood in the window of her chamber and watched them. She saw Sir Hugh spread his hands wide and shake his head; no doubt they were discussing Richard's murder. But Kathryn was under no illusions. No doubt the earl knew all there was to know about that foul deed . . .

Richard was buried that afternoon. The day was a fitting one for a funeral. Storm clouds hung perilously low and ominous. Though the hour was still early, a misty fog had begun to roll in from the sea. Father Bernard from the village church presided over the gravesite; Richard had refused to have a priest in residence at the keep. Beside her, softhearted Elizabeth dabbed at an occasional tear, while Kathryn stood still as a statue. It was odd, she thought vaguely. She felt nothing—not relief that Richard was dead and could no longer interfere in their lives, nor even hate that he once had.

It was a solemn procession that wound its way back inside the walls of the keep.

Inside the solar, Kathryn tore off her cloak and dropped it on a stool. Elizabeth stood in the center of the room, hugging herself as if for warmth.

" 'Tis hard to believe that Uncle is dead." She shivered. "Who do you think killed him, Kathryn?"

Kathryn's mind sped straight to one man . . . The earl had come to Ashbury to seek revenge for his wife's death. He had come to kill Richard . . .

And he had.

Her laugh was without mirth. "Who do you think? The earl came here for one purpose only— and today he has seen the deed done!"

Elizabeth said nothing, merely hugged herself more tightly.

Kathryn would have said more but some slight sound behind her alerted her. She whirled around.

The earl stood there. Tall. Dark. His presence as commanding as ever.

His gaze flickered to Elizabeth. "Lady Elizabeth—" His voice was pleasant. "—would you mind leaving us alone for a moment?"

Elizabeth bobbed a curtsy and fled.

Kathryn stood her ground boldly. When they were alone, those devilishly slanted brows rose slightly. "Mayhap," he murmured with a strange half-smile, "you'd like to accuse me to my face of murdering your uncle."

"You think I will not?" Kathryn drew herself up proudly. Her tone was as fierce as the blaze in her eyes. "You swore by all that is holy that there would be no murder done at Ashbury. But you lied, O mighty lord. You murdered Richard and for that you will rot in hell."

His smile vanished; in its stead was a cold, merciless mask. It was with a great deal of restraint that Guy held fast to his temper. There were few who would have dared to call him a liar without fear of grievous punishment indeed. He would allow Kathryn this transgression—but this one time only.

He rubbed his chin, the gesture curiously offhand considering the pulsating tension in the room. Those strange silver eyes fixed upon her. "Why," he queried softly, "are you so incensed? I would have thought that you, of all people, would be happy that Richard is gone."

Kathryn inhaled sharply. "I hated him, yes," she said evenly. "But you, milord, you are the one who is glad he is dead!"

She never dreamed that he would turn her words around on her. He merely raised his brows once more and inquired mildly, "And you, dear Kathryn? Can you not say the same?"

Kathryn said nothing. She had oft wished that Richard was gone from their lives—that he had never been born! But she had never wished him dead. And yet—may God take her soul, she could not feel true remorse that Richard was gone.

The earl's laughter grated. "You see? I am right. Furthermore, I do believe I underestimated you, Kathryn. When you told me last eve that you would do anything to be rid of your uncle, I never dreamed you'd be so quick about it. And he was killed with a knife . . . could it be you were frustrated at being foiled by me and decided your uncle should be the one to taste your handiwork instead?"

Kathryn was at first puzzled; then a flare of

white-hot rage spiraled within her. Did the man think she was daft? Oh, she knew his ploy. He sought to transfer the blame from himself to her. And *this* was what men called honor?

It appeared she was the one who had underestimated him. Sir Hugh had said his lord was fair and just, but the earl was conniving and deceitful, like all men.

"You bastard," she said feelingly. "By God, I'll not listen to this." She spun around and stalked toward the door, determined that he would bait her no more.

But Guy was right behind her. She hadn't gone more than two steps before he grabbed her and pinned her shoulders to the wall.

"Let me pass," she cried bitterly. "I had naught to gain from murdering my uncle."

"Naught but revenge."

"The same could be said of you! All I wanted was my home back—but now Ashbury is yours!"

"And will remain mine." His smile was frigid.

She hated him for reminding her. "How can you be so cold?" she cried in despair. "Have you no shame? No heart? You're no better than Uncle," she accused. "A man who kills but for the sake of killing. Nay, I've no doubt you killed him. You had every reason to want him dead!"

That he did, Guy silently admitted. But he didn't deny her accusation. Perhaps it wouldn't hurt to lower her confidence a bit.

Kathryn shoved at his shoulders, but he held her firm. Curiously, no smirk of satisfaction curled those thin lips. His countenance betrayed little evidence of his triumph. Yet his very lack of expression sent a prickle of unease trickling down her spine.

And then he laughed, a sound that sent chills

rippling over her skin. "If that's what you believe, milady, perhaps you'd be wise to watch your back as well."

He let her go, making no attempt to veil his contempt. Stunned, Kathryn slumped against the wall and watched him leave, her face stripped of all color. *Mother of Christ*, she thought numbly. Was she mistaken or—or had he just threatened to kill *her*?

Guy was furious that someone had managed to get to Richard before he did. In his mind, whoever killed Richard had robbed him of his greatest wish—that Richard die at his hands.

Hugh was just as troubled as he watched his friend seek solace in drink, consuming far more wine than he was normally wont to do. The two of them remained in the hall long after the other knights had sought their pallets.

The night was damp and chill; the heat of the fire had cooled to the faint glow of embers. Hugh tossed another log onto the fire. Hooking his fingers into the tie at his waist, he glanced at his friend. Now, he decided, was the time to pose the question that had been on his mind all day.

"Guy, now that Richard is dead, what comes next, my friend?"

Bleary gray eyes lifted slowly. Hugh moved to sit at the bench across from Guy.

Guy's eyelids felt as if they'd been weighted with stone. He stared into the flickering flames of the fire. "I'm weary of fighting," he said slowly. "If you must know, Hugh, my only wish now is to see Peter again. He is my son and I—I hardly know the boy." A fleeting yearning passed over his granite features.

"So you will return to Sedgewick and settle back into your estates?"

"Aye," Guy replied. "That I will."

Hugh frowned. "And what of Ashbury?"

It was a moment before Guy spoke. "I'm not about to hand over the spoils of victory," he said slowly. "But I need someone here whom I can trust." He raised his head to gaze at his friend directly. "I've a boon to ask, Hugh. I understand why you refused Ramsay, but what if you were to remain here at Ashbury as castellan? I plan to leave some of my troops in place here, and it would please me greatly if you accept."

Hugh's mind veered straight to Elizabeth. He envisioned the golden glory of her hair, the shining depths of the bluest eyes in the kingdom. He loved her sweet, gentle nature, the air of purity and goodness that surrounded her. He had yet to hear her laughter, but in time, he promised himself, he would . . . and it would be like the tinkling of a waterfall, light and lilting and music to his soul.

Nay, he thought, *'twould be no hardship at all to stay here with Elizabeth.* "How could I refuse such an offer?" The trace of a smile curved his lips.

"Aha! I've seen that expression a time or two before! You're smitten, my friend." Guy chuckled. He propped his elbows on the rough wooden trestle table and leaned forward. "So tell me, which do you favor? The raven or the dove?"

Hugh gave a hearty burst of laughter. "I much prefer the gentle cooing of a dove to the strident cry of a raven. Alas, I've a feeling 'twould take a falcon to be a match for the likes of the Lady Kathryn," he joked.

Guy said nothing.

"Indeed," Hugh went on, "a man like you, I'd say."

But Guy wasn't laughing. His smile was gone. He rose to stare broodingly out the window. Something in his features made Hugh eye him more closely.

"You've told me your plans for Ashbury," he murmured. "But what of the Lady Kathryn?"

Guy's jaw tightened. "If she thinks Ashbury is within her grasp, she's sadly mistaken," he said harshly. "She's selfish and stubborn—all she wants is Ashbury. And she's as cunning, calculating, and treacherous as her uncle."

Hugh cast a doubtful glance at his lord. "Oh, come now, Guy. She's but a woman—"

"A woman who tried her damnedest to see an end to me!" His voice grim, Guy told his friend how Kathryn had revealed her plans to marry Roderick and then wrest Ashbury from her uncle's grasp; how she'd then tried to barter her body with him—and how, at his flat refusal, she had sought to turn her knife on him!

"She also said she'd do anything to be rid of her uncle," Guy finished. "And she may have done exactly that!"

Hugh was startled. "You can't believe *she* murdered Richard," he protested. "Surely, if that had been her intent she'd have seen him dead long ago!"

"That's the only thing that stops me from being certain she did it," Guy admitted. "But I still don't trust her, Hugh. If I let her stay at Ashbury, she and her lover Roderick may well succeed in gaining Ashbury for themselves after all."

By now Hugh was growing alarmed. He recognized the unyielding intent reflected in Guy's features. He suspected that Guy did Kathryn a grave injustice in judging her so harshly—and yet he wasn't totally convinced Guy was wrong, either. But she was a woman, after all, and so he was inclined to leniency.

"You can't throw her in the dungeon, man. Despite everything, she's gently born—"

"Not gently bred, take my word for it!" Guy's laugh was brittle.

Hugh surveyed Guy uneasily. "So what will you do with her then?"

Guy's smile crept back, but it was a smile that didn't quite reach his eyes. Hugh was suddenly very sure that smile did not bode well for the lady in question . . .

"When I leave," he said flatly, "the lady goes with me."

The keep was ahum with activity the following morning. Yesterday's fog had given way to blue skies and sunshine. From her chamber window Kathryn watched a half-dozen grooms scurrying to and from the stables. The earl's soldiers were everywhere.

Alice, one of the household maids, was hurrying down the corridor when Kathryn stepped from her chamber. "Alice," she said, "the bailey is filled with the earl's soldiers. Do you know what's going on?"

"Aye, milady." Alice bobbed a small curtsy. " 'Tis the new lord. He leaves Ashbury this very morn for his home in Somerset." Alice dropped another curtsy and hastened on.

Kathryn longed to clap her hands with glee. Her first thought on seeing all the activity was that the earl was leaving, but she hadn't dared to hope it was true.

Near the stairs she passed Helga. The girl said nothing, merely cast a rather smug sidelong glance at her mistress, but even that wasn't enough to dim Kathryn's soaring spirits. She smiled all the way down to the great hall.

Hearing footsteps behind her, she stopped and

glanced over her shoulder. Elizabeth was only a dozen steps behind her. "Good morning, sister!" Kathryn sang out. " 'Tis a grand day indeed, is it not?"

Her fine golden brows lifting, Elizabeth joined her on the step. " 'Tis a fine mood you're in, to be sure," she said, peering at her closely. "Though I fail to understand why today is any different from yesterday."

Kathryn merely laughed. She snagged Elizabeth's arm and led her outside.

In the bailey, her eyes immediately fell upon the earl and Hugh. They both stood near the center well. The devil and his disciple, she decided scathingly.

It was Hugh who spotted them first. He raised a hand in greeting and began to approach, his features alight with pleasure.

"Lady Kathryn. Lady Elizabeth." He took both their hands in turn, bowing low over each.

The earl, slower to join them, displayed no such courtesy. He acknowledged their presence with an upward hike of one black brow.

"Ladies," he murmured. "You are just in time."

Kathryn swept him her best curtsy. "Good morning, my lord," she said sweetly. "As you can see, we've come to bid you a safe journey back to your home."

His gaze, cool and assessing, took in her agreeable demeanor. *Aha*, Guy thought. *Now that she thinks she's well rid of me, she's prepared to be gracious.*

It gave him immense pleasure to know that she was wrong.

Kathryn watched his slow-growing smile with mounting trepidation. It betrayed vast amusement, though for the life of her, she didn't understand what he found so entertaining.

A few of his troops had departed yesterday. From the corner of her eye, she noticed that another thirty or so appeared to be ready and waiting.

She stepped back. "Well," she said crisply, "the hour grows late. I'm sure you're anxious to take your leave. Why, Somerset must be several days' ride from here."

"Four," he corrected. "Which reminds me, Lady Kathryn, I think you should know that I'm leaving Sir Hugh in charge here, as well as a number of my knights."

Kathryn held fast to her temper. Meanwhile, the earl's disturbing smile widened further.

Beside her, Elizabeth grew increasingly uneasy.

His manner was wreaking havoc with Kathryn's nerves. Damn him anyway, why didn't he just leave! She was about to say something—anything!—to speed him on his way. But she'd barely opened her mouth when she spied her small palfrey being led from the stable.

Guy's gaze followed hers. "Your mount," he said politely.

Her heart began to hammer. What was going on here? she wondered frantically. Whatever it was, she'd not be a part of it!

She turned to the groom. "You must be mistaken, Will," she said with a shake of her head. "I didn't ask that Esmerelda be saddled—"

"But I did," interjected the earl from behind her.

Kathryn whirled, noting with satisfaction that he only narrowly escaped a jab in the stomach by her elbow. "For what purpose?" she demanded.

"I should think that would be obvious. You, Lady Kathryn, are coming with me."

"To Somerset?" Disdain mingled with incredulity.

"Aye. To Somerset—and Sedgewick." He leisurely crossed his arms over his chest and awaited her reaction.

As he'd expected, it wasn't long in coming. Her eyes narrowed. Her jaw snapped shut, only to open a scant instant later. "I have no intention of going with you to Somerset."

"And I have no intention of leaving you here at Ashbury. You and your Roderick could form an alliance that would be dangerous to my health, my lady fair, which is why you go where I go."

His utter calm was infuriating; his audacity knew no bounds. Kathryn's gaze swept around the bailey, seeking and coming to rest on Roderick, who stood near the entrance to the hall. She had no doubt that he'd heard every word she and the earl exchanged. He looked angry but he said nothing. Kathryn rebelled at the reluctant helplessness she sensed in him. A part of her raged at his acquiescence, and yet another part of her understood that to challenge his new lord was to forfeit his life.

Her gaze swung back to the earl. "You do this only because I have no knightly protector!" she cried.

Guy hadn't missed the look exchanged between the two. So, he noted angrily, she sought salvation from her lover.

His gaze flickered briefly toward Roderick. "Indeed you do not," he taunted softly.

His mockery cut deep. Kathryn dimly noted Roderick retreat into the hall; never had she hated the earl more.

She lashed out unthinkingly. "I'll not play nursemaid to your brat, do you hear?"

"I've not asked you to," he sneered. "You've Richard's blood in your veins, girl. I'm not sure I want you anywhere near my son!"

Shattered inside but determined not to show it, she met and matched the fiery hold of his eyes. If it had been anyone but the earl, she might have cried and pleaded for indulgence.

But she hadn't counted on Elizabeth. Wrapped in a red haze of fury, she was scarcely aware that Elizabeth had stepped forward.

"My lord!" Elizabeth clasped her hands together as if in prayer. "Surely you will not take my sister from our home!"

Guy's harsh manner softened ever so slightly. Elizabeth's blue eyes were huge, her expression utterly stricken.

His tone was gentleness itself. "I'm sorry, Elizabeth. But I fear I must—at least for now."

She cried out sharply, "But you cannot. Oh, please, you cannot take her from here . . . you cannot!"

Those devilishly arched brows rose high in silent question.

Elizabeth swallowed hard. The devious plan Kathryn had once thought to use against Richard leapt into her mind. Oh, Mother Mary, did she dare . . . ? Would she burn and rot in hell for bringing about such a lie . . . ? Yet she could not bear to be without Kathryn. Never in their lives had they been separated—never!

Dimly she heard his voice. "Elizabeth," he inquired, "why do you insist Kathryn remain here?"

"Because—because she is with child!"

Kathryn gasped. Guy sucked in a harsh breath; his eyes immediately cut back to Kathryn. Her gaze swiveled to lock on her sister. So shocked was she that she failed to notice the grim mask that descended over Guy's features.

"Kathryn!"

She actually jumped at the sound of his voice.

"I asked if the child has made you ill!"

Too stunned to be thinking clearly, Kathryn shook her head.

"Then my decision stands," the earl stated flatly. "You go with me to Sedgewick, since obviously the child will not be here for many months to come."

Though she was shaken and distraught, Kathryn quickly recognized his determination was as relentless as hers.

"I—I need a cloak," she said desperately. "I'll not keep you waiting long, I promise." A moment alone was all she sought—she knew the keep better than the earl or any of his men. She could flee and hide and they would soon tire of searching for her and be off . . .

But alas, it seemed *he* had anticipated everything! Before she could spin around, Helga appeared, her cloak thrown over one arm. Another servant followed in her wake, balancing a small chest on his shoulder. Kathryn's heart sank as she recognized it as her own.

Guy's patience was nearing an end. "Take your leave of your sister," he advised curtly.

A painful ache tightened Kathryn's throat as she turned to her sister. By now Elizabeth was openly sobbing. Kathryn wrapped her arms around her. "Shhh," she attempted to soothe her. "Be strong, Elizabeth . . . no, do not say me nay. You *are* strong, sister, stronger than you know. 'Twill not be so bad, you'll see. And I'll be back soon, I promise."

Elizabeth clung to her even more tightly.

Witnessing their painful good-bye, there was a slight easing of the hard line of Guy's mouth. He found himself stung by a prick of conscience. It wasn't because of Kathryn, he assured himself, but Elizabeth.

Kathryn forced back the burning threat of tears. She drew back, caught Elizabeth's hand, and pressed a kiss on her forehead. "Wish me well, now, sister," she whispered. "And may God be with you."

"Kathryn—" She choked. Kathryn squeezed her fingers, unable to manage any more. Then with a strangled cry, Elizabeth reeled and fled.

It was a moment before Kathryn was able to turn to Hugh, who still hovered nearby. Overwhelmingly conscious of the earl's all-seeing presence, she began to speak, her voice husky and low.

"I do not know you, Sir Hugh, and yet I—I sense that you are a kind man . . . I *hope* that you are, for I have no one else to turn to."

She paused to draw breath. "I've not yet told you how sorry I am about your sister." Her smile was a trifle watery. "And now, it seems, I must ask you to take care of mine." She gazed beseechingly into his eyes. "Will you do this for me, Sir Hugh? Will you watch over Elizabeth?"

A faint smile creased his lips. "I will, but I think it only fair to warn you, my motives are not entirely without selfishness."

His meaning was not lost on her. Kathryn was keenly aware of his flare of interest in her sister. She hesitated, a shadow flitting across her delicate features.

"Then there is something you must know," she said slowly. "Sir Hugh, it may not be possible to woo and win my sister, for Elizabeth is not comfortable with a man's attention—indeed, she is afraid of most men." She went on to hurriedly confide how Elizabeth had witnessed their mother's rape years earlier. "I fear," Kathryn ended, "that the memory has never truly left her."

Hugh listened, somberly intent. *Guy is wrong about her*, he thought suddenly. *His vengeance has blinded him to Kathryn's goodness—she could never willfully hurt anyone.*

"I'll not disappoint you, Lady Kathryn." His gaze met Kathryn's, unerringly direct. In that instant, a silent current of understanding passed between them.

She touched his cheek. "I'll keep both you and my sister in my prayers, Sir Hugh."

She stepped back. At a signal from the earl, her palfrey was led over. Kathryn laid a hand on the horse's mane; all at once the earl was there to assist her in mounting. At the touch of his hands on her waist, she twisted away. After what he had done this day, his effort at gallantry merely made her angrier. She mounted unassisted, unaware of the tightening of his jaw as his hands fell to his sides.

A moment later they were passing through the gates. Inwardly devastated, Kathryn didn't dare look back for fear she would burst into tears. Her gaze stabbed into his back where he rode at the head of his troops. It was easier . . . so much easier to focus instead on her hatred of him. He was wrenching her away from Ashbury—from all that she loved. Yet even as her heart yawned empty and cold, her soul burned with a rage more potent than any she had ever known. She had lost this battle of wills, she conceded bitterly.

She'd not lose the next.

Chapter 5

So Kathryn was pregnant . . . she was with child. Guy felt a flash of anger every time he thought about it, for it only proved she was the slut he'd known her to be. Oh, he could easily see how her predicament had come about—how her lover Roderick had been unable to resist her wiles. It struck him then that he assumed her Roderick was the babe's father . . . but what if he was not? Hadn't she offered herself to him just last eve, knowing she carried another man's child? Mayhap she had no idea who the father was! Indeed, she was a temptation few men could resist. Even he himself was not immune to her beauty.

And that was the hell of it.

She refused to look at him the entire day, but Guy had no such qualms. Time and again he found his eyes drawn to her, as if he'd been caught in a web from which there was no escape. Slim and straight, she rode her mount as if she were a queen, her carriage proud and erect.

Guy despised himself for his weakness, but he had only to glance at her to visualize those eyes that flashed like emeralds in the sun—to remember the fascinating heat of that sweetly curved mouth trapped beneath his, the delectable roundness of her breast beneath his palm.

His mood grew ever more vile.

Twilight hovered on the horizon before he called a halt to the day's journey. They stopped on the outskirts of the forest. Nearby was a clear, babbling stream.

Kathryn heaved a silent prayer of thanks. If the earl had chosen to go any further, she didn't think she could stand it. She wasn't used to riding more than a few hours at most; her thighs and backside ached unbearably.

The earl was busy giving orders to his men. Kathryn reined Esmerelda to a stop and prepared to slide to the ground. One of the earl's soldiers appeared. Hands spanning her waist, he lifted her easily to the ground. Kathryn smiled her thanks— his hands displayed a tendency to linger. A single dark look from the earl and the knight hastily backed away.

Kathryn's muscles protested mightily at holding her weight after so many hours on horseback. But once on her feet she became aware of a rather urgent need.

Most of the earl's soldiers swarmed in the clearing beneath the trees. Kathryn started off in the opposite direction.

The earl's voice stopped her cold. "Hold!" he shouted. Four long strides brought him to her side. He grasped her arm rudely. "What is this?" he demanded.

Of all the arrogant . . . ! Kathryn took a deep breath and struggled to control her rising temper. "I crave a moment alone." She couldn't look at him as she spoke. She could think of no way to convey her need to him.

His laughter grated. "What manner of fool do

you take me for, mistress? A moment alone—so that you may flee?" He laughed again. "Absolutely not!"

Kathryn twitched at her skirt. Vivid color stained her cheeks as she implored desperately, "For nature's call, milord."

"And I tell you again, lady, not alone."

His sharpness shattered her. He trampled on her dignity the way his soldiers trampled the fields. The knowledge that he would not allow her this privacy wounded her as nothing else had. At last she looked at him, dismayed and miserably embarrassed.

"I'll not flee, milord. This I swear."

His grip on her arm tightened. It was on the tip of his tongue to retort that, as Richard's niece, her vow meant nothing to him.

"Please," she whispered.

He saw her convulsive swallow—saw the way her throat worked and swore violently to himself. Damn, but the wench knew exactly how to probe his every weakness. Yet he sensed the word cost her no small amount of pride.

"Begone, then," he said curtly. "But be quick about it," he warned. "And do not think to escape me—" A devilish smile dallied about his lips. "—lest you come upon some wild, ferocious beast with a fancy for your lovely flesh." He turned his back and retraced his steps toward his knights.

Kathryn picked up her skirts. Bah, she decided as she marched toward a clump of bushes, it was altogether likely the only beast in these woods was the Earl of Sedgewick!

She returned to the clearing several minutes later. A group of soldiers was busily erecting a tent. A roaring fire blazed nearby. A spit had been fashioned above it, from which some delicious odor wafted her way. But Kathryn was too tired to take much notice. Fatigue weighted her body like a stone. She made her way toward a stately oak tree and lowered herself to the mossy ground, her shoulder propped against the tree trunk. Closing her eyes, she decided to rest for just a moment or two.

Some time later a shadow fell over her form. She was asleep, Guy noticed, a sight that gave him pause. Her head was tilted against the tree trunk in what appeared a most uncomfortable angle. Arms crossed over her breasts, she huddled beneath the threadbare wool of that damnable excuse for a cloak. Perhaps it was the childlike pose, but she seemed very vulnerable and very young just then, and he experienced a sliver of remorse. He'd set a breakneck pace that day, stopping only to water the horses. Weariness was plainly etched on his men's faces, yet Kathryn had uttered not a single word of protest or complaint—another time, perhaps, and he might have admitted to a twinge of admiration.

She was clearly exhausted. He debated whether or not to let her sleep, but decided she needed nourishment, if not for herself, then for the sake of her babe.

He clamped a hand to her shoulder and shook her. Her lashes fluttered open slowly; eyes as green as fresh spring leaves stared up at him in obvious confusion.

It hit him like a blow to the stomach just how lovely she was—beauteous enough to turn a king's eye. Her lips were parted; Guy fancied he could see the gentle rise and fall of her breasts. Her cheeks were sleep-flushed and pink. But her beauty, he reminded himself scathingly, was only on the surface, for hadn't she proved once already how treacherous a creature she really was?

He had no doubt she would prove it yet again.

"Here. 'Tis time to eat." He thrust a trencher of wild fowl and crusty bread into her hands. A moment later, his own meal in hand, he sat cross-legged on the ground beside her.

At least, Kathryn thought, he didn't propose to starve her. Nearer the fire, the knights' talk and laughter grew boisterous. She risked a peek at the earl from beneath her lashes. The rigid cast of his profile discouraged conversation. Not that she was so inclined, she thought with a sniff. Only she'd had no one to talk to the entire day . . . But she'd keep her silence for a twelvemonth before she'd deign to converse with this arrogant lord! On that thought, she confined her attention to her food.

Once the meal was done, his men began to disperse. When she saw them preparing to retire for the night, her gaze traveled uneasily to the earl. He had retreated to stand several paces behind her near the tent.

Kathryn pushed herself to her feet. She wet her lips nervously. "Where am I to sleep?"

In answer he swept open the flap of the tent. "A trifle humble for her ladyship's taste, I'm sure," he drawled, "but since I've always found it comfortable enough, I'm sure you shall, too."

Kathryn's eyes narrowed. She wasn't quite certain she liked the sound of that. "And you, milord?" she inquired stiffly. "Do you sleep within the tent?"

He bestowed on her a look so withering it would have made many a man cringe and creep away. His mood was as black as his soul, she thought.

"I do," was all he said. Crossing his arms across the breadth of his chest, he merely raised his brows and waited for her to precede him into the tent.

She squared her shoulders. "Then I sleep without," she announced. Her nose in the air, she spun about and began to resume her place beneath the oak tree.

He never gave her the chance. She found herself shackled about the wrist and dragged to the tent before she could draw breath.

"I thought we settled this the other night," he said through his teeth. "I'd sooner cut off my hand than lay a finger on you, Kathryn. Do you think me so enslaved by your beauty that I forget who you are? You stir nothing in me save my temper . . . most certainly not my passions! In a word, you leave me cold, mistress."

Cold, is it? jeered a voice inside him. He decried her . . . even as he desired her. Why, the very thought of bedding her sent a scalding rush of heat to his loins. Indeed, he half-feared the Lord would strike him down for daring to speak such a falsehood!

She remained where she was, as cool and haughty as ever. His words seemingly touched no part of her.

"I suppose 'tis only right that I warn you, Kathryn . . . out here in the open you render yourself fair game for any of my men-at-arms." His tone carried a note of bored impatience. "While I am quite discriminating about the lady who shares my bed, my knights are not always so . . . discriminating. My guess is that it's been a while since they partook of the pleasures of the flesh—so likely as not, most any woman will do."

Even you. There was no need for him to speak the words aloud—his derisive half-smile reeked of smugness. And all at once Kathryn was remembering the lewdness of his men that night at Ashbury, when she had sought to leave the great hall with Elizabeth.

But the earl's scorn made her long to slap the

arrogant leer from his visage—oh, if only she dared!

"You are as crude as I expected." She swept past him with an icy disdain, bent low, and entered the tent. She contented herself with the certainty that her choice was the lesser of two evils . . . she hoped.

The earl did not follow. Inside, the tent was large and surprisingly spacious. There was a small pile of furs near the entrance. Kathryn selected one for herself and moved to the far corner. Despite the earl's assurances that he'd not lay a finger on her—as if she would even allow him!—she had no intention of disrobing. She lay down, cloak and all, and pulled the fur over her shoulders.

It wasn't long before the earl entered. Kathryn lay on her back, determined to ignore him. The flames from the fire outside cast a faint glow inside the tent, just enough for her to make out the outline of his form.

Every muscle in her body tightened when he moved past her. She heard his scabbard drop to the ground. The next thing she knew he was pulling his tunic up and over his head—it slipped to the ground with a rustle. Now his hands were on his chausses . . . She felt her jaw go slack. Surely he didn't mean to sleep naked, with her not three feet away . . .

Outside someone threw another chunk of wood onto the fire. The blaze burned brighter still.

For the space of a heartbeat, his form was outlined in far more detail than she cared to see. Long legs. Wide chest. Powerful shoulders. A brazen masculinity . . .

She squeezed her eyes shut and turned to her side. Her heart was thudding so that she feared it would crash through her chest at any moment.

She had thought not to sleep a wink that night,

with the earl so close at hand. But it wasn't long
before her exhaustion wooed her into slumber.

Such was not the case two nights hence. Kathryn
curled herself into a tight little ball to keep from
tossing and turning—and waking the earl.

For if he woke now, all would be lost.

If Kathryn was feeling a trifle proud of herself,
she had reason to. She had used these past two
days well; it was a time to lull the earl into a
false complacency. He appeared to have relaxed
his guard a bit. He no longer warned her sharply
whenever she sought refuge for her private needs.
His gaze no longer shadowed her slightest move
around the camp at night.

But Kathryn did not seek to play the meek and
humble maiden. Oh, no, she suspected he was too
wise to accept such a drastic change in her. She was
no match for him in physical strength and so she
continued to battle him with what weapons were
at hand—with words and wit.

The time had passed agonizingly slowly that
night. It didn't take long before the earl's breathing
grew deep and even, but Kathryn waited hours
to make certain he was plunged deep into the
netherworld of dreams.

It was now or never.

Scarcely daring to breathe, she slipped from her
furs. Not once had the earl mentioned her penchant
for sleeping in her clothes—this was a boon she
hadn't considered that first night.

She crouched low and began to move stealthily
toward the entrance. Behind her, the earl flung
himself over on his back. Kathryn froze, her breath
tumbling to a standstill. She waited—forever, it
seemed!—before daring to creep forward again.

Outside the tent, moonlight spilled down from

the sky in shining splendor; the clearing was nearly as light as day. The horses were tethered on the far side of the encampment, some distance away from the knights. It was there that Kathryn directed her silent footsteps. Her fingers were shaking as she found Esmerelda among the horses and released her. Moments later they vanished into the shadows with ghostly ease.

Only the moon bore witness as Kathryn tossed back her head and let a bubbly laugh escape. She was free . . . *free!*

And as she rode onward into the night, her single thought was that escape had proved not nearly as difficult as she had expected . . .

Not once did she consider it might have been too easy.

Guy woke shortly after dawn the next morning. For a moment he lay perfectly still, his half-closed eyes absorbing the purplish ribbon of light visible through the flap. Then, with a yawn and a mighty stretch, he rose and began to dress.

Not once did he glance at the empty pile of furs beside him.

Outside, the camp was stirring to life. Guy called for his squire Tom to bring food to break the morning fast. The boy started to scurry away, then paused to glance back at his master.

His gaze flitted toward the tent. "For the lady, too, milord?"

He shook his head. "The lady is not here, Tom." The boy gaped.

A smile curled Guy's handsome mouth. "It seems the lady has decided to take a slight detour on her way to Sedgewick, Tom."

"Milord?"

Guy was sorely tempted to throw up his hands.

The boy showed promise with the sword and lance, but he had much to learn about the ways of his enemies.

"She fled during the wee hours of the night, Tom. She thinks to return to Ashbury."

The boy let out a wheezing laugh. "Why, she ought to know she can't escape from *you*." He laughed again, as if he thought the idea of a mere woman besting his lord highly amusing indeed.

Guy was not so amused a short time later as he ordered Sir Jerome to lead the rest of the party back to Sedgewick. They parted company in a flurry of dust—Sir Jerome and his men-at-arms speeding to the north, Guy to the south.

Aye, he affirmed grimly, urging his destrier still faster, he would bring the Lady Kathryn to heel. And while he was about it, mayhap he would put the fear of God into her soul.

With luck, Kathryn decided, the earl wouldn't discover her absence till morningtide. She had gleaned from his speech with his men-at-arms that they would reach Sedgewick by noon the next day. It was her most fervent prayer that, upon discovering she had fled, he would make only a token search for her. After all, he'd made his opinion of her abundantly clear. Since he was so near his home, she hoped he would decide she wasn't worth the trouble of recapture, abandon pursuit, and forget her existence . . . as she planned to forget his.

The day dawned bright and gloriously warm. Kathryn kept the rutted roadway in sight, but rode amidst the woods guarding the side of the road, for no decent woman would ride about unescorted. Her nerves were tightly wound, for several times she detected the dull clopping of hooves and was forced to wheel Esmerelda and take cover where she might find it.

By late afternoon, the sun beat warmly upon her head. Anxious to seek respite from the nagging worry that the earl lurked but a footstep behind her, Kathryn decided to seek shelter for the night while it was still light. She found a secluded glade that would serve quite well. Gnarled oaks arched high above. Hazy spears of waning sunlight cast the clearing in a golden glow.

A gently rushing stream flowed nearby. She led Esmerelda to the cool gushing waters and allowed her to drink her fill. The palfrey slurped gustily, wringing a laugh from Kathryn. When Esmerelda had finished, Kathryn secured her near a patch of grass. While the horse grazed, she dropped her pouch on the ground and began gathering wood for a fire. The task completed to her satisfaction, she gazed longingly toward the stream.

Wildflowers grew in sweet profusion along the bank, pushing up amidst leafy moss and tufts of luxuriant green grass. The air was sweetly scented. Above the treetops, the twilight sky darkened to pink and gold. Here in this beautiful lush setting, Kathryn felt the strain of the day begin to seep from her weary bones.

She fancied the dust from her days of travel lay thick and heavy on her skin. Succumbing to temptation, she stripped to her chemise and bent to the stream. Cupping the cool, clear liquid in her hands, she rinsed her face. Again and again she scooped the water from the stream. Tiny rivulets streamed down her arms and the calves of her legs. She ended by splashing her chest—once, twice, again, gasping a little at the chill. And though she felt cleaner, she didn't feel as refreshed as she'd hoped to.

She darted a hasty glance around the glade. High above, birds chattered and flitted to and fro among the branches. A furry rabbit scurried through the grass. On impulse, Kathryn quickly shed her chemise and dropped it on a rock. She was safe here. There were no prying eyes to invade her privacy.

That was hardly the case.

From behind the concealing breadth of a black oak, bold gray eyes consumed her every move. The thin linen of her chemise hid little of her sweetly feminine form. His mind besieged by lustful imaginings, Guy sucked in a harsh breath when she cast the hem of her chemise up and over her head. His gaze roamed hotly over the visual feast she provided his eyes.

She had twisted her hair into a long rope and drawn it over her shoulder. Her ivory skin glistened like a lustrous pearl. She was slender almost to the point of thinness, and yet her hips flared out from a waist that was incredibly narrow. Her breasts were full and perfectly formed, round and alluring and tipped with nipples the color of a creamy pink rose. She was as breathtakingly flawless as he had imagined—and there was the rub, he thought with a twist of his lips. He despised her, and yet he *had* dreamed of seeing her like this. Naked and open to him. Bare as a babe . . .

In the instant before she waded into the stream, his gaze swooped to the naked flesh below her waist. His lips thinned to a stern line. There was no sign of a babe swelling ripe and round in her belly—none at all! Between the span of her hips, her belly was concave and hollow. And yet . . . Doubt gnawed deep inside him. He wasn't entirely ignorant where childbirth was concerned. He reminded himself that it might be weeks before she grew heavy with her burden.

Slipping from the stream, Kathryn wrung the water from her hair. Shivering a little, she hurriedly donned her garments. Hunger gnawed at her stomach as she built a small fire. She hadn't much food, only what she'd managed to slip into the small pouch tied to her kirtle, but it would be enough to get her back to Ashbury. She gnawed on a hard crust of bread, making it last until darkness settled over the earth.

The moon climbed slowly aloft. The night was dark and crystal-clear. Flung against the ebony sky, the stars glittered with bejewelled brilliance. But although the day had proved warm and pleasant, with the setting of the sun the night's chill soon pulled her within its grasp. Huddled beneath the scant protection of her cloak, Kathryn edged closer to the fire, drawing her legs to her chest and wrapping her arms around her knees for warmth.

A low mist began to gather, hovering just above the ground. A keening howl pierced the air—a wolf. An eerie feeling prickled along her spine. She had thought the glade to be safe, but was it? These woods were filled with all manner of beast—including two-legged ones, as she well knew! And all at once every tale of cutthroats, murderers, and renegades she'd ever heard rampaged through her mind.

She was suddenly on guard, her nerves sharpened to a screaming pitch of awareness. A slight sound from across the glade brought her upright. She lurched to her feet, her eyes frantically searching the night-shrouded stillness. But she spied naught but trailing fingers of frothy mist swirling through the trees.

It was into that gossamer mist that a masculine form took shape, tall and powerful. Kathryn stood as if paralyzed. She wanted desperately to run, but her legs refused to do her bidding. Against the midnight gloom, the man appeared dark and featureless.

And then he stepped forward, close enough that the flickering firelight cast granite-hewn features into stark relief.

Kathryn stared, stunned and disbelieving. The beat of her heart grew still and silent, then leaped wildly to her throat as horror clutched at her insides.

"No," she whispered. A low sob tore from deep inside her, a cry of desolate despair. *"No!"*

Panic raced through her. She rushed blindly into the encroaching forest. Branches whipped across her cheeks, stinging her eyes. A cry escaped her as she stumbled. She quickly pushed herself from the damp ground. Did she only imagine the pounding footsteps behind her . . . or was it merely the rampant thunder of her heart? Her mind beset by frenzy, she had but one coherent thought . . . She would not yield herself over to him so easily. She had to keep running . . . She had to escape!

But alas, there was no hope for it—no hope at all.

He was upon her, his arm about her waist like an iron band. She found herself lifted and tossed over his shoulder like a sack of grain. Kathryn screamed and struggled and squirmed, clawing and pounding his back with fists and nails. But his jarring steps never faltered. In desperation she sank her teeth into the flesh of his back.

"Bitch!" Guy muttered. He gritted his teeth and flung back her skirts. He brought his open palm down hard on her bare rump, hard enough to make his hand sting. He felt her spine go rigid—but she pummeled his back no more.

By no means had he quelled her intent. He deposited her rudely on her back near the fire. Kathryn tried to roll away, but he was there above her, pinning her beneath outspread legs. Though she was gasping and winded, sprawled beneath him like a bird on a spit, she wasted no time venting the full force of her fury on him.

"I loathe you, de Marche! You are the spawn of the devil, the son of a warted toad! May your soul rot in Hades for all eternity—"

"Should my soul end up in hell," he interrupted smoothly, "rest assured yours will dwell alongside mine."

His gaze, cool and relentless, touched the fire in hers.

Kathryn struggled upright. He stepped back a pace but made no move to help her. Once on her feet, she choked back a cry of bitterness. "Damn you! Why couldn't you simply let me go? Why did you have to hunt me down like—like an animal!"

"Nay, not like an animal. Were that the case, I'd have homed in for the kill hours ago." He smiled at the confusion he read in her expression. "You did not realize that I followed close behind, eh? You could have been back within my grasp well before the sun reached its zenith—indeed, before you left my tent last night."

She regarded him numbly. "What are you saying? That you *let* me escape? That you were but a step behind me the entire day?"

His smile widened in silent assent.

Kathryn's eyes rounded. God in heaven . . . ! Had he been at the stream while she stripped and bathed? At the realization that he had seen her nude, her face began to flame.

"You tricked me!" she accused. "Why? Why would you do such a thing?"

"Why?" He arched a heavy black brow. "I should think the answer is obvious. You acted like a child who would test the limits of discipline, and so I thought to teach you a lesson—that you go nowhere lest I say so. 'Tis my will which will triumph over yours, Kathryn."

"Never," she vowed.

"Always."

He moved before she realized his intention. His hand locked around her wrist. He jerked her to him with a force that ripped the breath from her lungs.

"You escaped me once, milady. Do not think to do so again, for I vow I'll not be so lenient the next time."

She shrank back instinctively—she could not stop herself. Until that moment she did not realize how truly angry he was . . . His eyes seemed to burn with all the fires of hell.

His laughter was a terrible sound. "Afraid, Kathryn? Ah, lass, you should be, for you try my patience as no other before you. You have put me to much trouble—much trouble indeed. And I begin to wonder that you are worth it."

Somehow she managed to raise her chin and match his stare bravely, but her knees were shaking. Never had a man been more threatening by simple virtue of his sex. He towered over her, tall and powerful. His jaw was set tight. His silver eyes pierced through her like a lance. She read in his eyes the desire to punish her. She resented him for his power over her, even as she despaired her own weakness.

Courage come to her then—a reckless semblance of it, at least.

"Go ahead!" she taunted him unthinkingly. Let them meet as the enemies they were. "It won't be the first time I've felt the bite of the lash or the cuff of a man's hand. Or mayhap now that you've killed

Richard, you've a mind to murder me as well!"

"I will only say this once," he growled. "I did not murder your uncle, though nothing would have given me greater pleasure. Yes, I sought vengeance! But someone cheated me of my revenge."

"And I am to believe you? This from a man whose code of honor includes trickery?" Her lip curled in disdain. She tried to wrench from his hold. He wouldn't let her.

His arms came around her, tight and unyielding, trapping her hands between them. His mouth enveloped hers, ruthless and punishing, the pressure of his lips against hers so demanding she felt the gnashing of his teeth against her own. His tongue dove deep within her mouth, deep and plundering. Unaware that she did so, she gave a tiny whimper of distress, and suddenly, the tenor of his kiss began to change . . .

The world about her seemed to spin and swirl. The fusion of his mouth on hers was no longer hard and brutal, but hungry and seeking. She fought against an insidious pleasure—in some far distant corner of her mind, she was appalled that she could feel such a thing with this man. Yet she was helpless to prevent her fingers from slowly uncurling against the breadth of his chest.

Guy nearly groaned aloud. She was so slight; his outspread hand at her back nearly spanned the width of her waist. Her bones were fine and fragile. She felt as if she would break in half, yet there was a lithe firmness about her that drove him to the brink of madness.

He'd only meant to remind her that her will was subject to his, or so he'd told himself. But now his blood pounded thick and heavy along his veins. His hands strayed below her waist, discovering the lushness of her buttocks. With a guttural moan, he lifted her into the cradle of his thighs, molding her full and tight against him.

Kathryn stiffened in shock. Something strange and alien stirred against the softness of her belly. Hardening. Growing . . .

A growl erupted deep in his throat. He wrenched his mouth from hers. "Damn you." He nearly flung her from him. "Damn you for tempting me!"

"Me!" Her cry was one of outraged indignation. "Why, 'twas you who kissed me—why do you blame me instead of yourself?"

The tension spun out endlessly. He hated this— this unreasoning desire he harbored for her. He longed to banish the taste of her from his lips, while another part of him longed to snatch her back and let things lead where they would, and the consequences be damned.

His gaze fairly stabbed into hers. "You, my love-ly Kathryn, are a slut. No lady of virtue would do what you have done!"

"And what, pray, have I done that you find so . . . so despicable?"

His voice was as cutting as his eyes. "You sought the pleasures of the flesh with Roderick without benefit of marriage—and now you pay the price!" Kathryn flushed as his gaze raked down to her belly and back again. "And need I remind you that only four nights past, you offered those very same pleasures to me. You played the whore for Roderick, but by God, you'll not do the same with me!"

Stung, Kathryn shrank back as if she'd been struck. A fervent denial trembled on her lips. Why, her embrace with Roderick wasn't at all what it seemed! And that night at Ashbury, she offered herself to him out of desperation, nothing more. But the distaste on his countenance shocked and shamed her. How could she tell him that she couldn't possibly be with child? He would brand her liar as well as slut.

But it seemed there was no need for explanations after all. He stalked to his destrier and grabbed something from behind his saddle. A moment later he flung a blanket at her feet.

"Go to sleep," he said harshly. "We leave at dawn."

Sir Hugh raised a hand and rapped on the oaken portal that guarded Elizabeth's chamber. There was no ensuing response, so he knocked again, this time more firmly. At last he heard a faint stirring from within. "Who is it?" called a faint voice.

" 'Tis I—Sir Hugh. I must speak with you, Lady Elizabeth."

All was silent for so long he was certain she intended to refuse. Then at last the door slid open. "Sir Hugh," she murmured. "You wished to speak with me?" Her eyes were lowered. She stood there, hands folded before her, her manner subdued and submissive.

"Aye, that I did." He stepped forward. "I was worried about you, Elizabeth. I thought to check on you and make certain you were not sick."

Her gaze avoided his. "I—I am well," she whispered, and turned her head.

Hugh caught his breath. Her skin was pale and colorless, her lashes spiked and damp. The fragile skin below her eyes looked almost bruised. "You've been crying," he said quietly. "Why, Elizabeth? Tell me why."

The deep shuddering breath she took made his heart wrench. Placing finger beneath her chin, he raised her face to his. She flinched at his touch, but didn't withdraw as he half-expected her to. He longed to pull her tight to his heart, but didn't think he dared. Instead he wrapped both her hands in his, and drew her across the chamber to the bench below the window.

"Tell me what troubles you," he implored. "I will seek to right it, I promise you."

Elizabeth bemoaned her foolish, foolish heart. No doubt Sir Hugh would think her weak and spineless, as Uncle had. "If only you could."

Her sweet gentleness held him captivated. Hugh longed for nothing more than the privilege of protecting her from any and everything that might do her harm. But he hated the air of sadness which clung to her.

"Aha," he said lightly. "Methinks I know what's wrong. 'Tis Kathryn, isn't it?"

At the mention of Kathryn's name, her lips began to quiver. There was no need for her to answer.

"Do you miss her so?" His voice was very soft.

Elizabeth nodded. Her eyes clung to his. "I—I know that I'm a woman grown," she whispered. "But it seems so lonely without Kathryn. I—I have no one to talk to."

"You wound me grievously, milady." Hugh feigned a great affront. "Why, I am at your beck and call, should you feel the need to talk, to rant and rave . . ." *If ever you need anything*, he avowed silently.

Her fleeting smile made his breath catch, but it faded all too quickly. "You are very kind, Sir Hugh," she said slowly. Her eyes lowered abruptly, falling on their joined hands. "I do not deserve your comfort," she confided, her voice very low, "for I have sinned greatly."

"You?" he scoffed. " 'Tis not possible."

Trembling with shame, she tried to pull away. He would not let her. Her eyes lifted to his. "But

I have," she blurted. "I—I lied to your lord."

Hugh studied her quietly. "If you did, I am certain you did so with good reason."

"There can be no good reason for such a sin," she cried in a voice thick with self-recrimination. "I am guilty of selfishness and greed, Sir Hugh, more than you can ever know!"

A slight crease appeared between his brows. "How so?"

"Kathryn is not with child, Sir Hugh. I—I said that only so Lord Guy would not take her from Ashbury—I gambled and lost! And now he has and—and I fear that Kathryn will now pay the price for my deceit!" Two scalding tears slipped down her cheeks.

Hugh was sorely tempted to slap his knees and laugh loud and gustily. But Elizabeth was so distressed he was compelled to offer what assurances he could. He wiped the tears away with the pads of his thumbs, resisting the impulse to let them linger.

"Do not fret so," he soothed. "I know both you and your sister do not yet have cause to believe it, but Guy is not without heart."

Her expression remained deeply troubled. "You do not know Kathryn. I fear your lord will be blind to the good in her, for she is ever willful and quick-tempered and sometimes far too outspoken for her own good."

She might have been speaking of Guy. Hugh suspected they had too much pride as well, both of them. He also suspected both he and Elizabeth saw the best of Guy and Kathryn, and the worst as well.

" 'Tis beyond our means now," he said with a faint smile. "Do not worry so, for 'tis not so bad as you would believe. And—" A light began to dance in his eyes. "—lock yourself away in your chamber no more, fair lady. It would please me greatly if you would come with me for a walk down to the sea tomorrow."

Her gaze flitted away. He sensed she was on the verge of refusing. Placing his knuckles beneath her chin, he guided her eyes to his once more. "Please, Elizabeth." The smile had left his voice—now his voice betrayed only the gravity of his plea. "You wound me deeply should you refuse."

Elizabeth's heart seemed to beat with the flutter of tiny wings. She gazed deeply into his eyes and saw strength tempered by compassion and gentleness . . . or did she see only what she wanted to see? She was afraid to trust in her judgment—and just as afraid not to.

Her lips parted. "I'll not refuse you, Sir Hugh," she said on a feathery breath of air.

Hugh's heart rejoiced, even as he heaved a soundless sigh. He longed to trap those quivering rosebud lips beneath his own, but he didn't dare.

Soon, he promised himself. Very soon . . .

Chapter 6

Kathryn's first glimpse of Sedgewick came late the next day.

She lagged slightly behind the earl as their horses picked their way up a gentle slope. Cresting the rise, he reined his destrier to a halt. He swung down from the mighty steed, then stared out at the small valley before them.

The sky was clear and cloudless, but twilight cast its rosy glow on the far horizon. Kathryn brought her palfrey to a halt but didn't dismount. Instead she pressed a hand to the small of her back and massaged her aching muscles as she followed his gaze. In the distance, endless patchwork fields of brilliant green and gold stretched to the north and east. A short distance away, dozens of stocky cottages were tucked into the fold of a hillside.

But it was the huge fortress atop the bluff that dominated her attention. In stark silhouette against the clear sky, its towering limestone walls glittered white in the early-evening sun. Four round towers stood at the corners. A wide moat surrounded the thick walls. Seeing it, Kathryn felt a little stab of awe. It was easily thrice the size of Ashbury.

His voice came to her then. "You see before you Sedgewick."

She thought to detect arrogance in his tone—
instead there was only that which bespoke strong-
ly of pride. A heavy weight seemed to settle on
her chest. Her unblinking gaze remained fixed on
the fortress and surrounding landscape. Sedgewick
truly was a breathtaking sight, she thought vaguely. Some might think it a wondrous haven . . .

For her it was but a prison.

Guy swung back on his destrier. "Let's be off,"
he said. "I'm anxious to be home."

That he was, Kathryn decided irritably. He dug
his heels into his destrier's sides; the pair leaped
forward as one, down the slope and out across
the valley. She found it more irksome still when
Esmerelda took off in fevered pursuit, at no urging
from her mistress! He slowed only when they
approached the castle. Kathryn brought Esmerelda
up beside his mount. Together they clattered across
the drawbridge and entered the dark tunnel beneath
the gatehouse.

With every step forward, her muscles began to
tighten. Her body gave an involuntary jerk when
the gaping iron teeth of the portcullis clanged shut
behind her, closing out the world as she had known
it . . . and sealing her in.

A squawking hen weaved across a dusty courtyard, a long-legged hound at her tail feathers. The
sounds that reached her ears were familiar ones—
the shrill squeal of animals in their pens, the echo of
the smithy's hammer, the scream of falcons in the
mews. But unfamiliar were the open stares directed
her way. A wide-eyed groom spotted them and ran
over to grab the destrier's halter.

"My lord." He looked up at his master with shining eyes. " 'Tis good that you are back."

The earl addressed the boy by name. "Jon," he
said easily. " 'Tis good to be home again." He dis-

mounted and tossed the boy his reins, then turned to Kathryn and extended a hand.

The weight of that cool gray stare made her spine go rigid. She stared at his steel-gloved hand, wanting nothing more than to slap it away. His eyes chilled, a silent promise of swift retribution if she dared . . . Kathryn gritted her teeth and swung her leg over the saddle. Her fingertips resting lightly on his shoulders, she suffered his hands at her waist and let him swing her to the ground.

He released her immediately—and she him—as if neither could stand the touch of the other. But to her dismay, his fingers curled around her elbow. He led her up the stairs and into the great hall.

The hall was ahum with activity. At their entrance, several knights rushed over to greet their lord. One of them, a huge hulking man with a reddish-gold beard, laughed and clapped him heavily on the shoulder. "God's blood, man, but you took your sweet time finding your way home! We thought you were lost!" The knight laughed heartily.

Guy's smile was rather tight.

The knight swept an appreciative gaze toward Kathryn. "And who might this lovely lady be?"

A trace of panic raced through her. What would he say? she wondered wildly. Would he brand her friend or foe? She tried to jerk her elbow away but his fingers dug into her flesh in warning. She could feel his eyes upon her, cold and totally without mercy.

"Sir Edward, may I present Richard of Ashbury's niece, Lady Kathryn. As I anticipate being granted wardship of her from King Henry, she will be staying here at Sedgewick for a while."

He spoke loud enough that everyone might

hear—he intended it that way, Kathryn thought half in anger, half in despair. He sought only to hurt and humiliate her.

With his announcement, there was a shocked silence. In the blink of an eye, their expressions changed from curious to condemning—knights and servants alike.

It was because of Richard—because she was his niece. It spun through her mind that even from the grave, her uncle possessed the power to hurt her . . . Her only sin was in sharing the blood of her hated uncle, yet Kathryn felt scorching shame as never before.

Her lashes lowered. She could look nowhere but at the rush-covered floor. She was scarcely aware when he called a servant.

"Show the Lady Kathryn to her chamber," he directed.

Kathryn climbed the stairs behind the woman. She spent the rest of the evening in her room.

Sleep did not come easily that night. She lay huddled in her bed, trying desperately to make some sense of all that had happened. Had the earl killed Richard? If not, then who? And why had he insisted she accompany him to Sedgewick?

His ruthless features filled her vision. *He despises me and mine*, she thought with a shiver. Now Richard was dead—murdered. The earl claimed he'd been cheated of his revenge on Richard. A horrible assumption formed in her mind; she went cold to the tips of her fingers. Was this to be a reckoning of accounts? Perhaps through her—through *her*—he sought to gain his revenge on Richard . . .

Those words she had flung so recklessly came back to haunt her. *Mayhap now that you've killed Richard, you've a mind to murder me as well* . . . She envisioned his hands, dark and lean and strong . . .

It would be so easy for him . . . He had only to wrap his fingers around her throat . . . or fell her with a single blow.

He could kill her and there was naught she could do to stop him.

A tight band seemed to wrap across her chest, stealing her breath. She made a choked sound deep in her throat. How could she endure it here? She couldn't stand it . . . she could not! Yet escape provided no alternative either—the earl had hunted her down once. She had no doubt he would do so again. So what was she to do? She was trapped, like an animal in a cage. There was nowhere to go, she realized bleakly, that the earl would not find her. No one to care . . .

She thought of Ashbury . . . and Elizabeth . . . dear, sweet Elizabeth . . . Would she would ever see either of them again?

Never had she felt so alone! She wished desperately that she could cry, but all her pain remained locked tightly inside her.

Kathryn surfaced slowly from beneath filmy layers of sleep. A sense of befuddled confusion nudged the fringes of her consciousness. Something was different, she thought hazily, for every morning of her life she woke to the whistle of the wind whipping round the tower. Still half-asleep, her ears strained to hear the restless wash of the surf scouring the shoreline.

Her eyes flew open as remembrance flooded her mind. She did not snuggle in the warm comfort of her bed at Ashbury—she was at Sedgewick. With a heavy sigh, she heaved onto her side beneath the covers . . . only to stare straight into a pair of eyes as blue and brilliant as the morning sky.

Her startled gaze beheld a small cherub face—

plump, pink cheeks, small nubbin nose and chin that even now proclaimed a hint of arrogance, and fine, black curls as dark as her own. Her heart lurched as recognition tore through her like a shock wave.

There was no doubt as to this child's identity—he was clearly the earl's son.

Kathryn pushed her heavy hair from her face and sat up, keeping the fur tucked around her nightrobe. The little boy displayed no fear. His eyes were round with curiosity. "Good morning," she said with a smile. She patted the rumpled covers beside her. "Come and sit beside me," she invited.

He clambered atop the mattress, curled up his legs beneath him, and gazed at her.

She tipped her head to the side. "My name is Kathryn," she told him. "What is yours?"

A hint of shyness crossed his features. He said nothing, merely bit his lip.

"Well, then," she went on lightly, "I suppose I shall have to guess. Is your name Eugene?"

He shook his head.

"William? Duncan?"

Again he shook his head. His eyes had begun to dance.

"I know. 'Tis Wickham!"

A broad grin crossed his face. The sight made her wounded heart lift and soar. Kathryn rattled off another name, still another and another, each more ridiculous than the last, until he was giggling outright.

It was in the midst of this scene that a knock sounded on her chamber door. Neither Kathryn nor the boy heard. The door swung open a second later.

"Peter! There you are, you little scamp!"

The boy was snatched from the bed by a young

serving girl of perhaps her own age, with chestnut hair and wide dark eyes. For an instant, Kathryn went utterly still. For the life of her she didn't understand why, but she had the feeling she'd just done something very, very wrong.

"Please forgive Peter's intrusion, milady," the girl said quickly, "and my own lax behavior in letting him stray so far from me."

Kathryn smiled at her. "I did not mind," she said softly. "Indeed, he and I were having great fun."

But no answering smile broke the straight line of the girl's generous mouth. Kathryn watched her, faintly puzzled. Was it her imagination, or did the girl clutch the boy even closer, as if she sought to protect him?

She tried once more. "As I just told the little lord, I am Kathryn." She winked at the little boy. "And I am heartily glad that I've finally learned his name is Peter."

The girl bobbed a curtsy. "I am Gerda, milady."

Kathryn suddenly felt very exposed in the big wide bed. "I see." She feigned a lightness she was suddenly far from feeling. "And do you tend to Peter, Gerda?"

"Aye, milady." Peter was struggling in her arms. "And milord has instructed that I attend you as well. Will you be needing a bath this morning, milady?"

Kathryn's smile froze. Although Gerda's tone and manner were far from lacking in respect, she was stunned at the coldness she sensed in the girl. "If it's not too much trouble," she murmured.

"I'll see to it then, milady." Gerda backed away, still holding the wiggly little boy in her arms. Kathryn inhaled sharply. It was impossible not to note the girl's clumsy, awkward gait as she withdrew from the chamber.

Alone once more, Kathryn pushed back the covers and rose. She'd been too weary to look about last night, but she did so now, and was unable to suppress a feeling of awe.

The chamber was easily twice the size of her chamber at Ashbury, and far more richly furnished than any she'd been exposed to. The bed was wide and long, curtained with crimson hangings. Her chest had been brought in, pushed against the far wall next to a bench. A beautiful woven rug lay upon the floor, finer than anything she'd ever seen. Wooden shutters framed the window to shut out the chill of winter; it was there that Kathryn directed her steps. She pushed the shutters aside and let the sun's warming rays shower down upon her, noting that her chamber looked upon the inner courtyard.

She was about to turn away when a tall figure intruded into her field of vision. She could have screamed when she recognized the earl. His graceful, long-legged stride carried him across the courtyard. He did not stop until he was almost directly below her window. The boy—Peter—suddenly appeared and darted toward his father.

Some inexplicable force beyond her control kept her rooted near the window. It was as if her entire being were riveted to the pair below as the earl awaited his son. She blinked as the hard edge fled his granite-hewn features. Was it a trick of her eyes? Peter raced toward his father as fast as his chubby legs would allow. With a squeal of excitement, the boy was snatched high into strong arms. The unexpected sound of low male laughter reached her ears. The features she had thought so grim and ruthless were filled with warmth and love—the harsh, unyielding man she had come to know might never have existed. One dark hand

gently cupped the back of Peter's head, a gesture
that bespoke all that words could not.

Yet something must have alerted him to her, for
at that moment he half-turned. His gaze climbed
inevitably to the place where she peered out. And
for the space of a heartbeat, the mask of icy coldness so familiar to her was back in place . . . and
back with a vengeance.

Kathryn recoiled as if she'd been struck with a
fist. The breath left her lungs in a rush. She stumbled back, feeling oddly shaken. It occurred to her
then. She was an outsider here at Sedgewick. She
did not belong . . .

The warm soak in her bath did much to ease
the soreness wrought in her aching muscles by
the long journey, but it did nothing to boost her
flagging spirits. She allowed Gerda to dress her
hair, though it was a luxury she hadn't known at
Ashbury. Again the girl displayed no sign of friend-
liness, no sign at all. When Gerda wordlessly began
to unpack her chest, Kathryn looked away, biting
back a swell of humiliation, unwilling to suffer the
sight of the girl's hands on her meager belongings.
She didn't see Gerda's smooth forehead crease in
puzzlement, or the confused glance she directed at
the newcomer. Kathryn ventured downstairs to the
great hall for a hasty meal, but the suspicious glares
she encountered there soon drove her back to her
chamber.

A narrow shelf had been fashioned just below the
window overlooking the courtyard. Kathryn discovered it was big enough that she could sit quite
comfortably, her legs stretched out before her. She
spent the remainder of the day cloistered there.

The evening's first star had just made its appearance when a knock sounded on the door. Thinking
it was Gerda with the evening meal, she bade her

come in. Feeling low and dispirited, she wrapped her arms around her knees and laid her cheek against her knees and watched a second twinkling star appear. She paid scant attention to the footsteps crossing the room.

By then it was too late. The hair on the back of her neck stood up in warning.

"So meek, Lady Kathryn. So humble. You surprise me, for I had thought you would have my household in a rampage by now."

She gritted her teeth against that velvet-honed voice of steel. "You know nothing of me." She delivered the words curtly, refusing to look at him.

"Indeed," he mocked. "A situation mayhap we should remedy."

"I think not."

"How quickly you forget, Kathryn! My will prevails, does it not?" Before she knew what he was about, a muscled arm shot out. He scooped her from her perch and deposited her before him. He then proceeded to inspect every detail of her appearance, from the glossy black hair concealed beneath her wimple to the much-mended seam in the shoulder of her woolen kirtle.

"You will do," he announced at last. He reached out to grasp her elbow.

She snatched it back. "Do for what?" she cried. "Where are you taking me?"

He merely sighed as if she were an unruly child. "Cease your prattle, Kathryn. I merely mean to feed you."

She spurned his touch when he would have reached for her again. Guy allowed it, though he clenched his fist at his side in order to do so. This was one wench who possessed pride aplenty—and if he were honest with himself, he would admit he found himself both intrigued and irritated by it.

In the hall, servants scurried to and from the kitchens, seizing empty platters and piling food onto trestle tables. Guy led her to the high table and saw her seated. Kathryn stole a quick glimpse in all directions from beneath her lashes, relieved to find that they attracted no more than a passing glance. When her gaze returned to the earl, she found it disconcerting to find herself the sole object of his scrutiny.

The way he arched a single black brow lent him a satanic look. "I trust your chamber is adequate."

It was on the tip of her tongue to blurt out that it was far more than adequate. She swiftly quelled the impulse. "Quite," she said shortly.

Neither spoke as his squire began to serve them. There was a mouth-watering stew, lamb and suckling pig, fruit and tempting cakes sweetened with honey. But Kathryn could scarcely eat more than a few bites. Her stomach felt as if it were tied up in knots. She couldn't relax—she could scarcely think with the earl so close!

The earl paused, his goblet suspended halfway to his mouth as he frowned at her. "Is the food not to your liking, Kathryn?" A hint of scorn laced his voice.

"The food is excellent," she pronounced flatly.

"Eat, then, for I would fatten you up—you and your babe."

Her babe. The words hit her hard, for she'd forgotten he thought her with child.

"I must have a care," she murmured, "else my weight will be too much for my palfrey to carry me home."

His brittle laugh further set her on edge. "You wish to leave us so soon? Milady, you wound me sorely!"

For a moment Kathryn said nothing. A hot ache

closed her throat as her mind turned fleetingly back . . . She had oft dreamed of the day she would finally be free of her uncle. But she had never dreamed it would be like this . . .

"God's blood, I—I wish I'd never come here!" Even if the longing in her eyes hadn't given her away, her fervent tone would have.

"But you *are* here and so I must insist you grace us with your presence." His taunt struck home. He brought the goblet to his lips; above the dull beaten silver, his eyes gleamed with satisfaction.

Rage began to simmer along her veins. Oh, he was so smug—so unutterably sure that he was lord and master of all he surveyed! More than anything, Kathryn longed to shove at his chest, topple his chair, and see him sprawled at her feet—ah, if only she dared!

Totally indifferent to her anger, Guy resumed his meal.

Something snapped inside Kathryn. Heedless of anyone who might be watching, she leaped to her feet, spun about, and stalked from the table.

He was right behind her. She could hear the determined echo of his footsteps. Her pace quickened. She silently gauged the distance to the top of the stairs. Her heart clamored like a drum, but she refused to flee like a trapped doe.

Alas, at the threshold of the dark corridor that led to her chamber, he loomed before her—thwarting her, stopping her cold.

"I did not grant you leave to depart, milady." He towered above her, his ominous presence surrounding her like a mantle of darkness. She tried to shake it off and could not.

"Oh, stop!" she cried. "I've no more wish for your company than you have for mine!"

A slow smile rimmed the hardness of his mouth.

"No?" he murmured, hiking a brow. "I'm not so sure, Lady Kathryn. I'm not so sure at all." His eyes boldly traveled the length of her body, lingering on breasts and belly and hips, taking liberties no other man had dared.

Anger brewed within her, like a storm gathering force and building to a tempest. Her teeth clenched anew. "Cease with this pretense, my lord earl! I know why you wanted me under your roof. The better to make me wait in dread while I wonder what you have in store for me—the better to toy with me the same way you would have toyed with Richard had you had the chance!"

"The better to watch you," he snapped. Her anger was vivid in her eyes, but Guy was annoyed she could think he would treat her so cruelly. Hadn't he shown her every care thus far?

"I do not trust you, Kathryn." His expression turned brooding. "That is all there is to it—no more, no less. But if you behave, who knows? Mayhap we can strike a bargain."

"I'd as lief bargain with the devil."

His gaze flickered over her. With her chin angled haughtily, her shoulders straight, small hands fisted at her sides, she was the picture of defiance . . . ever bold, ever sure of herself . . . ever beautiful.

"Mayhap you shall, Kathryn—" His smile was tight. "—and sooner than you think."

The light from the candle set high in the wall spilled down on him, outlining his arrogant profile, and the hardness of his mouth. He went on coolly, "And now I think 'tis time we returned to the hall."

Panic leaped within her. Though she was frustrated and infuriated, until that moment she had scarce given a thought to those who might have witnessed their departure from the hall—how humiliating it would be to return in his wake!

When she didn't move, Guy lost patience. He snared her about the waist, in the back of his mind marveling at how slight she was. He lifted her full off the floor and started toward the stairs. He had no qualms about carrying her kicking and screaming under his arm like a sack of grain—all the way back to the hall if need be.

But the tiny strangled sound he heard brought his eyes cleaving to hers in a flash.

Her palms opened on the soft wool of his tunic. "I cannot," she said, very low. In some distant part of her mind, she applauded the evenness of her voice. Pride alone kept her chin up.

The moment seemed to stretch into eternity, for inside Guy a violent tug-of-war was being waged. His jaw tense, he stared at her. The screen of her lashes shielded her eyes. If he were to raise her chin, he knew full well she could not hide her stricken entreaty. From the start, Guy knew he had been right about her. She was stubborn and strong-willed and defiant. Her willfulness could not be ignored, and he was just the man to bring her to heel. And yet, the feel of her body against his aroused a flurry of emotions.

She was so close he could feel the ragged tremor of her breath against the hollow of his throat. "Please," she whispered. "Do not make me." It was not her spoken plea, but the quiver of her lip that betrayed her tremulous emotions.

He lowered her to the floor but kept a steely arm tight about her waist. The grim tension had not left his features. If anything, his expression was even more implacable than before.

With his thumb and forefinger, he prodded her chin up. "Hear me, Kathryn," he said brusquely. "Hear me well, for I will say this only once. Do not expect leniency from me—do not think to twist me round your finger! You have tested me once already and lost. Should you wish to ever have my trust, you will have to earn it."

With that he was gone, as swift and silent as the night. Kathryn fled to the sanctuary of her chamber, her dignity in tatters.

She threw herself across the bed, furious at the helplessness of her position . . . cursing the man who had brought it about. The earl controlled her every move, as surely as a falcon on a jess.

And she could do naught but endure the fate that awaited her.

Chapter 7

In the fortnight which followed, all that sustained Kathryn was a thin trickle of hope. She prayed nightly that the earl might soon grant her leave to return to Ashbury, but he showed no signs of relenting. He was often gone during the day, seeing to the spring plantings and other duties. During the evenings, he was ever aloof, ever icy . . . ever distant. Even the servants were wary of her. Gerda, who attended her closely, was stiff but polite, obliging but guarded. Indeed, the girl was almost as suspicious of her as was the earl! Oh, she knew why—because she was Richard's niece. Still, their flagrant distrust hurt, especially Gerda's.

Sedgewick itself was grand—built both as a defensive fortress and as a comfortable home. But Kathryn's soul was empty and lonely. She could not rid herself the nagging restlessness inside her. She missed Elizabeth—and Ashbury. She missed the mist-shrouded headlands of Cornwall, the keening wail of the incessant wind, the muted roar of the sea.

Her only redemption was Peter. His shyness with her lasted only a day or two. Only with the little boy did Kathryn feel she could be truly herself, for he was the only one here with no preconceived notions about her.

Even the weather was an ominous reflection of her mood. Throughout the day yesterday, dark clouds scuttled across the sky, while wind-driven sheets of rain lashed the ramparts. But this morning, bright golden sunlight bleached the sky. Between the rain and her enforced confinement, Kathryn longed to be free of the castle walls, if only for a while.

When Peter peeked into her chamber a while later, she crooked a finger at him. He ran to her and she scooped him up in her arms. "How would you like to go on an outing today, my little lord?" She whirled toward the window and Peter laughed delightedly.

"Look," she urged. Standing before the window, she pointed to where a strip of lush woodland ran back into the hills. Sunlight glinted off the stream that meandered through the trees. "You see the stream there? We could take a bit of food along with us, and eat there beside the water. And while we walk, we could pretend we're two soldiers marching off to slay a fierce, fire-breathing dragon."

"Dragons!" he cried, clapping his hands in approval. A secret smile tilted Kathryn's lips. The fire-breathing dragon conjured up in *her* mind had hair as black as midnight and glowing eyes of silver.

Gerda, who had been hovering behind them, said quickly, "I will go too, Lady Kathryn. Shall I ask the cook for some cheese and a loaf of bread?"

Kathryn glanced at her sharply. There was something about her tone . . . She lowered Peter to the floor, her smile rather stiff. "Peter and I will be fine, Gerda. You need not come with us."

A look of anxious distress widened Gerda's eyes.

"If you do not mind, milady, I—I think I shall."

It was on the tip of Kathryn's tongue to snap that she *did* mind. Still, she suspected Gerda was only doing as she'd been told—no doubt the earl had ordered that she was not to venture outside the castle walls alone.

"Very well," she said curtly. "If you'll fetch some food from the kitchens, Peter and I will meet you in the hall." Gerda fled the room, and Kathryn's lovely mouth turned down. Damn the earl to hell and back! she raged silently. He need not be present, and still the dratted man was able to make her utterly miserable!

But her mood lightened once they left the castle walls behind. The sun spilled down in radiant splendor, bathing her face and warming her limbs. She chuckled as Peter tramped along the narrow pathway, wielding a stick he'd found as if it were a mighty sword. She decided to stop near a spot where massive oaks arched over the shallow creek. Gerda laid out a blanket she'd brought so they could sit, and soon they were ready to eat. Peter sat between them, grinning up at Kathryn between bites of cheese. Once again, Kathryn was struck by the brilliant translucence of his eyes; surrounded by indecently long black lashes, they glowed like sapphires.

When he ran off to play at the bank, she shook her head. "I've never seen such beautiful eyes," she murmured. "Were his mother's so incredibly blue?"

Something flickered across the girl's face. "Lady Elaine," she said quietly. "Aye, milady. The boy has his mother's eyes."

Kathryn had decided that the earl would not ruin this day for her, but she was suddenly intently curious about the woman who had been his wife.

"Gerda." She twitched at a fold in the blanket. "Did you know her—the Lady Elaine? I know you must have been rather young when she was mistress here . . ." Kathryn broke off, feeling very awkward.

There was a prolonged silence. An odd expression crossed the girl's face. "I knew her," Gerda said finally. She paused for the space of a heartbeat. "I was the last one to see her alive."

Kathryn started. The remembrance glaringly vivid, all at once she recalled the earl's words that night in Richard's chamber. *It was only by the mercy of God that my wife's maid escaped, along with my son . . . You gave orders that no one was to be spared— not women, not children—no one!*

The maid who had escaped with Peter had been Gerda, she realized numbly. Gerda had been there during Richard's rampage, while he ravaged and murdered . . . There was a sharp, stabbing pain in Kathryn's chest. She couldn't tear her eyes from Gerda, who sat very still, her hands folded, her gaze lowered. She longed to reach out to the girl, to ease the torment hidden deep inside—it didn't matter that she was a servant—but she sensed Gerda did not want that from her.

She drew a deep, unsteady breath, unsure of what to say. "Gerda," she murmured, "I—I do not make excuses for myself, but it shames me greatly to know that I am kin to a man such as Richard. I mourn your lady's loss, but I cannot mourn his. Will you tell me about her, Gerda? What she was like? I know it may seem a strange request, but I would truly like to know."

Gerda's huge brown eyes were fixed on her face. "If it is your wish," she said slowly, "then I will tell you." Her bad leg lay twisted at an odd angle away from her body. She adjusted her skirt over her knees before she began to speak.

"Lady Elaine was very small and fragile. The first time I saw her, I thought she was a glorious angel sent from the heavens." She smiled slightly. "Her hair was like nothing I'd ever seen before, not like the gold of the wheat fields—but pale and flaxen, like—like moonbeams flowing down from the sky." As she spoke, Kathryn's hand slipped unknowingly to the shining sleekness of her own dark locks.

"I'd never known a lady as good and kind and sweet as the Lady Elaine. She took me from my father and brought me into the castle so that he could no longer beat me." She touched her misshapen leg lightly. "I loved her dearly, as everyone who knew her loved her."

"Including the earl?" Kathryn bit her lip. Where the question came from, she didn't know. But it had slipped out before she could stop it.

"Especially the earl," Gerda said softly.

"Their marriage—it was arranged?"

"From the cradle. But it didn't matter, for it was well known that the earl fairly worshiped Lady Elaine."

Kathryn gazed out where the water rippled over the rocky creek bed, aware of an odd tightness in the pit of her stomach . . . Distress? Surely not! It mattered little to her that the earl had been enamored—enamored?—of his wife. If Gerda was right, he'd been madly in love with her!

"He must have taken her death very hard," she murmured.

Gerda said nothing, but Kathryn could feel her staring at her and began to flush. Thankfully she was saved from further embarrassment, for Peter ran up then, his boots and tunic wet from splashing in the creek. Kathryn stood. "We'd better get back and get him out of these wet things."

Not long after they had set off toward Sedgewick, Peter pleaded tiredness and begged to be carried. Gerda swung him up onto her hip but it wasn't long before she began to lag behind. Kathryn turned, and it was then she noted a spasm of discomfort cross Gerda's rosy face. A pang of guilt shot through her, for until that instant she hadn't given a second thought to the difficulty the trek might pose for Gerda.

She extended her hands toward Peter. "Here, Peter. Let me carry you." The boy came willingly into her arms.

Gerda blinked. "Milady . . . ?"

Kathryn arched her brows. "Your leg is paining you, is it not?"

It was Gerda's turn to flush. "Aye, milady, but you need not take the lad—"

"Oh, yes, but I do."

Gerda's jaw dropped. "But Lady Kathryn, why would you do such a thing? You are a lady and . . . and 'tis my duty to—"

"Gerda, I see no reason why you should suffer when I'm perfectly capable of carrying him instead." She tickled Peter under the chin. "Right, my little lord?" With that, she was off again.

Gerda stared after her, both troubled and bewildered. When Richard of Ashbury had slain the Lady Elaine, he had become the earl's enemy . . . and hers as well. She had thought to hate and despise any kin of Richard's, certain his family must be as evil, treacherous, and odious as Richard himself. But she had put aside her anger and resentment and served Lady Kathryn solely because of her loyalty to the earl.

But Lady Kathryn seemed neither evil nor treacherous nor odious . . .

And it was getting harder and harder to think of her as an enemy.

They had nearly reached the outer palisade when a strange feeling crawled up Kathryn's spine. She looked over her shoulder just in time to see a horseman not twenty paces behind them. He must have seen her turn her head for he quickly swerved behind a copse of trees. But Kathryn had already recognized him. It was Sir Michael, a handsome young knight who had been with Guy at Ashbury.

Every nerve in her body suddenly quivered with rage. The earl had had them followed!

Peter's body lay limply against her, his chubby cheek pressed against her shoulder—he had fallen asleep. She delivered him to his chamber, eased him onto his bed, and dropped a kiss on his forehead.

In the great hall, she stopped one of the maids and asked if she knew the whereabouts of the earl. The girl shrugged. "Try the counting room."

Guy was busy tallying rents from one of his manors—forty ambers of ale, ten vats of honey, ten withers . . . The door burst open. A small figure stormed inside and planted herself squarely before him.

"Is it necessary to post a guard to watch my every move?" she demanded.

Guy leaned back in his chair. She was in a temper, by the look of her. Two spots of color stood out on her cheekbones; her eyes were the deep green of a stormy sea. Well, that was fine with him. If nothing else, their altercations were never boring.

He dropped his quill, his smile tight. "Perhaps it is for your own protection."

Her mouth thinned with ill-concealed annoyance.

She spoke but one word. "Bah!"

"If I say it is necessary, then it is." His voice carried as much warmth as a winter wind blowing from a mountaintop.

In her anger she jammed her hands flat on the planked tabletop. "Gerda was with me today. Was that not enough?"

His eyes were the color of stone—and just as unyielding. "But you wield a dagger so well, Kathryn. I fear the damage you might do to a poor girl like Gerda."

The glitter in his eyes caused a shiver of reaction in her. With an effort, Kathryn willed the tremor from her voice. "I would know my status here, milord. Am I your prisoner? Or am I a guest here?" Even as she spoke, her heart cried out in angry despair. Did it really matter? Either way, she couldn't leave.

His expression was cool and remote. She could read nothing of his thoughts. "Your actions will dictate the answer, Kathryn."

Kathryn wanted to scream in outrage, but inside her heart was breaking. He gave no quarter . . . and she would ask none of him. She snatched her hands away and whirled to leave. The sound of his voice stopped her. When she spun about, she saw that he had placed his elbows on the trestled tabletop so that his fingers rested tip to tip. He tapped them together lightly.

"It occurs to me, Kathryn, that there is a way to get what you want."

He had risen to his feet and was coming toward her. Kathryn eyed him, wary of the gleam in his eyes. "How?" she asked, uncaring that he heard the suspicion in her tone.

He stood before her, blocking her path to the door. Despite the tension—or perhaps because of it—she was suddenly overwhelmingly aware of the power of his presence.

"Tell me," he said abruptly, "do you still pine for your Roderick? Do you love him still?"

She couldn't tear her eyes from the tanned hollow of his throat, where a wild tangle of curly dark hairs spilled over the neckline of his tunic. All at once she found it difficult to swallow. "I love no man," she stated unevenly.

A dark eyebrow arched high in amusement. So she scorned love, did she? Somehow Guy was not so inclined to believe it.

"Aha," he murmured. "So you love no man . . . or mayhap you love all men."

That drew her gaze up in a flash. She bristled when she discovered his mouth curled in a mocking smile.

He laughed softly. "In either case, a trifling kiss should be no hardship at all."

It was her turn to curl her lips. "A kiss, milord? Surely you jest."

"Nay, Kathryn. A kiss—and mayhap you'll gain what you wish. That's the way of it, I'm afraid."

God, how she hated his self-satisfied smirk. She wanted to scream that she'd sooner kiss a toad, a snake—the most wretched creature unimagined! Yet when at last she spoke, neither words nor action were what she intended.

She averted her face, her voice very low. "Why do you torment me so?"

Guy's mouth twisted. Perhaps a better question was why he tormented himself so. He hadn't wanted to examine his reasons for insisting she accompany him to Sedgewick. Yet for the first time Guy wondered if he hadn't made a grave mistake. So close at hand, he couldn't forget her. Pregnant or no, enemy or no, she provided a temptation that threatened his

good judgment. If he were wise, he'd send her back
to Ashbury and forget he'd ever laid eyes on this
deceitful little wench . . .

Her head was lowered, the sweep of her lashes
veiling the incredible jade of her eyes—the humble
maiden again, he thought, aware of his emotions
hardening. Why did she bother, when he knew she
was little more than a strumpet? But she was a
beautiful one, and there was the rub! With that black
mane of silky hair, that lissome young body so
enticingly curved to fit a man's hand, she radiated
an earthy sensuality that brought his keenly honed
senses primitively alive. Like a male animal who'd
just caught the scent of female, his nostrils flared
wide. An elemental heat welled up inside him.

His hands were on her shoulders, searing her
with their warmth. "Torment, you say? I ask you,
what torment is there in this? I merely suggest that
if you sheathed your claws, little cat, the lion in me
would be less likely to pounce. Men, you see, for
all that we claim to be so fierce and warlike, are
not so very different from the fairer sex after all."
The pitch of his voice lowered, as soft as fleece.
"We, too, crave sanctuary—in the soothing touch
of a gentle, feminine hand, in the softness of lips
warm and willing . . ."

Kathryn inhaled sharply. She went hot inside,
then icy cold. Mother of Christ! Was he suggesting
that she seduce him?

Her mind raced apace with her heart. He loomed
above her—with the prominent angles of his cheekbones, the jutting forcefulness of his jaw, he exuded
a ruthless and powerful vitality. And the flame in
his eyes—was it desire? All at once she remembered what her uncle had told her—that a man
need not feel love to desire a woman. Oh, she knew
how thoroughly the earl despised her. Yet when her

gaze locked helplessly onto that hard face, she saw no revulsion, no malice, only something heated and intense . . . something that frightened her.

His smile was wickedly seductive. "A kiss is all I ask, Kathryn. The merest touch of your lips upon mine."

"Ask?" she cried. "As you are so fond of reminding me, milord, your will prevails, does it not? Nay, you do not ask, you demand! Oh, it matters not that your words are sweetened with honey. I have no doubt the outcome will remain the same. You will have your way, whether I wish it or not!"

She did not trust this unexpected turnabout, not a whit! But if she thought to goad him into anger, she failed miserably. The pressure of his hands on her shoulders increased every so slightly. She raised her hands to push him away, but he caught her wrists. "Methinks," he said softly, "that you are still afraid of me."

"I was never afraid of you!" she said without thinking.

"Then let it be done," he whispered.

She had no time to prepare, no time to even think, before his mouth closed over hers. Always before when he had kissed her, she sensed a seething undercurrent. His lips had been ruthlessly intent. Yet there was nothing hard or punishing in this kiss. Oh, the demand was still there—she could feel it in the gently coaxing pressure of his lips on hers. But the contact was subtle and persuasive, compellingly seductive.

In a battle of wit and words they were evenly matched. But in this, her inexperience failed her . . . Against all reason—against all instinct—she longed to succumb, to let this yearningly sweet kiss that promised so much lead where it would, forgetful of all else. But in her heart, she knew this was no sweet seduction—he merely sought but another means of dominion! And so she strained her every muscle against him and kept her lips tightly closed, desperately denying the treacherous warmth that threatened her tenuous control.

But Guy was aware of her resistance. He decided to intensify his assault, but first a change in tactic was needed. He raised his head to stare down at her.

"What!" he mocked softly. "Didn't your Roderick teach you how to kiss?" A hand came up to frame her face. With the pad of his thumb he tugged her bottom lip downward. "Open your mouth," he whispered.

She had no choice but to grant him entrance, and when she did his tongue dipped boldly within, swirling far and deep in a breath-stealing foray that robbed her of strength. Her thoughts scattered. The pressure on her cheeks eased. Hard arms came around her and he was dragging her close—closer!—so close she could feel the sinewed strength of his thighs welded against hers. She began to tremble. There was a peculiar tightness in her middle. Her skin felt hot and tingly all over, as if she were ill with fever, though she knew it was not so.

She gave a tiny little moan of distress . . . but not displeasure. God help her, not displeasure . . . The strangest sensation spilled through her, as if someone else had taken over her body—as if *he* had. She sought to pull away but he allowed no retreat. Caught fast within his binding embrace, he held her captive with the searing pressure of his mouth. Over and over he kissed her, deeper and deeper, until she was breathless and dazed.

The effect of finding her so willingly compliant was heady nectar indeed, Guy thought dimly.

His heart was pounding as if he'd been plunged into the thick of battle. His blood ran hot through his veins, spawning a heavy ache that swelled his loins . . . and this from a mere kiss yet! He was not a stripling lad whose staff leaped apulse at the mere thought of an easy tumble. He was a man who knew how to master his hunger; a man who had learned the pleasure to be gained from slowly savoring his passion. So why was it that Kathryn made him feel as if he were a forest gone aflame?

Never had he hated a woman as he hated her . . . or desired one as fiercely as he desired her. Yet desire was the one thing he did not want to feel for her, for he could never forget that Richard's blood flowed in her veins.

He released her. Dispassionately, he raised his head and stared down at her. Her eyes opened, heavy-lidded and dazed. The twinge of guilt which cut through him was banished as quickly as if it had never been.

"You must learn to try harder, Kathryn. Perhaps then the next time I'll be inclined to grant your wish."

His cool words seeped in slowly. He was smiling, that arrogant half-smile that never failed to prick her temper. Yet for a timeless instant, Kathryn stared at him, unable—or unwilling, mayhap?—to grapple with the lightning change in him. But then wave after wave of angry hurt swept over her. His rejection left her feeling filthy and ashamed—above all, humiliated. Not because he had kissed her, but because she had wanted it to go on and on . . .

"I pray with every breath in my body for the day I would be rid of you, milord." Her glare bespoke her hatred as keenly as her taunt. "But there is naught that could make me so desperate I would intentionally suffer your touch again."

She whirled and swept from the chamber, seething as his laughter followed her through the opening. Somehow, she vowed fiercely, he would pay. She knew not when. She knew not how.

But someday he would pay . . . and pay dearly.

Chapter 8

⎯⎯⎯◈◈◈⎯⎯⎯

Kathryn took her meal in her room that evening. She half-expected the earl to demand her presence at the table, but he did not. Nor was he present when she and Gerda departed the bailey to take Peter down to the stream again the next afternoon.

Gerda was appalled when Kathryn insisted she and Peter ride her palfrey. "Lady Kathryn," she blurted, " 'tis not right that you should walk and I should ride . . ." She quickly discovered that arguing with Kathryn was fruitless.

On their return, Gerda slipped down from the horse just outside the gates, but Peter balked. "Ride," he pleaded. "Ride!" Kathryn laughed and clasped his chubby fingers firmly around the pommel. "Hold tight!" she warned. "Do not let go!"

She led the palfrey toward the inner bailey, glancing back every so often to see how Peter fared. She smothered a chuckle, for Peter sat upon her palfrey as proudly as an armored knight. His eyes were shining, his little chest swelled with pride. When they stopped near the stable, Kathryn extended her arms. He looked so stricken she had to bite back a laugh.

"We will ride again tomorrow," she promised. "And mayhap we'll wade in the stream again, too." His face lit up as she lifted him down. He liked that almost as much as he liked riding. Gerda took his hand while Kathryn paused to speak to the groom who had taken Esmerelda's reins. Together the three of them started back toward the hall. But all at once, Peter jerked free of Gerda's hand.

A groom was leading the earl's destrier toward the stables. It all seemed to happen in slow motion—Peter darting back toward the stables, the squawking hen zigzagging across the bailey, crossing in front of the destrier . . . The huge horse tossed his head and snorted, wrenching the reins from the startled groom's hands. At all the commotion, Peter halted abruptly, perilously near the massive destrier. The hen lurched and charged again, and someone shouted; the destrier lunged and reared. Beside her, Kathryn heard Gerda gasp.

She had no recollection of moving. The next thing she knew she was hurtling through the air, arms outstretched like a madwoman, as if she sought to fly . . . She slammed onto her stomach and shoved Peter clear, the impact knocking the breath from her. She pushed herself up on her hands, gasping for air. The destrier's scream seemed to come from very far away . . . In the split second it took to recognize the danger, Kathryn flung her arms around herself and prepared to roll away. Above her, the muscles in the destrier's muscular chest rippled with power. Flailing hooves lashed the air.

She almost made it. The ground beneath her vibrated as those flashing hooves came crashing down—one glanced across her shoulder. A terrible, gouging pain ripped through her; earth and sky whirled around her, a sickening kaleidoscope of sound and color. The world receded into a gray mist.

She was only vaguely aware of someone shouting.

"Kathryn . . . *Kathryn!*" A strong arm slid beneath her. She felt herself lifted and cradled against a solid warmth. Her head was reeling. She struggled to focus on the lean face hovering just inches above her own. The earl, she realized, staring dumbly. Unbelievably, his features bore no trace of his familiar hard-featured reserve. She had never seen him like this, his expression almost frantic.

She felt suddenly weightless, her weight borne upward in a surge of power. She gave a muted sound of protest but the earl paid no heed, striding into the great hall and up the stairs. Kathryn's arms tightened around his neck. She buried her face into the curve of his neck. She was not herself, she decided fuzzily. Held so securely against his chest, she was aware of a strangely pleasurable feeling of contentment, despite the wrench in her shoulder at every jarring step.

When they reached her chamber, he shouldered the door open and kicked it shut with the heel of his boot. Crossing to the bed, he began to lower her. She bit back a tiny moan as her shoulder connected with the mattress. Then it dipped again as the earl sat beside her.

There was a glint of steel as he pulled his dagger from the sheath at his waist. Kathryn paled and instinctively flattened her back against the pillows propped behind her back. "Milord," she cried, "what do you—"

Guy's jaw clamped shut. For just an instant, his expression darkened. "Good God," he exploded. "My only intent is to see to your shoulder and this is the quickest way to do it. Had I sought to put an end to your existence, I'd have done so long before now!"

It was on the tip of her tongue to plead with him not to ruin her gown, but he looked so grim she decided against it. "Milord," she said faintly, "I am fine. Truly, I am. There is no need—"

He paid her no heed. The blade slipped beneath the neckline of her kirtle. A quick slicing sound drowned out her protest, then another as the same motion slashed through the strap of her thin linen chemise. Impatiently he flicked aside the material, baring her shoulder and the top half of her breast. Kathryn stared in mute horror at the gleaming mound of one breast. The sight of her own flesh, so pale and smooth, seemed to mock her. The heat of embarrassment rose within her like a flooding tide, but she held her breath, afraid to move, afraid even to breathe for fear of exposing herself further.

Guy scarcely noticed. His entire frame tense, he drew in a harsh breath, his gaze locked on the place where his destrier's hooves had landed. Already a series of angry bruises darkened and discolored the ivory skin of her shoulder. Blood oozed bright and crimson from half a dozen long ugly scratches that trailed across her collarbone. The sight of such pale, perfect flesh mottled with purple shadows made his stomach clench.

His insides twisting with sick dread, he laid a hand to her shoulder, anxious to assess the damage he could not see. Fingertips skimming lightly, he began to gently press and probe, feeling the delicate bone structure beneath her broken skin, watching her every reaction.

He cursed beneath his breath—he could see how swollen and tender she was. This hurt him almost as much as it was bound to hurt her. Yet even as the realization tolled through his mind, he wondered why it was so . . . He gritted his teeth and began anew. His fingers had scarcely moved before he felt her flinch, though she did not cry out.

"Damn! I'm sorry, lass, I know it must hurt like the very devil, but I do not mean to hurt you, I swear . . . I'm sorry . . . Just hold tight and it will soon be over."

Regret lay thick and heavy in his voice, but mingled within was an unexpected tenderness that caught her totally off guard. It was this which made Kathryn look helplessly to his face. She willed away the ache in her shoulder, unable to tear her gaze from his rugged features.

His brow was furrowed in concentration, his winged black brows drawn together over the jutting blade of his nose. His jaw was set as firmly as ever, yet for once, she could detect no coldness in his manner. The mouth she had always considered so cruel was set a bit sternly mayhap, but it was beautifully shaped nonetheless. And his eyes were as crystalline-clear and pure as the rushing waters of the nearby stream, his lashes as long as Peter's.

An odd little tremor shot through her. Why? she screamed inwardly. Why did she notice all these details about him? It was as if something inside her had hoarded all these subtle little nuances, only to spring them upon her now when she least expected it. What was it about him that affected her this way—and he a man she hated with all her heart! She had lived her life surrounded by men . . . and the earl was but one more man, much as any other man.

Nay, whispered a niggling little voice in her brain. *He is not as any other man, for he has trapped your lips beneath his . . .*

But Roderick has kissed me, too! she countered silently.

Aye. But you did not feel the same—as if a storm had seized you and swept you from the earth in a mighty tempest of sweet sensation . . . And the earl has touched you as no other has . . .

Guy felt her tremble beneath his hand. "There," he said softly. " 'Tis done. It appears nothing is broken but you'll bear those bruises for several days." He leaned back, worriedly scanning her face. Her lovely mouth, he noted, was pinched tight. With a frown he saw that her face was blanched of all color.

Kathryn felt the weight of his gaze as surely as she'd felt the weight of his hand on her body. She felt curiously awkward and exposed, only this time it had little to do with the torn remnants of her kirtle. Still, her hand fluttered protectively over her bare flesh. She knew he saw the reflexive movement but he said nothing. She tried to summon a smile but found her lips reluctant to do her bidding.

" 'Twasn't so bad," she murmured. "And 'tis just as I told you—I am fine, milord."

"Fine, is it?" He snorted. "Girl, you are luckier than you know. My destrier might have crushed those fragile bones of yours as easily as mush." The very thought made him want to break out in a cold sweat.

There was a knock at the door and he rose to answer it. It was Gerda. Kathryn couldn't hear their low-voiced conversation, but when he returned to her side, he carried a small basin of water. He pulled up a small bench and placed the basin atop it, then resumed his place beside her.

Kathryn bit her lip, her expression anxious. "How is Peter? He was not hurt, was he?"

"Peter is fine," he said briefly. He continued to regard her, his dark head tipped slightly to the side. "I must thank you for saving his life—" She was startled to see a slow smile creeping across his lips. "—indeed, I've noticed you do not seem averse after all to occasionally playing nursemaid to my brat."

Kathryn could take no offense, for the faint light in his eyes robbed the words of any sting. Aware of her pulse picking up speed, she could not help but retort in kind. "Your son," she replied, "is possessed of a sweet, gentle nature, milord."

"Aha. Unlike his father?"

Her tiny smile matched his. "Your words, my lord, not mine."

He stunned her further by throwing back his head and laughing. Kathryn watched as he dipped a cloth in the basin, then wrung the water from it. Her shoulder was throbbing, but she gasped when he laid the cloth on her—the cold stung her torn flesh so much that her eyes watered. She squeezed them shut, afraid the earl would see and mistake the moisture for tears.

It was impossible for Guy to ignore the tension constricting her muscles. "The cold will dull the hurt," he murmured. He lifted the cloth, dabbing gently to remove the blood from her flesh. He rinsed it, then wrung it out and replaced it on her shoulder, this time leaving it in place.

Eventually she leaned back against the pillow, let out a sigh, and opened her eyes. Her gaze, wide and unwavering, melded with his. Guy felt as if a fist had plowed into his stomach. He couldn't think when he'd seen anyone with eyes so pure and green, the color of lush spring grass. He could not stop himself from wondering what truly went on beneath the lure of those beautiful green eyes . . . what secrets she concealed from him. And yet, it appeared they held no secrets now, at this moment . . . Her expression was half-troubled, half-watchful, as if she trod an unfamiliar path with no clear destination.

He almost welcomed the mild irritation that flared as he rinsed and replaced the cloth again, for she kept her slender fingers doggedly clamped to her breast. Why she attempted to preserve her modesty, he had no idea—he'd already glimpsed every delectable inch of her the night she sought to flee to Ashbury. And well they both knew she was far from chaste and virtuous.

At last he laid the cloth aside. With his fingers he began smoothing a healing unguent into the curve of her shoulder, down to where the arcing top of her breast began its thrusting ascent. There was nothing sexual in his touch—his features bespoke a shuttered detachment—but Kathryn flushed from the intimacy of his ministrations.

He had scarcely finished when another knock sounded. Gerda passed a small tray into the earl's hands. A moment later he extended a small goblet toward her. Plumes of steam curled toward the ceiling. "Here," was all he said.

The delicate sweep of her brows rose a fraction as Kathryn eyed it askance. She sniffed, but she could detect no noxious odor. "Ha!" she muttered. "Methinks I want you to taste it first, lest it be riddled with poison."

"Poison, eh? Your opinion of me sinks ever lower, Kathryn. I must admit, the idea has never crossed my mind." Guy laughed, unwillingly amused. He could think of a great many things he would like to do to this bewitching little wench . . . poison was not among them.

The pitch of his laughter was low and deep. Her heart gave an odd little flutter as her eyes met his. Time spun out slowly while they stared at each other, as if neither were able to break the strange spell that had cropped up. Something passed between them, something that seemed to pain both of them . . . something neither could deny.

It was Guy who spoke first. "Drink," he ordered quietly. "Gerda has a way with herbs. It will do you good." His arm slid around her back, easing her forward. He pressed the goblet to her lips and held her so she could drink—the brew was warm and tasted faintly of mint. But she found his touch and their closeness both comforting and disturbing. She drank it quickly, willing her mind from the way she leaned against him, trying desperately not to think about how the tips of her breasts grazed his chest, kindling a tingly sensation that was not entirely unpleasant. Rather, it was highly pleasant indeed . . .

The throbbing in her shoulder diminished to a dull ache. Her lids began to droop. She was aware of the waning rays of sunlight seeping through the window. It was not yet dark, so why was she so tired? Her limbs felt as though they'd been weighted with lead. The edges of her vision were tinged with gray. The earl's dark visage shifted and swirled. Nor could she seem to think straight. She shook her head to clear it.

Her eyes flew wide. Her gaze sought the earl's, though all she saw was a looming shadow. "The drink," she muttered. "There was something in it . . . I knew it! You truly seek to poison me . . ."

Soft, mocking laughter reverberated in her brain. "Milord?" Even her tongue felt thick and clumsy.

"Here, Kathryn."

There was a touch against her cheek, like the wispy trailing of a feather . . . or did she only imagine it? She flung out a hand, groping as if she were blind. The next instant warm fingers closed about her own. "Do not . . . leave me," she heard herself say. In some far distant corner of her mind, she knew it was totally illogical that she should so cling to this man whom she hated, yet she could not stop herself. That was the last thing she remembered as she drifted into oblivion.

Guy studied the small hand curled so trustingly within his own, listening as her breathing grew deep and even. He felt compelled to linger, though he didn't know quite why. Perhaps it had something—everything?—to do with Kathryn casting aside her own safety for the sake of his son . . .

With his free hand he trailed a fingertip along the downy curve of her cheek, the slender grace of her throat. He was reminded of what she had said that night in the forest. *'Tis not the first time I've felt the cuff of a man's hand* . . . The remembrance made a muscle tighten in his jaw. The thought of that tender white skin marred and bruised filled him with rage. Who, he fumed angrily, had dared to strike her? Richard?

It was inevitable that his thoughts would turn to Elaine . . . *Elaine*. Even as a wrenching pain squeezed his heart, he could scarcely summon the vision of her face, her flaxen hair swirling about her like an angel . . . Instead, his mind was besieged by this witch—Kathryn—whose hair shone dark as the wings of a raven . . . and he bitterly resented her for it.

And yet she possessed an allure he could neither deny nor submit to. His gaze lingered on lips stained a deep, vibrant pink, so dewy and moist she looked as if she'd been well and thoroughly kissed. Her cheeks were pink and flushed from sleep, her hair streaming wildly over the pillow. Seized by a sudden greed for the feel of it, he reached out and lifted a silky black strand. It curled around his fingers, sleek and vibrant, as if it possessed a will of its own.

As always, he could not look upon her without remembering that her flesh was the fairest of ivory; that her legs were supple and long and made to entwine with a man's. He longed to test for himself the cushioned softness of breasts ripe and firm, like the sweetest of fruit; he ached to sample the honeyed sweetness of rose-hued nipples against the twine of lips and tongue. He wanted to slide his fingers through the springy thatch that guarded her womanhood; settle himself between her slender thighs and seat the burning shaft of himself deep inside her . . . deeper still . . . while passion slaked its relentless thirst.

Too late he realized his mistake. His temples began to pound. A ravenous hunger surged inside him, so heady and strong he felt engulfed in a raging heat. Disgusted with himself, he crushed the lock of hair in his fist and dropped her hand, then prowled restlessly around the room.

What was he to do with her? In all truth, he didn't know. She was too much a lady to turn into a servant. At Ashbury, it had been in the back of his mind to make her his mistress—the obvious solution, for that would satisfy this accursed craving he had for her! But that was before he had discovered she was with child—and he couldn't make a woman who was with child his mistress . . . or could he?

The rational part of him rebelled at taking another man's leavings—for wasn't that what she was? But the physical part of him, the part that ruled his senses, was something else entirely. And it was this part of him that argued it would be some months before the child hindered his use of her. Surely by then—why, long before then!—this ludicrous longing for her would be extinguished . . .

He was standing at the bedside before he knew it. Desire tightened his expression as he stared down at her with undisguised yearning. The blood pooled thickly in his loins, swelling him until he was rigid as stone. As he'd longed to do almost from the instant they'd entered this chamber, he bent and pushed aside that vexing swath of cloth from her shoulder, exposing one perfect breast to his avid gaze.

Her chest rose and fell with every breath, offering up the exquisitely rounded flesh like a tempting sacrifice, causing his own breath to dam in his throat. That swelling mound was softened now, but still enticingly full and sweetly curved. Her skin was pale and finely textured, almost translucent, that single breast tipped by a delicate rosebud nipple the color of coral. Guy swallowed, beating down the rush of desire that threatened to overcome his good judgment. But he could not help himself. He knew he had to touch her or die . . .

With lean, tapering fingers he staked his claim. For an instant he stared at his outspread hand, the contrast between his bronzed fingers and her pale flesh striking. He filled his palm with her softness, caressing ever so slightly, gently kneading, seeking—sweet Jesus, she felt like velvet and silk! Clamping his jaw tight, he fought a violent battle with white-hot desire. The urge to bend over, to close his lips around that tantalizing pink nipple and feel it quiver to erectness against his tongue, was almost overpowering. But he knew that if she woke, words would fly like clanging swords. And so instead, he raked his thumb across the crest, the merest butterfly caress, while Kathryn slept on, as trusting and innocent as a child.

But a child she was not, and the ripeness of the flesh beneath his hand was a silent testimony. Nor was she innocent, and well he knew. He went very still inside, aware of some inexplicably dark emotion slipping over him, like a murky veil. The heat within him began to cool.

Unbidden, unwanted, an image in his mind began to swirl, slowly taking shape. He saw Kathryn and Roderick as they had been that first night at Ashbury, his hands twisted in her luscious black name, their lips fused in fevered splendor, their bodies clinging recklessly in the wanton way of lovers . . .

His lips grew ominously thin. His face settled into a cold hard mask. Disgusted with himself, Guy snatched his hand away, scorning the passion he felt for this tempting little sorceress. It was lust, he told himself, purely carnal, purely erotic. He dismissed her scathingly. Kathryn meant nothing to him—nothing at all.

And because he willed it, it would be so.

Chapter 9

Matters were just a little different with Sir Hugh. While his dilemma, too, concerned the fairer sex, his problem was that his chosen lady scarcely knew he existed.

He likened her to a tiny, rare flower, the kind that appeared only once in a lifetime—so breathtakingly lovely one could not look upon her without coveting such beauty for his own, yet so fragile and frail that but a single fleeting touch would make her vanish and disappear, forever beyond his reach.

He knew she feared him—he knew because Kathryn had told him why. But he hadn't realized how very delicate she really was . . . He had learned in a way that was no less than painful.

Their walks around the grounds had become a habit. Her sweet shyness tugged at his heart. It was eminently clear that the only person Elizabeth truly trusted was Kathryn. She trembled when he touched her, even the most casual touch. But— miracle of miracles—he felt he'd finally begun to draw her out.

Twilight veiled the land one evening as they left the keep behind. Hugh's aimless steps soon carried them to the crest of a craggy bluff. High above, gulls soared against the wind-whipped current, while far below, a huge pile of granite seemed to have tumbled into the churning waters of the sea. He filled his vision with the wild and rugged landscape before returning his attention to Elizabeth.

He knew instantly that something was wrong. He could see the way she huddled beneath her cloak. She clutched her hands about her body as if she were frozen to the bone.

"Elizabeth?" He touched her shoulder, a silent gesture of reassurance. She made no sign she heard him. Her eyes were dilated and glassy, fixed on a point just beyond his shoulder. Seeing her thus, Hugh felt a curious chill run up his spine. It was as if she had retreated to another place, another time.

"Elizabeth." His tone was sharp. "What is it? Tell me what's wrong."

She stood frozen. "This place," she said jerkily. He saw the tremendous effort it took for her to swallow and focus on him. "Why?" she whispered. "Why did you bring me here? What have I done that—that you would hurt me so!"

"Elizabeth, how can you say that?" Hugh was utterly perplexed. "I have no wish to hurt you. Tell me what I have done that distresses you so—"

He broke off as she suddenly whitened, every vestige of color stripped from her face. Her eyes swept frantically all around then, as if she sought to find something elusive and hidden, something beyond this world. "I cannot stay here," she cried, panting raggedly. "Oh, God, I . . . I cannot!" With a panicked cry she whirled, running as fast as her legs would carry her. Hugh attempted to follow, only to wrench his knee as he stepped on a rock. He shouted after her, but she refused to stop.

After that she neither spoke nor looked at him. It didn't take Hugh long before he realized he must have led her very near the spot where her mother was raped. He knew he had made a mistake . . . one that would cost him dearly.

For the third night in a row, Hugh's mind refused the balm of sleep. In abject frustration, he moved to his chamber window, watching as the moon traversed the leaden sky. Hours passed before he finally stepped toward his bed. He had just stripped off his tunic when the sound of a muffled cry reached his ears . . . Elizabeth! He tore down the passage and burst into her chamber. Hand on his dagger, legs spread apart, he strained to see, searching the shadows for a hidden assailant. It took but an instant to realize there was none. Elizabeth was tossing and turning on the bed, moaning and sobbing, clearly in the throes of a nightmare. All at once she bolted upright, her breathing jagged and rasping.

Hurriedly he lit the taper in the wall sconce, then dropped down beside her. Her eyes were open, filled with terror as if she confronted all the demons in hell. Then something inside seemed to collapse. "Mama," she whispered brokenly. "They're gone now . . . I'll not let them touch you or—or hurt you anymore." She whimpered. "Oh, God, you're all bloody . . . Mama, please, get up . . . *Mama!*"

Her shrill, desperate scream rent the air. There was such anguish in the sound that his throat closed with a hot, unfamiliar ache. Compassion and rage warred within him, compassion because the terror of her mother's death had remained locked in her mind throughout the years—rage because he knew instinctively that Elizabeth relived the heartbreak of that loss in each and every nightmare.

He shook her, not ungently. "Elizabeth!" he said harshly. "Wake up. Wake up, love, please!"

Her eyes were still half-wild, but he knew the instant awareness returned. Her gaze dropped to his naked chest and she stared as if in shock—until that moment Hugh had completely forgotten his state of undress. "It's all right," he said before she could say anything. "I heard you screaming, Elizabeth. But it's just a dream, love, just a dream."

"Just a dream," she repeated, and then her face seemed to crumple. "Oh, God—" She gave a half-sob. "—why isn't Kathryn here? It—it never seemed so awful when I woke up and she was here . . . oh, Lord, I'm afraid to close my eyes again . . ."

Hugh didn't give her time to reject him. He simply wrapped his arms around her and pulled her close. "There's no need to be afraid," he whispered, lips against her temple. "Kathryn's not here, love, but I am. And I'll hold you the night through if it will make you feel safe."

Safe, Elizabeth echoed silently with a little shiver. Hugh was so tall and lean. Sometimes just looking at him made her stomach knot with a feeling that she had always assumed was fear. For so long now she had associated male brawn and strength and muscle with hurt and fear and pain; she had never once dreamed of associating the latent power of a man with shelter and security and safety.

She did so now. And it was with a dawning wonder that Elizabeth realized that was exactly how she felt—safe and warm, as if she'd crawled deep into a haven where nothing or no one could hurt her. She let her fingers slowly uncurl against his muscular bare chest. It was strange to feel his hard arms about her back, almost as strange as the firm resilience of his flesh beneath her fingertips . . . strange, but wonderful.

"This dream, Elizabeth . . . it comes to you often?"

Her head tucked beneath his chin, she paused. "Sometimes," she whispered hesitantly.

"Tell me about it."

She stiffened and would have pushed away, but he wouldn't let her. His arms tightened. "This dream," he whispered. "It has to do with your mother, does it not? I know you were there when she was attacked, Elizabeth, that you hid so the men would not find you. Is that why you ran from me that day on the bluff—is that where it happened, love?"

Shock held her motionless, but only for an instant. She twisted around to stare at him numbly. "How can you know this?"

Hugh prayed he hadn't made another fatal blunder. "Kathryn told me the day she and Guy left for Sedgewick."

"Kathryn," she moaned, her expression stricken. "Oh, how could she do this to me—"

"She told me because she trusted me to look after you." With his fingers he tipped her chin to his, searching her face. "Can't you do the same?" he asked gently. "I know the memory still haunts you. But sometimes the pain and fear are not so great when shared with another."

She closed her eyes in shame. "You want me to tell you what—what I saw," she stammered.

"Aye, love, I think 'tis just the medicine you need."

Her eyes opened, huge and pleading. "I cannot," she choked out miserably. "Sir Hugh, what I saw . . . why, I've not told even Kathryn . . ."

"Then tell me as little or as much as you want. Elizabeth, if it proves too painful, you can stop whenever you want, I promise I'll not press you. But I honestly think 'twill do you good."

As he spoke, with his hand he brushed wisps of hair from her temple. How, Elizabeth wondered was it possible that a man's hands could be so achingly gentle? She didn't know why, but she sensed that this moment was of grave importance to both herself and Hugh. She bit her lip, searching her heart and mind, praying that she made the right choice . . .

Her voice, when at last she began to speak, was very low. Hugh listened quietly, sick at heart as she related the atrocities done to her mother. Christ, it was no wonder Elizabeth was so frightened of men—any man! When she had finished, a convulsive shudder shook her body. Hugh pulled her down beside him on the bed, arranging her body against his, tucking her hand in his, feeling her heart beating like a trapped bird. Shiver after shiver shook her body, but surprisingly, there were no tears. After a long while, he felt her body melt into his and knew she slept.

Instead it was Hugh who lay awake until dawn streaked the eastern sky. His eyes were bleak, his chest hollow, his mind filled with but one thought . . . He would gladly lay down his life before he'd let any harm befall this beautiful creature in his arms.

He would protect her from anything . . . even himself.

Amidst the dark, tangled woodland, streamers of sunshine flitted through the treetops, lighting the clearing a glorious shade of sun-dappled gold. The gurgling rush of the stream blended with the sound of high-pitched giggles and soft, husky laughter.

"More!" came the childish demand.

"All right, my little lord," a feminine voice replied with a chuckle. "But once more and that is all. I am so dizzy I can hardly stand!"

Just beyond the glade, a dark figure sat upon his horse. For the fourth day in a row, Guy surveyed the scene played out before him, his features drawn into sharp lines.

He watched broodingly as Kathryn bent with grace, leaning and then straightening to swing his son in a wide circle, around and around. He had yet to tear his gaze from the enchanting picture she presented. She wore no wimple. Her hair was loose, tumbling over her shoulders and down her back in an artless profusion of silken waves well past her hips. The old and worn material of her gown did little to detract from her appeal. Indeed, it only emphasized her enticing slenderness, the supple fullness of breasts and hips.

His hands tightened on the reins. A pulse ticked hard at the base of his throat. What madness was this that he was so entranced with her . . . and she a woman who carried another man's brat? And yet, he had never seen her more lovely . . . or more desirable. The notion spun through his mind that if he were not careful, she might well become an obsession . . . Christ, she was already! jeered an inner voice. He woke in the morning with the image of her face before him. In the heat of the night he imagined her slim young body beneath him, arching and twisting.

But Guy was ever aware that he'd best be wary of this dangerous attraction between them. He dared not touch her again, for he knew not what would happen. He wanted her, aye, in the age-old way where male dominates female. But he also wanted her in passion and tenderness, to touch her with caresses that flamed as well as soothed. It was as if a simmering heat had been lit between them, and it would take but a spark to set the flames raging—

and Guy possessed experience enough to know that—whether wanted or unwanted—Kathryn felt it, too.

His hand lifted. He nudged his horse further into the clearing. He knew the exact moment she took note of his presence. Her laughter faded. Her smile withered. The spark was extinguished from her eyes as if it had been doused by a wall of water.

Guy was abruptly furious—with himself and with her. With Peter, she was ever vibrant, ever gay and laughing. But those wide green eyes were never tender, never laughing or indulgent when they chanced to meet his . . . and why the hell did he wish it were so?

Kathryn lowered Peter slowly to his feet, fighting an inexplicable sense of betrayal when the boy's chubby legs took him toward his father, his arms outstretched. The earl swiftly dismounted and caught the boy high in his arms. His hard expression softened as he whispered something in Peter's ear. Kathryn had gone very still. At the sight of those two dark heads bent together, there was an unexpected catch in the region of her heart.

The earl turned slightly and beckoned. Another mounted rider came into view, and Kathryn's mouth tightened. She should have known, she thought bitingly. It was Sir Michael, her ever-present shadow. She said nothing as the earl handed Peter to the younger knight. Sir Michael settled the boy before him on his saddle, wheeled his mount, and galloped away.

Kathryn had no chance to speculate why the earl sought her out. His attention had returned to her, his features as distant and remote as ever. "Your shoulder," he inquired coolly. "It pains you no more?"

She drew a sharp breath, dismayed by the thought which leaped into her mind. Her shoulder, no . . .

But her heart . . . ah, her heart was another matter. Exactly why she didn't know. But somehow it was all twisted up inside with the confusing blend of enmity and fascination that so dominated her feelings for this man.

"No," she said faintly. " 'Tis healed completely. I feel no pain at all."

She waited nervously as he came within inches of her. As always, her body displayed an alarming reaction to his nearness. An odd restlessness burned fitfully inside her. He touched her nowhere, but she felt as if he did.

"I've yet to hear what you thought of my gifts."

The change in subject caught her off guard. It took an instant before she gleaned his meaning.

Yesterday the earl had taken her, Gerda, and Peter to the weekly village market. While the earl took his business elsewhere, they were left to themselves. After Peter tired of watching the jugglers and a dancing bear, they browsed among the merchants' stalls. Kathryn lingered at one displaying numerous fabrics. A bolt of velvet snagged her attention and she couldn't help running a caressing hand over the supple folds. The color was a vivid midnight-blue, shot through with threads of silver.

The merchant stepped up eagerly, looking her up and down. "A fine choice, mum. With such dark hair and a fair complexion like yours, I vow it's just the thing. And I've the entire bolt—why, there's enough for both a gown and a cloak, too." The price he named was outrageous.

" 'Tis beautiful," she said, smiling slightly. "But I think not." She couldn't resist smoothing it once more with the back of her knuckles, unaware of her wistful expression. It was only when she turned to leave that she discovered the earl had been watching, standing but a few paces distant. The urge to hang her head was overwhelming. The earl's garments were fine. Next to him she felt almost poor and ragged.

Today, just after the morning meal, Gerda had bid her return to her room. There, spread upon the bed, were a dozen or more bolts of cloth— including the midnight-blue velvet—and all finer than anything Kathryn had ever seen in her entire life. She stared, dumbfounded when Gerda told her they were from the earl. Then, as now, she was at a loss for words.

She regarded him uncertainly. "Milord," she murmured, "your generosity overwhelms me." *And confounds me as well*, she added silently. "But truly, there was no need for you to do such a thing."

Think again, sweet wench, Guy thought grimly. He was tired of seeing her garbed in such worn, threadbare attire and longed to pitch her entire wardrobe, what little there was, into the nearest fire!

He sighed. "If the cloth is not to your liking, you can choose something else—"

" 'Tis not that," she interjected quickly. " 'Tis beautiful, all of it, exactly what I'd have chosen myself." The confession slipped out before she could stop it. She understood the reason for such a lavish endowment—only too well! She had saved his son from being trampled by his destrier, but a man such as he would not like being beholden to another—especially her! No doubt this was his way of discharging what he felt was his obligation to her!

If only he had done it—not because of Peter—but out of the goodness of his heart. How much more it would have meant if he had! She did not understand why she was so hurt—she knew only that she was. Nor could she find it in her to be angry.

But it would be just like him to make her explain, and that was the one thing she did not want to do. She lowered her lashes, but not before he glimpsed her distress.

His hands came down on her shoulders, stopping her when she would have eased away. "Kathryn," he murmured. "What is it? I thought you would be well pleased."

"Pleased! I—I know why you did this—'tis only because I saved Peter from your destrier. Mayhap you feel obliged to make some form of—of recompense! But I asked no repayment of you and I—I want none either! And 'twould be just like you to think that I . . . I did what I did . . . not for Peter . . . but for what reward it might bring! And you offend me sorely if that is what you think!"

Guy stared at her, aware of a twinge of admiration for such outraged pride. "Disabuse yourself of that notion," he growled. "I am grateful for my son's life, aye! But the cloth is a gift, Kathryn, not a reward! I did it because it pleased me to do so—because it will please me even more to see you garbed in such cloth."

Both his words and his vehemence matched hers, making her breath catch. She didn't dare put an interpretation to it . . . or did she? She could feel the warmth of his fingers searing through her kirtle, and an unwelcome shiver of desire played upon her skin.

"I still cannot accept a gift of such extravagance," she said stiffly.

"And why not?"

All at once the dignity that had served her so well was in short supply. She struggled for a reply, her voice very low. "Because you know that I—that I cannot repay you."

"And I repeat, Kathryn, the cloth is my gift to you—and a gift requires no remuneration. I would also add that 'tis you who now offend me by implying that I would expect such!"

Kathryn swallowed. "I'm sorry," she whispered.

"I find, however, that I am not averse to a small token of thanks."

His voice had deepened to huskiness—it was not at all what she expected.

Her gaze flew questioningly to his. She was expecting his usual mockery—what she got was something else entirely. A tiny smile lurked on his lips, aye, but with none of his usual vindictiveness. And his eyes were almost . . . tender.

A fleeting panic touched her spine. *No*, she thought helplessly. *Oh, lord, what is happening to me*? She was shaken and confused—yet again. His mouth hovered just above hers—she remembered with scorching intensity exactly what it was like to have that hard mouth trapped against her own. She fell prey to a perilous curl of heat in her midsection, but when he tapped a finger to the tanned hollow of his cheek in silent indication of his wish, she wasn't sure if she was relieved or disappointed.

Summoning all her courage, she levered herself up on tiptoe, prepared to deliver a brief, hasty peck on the cheek. But just as her mouth grazed his cheek, he turned his head . . .

Their lips met; the contact went through her like an arrow of fire. It was her intent to draw back quickly, for she feared what his touch did to her. But she did not and it proved to be her downfall, for he was ever quick to press home the advantage.

Nor was this the chaste contact she intended; indeed, the kiss was no longer hers to control, had it ever been so. With a gasp her lips parted beneath the sweeping entrance of his tongue. He explored the silken interior of her mouth with such breath-stealing thoroughness that her taste was no longer hers, but his. It spun through her mind that she should wrench away—run while she had the chance. Her hands came up in a quick, reflexive movement, as if to suit the deed, then all at once her fingers twisted helplessly in the front of his tunic.

His arms were like iron bands around her back. His mouth possessed hers, stark and blatantly sensual. His head angled first one way, and then the other. With the pressure of his lips he coerced, then seduced; demanded, then persuaded. A dark, forbidden thrill ran through her. It was as if his kiss were no longer confined to her mouth, but blazed all through her. The sound of her breath, quick and ragged, filled her ears.

His mouth slid with slow heat to the tender place where her shoulder met her neck. Her head fell back with a delicious shiver; she felt his burning touch on her throat, even as his hand stole around her waist, then upward . . .

Kathryn's heart tumbled to a standstill as those treacherous fingers paused, hovering directly over the pouting peak of her right breast. She was shocked to realize that beneath her kirtle, her nipples were hard and pointing—they tingled, nay throbbed! From some little known place inside her, there came the urge to crush that lean, dark hand down upon the aching swell of her breast . . .

She began to tremble, shaken and confused by the yearning inside her, a yearning she did not understand. Through a haze she felt his head come up. He released her slowly. It took every ounce of courage she possessed to meet his gaze, for she knew well and true the gleam of triumph would be high and bright in his eyes. But his scrutiny hinted more of puzzlement than victory.

His fingers were beneath her chin. The back of his knuckles grazed her cheek. "What is it?" he murmured. The caress was but fleeting, yet Kathryn felt she would break from the tenderness of that touch, and it was suddenly more than she could stand.

She turned her head aside. "I believe you have your thanks now, milord." Eyes downcast, she was only barely able to keep the quaver from her voice.

For one horrible moment there was naught but silence. She feared yet another battle between them, but then he merely cupped her elbow and began to lead her back to the castle. She was glad he did not insist they ride. Instead he led his horse and walked beside her.

Guy could not help but notice her change in mood. She was subdued and quiet and totally unlike herself. He pulled her around to face him. "Why this melancholy mood, milady? Are you sulking?"

Her mouth opened, then snapped shut. "I do not sulk, my lord!"

He merely raised his brows in that sardonic way that never failed to rouse her dander, staring at her as though he would seize her thoughts for his very own. "What then?" he demanded. "You hide something from me, Kathryn. I know it." Before she could respond, he frowned and asked. "Has someone treated you ill?"

"Aye," she flared. "*You* have!"

His expression hardened. "Indeed, my dear Kathryn. 'Tis food from my table that fills your belly—*and* your babe's. My roof that keeps the cold and wind from that delectable little backside of yours during the long hours of the night." His gaze swept her from head to toe, as frigid as his voice. "Why, I've seen to your every need!"

It was on the tip of her tongue to scream that there was no babe in her belly, but as always, his cold demeanor fired her temper. What difference did it make anyway? Men dealt in lies . . . and this wasn't even *her* lie!

"Aye," she said bitterly. "You've seen to my every need—all but the one that matters most to me."

His eyes were like twin chips of ice. "And what would that be?"

"The truth, milord?"

The truth, he echoed silently. His mouth twisted. Aye, the truth, he affirmed silently . . . such as it was.

She tossed her head and faced him boldly, uncaring that a sudden breeze whipped her hair and molded her gown to her body. "You wrenched me from Ashbury—from my home—from the arms of my only sister! And now you refuse to let me return!"

Ashbury . . . *Ashbury!* Guy wanted to grind his teeth in impotent fury. The chit thought of little else, save her own selfish wants!

"The truth, eh? I see the truth a little differently, for I've had it from your lips once already, Kathryn. Do you forget so soon how you planned to wrest Ashbury from your uncle—how you planned to use your lover Roderick to that end?" He gave a harsh laugh. "You covet Ashbury for your own, Kathryn. *That* is the only truth I see."

"I've made no secret of that!" she replied with a toss of her head. "Ashbury belonged to my father, and his father before him! It should have been mine—mine and Elizabeth's upon his death. But Richard stole Ashbury from us as surely as you have stolen it from us yet again!" Thinking of Ashbury and Elizabeth made her chest hurt. But her anger at this—this arrogant interloper overrode all else. "You killed Richard—

you have your revenge! Isn't that enough? I've
seen enough to know that you have no need of
more lands. Why must you claim Ashbury as
well?"

"So instead you would have me cede Ashbury to
you?"

"Aye!"

He laughed outright. "You cling to Ashbury like
a mother to a suckling babe, but you forget that you
are but a woman, Kathryn. Or is it your intention
to scurry back and marry your precious Roderick?"
He smiled cruelly when she said nothing. "No? It
seems I was right after all, Kathryn. You sought
not the restrictions of marriage but the pleasures.
How long, then, before your knights deserted you?
And what of your tenants? They look to their lord
for guidance and protection in time of siege. How
would you defend your precious Ashbury from
attackers with no knights to rally to your defense—
with no husband to command your army?"

He was cruel to taunt her so. He ridiculed her
helplessness, yet it was he and others like him who
thrust it upon her! His speech infuriated Kathryn,
yet she could find no answer to refute him.

Guy met her stare mercilessly, yet as time spun
out, he found himself torn between the urge to
shake her senseless and cradle her tenderly to his
chest. "That is the way of the world, Kathryn. I
suggest you accept it, since you cannot change it."

The ache of tears in her throat was nearly unbearable. "And so Ashbury is your prize? And I am
your possession?"

She glared at him, yet her eyes betrayed a suspicious glitter. Tears? Guy scoffed. Surely not, for
she was a shrew whose heart lay cold as death.

He smiled sardonically. "I see we understand
each other, Kathryn."

Kathryn gave a choked little cry. She should have known better than to expect lenience and understanding from him. He was a man with a heart of stone!

"You keep Ashbury only to spite me," she cried. "And you keep me here only to spite me. Damn you, why can't you let me go?"

His jaw tensed as he watched her flee. He'd been right about her after all. She would not bend, he thought furiously. And if she would not bend, then she must break . . . Christ, the wench was more trouble than she was worth!

If he were wise, he'd do exactly what she wanted and send her back to Ashbury. Yet even as the thought burned through his mind, he knew he would not.

Would not, or *could* not . . . ?

Chapter 10

It was late that night when Guy entered Peter's chamber. He paused by the side of Peter's bed to let his knuckles drift back and forth across the downy curve of his son's cheek, his features incredibly tender. Gerda looked on from the foot of the bed, aware of a painful heaviness in her chest. It had been a long, long time since she'd seen that expression on his face . . . He had been through so much heartache, she thought. She prayed nightly that at least some small measure of happiness would come to him.

He looked pensive when he straightened. Gerda summoned a smile. "He is never still, my lord. He plays so hard, he is worn out by nightfall."

His nod was rather absentminded. "Gerda," he murmured, "someone mentioned that you've assisted with a number of births these last few years."

Gerda frowned, unsure what he was after. "Aye, my lord."

"You have more experience than I in these matters then. When would you guess that Lady Kathryn's babe is due?"

The girl's jaw sagged. She gaped disbelievingly. "Lady Kathryn's *babe*? My lord, I . . ." A fleeting

173

puzzlement crossed her features. "How can this be when she . . ." She broke off, blushing hotly.

"What?" Guy demanded. "Gerda, if there is something I should know, spit it out, girl."

Utterly mortified, Gerda stared at the floor, then finally decided there was nothing for it but to blurt it out. "My lord, she had her monthly flux just a few days after you brought her here! I—I do not see how she can be with child . . ."

Guy's whole body went rigid. *How, indeed,* he echoed silently. Aloud he said, "Gerda, are you certain you are not mistaken? You're positive this was her monthly flux?"

"I am not mistaken," she said faintly. "My lord—" She got no further. Stunned, she watched him whirl and stalk from the chamber. There was an air of leashed savagery about him that she feared did not bode well for Lady Kathryn . . .

Snug in her chamber, Kathryn held luxuriant blue velvet. She rubbed the swath across her cheek, still rather stunned by the earl's unexpected kindness—and her own response to it. She had no desire to be beholden to him. She wanted nothing from him, save that he remove himself from her life! It was inevitable, perhaps, that she should be reminded of what had passed between them in the forest. His ardent kiss had shaken her sorely. But in truth, it was his achingly tender caress of her cheek that sent a tremor through her anew. She had not realized that a mere touch could be so painfully sweet, so gentle . . . that *he* could be so gentle. A bittersweet pang pierced her breast.

He had threatened her, dragged her to Sedgewick against her will. Ah, but she preferred that he rant and rave, strike her, even beat her, for she could rally her defenses against his anger . . . Twice now, she had glimpsed a side of him she had never dreamed might exist in this iron-hearted knave. For all that he was fierce and warlike, he had shown her he could be gentle . . .

She feared his gentleness far more.

The heavy footfall of steps in the passage outside jarred her from her musings. Her door crashed open. Kathryn drew no more than a quick startled breath than the earl stepped within, his powerful frame filling the doorway. His dark head nearly touched the crosstimber; his shoulders eclipsed her view of the passage.

His presence was dark and menacing. Kathryn stared as if she'd come face to face with her executioner. And indeed, she thought faintly, perhaps she had, for was it not true that her very life was subject to his every whim and will . . . ?

The moment of weakness passed, mercifully quick. She squared her shoulders and fixed him with a blistering glare. "Do you not knock, my lord? It occurs to me that for one so nobly born, your manners are no better than the lowliest villein's."

Guy was in no mood for the tartness of her tongue. He was furious with himself for feeling any softness toward her—for feeling anything at all! He need not think long and hard on her trickery to be filled with a rage darker than any he had known. She had deceived him, made a fool of him!

He jeered openly. "I am lord here, Kathryn. I go where I please. I ask what I please. I *do* what I please. And it occurs to me that a reckoning of accounts is due—from you, my lady, you who profess to be such a great seeker of truth."

Two steps brought him before her. Her hands still clutched the blue velvet. He snatched it from her grasp and flung it across the room. Shaken by the venom in his eyes, Kathryn dared not move as he walked in a slow circle around her. For all the violence of the act, when at last he spoke his tone was feathery-soft, belying the ruthless tension constricting his features.

"Your child, Kathryn. When do you expect it?"

Kathryn blanched. Surely he did not know, she thought in panic. Yet something deep inside her cried out a warning... A strangled exclamation broke from her lips. "You know, don't you? Oh, God... you know..."

"What, Kathryn? What do I know?"

He stopped before her. His hands lifted, circling her neck. With his thumbs he traced a path up and down the slender column of her throat. Suddenly she felt fearful. She pictured his fingers, tanned and powerful, against her skin. Ah, he played the game so well. He toyed with her as a lion toyed with his prey before pouncing for the kill. He had only to tighten his grip and the life would be crushed from her. Her presence on this earth would be no more... She closed her eyes and wrenched her face away. "There is no child," she choked out.

His thumbs ceased their caressing motion. She heard his voice, caustic and grating, above her head. "There never was, was there?"

She tensed, afraid of the moment she would breathe her last, even as his accusation splintered through her like the tip of a lance. She shook her head mutely, then opened her eyes.

The cold condemnation on his face stabbed at her. "It was a plot, then, conjured up by you and your sister—"

"Nay," she cried. "Not in the way that you think... I admit I planned to tell Uncle I was with child so that he would allow Roderick and me to marry. But then there was no need to go through with it—" She floundered helplessly. "'Twas Elizabeth who told you, not I, my lord!

Why she did so I—I do not know!"

Oh, she lied so prettily. But Guy would never again be so gullible. His lip curled in disdain. "No doubt your sister sought to save you from my evil clutches. Perhaps she feared that I would ravish and defile you—take you unto me and use you . . . like the whore we both know you are!"

She flinched, bitterly stung by his contempt. His quiet rage was worse than if he'd bellowed with fury. His hands fell away from her, as if he found her revolting. He stalked away to survey her coldly from across the room. Deep within her, a reckless courage surged to the fore.

Her chin angled high, she matched his stare as boldly as a warrior with sword at his side and shield at his breast. "You've found me out, my lord earl. So punish me," she challenged clearly. "Aye, do your worst to me. Beat me, whip me, thrash me, I care not. Indeed, I welcome it, for it will kindle my hatred for you. But know that someday—someday I will be free of you and your hold over me. And then vengeance will be mine."

Guy sucked in a harsh breath. He wondered if this rebellious chit truly realized how very much she risked, that she dared to threaten and defy him now, when he was so close—so very close— to venting all his pent-up wrath.

He stared into those flashing sea-green eyes, eyes that had scarce given him a moment's peace since the day they'd met. And then every thought in his mind blurred beneath the onslaught of just one.

He did not welcome the seething pulse of desire that leaped within him, but the burning in his soul would not be silent. It struck him then— this was something he could control, something easily quenched . . . And now there was no reason not to.

His time of waiting had come to an end.

"That would please you, would it not? For me to lay my hand on you in anger. But you may rest easy, lass, for 'twould give me no satisfaction to see that lovely skin bruised." An ugly smile distorted the chiseled beauty of his hard mouth. "But I promise you, sweet, you *will* feel the touch of my hand this night."

Her breath tumbled to a standstill. She had to struggle to find voice. "What—what do you mean?"

"Do you remember Ashbury, Kathryn? The eve you came to my chamber?" he asked, striding toward her.

She blanched. Dear God, she thought numbly, how could she forget? Through a haze she heard him continue. "How shall I put this . . . You sought to ease the loneliness of my solitary bed . . ." Eyes starkly brazen, his gaze raked over her from head to toe.

Kathryn went rigid. Icy fingers of dread crept up her spine. She read his intent in the flaming glitter of his eyes—he meant to bed her! "Nay," she cried. She flung out a hand as if to ward him off. He caught both her wrists and dragged her up against him.

"Yes," he mocked. "Oh, yes."

She struggled against him but his hands curled around her wrists like manacles of iron. "You detest me," she reminded him desperately. "And you denied me that night, milord. You did not want me—"

"Oh, but I did, sweet witch. It's true I am an unwilling victim of desire. I swore that night that you would be mine, Kathryn, but the time would be of my choosing. Then I learned of the child you were to bear. I told myself I could not take a woman with child . . . But now that obstacle is no more, and tonight, sweet witch, tonight we shall finish that which you started so long ago."

Her heart lurched sickeningly. Too late Kathryn realized her position. His time of waiting had come to an end. And there was naught she could do to stop him.

There was no gentleness in him now. There was nothing but cold, implacable purpose that sent terror coursing through her body. He towered over her, big and powerful, and suddenly she was frightened of what she sensed in him. She feared the anger leashed so tightly inside him, as if a tempest raged deep within.

She wanted to twist away, to flee as far and fast as her legs would carry her. But she couldn't move. She was held chained by the realization that it was too late—that there was nowhere she could go where he would not find her.

"I will not lie with you. Do you hear? I will not!"

It only frustrated her further that he found her outrage so amusing. "Come, Kathryn, I'm but a man, much the same as any other. Why should you withhold from me that which you gave so eagerly to your lover, Roderick? Besides, there are many who feel I am quite skilled in the arts of bringing a woman pleasure."

"Pleasure!" she flared. "I'll derive no pleasure from your touch, you conceited lout! You tout yourself and your manhood like a merchant selling his wares, but you are as repulsive as a toad. You—you disgust me!"

Her taunts hit home. Guy swore softly under his breath. Never before had he struck a woman, but she tried him sorely. An arrogant smile crept across his lips. "We shall see," was all he said. "We shall see."

The next instant his smile was gone. He crossed his arms over his tunic and arched a heavy brow. "Strip," he ordered curtly.

Kathryn gaped at him. She felt as if the ground were falling away beneath her feet. "You are mad," she gasped.

"Aye," he agreed coolly. "Mad with lust for you. Now strip, Kathryn, else I shall do it for you." His half-smile was frigidly brutal. "The choice is yours, milady."

The choice was hers? He offered no choice but submission! Oh, God, she should have known . . . he would dare anything . . . he would *do* anything! Her composure badly shaken, her pride sorely bruised, she gave a strangled cry of ire and presented him with her back. Even as she berated herself for her weakness, her fingers clumsily fumbled with the sash at her waist.

His voice drifted to her. "I still await, Kathryn. And I grow ever more impatient."

Prolonging her fate though she knew she risked much, she scorned him silently. Bending slightly, she tugged at the garter below one knee and pulled off her hose; the other followed suit. She slowly pushed her gown from her shoulders where it fell to the floor. She did the same with her linen chemise, letting it drop in a heap about her ankles.

Eyes downcast, she was quiveringly aware of the earl's approach. In a hurried bid to retain some semblance of modesty, she sought to tug her hip-length hair across her shoulders. But she had scarce lifted her hands than she found them ruthlessly jammed back to her sides.

Kathryn stood mutely. The humiliation that gripped her was scalding. Eyes the color of storm clouds pored over her nakedness in a leisurely, deliberate examination, leaving no part of her untouched. Never before had she been so despairingly aware of her vulnerability as a woman. Her throat closed with the aching threat of tears. She willed them away, resolving that no man would ever see her cry—most especially not this one!

The breath left Guy's lungs in a rush. The candlelight from the wall sconces flickered over her, bathing the whole of her in ivory and gold. He'd thought her beautiful before, but she was truly exquisite—slight but long of limb, slender but with enticingly full breasts, tipped with dusky-rose nipples. His blood began to heat, exciting him to a fine frenzy. It was all he could do not to pull her against him, tug those deliciously long legs around his waist and plunge hot and deep inside her then and there.

A lean hand clamped her bare shoulder. Kathryn had thought herself well steeled for his touch, but her entire body jerked. In all truth, her nerves were scraped raw. Oh, she knew why he did this—he longed only to assert his dominion over her—to squelch her rebellious pride and prove that his will would ever triumph over hers. He had never seemed more dangerous than he was at this moment—the thought of him possessing her body was terrifying. For the first time she regretted that he despised her so, for his desire was spawned of anger. He would channel all his pent-up fury into this single act. His pleasure, she thought wildly, would be gained from her pain.

She bit back an anguished sob. Panic gripped her mind. Her only thought was to escape this madman's vengeance. She spun about and lunged wildly for the door but he was too quick for her. His arms snaked out and caught her, pinning her back against him.

He laughed huskily. "You think to flee so late in the game? And where would you go undressed as you are—you'd surely give my knights an unexpected treat. Why, they'd be lined up clear beyond the outer walls to taste your bounteous charms. But alas, 'tis their loss and my gain, for I shall be the one to claim the honeyed treasure between your thighs this night."

"You braying jackass!" she raged in impotent fury, but her arms were useless, trapped against her body by the muscled forearm banding her waist. She twisted and kicked backward with her bare feet but the effort was futile. "You—you are crude!"

That iron-thewed arm tightened further. "Whatever," he muttered, and his voice had gone low and deep. "But I've waited a long time for this night and I'll not be cheated of it." He lifted her clear from the floor.

The next thing she knew she lay sprawled on the bed; his big body followed hers down. She lay stunned, unable to move for an instant, her breath slammed from her lungs by the oppressive weight of his body atop hers. Then she came alive, trying to jerk her arms and legs free. In desperation she sank her teeth into his shoulder. She heard a satisfying grunt of pain before he pulled back slightly, and then victory was but a fleeting memory. With a vicious oath he curled his foot around both her legs and yanked her arms beneath her back. Kathryn soon discovered that the slightest movement made her arms feel as if they were being wrenched from their sockets. Her struggles subsided, but she stiffened every muscle in her body against him until her arms went numb and her mind was spinning from lack of air. She turned her head aside with a half-sob.

Feeling her body go limp beneath him, Guy waited tensely, gauging her for further trickery. A pang of remorse shot through him as he loosed her wrists and raised himself slightly. He crouched above her, ripped off his leather jerkin, and flung it aside. Not once did he take his eyes from her as he stripped. She lay before him—spent, trembling, her eyes wide and unblinking as she stared sightlessly toward the wall. Not for the first time, Guy was struck by the air of innocence which clung to her. Some strange twisting emotion unfurled inside him, fazing his certainty . . . He could almost believe that she was frightened. She appeared defenseless and helpless, and so very, very young . . . A niggling little voice in his mind taunted that he'd been well misled before by her trickery. Nor was she innocent in the ways of men, and the knowledge served to harden Guy's heart.

It did naught to cool his ardor.

"Kathryn." There was that in his tone which commanded she heed him. With pained reluctance, she moved her head and encountered the enigmatic attraction of his sheer masculine presence.

He loomed above her. Dark and strong. Fiercely compelling. Kathryn's heart began to pound. Naked, he was an awesome sight, more powerful than ever. His shoulders gleamed smooth and hard, like oiled walnut. A dense layer of dark curly hair matted the whole of his chest and abdomen. Swallowing, her gaze touched the corded swelling of his arms, then strayed helplessly downward . . . the rigid thickness of his manhood was starkly, daringly explicit. One terrified glimpse was enough to send her eyes flying back to his face. Oh, God, she thought. He would hurt her. Impale her like a fish on a hook and tear her asunder . . .

His lips twisted into something that bore little resemblance to a smile.

He stretched out beside her. Kathryn shrank away instinctively, but he would have none of it. His hands closed around the soft flesh of her upper arms; he dragged her against him. She gasped as her naked breasts encountered the furry roughness of his chest.

Their eyes locked. There was a taut silence as they stared at each other appraisingly.

It was Kathryn who broke free from the hold of his gaze. "Damn you," she cried. "Just do it . . . do what you will and be done with it!"

His head descended. All at once he was so close it was as if they shared the same breath. He nuzzled the delicate skin of her temple. "But there is so much that we would miss," he whispered, and she thought she felt him smile against her cheek. "And I'd not deprive you of your pleasure."

I'll feel no pleasure, she longed to screech. Her eyes blazed. She opened her mouth to curse him at the same instant he sealed her lips with a binding kiss.

She fought him. Oh, she was well aware she could not overcome his physical strength. But she fought him in the only way she knew how. She emptied her mind and concentrated instead on Ashbury—recalling how dreadfully she missed Elizabeth, how she longed to walk along the cliffs with the sea wind whipping her skirts and hair.

With the pressure of his chest, he urged her onto her back. She lay stiff and unresponding as his fingers slid into the unbound glory of her hair. His tongue flicked across her lips, insistently seeking. She clamped her lips tight and barred him entrance.

He raised his head to stare at her. Though his features were dark and shadowed, the jutting clench of his jaw bespoke his displeasure. His fingers tightened almost painfully on her scalp. "Yield to me, Kathryn." There was no softness in his voice, none at all. "Yield . . ."

"Never," she vowed. "You are crude. A vulgar oaf—" Her imprecation was smothered by the hot seal of his mouth on hers. But this time he did not seek, he demanded . . . ah, but with such seductive persuasion! With an ease that proclaimed the experience he had boasted of, he set about rousing forbidden fires. His mouth was wildly consuming, devouring and fierce, hard but not hurtful. He kissed her endlessly, deep, drugging kisses that seemed to go on forever and melted her resistance like tallow beneath a flame.

Somewhere in the deepest, darkest recesses of her being, a stranger fluttered to life, a stranger she scarcely recognized as herself. A curling ribbon of sensation unfurled like the buds of a flower beneath a warm summer sun. It was but a kiss, she tried telling herself. But no longer did she merely endure the browsing glide of his tongue. She could feel her senses widening, expanding, opening to absorb the heat and essence of the man himself . . . She gave a low moan and allowed her arms to creep around his neck. She helplessly surrendered all that he sought, for she could summon no more strength to resist his will and her own traitorous need.

With a groan Guy crushed her to him. The sweet clinging of her mouth against his was almost more than he could bear. Her breasts burned like twin peaks of fire into his chest. He could feel the tender press of her thighs against the part of him that needed her most—he was so achingly full he thought he might explode. It was both heaven and hell to hold her thus and not give in to the need clamoring wildly in his veins, but all at once he did not want this passionate encounter to end so speedily.

He brought his hand to her breast, slowly rotating his palm around the swelling peak, cupping the

cushioned fullness in his hands—Christ, her skin
was like warm velvet. He had a sudden, consuming
urge to taste such tempting fruit.

Kathryn's eyes flew open. The touch of his hand
there sent a jolt of lightning streaking through her.
She had not dreamed that he would touch her
there . . . She emitted a startled gasp of bewildered
shock when he abruptly lowered his head, his tar-
get her left breast. What madness was this, that he
would suckle her like a babe . . . ?

Her fingers curled against the sleek flesh of his
shoulders, but she did not stop him. His breath
caressed her first, wafting across the aching tip like
the first faint whispery wings of night. A quivering
excitement shot through her. She was stunned to
discover her breasts seemed to swell, her nipples
tight and aching and tingly. By the time his mouth
fully encompassed the straining peak, she was so
acutely sensitized there she nearly cried out.

He laved her nipple to quivering erectness with
the lashing stroke of his tongue, all the while
taunting the other with his fingertips, circling
and teasing it. The dual assault left her gasping.
She inhaled sharply, the flood of sensations inside
threatening to choke her.

A restless longing began building inside her, an
acute yearning she did not fully understand. She
forgot that he was her enemy. She forgot that she
hated him. She told herself that she shuddered in
loathing, but she knew that she trembled with a
perilous excitement that far surpassed anything she
had ever known.

He lured her into a realm from which there was no
escape. His hands roamed at will—stroking, soothing, coaxing, and caressing. Kathryn did not stop
him. To her horror, she found she did not want to.
At times his hand was a fiery brand, claiming her for

his own. Then suddenly his touch was tantalizing and tormenting, maddening and elusive, drifting like smoke and making her shiver inside and out. He seemed to know exactly where to touch—when to tease—it was as if he knew her own body better than she herself . . . She was no match against such an unfaltering, practiced lover. When his mouth reclaimed hers, he drew from her an unbearably sweet response she was incapable of withholding.

Lean fingers traced a nerve-shattering path across the concave hollow between her hips. Then, as bold and brazen as he himself was, those daring fingers trespassed through the downy thatch below. Kathryn's heart slammed to a halt—the intimacy was unbearable! She tried to close her thighs against his encroaching hand, but he would have none of it. Soft triumphant laughter rumbled against her lips. A lone finger dipped and swirled, intent on a mind-stealing rhythm that robbed her of breath. Waves of scorching heat coursed through her. The rampant thunder of her heart echoed in her ears. She began to tremble. Sweet Jesus, what was he doing to her?

Her fingers curled against the hard flesh of his shoulders. She uttered a choked plea. "Do not, milord. Oh, please—"

His head lifted. "I have a name, Kathryn." His voice sounded odd and strained. "Why do you never use it?" Oh, he knew why. It was but one more barrier that she threw up against him, yet another way to defy him. But until that moment Guy did not realize how he longed to hear it spring forth from those sweet lips . . . nay, not in anger, but in whispered passion . . . in the heat of slumberous desire.

Kathryn stared up at him, taken aback by the urgency she sensed in him. It seemed such a small thing . . . "This would . . . please you?" In some far distant corner of her mind, she marveled that she could speak at all.

His eyes darkened. "Aye." He bent and kissed the wildly thrumming pulse at the base of her throat. "Say it, Kathryn," he muttered hoarsely. "Say my name."

Guy . . . His name trembled on her lips. Her teeth dug into her lower lip to keep it from spilling out. His eyes looked down on her, fiery and glittering—she saw in them all that she feared. He had ruthlessly set about the task of setting her blood afire, not because he harbored any tender emotion toward her . . . but because he sought only to tame her to his hand! Pain sliced her chest, as if a knife had passed through it. She could not—would not!—lead him along the path to triumph so easily.

His head lowered. A flurry of panic traced through her—he meant to kiss her into weak, willing submission! "Nay," she heard herself say. For all that it was but a whisper, she denied him fiercely . . . and then again. *"Nay!"* And she wrenched her head away, spurning him outright.

A veil of red-hot mist swam before Guy. A brutal rage erupted inside him. If she would not allow him to give her pleasure, then so be it, he decided harshly. He shifted his weight atop her. With his knee he splayed her wide open . . . he shifted again, the searing tip of his shaft poised at the very heart of her . . .

A mighty thrust buried him deep inside her.

Blinded as he was by rage and passion, his tardy mind was slow to register her body's fragile resistance to his invasion.

Kathryn never heard the bitter oath that stung her ear. She strained away instinctively, but he was like a rock above her, a white-hot lance inside her. With a strangled cry she jammed her palms frantically against his shoulders and chest, desperate to dislodge the throbbing shaft that burned and stung like fire, clear to her womb.

Above her, Guy had gone rigid, his features dark and hard, twisted into a grimace that closely resembled pain. His breath was harsh and scraping, the cords in his neck starkly visible. The roped sinews of his arms stood out as he braced himself above her.

"Kathryn—" He reached up and clamped his fingers around her wrists, pinning them to the mattress. A convulsive shudder racked his form. He gritted his teeth and tried not to think how small she was, how tightly embedded was his swollen length in the hot silken prison of her flesh.

It was no use. The thundering pulse within him governed all else. "I cannot stop," he muttered thickly. "God help me, I cannot!" With a frenzy he could not leash, he drove mindlessly into her. Once. Twice. Again. For once he had no control over the dictates of his body. He came quickly like a stripling youth, drenching her with the wet heat of his seed even as he collapsed against her.

His grip on her wrists relaxed by subtle degrees. Sanity returned much more quickly—and with a vengeance. The magnitude of what he had done washed over him like a thundercloud. He withdrew from her abruptly and rolled away, rising to his feet. He had to force himself to look at her. She lay stiff and passive, her eyes squeezed shut, her lashes fanned out like thick black fans against skin that was almost colorless. Revulsion twisted his insides as he spied the blood smeared on her pale thighs.

Self-loathing poured through him like boiling oil. He relived the agonizing remorse of that split second when she shed her maidenhead—Christ, he had taken her with all the finesse of a battering ram slamming through the gates! Bitterly he wondered if she knew the act had brought him little satisfaction.

He moved away, only to return a moment later, a wet cloth in his hand. Her entire body jerked as he pressed the cloth between her thighs and began to wipe away the traces of his possession. From the corner of his eye he saw her fingers wind into the sheet. With a convulsive swallow she turned her face aside.

Something twisted inside him. Where was that haughty spirit that so drove him to insanity? Right now she looked like a frail spring blossom he'd crushed with his heel!

Never had she been more exposed and powerless than she was at this moment, and he hated her for it, and for the foolish uncertainty which suddenly plagued him. She had led him to believe that she and Roderick were lovers . . . or had she? Had he believed it simply because he was convinced it was so? Yet she'd made no effort to set him aright!

"A virgin," he muttered furiously. "Damn it, a virgin!" The words tumbled forth in a rush of frustrated, bewildered anger.

Kathryn's eyes opened, huge and wounded. She was shattered to find his expression taut and inscrutable. It conveyed no tenderness, no remorse or even apology. As always, he condemned and accused . . . A stab of anger pierced through the hurt and humiliation. She lurched to a sitting position, snatching a fur to her breast to shield her nakedness.

His jaw clenched. "You should have told me," he began.

He got no further. "Why? Would that have stopped you?" She was suddenly shaking in her anger. "You meant to punish me—to hurt me. You *wanted* to hurt me . . . and you did!"

Guy went numb with shock. Mother of Christ, did she really think him so vile? "I wanted you, aye! But I never meant to cause you pain." He stretched a hand toward her but she scrambled back, as far away as she could.

"Who lies now, milord?" she flung at him scathingly. "Just get out . . . get out!"

His expression went rigid. The air seethed as their eyes locked in furious combat. With a violent curse, Guy flung the bloodied cloth to the floor, grabbed his clothing, and stormed from the chamber.

The cloth landed atop the rumpled heap of midnight velvet. Kathryn saw it there an instant later. She kicked it aside with a muffled cry, snatched up the velvet, and held it fast to her breast. She slumped to the floor amidst its folds, the taste of bitter tears upon her tongue.

And when she spoke his name, it was not a whispered lover's plea, but a blistering curse. "Damn you, Guy," she choked. "Damn you to hell!"

Chapter 11

Kathryn struggled to wakefulness the next morning, her mind befuddled with sleep. Dust motes fluttered within the pale shaft of sunlight that found its way between the wooden shutters. Some elusive memory tugged at her but she fought to keep it at bay, sensing that if she did not, something awful would happen . . .

Dear God. It already had. Last night's humiliation came back in scorching remembrance. Guy had taken everything from her—her home, her family— and now her body. She willed away the scalding rush of tears—she had cried throughout the night. In the wee hours before dawn streaked the eastern sky, she vowed that never again would Guy de Marche bring her to tears. In some strange indefinable way, it was but one more way she bowed to his will, and she would not let him force her to such weakness. And yet . . . she felt changed somehow. As if by that single invasion of her body, he had laid claim to some secret part of her. She had the strangest sensation she would never again be herself . . .

There was a tap on the door. Kathryn froze, the covers clutched beneath her chin, half-afraid it was

Guy. But it was only Gerda.

" 'Tis late," Kathryn murmured with a faint smile, pushing her heavy hair from her face. "You should have woke me earlier."

"My lord said to let you sleep," Gerda told her.

Kathryn's smile faded. She made as if to leave the bed, then realized her chemise was in a heap across the room where Guy had made her disrobe. Gerda went to fetch it, her smooth brow creased in a slight frown. Kathryn bit her lip. Such untidiness was so unlike her that she could almost see the thought running through Gerda's mind. But if Gerda thought it unusual, she said nothing. Kathryn accepted it, thanking her, and pulled it over her head. Pushing aside the covers, she rose, wincing a little at the slight twinge between her thighs.

Behind her, there was a quick indrawn breath. Kathryn turned abruptly . . . They both stared in horror at the pale-red stain upon the sheets. A crimson tide of embarrassment stung her cheeks. It shouldn't have mattered what Gerda thought, but it did. Since the day she had saved Peter from being trampled, there had been a change in the servant's manner toward her—Gerda's softening had been more subtle. But Kathryn did not delude herself that, in a test of Gerda's loyalties, she would ever win out over the earl.

She sensed Gerda's gaze returning to her, but she could not face the girl, for suddenly she knew not what to expect from Gerda. Pity? Or condemnation? She could stand to see neither right now.

She started when a gentle hand touched her arm. "Milady," Gerda said softly, "mayhap you'd like a warm bath this morning." Kathryn dredged up the courage to glance at her. Gerda was gazing at her with something akin to concern. More than ever, Kathryn longed to cry.

"Thank you," she murmured. "I'd like that very much."

The steaming waters of the bath soothed the ache in the tender petals of her womanhood. The feel of the earl was still about her body and the scent of him still clung to her. She scrubbed herself furiously, anxious to rid herself of every trace of him. But to her horror, she found she could not blot out the memory of the night so easily. She shut her eyes but it was no use. She could still recall the shape of him—so tall, his body pared of all fat, all sleek, hard muscle densely covered in hair . . .

Her hand stilled, unknowingly coming to rest directly over her heart. Deep inside her, a squall of emotion blustered and raged. She felt . . . oh, so many things! She had expected to feel only revulsion and disgust for what he had done. Her throat tightened oddly. Now, she only felt . . . cheated somehow. As if there were something more . . . She cried out silently. What magic did he possess that he so addled her brain? She had sworn she would partake of no pleasure at his hand—and yet she had, a pleasure so pure and sweet it made a quickening heat storm through her all over again. With stark, vivid clarity, she remembered the daring foray of lean dark hands that roamed her flesh—how they first explored with flaming caresses and breath-stealing discovery—then later, how he bound his hips to hers while he thrust inside her . . .

The heat inside her grew cold. His touch had promised so much . . . but in the end, it delivered only pain.

When Gerda returned, Kathryn was standing at the window gazing out upon the bailey. "I've not seen the earl this morning," she remarked. She strived for an even tone and somehow managed to achieve it. "Do you know where he is, Gerda?"

"He is gone, milady."

"Gone! Where, Gerda?"

"To visit several of his manors to the north, milady. He expects to be gone a fortnight, maybe a little less."

"A fortnight," Kathryn repeated numbly. "But he said nothing—" She broke off abruptly. *Fool!* A voice inside her fiercely berated her foolishness. Why should he apprise her of his plans? She meant nothing to him—nothing! Hadn't his abrupt withdrawal last night proved that? Once again his face loomed above her, his expression frigidly angry as he pulled away from her body—the remembrance slipped beneath her skin like a needle. If only he had displayed some small scrap of tenderness, a hint of compassion instead of such callous disregard, she might have forgiven him . . . She hardened her heart against him. Aye, she was glad he was gone and heartily so. He could leave for a twelvemonth and she cared not a whit!

She was stunned to learn that Guy had relaxed his restrictions before he left. Sir Michael no longer followed when she left the castle walls. It bruised her pride to admit that perhaps he knew her better than she thought. Had he tightened the noose around her neck, her first reaction would have been to bolt at the first opportunity that presented itself.

She had to force herself to begin fashioning the cloth he'd given her into gowns for herself. She and Gerda spent most mornings sewing, while Peter played at their feet. But she went for a ride nearly every afternoon, sometimes alone, sometimes with Gerda and Peter.

One warm, sunny afternoon after she and Peter had finished playing at the stream, she impulsively decided to do a little exploring. When Sir Michael had been in attendance, she had always refrained. Oh, he was always impeccably polite and obliging, but she'd been unable to quell her resentment at being shadowed.

Now, standing beside Esmerelda with Peter, she paused and sent a sweeping gaze around the tree-studded landscape. Beyond the treetops, lush green hills stretched as far as the eye could see, fold upon fold.

"What do you think, Peter? Shall we stay out a while longer? We could ride there to the top of that hill—" Her arm stretched out. "—while you pretend that you're lord of the manor out surveying his demesne." She crouched down before him and tickled him beneath the chin. "Because when you're a man full grown, you will be, you know."

The boy gazed up at her eagerly. "Will I be a brave knight like my papa?"

Kathryn didn't understand the pang that shot through her. "Aye," she murmured, ruffling his black curls. "Just like your papa."

"Will you be here when I am lord?"

His question startled her—it disturbed her far more, for until that moment she had staunchly refused to consider her future.

She did so now.

Despite the warmth of the sun beating down on her head, she felt as if a cold wind swept across her heart. She did not belong here at Sedgewick, she thought despairingly. And the earl had seen to it that she no longer belonged at Ashbury. Her future loomed before her, empty and barren. Never had she felt so lost and alone!

But Peter still awaited her answer. "Peter—" She strived for a jesting tone, and miraculously achieved it. "—when you are a lord, I shall be old and ugly and wrinkled—"

She broke off in amazement when he shook his head. "Not ugly!" he said with surprising forcefulness. "You are boo . . . booty . . ." His little brow furrowed as he struggled to find the right word.

"Peter," she said chuckling, "are you trying to say 'beautiful'?"

His eyes lit up. "Aye!" he exclaimed. "You are beautiful! Papa said so!" He grinned from ear to ear, threw his arms around her neck, and laid his cheek against hers.

Kathryn hugged him back, aware of a funny feeling constricting her chest. All at once her heart was thudding. *Guy* had said she was beautiful? Nay, she thought dazedly, surely not. Yet Peter was so adamant she was sorely tempted to believe him . . .

They never completed their journey, however. They hadn't gone far when Kathryn spotted the road through the spindly branches of a half-rotted tree. She had barely nosed Esmerelda in that direction when all at once the forest woodland became eerily quiet—insects ceased their hum; the trilling notes of a bird warbled to a close. Kathryn's only thought was that it was like the ominous calm before a storm.

It was then that she heard it—the thump of hooves, the raucous sound of voices and grating male laughter. Acting on instinct alone, she hurtled from Esmerelda's back and reached for Peter. Clutching him tight, she tugged on Esmerelda's reins and huddled behind a dense thicket, praying it was tall enough to shield the palfrey. Young as he was, Peter sensed that something was wrong. He stared at her with wide, frightened eyes.

"Peter." She spoke in low, hushed tones. "You

must listen to me and do exactly as I say. I thought I heard someone but I don't know who, so I must check and see. I want you to stay here with Esmerelda—go nowhere else and do not say a word, do you understand? Can you be a brave lad and do this for me?"

He nodded. Kathryn pressed a hasty kiss on his forehead and crept away. The men had stopped in a clearing a short distance away. She concealed herself in the waist-high underbrush and peered through the endless tangle of vines. Her heart drummed so loudly in her ears that she could scarcely hear, but she went very still and concentrated on calming herself. No less than six of them clustered in a circle, mean and evil-looking. Their tunics were torn and dirty, but for all their ragtag appearance, they were heavily armed.

"There's a village just up the road a ways," one of them said. His laugh was chilling. "I say we torch it and have done with it."

"Aye," chimed in another. "Let's roust the place now!"

"Are ye daft, man? You'd have the Earl of Sedgewick down on your head before you could lay your first maid!"

"So let him come! I'm a match for any man," boasted another. With an ugly smile he ran his fingers over the handle of his sword.

"I'd rather have the king himself on me arse!" proclaimed the dissenter. "I say we do as we planned— ride through to the north."

Kathryn inhaled sharply—she'd been right to be so leery. These men were raiders, unsavory wretches who preyed on the unwary and the helpless, those weaker than they and unable to defend themselves. An icy knot of dread coiled in her stomach. If they discovered her and Peter, they would likely as not slay them both!

Though she strained to hear, she could not make out their decision. She stayed in her hiding place until they mounted up and rode off—in the direction of Sedgewick! Then she crawled back to Peter and Esmerelda.

Thank heaven Peter had not moved! His lower lip had begun to quiver, though, so Kathryn pulled him close and whispered reassuringly as she placed him on Esmerelda. "Guess what, Peter? We are going to play a game, you and I—and Esmerelda, too! We are going to pretend that we are hiding from all the world, so you must be very, very quiet again and not say a word."

As soon as she was mounted behind him, she urged the palfrey into a gallop, heading in the opposite direction from the one the raiders had taken. Such a course would take them further from Sedgewick, but she dare not take any chances that she would run into them. She would double back to Sedgewick shortly.

She rode Esmerelda hard, deeper into the encroaching forest where the dense crisscross of tree boughs overhead masked the waning of the sun. It wasn't until she stopped Esmerelda for a rest that she realized the lateness of the hour. Shadows leaped and twisted everywhere. Towering trees crowded menacingly all around, seeming to close in on them. With every moment, the veil of gloom settled deeper over the earth. Soon it would be dark.

She stuffed a fist into her mouth to keep from crying out. She was certain she could find her way back to Sedgewick, but not in the dark! With a sinking feeling in her breast, she dismounted. They had no choice but to spend the night here and begin the journey back to Sedgewick in the morning.

She had taken but three steps forward when she spied a tiny hut a short distance away. Outside the hut, she tethered Esmerelda to a tree. Moments later, she and Peter were standing in the doorway. The hut was old and shabbily constructed, scarcely higher than her head and no more than eight feet across, but at least it offered shelter for the night.

Peter tugged at her skirt. "I want to go home," he whispered pitifully.

Looking down into his forlorn little face, Kathryn felt her heart melt. He had been so good, doing all that she asked with nary a peep. "I know you do, love," she said, kneeling before him. "But I'm afraid we must wait till morning and it's light. Esmerelda can't see very well in the dark, you know, and I'm afraid I can't either." She smiled ruefully and smoothed his hair. "Are you hungry?"

He nodded eagerly. Kathryn fished for the hunk of bread she'd thrust in her pocket just before they left. She watched him gnaw it hungrily, grateful that it satisfied him. When he'd finished, she propped her back against the wall and held out her arms. Within minutes he was asleep, his cheek resting against her shoulder, one small hand curled on her breast.

The night's chill crept into the hut; Peter shivered against her. She wrapped her skirt about him as best she could, wishing wistfully for the warmth of a fire. She stroked his back and stared into the darkness, uncomfortably aware of a sliver digging into her spine. She did not move for fear of waking Peter. Amazingly, her lashes soon drooped. Her mind spun adrift, snatches of reflection floating in and out of her consciousness . . . The raiders—at least some of them—had no wish to confront Guy. Perchance it was true that his was a name

to be reckoned with . . . She prayed they would not
loot and plunder the village, but ride on and leave
it untouched . . .

Guy . . . His name whispered through her mind,
again and again, like a silent litany . . . Had he really said she was beautiful . . . ?

That was her last thought before slipping into the
arms of Morpheus.

A mighty crash sent the door careening wildly
from side to wide. Kathryn's eyes popped open.
She flung up an arm to shield against the glaring
sunlight pouring through the opening. It was then
that she spotted the imposing male form looming
in the doorway. With the sun at his back, his face
in shadow, he appeared dark and featureless and
wholly menacing.

The scream that crowded her throat never made
it to fruition. Before she could draw breath, Peter
was snatched from her arms and handed to someone behind him. Kathryn found herself plucked
from the floor like a hen from its nest. It was a
rude awakening, in the truest sense . . .

Pale silver eyes impaled her with their fierce-
ness. "You," she gasped. "I did not know you were
back."

"Obviously I came too soon for you to make good
your escape." There was no mistaking the anger
that fed his accusations. "God's blood, woman, you
have the gall of no other! Did you really think you
could do it—did you think I'd let you fly like a thief
in the night . . . and take my son with you?"

His eyes tore into her, like the slash of a
swordpoint. She gaped at him, stunned. "What—
what are you saying? Surely you cannot think
that I—"

He seized her arm in a bruising grip. "Say no

more, lady! By God, I'll not vouch for my temper right now!" He hauled her outside where a small party of his men awaited, then proceeded to set her on Esmerelda's back so jarringly her teeth came together with a snap.

It took more than an hour and a half to reach Sedgewick. Kathryn rode with her head held regally high, her spine so rigid she felt it might crack.

Not one word was said to her the entire time.

A small cluster of servants waited in the bailey, Gerda among them. The earl handed Peter into her waiting arms. Kathryn could not bear to look at her, certain she would be as silently condemning as the earl. She slid down from Esmerelda unassisted. The next instant a hand touched her shoulder. She started as she saw that it was Gerda, her eyes wide with concern. "Are you all right, milady?"

"I'm fine," she choked out. She could say no more, for suddenly her throat was clogged tight. She pressed the reins into the hands of a waiting groom, whirled around, and rushed for the stairs.

A voice like a whip halted her dead in her tracks. "Where do you think you are going, milady?"

A feeling of sick dread knotted her stomach. She wasn't ready for this, she thought numbly. She was exhausted and cold and hungry. Instinct urged her to run like a hunted animal—the better side of reason dictated otherwise. She awaited his approach, still as a statue, not daring to look around. With nary a pause in his stride, he hooked steely fingers into her elbow and pulled her forward.

Kathryn wrenched her arm from his grasp. "There's no need to drag me," she hissed.

He glared at her but freed her arm. Nonetheless, his pace was so rapid she had a hard time keeping up with him. By the time he slammed the door of the counting room, there was a painful stitch in her side. She stopped in front of the long wide table, while he crossed to the other side.

He drummed his fingers on the trestle table, never relieving her of that unnerving silvery stare. "Well, madam," he said harshly, "what have you to say for yourself?"

Kathryn pressed her lips together. He seemed to have all the answers. Let him supply it!

"What! Does your memory escape you so soon? Or do you need more time to concoct your story?"

Kathryn gritted her teeth. Her stinging resentment increased by leaps and bounds. Always he mocked her—always he judged her. What use was there in trying to explain?

"Well, milady, what was your plan?"

If he sought to prick her defenses, he succeeded well. She found she could not back down from the challenge inherent in that diamond-hard gaze.

"There was no plan," she said curtly. "Peter and I were at the stream. We decided to ride to the nearest hilltop but we did not get that far. We nearly ran into some men, a band of raiders—"

"Raiders!" A lazy smile of amusement curled his lips. "My lands are safeguarded well, Kathryn. I pride myself upon that. If there were raiders near here, my men would have seen to their demise."

His arrogance never ceased to amaze her. "You think you know so much but you know nothing! I rode deeper into the forest so they wouldn't discover us. But darkness fell and I realized I couldn't find my way back to Sedgewick at night. We found the hut and so I thought it best to spend the night there and return to Sedgewick this morning." When he said nothing, she smothered a cry of indignant outrage. "I heard them, I tell you! There were six of them. They were divided as to whether or not to raid the village here or ride north!"

"As you saw, Kathryn, the village is unharmed and secure."

"Then they clearly decided to head north instead!"

The smile continued to dally about his lips.

Tears rose in her eyes but she clenched her fists and blinked them back. "You—you wrong me grievously," she said, her voice low and intense. "Peter is just a child. To think that I would hurt him—"

His smile withered. The ice in his gaze chilled her to the bone. "I do not believe you would intentionally do him harm," he said coldly. "But he is my son, and I believe you would do anything you could to seek retribution against *me*."

"Including running off with Peter? Think, my lord! You've been gone a fortnight. If that was my intention, I'd have done it the moment I discovered you gone!"

He made no reply. Kathryn found his silence brutal. She did not know that, unbidden, the memory of their last encounter had soared aloft in his mind. Guy damned himself for tormenting himself these past days—for wondering if she were all right—for fleeing like a coward, loath to face her after what he had done. A hundred times he'd heard her stricken cry as he tore through her maidenhead. And now, seeing her in the flesh once again . . . Despite her militant stance, he was reminded how fragile and delicate she had felt in his arms, how small and tight was her woman's sheath as he drove inside her . . .

And he thought of his tender, loving initiation of Elaine. Elaine, his wife, his beloved . . . A clawing pain ripped at his insides. He was not sure who he despised more, himself or Kathryn. He had lain with her, she who was kin to his wife's murderer . . .

And not once had he thought of his wife.

Yet Kathryn was so convincing, he could almost believe her. But doubt had clouded his mind for so long it was difficult to see the truth. Ah, but what was the truth? With her, he never knew. Nay, he decided harshly, he dared not trust her. He dared not believe her, for she had already proved that she was as cunning and treacherous as her uncle.

"I do not pretend to know what is in your mind," he told her. "Indeed, not until I returned to find you gone did I realize I might have given you cause for your hatred of me to run deeper than ever." His brows rose when she frowned at him blankly. "I'd rather thought of it as unforgettable," he went on smoothly. "Am I wrong then, in assuming you remember our coupling with fondness?"

His indifference sent hot shame coursing through her. Oh, he was a callous beast to remind her so cruelly!

"Unforgettable, aye, that it was!" she said fiercely. "But I do not recall that night with fondness. Nay, I think of it with naught but loathing and disgust!"

He smiled grimly. "So I thought, which is why I sought to appease you by removing your guard while I was gone." His tone turned as cutting as his eyes. "And how did you repay me? I returned to find you gone—and my son along with you! Now tell me, Kathryn, which of us has been wronged here?" He slammed his palms down on the table so hard she jumped. "Christ, I should never have brought you here!"

She closed her eyes as if she were praying. "Then send me back to Ashbury," she whispered. The plea slipped out before she could stop it, and then she didn't want to. She opened her eyes to stare at him mutely. She went on, unaware of the naked longing that dwelled in her expression. "I've been here more than a month. I've obeyed your rules and done your bidding. And yet you continue to keep me prisoner!"

He scorned the leap of hope in her eyes. *Ashbury*, he thought savagely. *It is always Ashbury with her* . . . She would not cast aside this foolish notion that she could hold title to it!

"Prisoner, is it?" His laugh was grating. "The term intrigues me, Kathryn, especially since I've shown you every kindness."

Her tone was stiff. "Oh, you do not stoop to physical harm. But you keep me here against my will. What kindness is there in that?"

"Egad, woman, you have abused my trust! Yet you expect to be rewarded?"

She stamped her foot. "I've abused nothing! After all that has happened between us, you cannot expect me to remain here—"

"Ah, that's where you're wrong, Kathryn." His mouth twisted. "I can and I do."

She stared at him with eyes both accusing and pleading. Her anguished cry seemed to echo from the furthest depths of her soul. "Why? Just . . . tell me why!"

He ignored her completely, moving to sit at the chair on the opposite side.

She slapped her palms before him on the table. "I'll not be your mistress," she burst out. "Your prowess as a lover was much overrated, my lord. Indeed, I found it sorely lacking!"

Slowly his gaze lifted, tangling with hers. His features were set in a cold hard mask, but within those silver depths a molten fire burned hot and searing. "Do not seek to test me, Kathryn—" His lips curved into a wicked smile. "—for you would give me no choice but to prove the falsehood you speak, which I would do, I'm sure, with a great deal of pleasure indeed."

Oh, how her fingers itched to slap that insolent smirk from his mouth. "You bastard." She glared at him, her lips barely moving as she went on. "How long do you intend to keep me here?"

Her eyes were the dark green of a stormy sea. Her stance was defiant, small fists jammed at her sides. For the first time he noted the exhaustion that rimmed her eyes. He ignored it, driven by fury and some nameless emotion he refused to recognize as disappointment. He'd far rather meet her on these terms, for this was the woman he knew—coldly enraged and icily distant.

"Who knows?" He gave an offhand shrug. "A week. A month. However long it may or may not be, know that it will be my choice, Kathryn—" His smile grew brittle. "—mine and no one else's."

"I see," she said tightly. "Your will again, I take it." Her breath came fast and shallow. She was suddenly so angry she was shaking. "Well, your will be damned, my lord earl—*you* be damned."

To her shock, he rose and handed her a tiny dagger. He spread his hands, leaving his chest wide open and exposed. "Go ahead," he invited in a silky tone that was all the more deadly for its very softness. "Shall we place a wager on the victor?"

Green eyes clashed with eyes as cold and gray as a wintry sky. The tension that pulsed between them was like thunder in the air. Though his posture was relaxed, Kathryn knew that if she made one false move, those powerful muscles would quiver to life—he would not hesitate to subdue her. Kathryn's fingers tightened around the handle of the dagger—she was stunned and then sickened at the violence that surged like a tide inside her.

She stabbed the blade into the table. *God!* she thought brokenly. What was the use? She couldn't wound this ironhearted knight physically or otherwise. She spun around with a jagged cry.

"Kathryn!"

She half-turned.

His expression was stony, the fiery probe of his eyes unendurable. "Do not run from me again," he warned. "Next time I will lock you in your chamber." He took his time perusing the slender curves of breasts and hips outlined beneath her kirtle. "Better still, I'll lock you in mine."

She choked back an impotent cry of rage. "I've heard tell that King Henry travels far and wide across the land," she flung at him. "I will pray nightly that he calls you to his side."

Chapter 12

The battle lines had been drawn once again.

Guy went his way. And Kathryn went hers. She saw little of him in the days that followed, except occasionally during the evening meal, which was always a strained affair. She was bitterly stung that she was no longer allowed to be alone with Peter; no longer was she allowed outside the walls without Sir Michael trailing along behind her.

It was but more fuel to fire her smoldering resentment of the earl. And for that—and for so many other things—she could summon no forgiveness.

There was nowhere she could escape his presence, whether he was present in the flesh or no. His will bound her to him as surely as chains of steel. She had even lost the peaceful sanctuary she'd once found at the stream, for he had invaded this domain as well, often riding there with Peter.

She watched him from afar one day, tossing Peter high in the air while the boy squealed with delight. Seeing him thus, laughing with his son, she could almost imagine how he might have been with his pretty young wife . . . Elaine. Gallant and teasing, those pale silver eyes alight with laughter and love and adoration . . .

A tight hollow band seemed to creep around her chest. She had never seen that side of him, she realized. She would *never* see that side of him.

And why . . . oh, why . . . was the certainty like a knife plunged deep in her breast? She could not forget what Gerda had told her—that Guy had loved Elaine dearly, loved her with a tender regard that was rare and precious and attained by so very few. Always, always, it was in the back of her mind, like a sliver beneath her skin. Every time she thought of Guy—and Elaine—there was an odd little catch in her heart. She did not understand it.

As the days became weeks, the tension became almost more than she could bear. Sometimes there was a strange restlessness inside her that would not be denied. She told herself it stemmed from being torn from her home. She ached to see Elizabeth once again—she missed Ashbury. But when she mentioned her longing once in all innocence, Guy became enraged and walked out on her. Nay, she would not cry, or plead, or beg for mercy, for he had none. Still, she began to fear he meant to keep her at Sedgewick forever—his purpose eluded her. But being on guard so often was taking its toll on her nerves—they were scraped thin. To make matters worse, she, who was sick but rarely, had been feeling poorly of late.

She was combing her hair, preparing for bed one night in early August, when a knock sounded on her door. It was unusual for her to be disturbed at this hour. "Who is it?" she called.

"Sir Michael," came a voice from the other side.

Finely arched brows shot up. *What!* she thought testily. Had Guy decided to post a guard outside her door at night, too? She opened the door a crack and peered warily at the young knight.

"Forgive the lateness of the hour," he said with an apologetic smile, "but Sir Guy wishes to see you in his chamber."

Visit the beast in his chamber? She could think of one reason and one reason only why he would make such a request—his arrogance knew no bounds! Kathryn opened her mouth, prepared to deliver a biting refusal, when Sir Michael caught sight of her flushed cheeks.

"There's been a slight accident, milady," he said quickly. "He has need of your assistance."

The earl had not been at dinner, but Kathryn wasn't sure she liked the sound of this any better. But if she refused, she had no doubts whatsoever that he would come and fetch her. She inclined her head slightly and joined Sir Michael in the passage. The young knight escorted her to the earl's chamber, closed the door, and withdrew.

She did not see him at first. The candles in the iron-spiked wall bracket cast flickering spears of light into the room. He sat on a chair before the fire, his long legs thrust out before him.

"My lord—" She sought to adopt a formal tone and failed miserably. "—you wished to see me?"

"Aye, Kathryn." There was a slight pause. "Come here."

She shuffled forward, feeling as if her legs were made of wax. She stopped what she considered a safe distance away. It was disconcerting to discover him regarding her rather quizzically.

"Kindly refrain from looking like a lamb on its way to be slaughtered," he said with sour humor. "I admit I'm in dire need of a woman's tender hand, but it's your skill with the needle I've need of right now." He turned slightly and inclined his head toward his right shoulder, where the flesh had been sliced wide open. The gash was easily the length of his hand. Though he had recently cleansed it, blood continued to well from the shredded edges of the wound.

"The damn thing won't stop bleeding. I don't think it will unless it's closed up."

Kathryn's eyes were wide. "You want me to *sew* it closed?"

Her tone reflected the horror she felt at the prospect but he paid scant heed. "Aye," he murmured.

"But I've never done anything like this before," she blurted.

"Gerda tells me you're quite skilled with the needle. Lord knows you probably sew a cleaner seam than my squire, and if you'll not do it, I'm afraid I'll have to submit to him." He offered a crooked smile. "Think of it as a chance to torture me, Kathryn. You'll get to poke and prod as you please and I dare not say a word against you."

"I'll hold you to it," she murmured. She fetched needle and thread from her room, then hurried back to his chamber. He had not moved while she was gone; he still sat before the fire.

His tunic lay across his lap; he wore naught but braies and chausses. His chest was bare, all solid muscle and dense dark fur. Kathryn tried not to notice as she knelt down, anxious to be done with the task and safely back within her own chamber. "How did this happen?" she murmured.

"We ran into several poachers in the forest. One of them decided he'd like to relieve me of my sword arm."

Poachers—not raiders. Kathryn could not help but feel a twinge of resentment. It was still a sore spot that there had been no trace of the raiders she had seen that long-ago day. She did not inquire as to the fate of the poachers he'd encountered today. She had no doubts his prowess as a warrior

was well earned; nor was he a man to let another
get the best of him. Despite his relaxed posture,
he radiated an aura of power and pure strength.
His shoulders looked impossibly wide, his biceps
sculpted and keenly defined. A quiver shot through
her at the prospect of running her fingers over
his muscular arms. Tentatively, she extended her
fingers, pressing gently to gauge the depth of the
wound.

A bowl of water and a linen cloth lay on a narrow
bench near his elbow. Kathryn dipped the cloth in
the water and wrung it out, then blotted the blood
away. When the wound was cleaned to her satisfaction, she picked up her needle and threaded it,
marveling that her hands were so steady. She bent
slightly. Guy didn't make a move when the point
of her needle punctured his skin. Instead it was
Kathryn who winced, wanting nothing more than
to jump up and abandon him. Willpower alone
kept her there at his side.

It occurred to her that she was finding this more
painful than he. She glanced at his unyielding profile. He remained as still as a statue. If the dip and
pull of needle and thread caused him any pain, his
features bore no trace of it. She tied and cut the last
thread, then sighed. "There," she murmured. " 'Tis
done."

He flexed his shoulder. An involuntary shiver
shook her body as she watched. Candlelight from
the wall sconce flickered over his shoulders, outlining sleek muscle and sinew. Her gaze strayed
helplessly to his chest; he had bathed recently. The
scent of soap still clung to him. Water glistened in
the dark hair on his chest, glittering like tiny jewels.
Kathryn swallowed, her mouth dry as parchment.

His hands had come out to steady her waist as
she worked. She could feel their warmth burning

through her kirtle. Guy was caught up in that very same current of awareness, aware of a brooding ache inside him. For weeks now he'd run the gamut between rage and confusion. He had possessed her, as he had sworn he would do . . . but it had not banished the longing inside him. Her aloofness and distance only made him want her all the more.

Her lips were dewy and damp, the downy curve of her cheeks as petal-soft as roses. The tip of her delicate pink tongue darted out, betraying her nervousness. A shaft of longing, desire like a sword of molten steel, cut through him. He longed to touch her, to hold her, to mold her sweetly curvaceous body naked and tight against his own, as he had once before.

She made as if to straighten. His fingers tightened around her waist, just enough to remind her she wasn't free. Kathryn froze, torn in two very different—and conflicting—directions. She wanted to run and hide, to seek refuge in her chamber. Yet another part of her bade her stay and wait—wait for what the moment would bring . . .

The air was suddenly close and heated. His eyes did not free her. Nay, he watched her with an intensity that made her tremble. His mouth was unsmiling, yet was not so very grimly forbidding. A frisson of panic raced through her. Kathryn was not sure if she was relieved or not. His expression was unreadable, his eyes dark and unfathomable. With him seated, her looking down at him, she should have felt she had the advantage—that was certainly not the case! Never had she felt so exposed and vulnerable.

"What do you wish of me, milord?" Her voice was no more than a tremulous wisp of air.

He tipped his head to regard her more fully. The silence heightened to a screaming pitch before he finally spoke. "Methinks you already know, Kathryn." For all the softness of his voice, his eyes seemed to delve even further into hers, as if he sought to reach inside her, clear to her soul . . . She could not stand it—she could not! She gave a muffled sound and tried to step backward.

His uninjured arm caught at her waist. He checked her movement and brought her down onto his lap in one fluid move. Her hands came up instinctively. One arm slid around his neck for balance. The other caught at his shoulder. Beneath her fingertips, she registered the feel of firm resilient flesh, the shape and feel of him. She drew a deep, startled breath and sought his eyes. To her dismay, he turned his head and her lips brushed the raspy hardness of his cheek. The contact was fleeting, but all at once her senses were thrumming.

He stared at her mouth.

She stared at his.

His head began to lower. Closer . . . so close it seemed they shared the same breath. "No," she whispered, as if to deny it—to deny *him*. "Oh, no . . ."

Like a thief in the night, his fingers plied their way across her nape, then came up to weave in her hair. As if he sought to stop himself, he pulled her head back slowly. Riveted by the undisguised hunger on his face, she could not tear her eyes from his.

A quickening heat stormed through her. Kathryn could not fight it—she could not fight him. His mouth trapped hers, both hungry and tender all at once, eroding any notion she might have had of resistance. The intimate glide of his tongue against hers set her heart to pounding. Her lips parted to allow him access to the honeyed interior of her mouth.

With a surge of power he was on his feet. Kathryn's head was whirling, along with her senses. She clutched at him as the only solid object in a wildly spinning world. Without breaking the searing fusion of their mouths, he crossed to the bed.

The mattress was soft beneath her back. Above her, his body was hard and heavy against hers, silent testimony that spoke of years of swordplay and hours at the tiltyard. With an ease that robbed her of breath, he tugged her kirtle to her waist and freed the naked bounty of her breasts. Inexperienced as she was, he had taught her well the pleasures he could heap upon her body. Even before his hand encompassed the weight of one breast, it was taut and tingly and aching; he kissed her endlessly, all the while his fingertips toying and skimming first one nipple and then the other into tight little buds. It shocked her to realize that she wanted not only his hands on her breasts, but the play of tongue and lips, tugging and laving and teasing . . .

She broke free of his mouth with a low moan—a sound of frustration? Protest? Or surrender? Her mind was churning so that she could scarcely think. God help her, she didn't know!

He raised his head. She tried desperately to drag her scattered wits about her, but for a timeless moment all she could do was stare in vague fascination at the dark hand that lay claim to the burgeoning softness of her breast—as if it had a right to be there—as if he had a right to her. She squeezed her eyes shut against the sight. She did not want this. She did not . . .

"Let me go." She despised the pleading in her voice, yet within was a fervent demand.

The silence was overwhelming. He did not move. Indeed, he did not even appear to hear . . .

Kathryn's eyes flicked open. She had expected anger. At the very least, his familiar, cutting sarcasm. In truth, she expected anything but the hint of defeated resignation that flitted across his features.

"You are a witch," he said slowly. "A sorceress who seeks to work her spell of enchantment over me." He searched her face as if convinced some damning evidence could be found there. "You tempt me, Kathryn, though you scorn me outright and pretend I do not exist. You tempt me when I am miles away and—"

Disbelief shot through her. "*I* tempt *you!* Oh, I think not, my lord, for I have done naught but try to stay clear of you!" Her cry verged on anger. "You blame me, milord, but 'tis you who seek me out— always! 'Tis you who bind me to you—you who refuse to let me return to Ashbury!"

Something dangerous flickered in those strange silvery eyes. His fingertips moved ever so slightly on her breast, warm and tormenting, even as his gaze grew cold. "And that is still your wish? To return to Ashbury?"

Kathryn was beyond heeding any warning, verbal or otherwise. "Aye!" The sound tore out of her throat. "How can you believe I would wish to stay here?"

His mouth twisted. How indeed, he thought. But even as the dark shadow of some nameless emotion gripped his soul, his body throbbed with desire. She stared up at him, her features delicately exquisite. His avid gaze swept over her, lingering on her breasts. Her skin was smooth and creamy, her nipples pure enticement, a deeper darker rose than he recalled. With his eyes he traced a visual path over her swelling softness—his memory failed him again, for though she was still small, she was fuller than he remembered.

Never had he felt a passion so deeply, so intensely that it robbed him of sanity, stripped him of pride and reason and controlled his every thought . . . as *she* controlled his every thought.

Let her go? he thought in amazement. He was awash in indignant outrage . . . and a despairing bleakness. Did she really believe that he would willingly send her back to Ashbury . . . ?

Not now. Not yet. And maybe never . . .

Though her chest ached with the force of her scrambled emotions, Kathryn swallowed and lifted glistening eyes to his.

"Please." Her voice was very low. There was a faint catch in her voice. "Please do not do this. You do not want this any more than I—I see it in your face!"

Tension gripped his features. He closed his eyes, as if he fought some gut-wrenching inner pain. When they opened, his expression was curiously hollow.

He bent and brushed her lips with his, a touch so achingly gentle she nearly cried out. "This thing between us," he whispered, " 'tis more powerful than both of us. I cannot stop it, Kathryn." He nuzzled the baby-soft skin behind her ear. "Nor can you."

His lips returned to capture hers, and this time the contact was firmer. Deeper. Intimately knowing . . .

"I want you," he said into her mouth. And then again, "*I want you* . . . "

Her lips fluttered against his; her tongue shyly touched his. It was all the invitation Guy needed. His mouth opened wide, his tongue dueling with hers in an unbridled skirmish that made his heart leap anew. She could deny him with mind and heart and soul—but she could not deny her physical need for him. His arms came around her. He dragged her against him, suppressing a groan at the feel of her breasts crushed against his chest.

Kathryn yielded with a low sobbing moan. Her feeble resistance could not rival his strength—or her own forbidden yearning. She forgot everything but the hungry heat that raged between them. She caught his head and guided his mouth to hers, her kiss tinged with a dark desperation.

Her clothing was a barrier neither could tolerate. He stripped her kirtle from her hips and cast it aside. She quivered as he traced a flaming line from her hip to the pouting crest of her breast. Her body bowed. Her fingers dug into the binding hardness of his arms, communicating a wordless plea. His laugh was low and throaty, for he well knew exactly what she craved.

His thumbs raked across her nipples; they felt swollen and engorged. Her breath spilled out in a rush. It was an exquisite torture to wait while his mouth slid with slow heat down her throat. He blew gently on the sensitized peak; she thought she would drown in sheer sensation at the slightly abrasive texture of his tongue curling around the pebbled nub.

A whimper rose in her throat. Her legs shifted restlessly. He inhaled sharply as her untutored movements brought her slender thigh flush against his straining fullness. Christ, she was driving him mad! He levered himself away and raised his head to stare at her, silver eyes aglow, aflame with wanting.

His shoulders loomed above her, wide and sleek and golden. He possessed a dark magnificence which should have frightened her, yet did not. Indeed, it robbed her of breath. He was so tall, so powerful, she thought wonderingly. With the candlelight flickering over his bronzed skin, he seemed more god than human. She knew a shocking urge to weave her fingers in the curling mat of hair on his chest and abdomen. Her gaze slid helplessly lower, just as he stripped off his chausses.

His manhood sprang free of its confinement, stiff and rigid and swollen.

Her eyes widened. Her golden haze of pleasure evaporated, like mist on a blazing morn. To her horrified eyes, he was shockingly—brazenly—aroused. She shuddered as the memory of their first time together came crashing down around her. She'd not soon forget the fiery prelude that promised so much, but delivered only pain. He would invade her body with his mighty weapon, a thrusting blade that split and tore. Too late she realized where her passion had led her.

He began to lower himself over her. With a gasp her hands came up against his shoulders, thwarting his forward movement. "Nay," she said faintly. "Oh, please, I cannot—"

His lips swallowed her breathless little cry. "Hush," he murmured. "I'll not hurt you, Kathryn."

She drew a deep, shuddering breath. Her heart beat furiously. "I fear you cannot help it!" she cried wildly. Just thinking of his size made her tremble. "You are so . . ." She could say no more. With a ragged moan of distress she turned her head aside.

Regret seized him, even as her innocent words sent his ardor spiraling. A finger beneath her jaw dictated that she meet his eyes; hers were huge and frightened. Beneath him, Guy could feel her shaking.

His hand slid down her throat. "That pain you felt, Kathryn . . . it was naught but the pain of first love."

The timbre of his voice sent a shiver through her. *Love?* she thought wildly, vaguely alarmed. It spun through her mind that she felt many things for this man who so dominated her life . . . but love? Nay, not that . . . never love . . .

"Please—" Her fingers curled and uncurled in the springy dark hair on his chest. What she pleaded for, she did not know.

"I thought I could forget that night, sweet witch. But a hundred times I've heard that tiny little cry you gave." His whisper was low and vibrating; it swirled all around her, reaching clear inside her. "And a hundred times I've wished it could have been different." He raised his head to stare down at her with burning eyes. "I don't want you to remember that night as it was. I want you to remember this night instead—to know the way it can be between us—the way it *will* be."

She was trembling, every muscle in her body tensed against him as his mouth slowly descended to hers. Yet his kiss was so tender, so achingly sweet it brought tears to her eyes. With a choked sob, she turned into his chest and locked traitorous arms around his shoulders, clinging to him as if he were all she'd ever wanted in this world.

His tongue flicked at her lips, demanding entrance, stealing deep within her mouth with a ravaging rhythm that made her go weak inside. Once again she fell victim to the same driving need she sensed inside him. His hand slid down her body, shaping and molding, reawakening dormant pangs of desire, trailing fire wherever he touched. She felt as if he led her through a vague dark mist where she could not find her way alone; 'twas his hand, his binding touch that guided her, and only through him could she find the path she sought.

Sensations hitherto unknown to her clamored through her. When his lips at last closed over her straining nipple, she bit back a cry of sweet bliss. Her fingers threading through the midnight darkness of his hair, she clamped him to her breast.

He laved her breast with his tongue, while his knuckles grazed the flatness of her belly, over and over before tangling in the downy fleece guarding her womanhood. Her heart tripped over itself when a bold and daring finger ventured still further. She instinctively tried to clamp her thighs closed.

"Don't fight it, sweet." His hot breath feathered across the delicate sweep of her cheek. "Don't fight me." Guy clenched his teeth. The dewy warmth his hand encompassed nearly shredded his control. His manhood was full to the point of bursting; he was near-crazed with the need to bury himself to the hilt inside her. But he held off, wanting to make certain her desire echoed his.

He sealed his lips with hers, devouring her mouth with fierce possessiveness. Her breath caught when that shamefully invading finger delved deep within her furrowed warmth, sweeping her away with bold, torrid strokes that turned her limbs to water. It was an exquisite torture. She began to writhe and twist, searching for something tantalizing and elusive—exactly what she did not know. He raised his head to drink in her response, reveling in her softly panting cries, the way her head thrashed back and forth on the pillow. A thrill of purely male triumph shot through him as she convulsed around his fingers.

Weak and dazed by what had happened, Kathryn opened her eyes. His dark features hovered above her, taut with strain. She felt him nudge her thighs apart, felt his manhood like a searing brand against her thigh, and inwardly braced herself for the pain she knew would follow.

The scorching heat of him sank slowly within moist, feminine petals. She gasped, certain she could not take all of him. Indeed, she felt her body stretch to the limit to accommodate his velvet-and-steel hardness, but there was no pain . . . She sensed his restraint as he slowly withdrew, then eased inside again. Within her belly, a heavy warmth unfurled. With each carefully measured plunge of his body into hers, heat shimmered along her veins. She caught her breath at the silken friction, until at last her hips arched in involuntary response, instinctively seeking his.

Above her, he went very still, so still she feared she had done something terribly wrong. His breath was harsh and rasping in her ear. She could feel the frantic thunder of his heart against her own. Her fingers curled helplessly in the hair that grew low on his nape, an involuntary caress.

"Guy?" She waited, scarcely daring to breathe.

At the sound of his name, something seemed to give way deep inside him. With a groan his mouth sought hers, not rough, just . . . urgent. He drove into her with a force that resounded in the chambers of her heart. Again and again, his thrusts wild and almost frenzied, as if he'd lost all control. She clutched at the hardness of his arms and buried her face against his shoulder, and she no longer cared that he was not gentle. Because she was suddenly out of control, too, clinging to him in wanton splendor. The flames inside her blazed high— sparks showered through her, inside and out. She spun away in mindless wonder, even as he gave one final shattering plunge. The spewing heat of his seed bathed her womb with honeyed fire.

Time ceased to exist. The heavy weight of his body eased. Kathryn was only vaguely aware when he moved to his back, pulling her up against his side. She lay curled against him, her head pillowed on his shoulder.

An hour earlier she'd have deemed it nigh impossible . . . She fell asleep to the lulling drumbeat of his heart beneath her ear, the soothing caress of his fingers trailing her spine.

She woke alone.

Last night's events flooded her mind in vivid detail. She shut her eyes. Her heart cried out. How was it possible to despise and hate a man so, and yet experience such wondrous elation at his hand? When he made love to her, she could hold back nothing—nothing!—and it was frightening. In the cold light of day, she could not condone what she had done. Never had a battle been so easily won! she conceded bitterly. Ah, there had been no need for force—or even subtle coercion. He need not even ask . . . and she willingly surrendered all that he sought. Clutching her pillow to her breast, she rolled to her side and stared at the tepid sunshine creeping through the shutters.

He called her witch. He branded her sorceress. Ah, but he was the sorcerer, for something happened the instant he touched her. He leeched her will from her with but the touch of his lips, the seductive stroke of his hand.

It was in the midst of this disturbing frame of mind that the door opened. Kathryn knew instinctively it was Guy. Along with his entrance came a seething tension. The heavy footfall of steps preceded his appearance at the bedside.

An icy dread clutched at her. She smothered the urge to throw the covers around her head and huddle like a child, for she knew not what to expect from him! Instead she curled her fingers over the edge of the furs to shield her nakedness and forced herself to look at him.

In some distant corner of her mind, she was surprised to see that he wore his hauberk, as if he prepared to do battle. In the next instant, all her attention was focused on the rigid cast of his jaw, the taut constriction of his body as he towered over her. Nothing in his expression gave any indication of what had passed between them only hours earlier.

The passionate lover of the night before had vanished. Before her was the cold, merciless knight she hated and despised. Her heart plunged to the floor. She quickly pushed away her weakness, berating herself furiously. It was foolish to expect any tenderness from him—foolish to expect anything at all!

He stared down at her, his tone as chilly as his regard. "A messenger arrived early this morn."

Kathryn frowned, raising herself up on an elbow, careful to keep the fur around her naked breasts. She could not think why he would tell her unless . . . Her eyes widened. "Oh, no! Has something happened to Elizabeth?" She bounded to a sitting position and clutched at his arm. "Tell me, my lord! Is she hurt?"

Guy's lip curled. He swore viciously—did she think of nothing else? "Set your mind at ease," he said harshly. "This has naught to do with Elizabeth . . . or Ashbury!" This last was fairly flung at her.

Stunned, Kathryn stared at him numbly. He was angry with her . . . why? She did not understand it—she did not understand *him!*

She moistened her lips and eyed him warily. "This message," she said stiffly. "If it does not concern me, why are you here?"

His laughter held no mirth. "Ah, but it does concern you, milady, for it seems the king himself has granted your fondest wish." His lips twisted. "Henry has summoned me to his side."

Kathryn blinked. "What! You mean you . . . you must leave Sedgewick?"

"Aye." He uttered the word like a condemnation, not an affirmation. Ruthlessly he searched her face for the triumph he was certain he would find there. But those rose-hued lips were slack in surprise. Those lovely green eyes reflected just the right amount of bewildered astonishment . . . ah, but she played her role of innocent with consummate ease!

With brutal fury he wondered if she knew this cost him dearly. He had no wish to leave Sedgewick, yet he could hardly ignore his king. Damn! If only Henry's summons had come on the morrow, or the day after. Better still, not at all.

Yet what did it matter? he asked himself bitterly. Last night she lay pliant and weak in his arms—she had abandoned herself to him ever so willingly—aye, even eagerly! But when dawn streaked the eastern sky, there was naught of victory in his heart, no deliverance from this hell into which she'd cast him.

In his arrogance he had convinced himself that he alone commanded her body. Even now he wanted to tear the covers from those bare, silken limbs, plunge his fingers into her black mane and smother her lips with his. He longed to explore the sleep-scented hollows of her body and forget his king existed—forget everything but the driving need to bury himself in her honeyed cave of velvet heat . . .

And he knew he could do it—oh, she might pretend resistance again, but she would melt soon enough.

Only one thing stopped him—he found himself tormented by the thought which had plagued him the night through . . . Mayhap she yielded her body only to gain what she wanted. Mayhap this was her way of molding him to her will, for wasn't that what she had planned with Roderick? She had sought to lure and entice Roderick into her web of enchantment, then turn around and play him against her uncle, like a puppet on a string!

He pulled the furs from her clenched hands. "Get dressed!" he commanded curtly. "I want you in the bailey as soon as you're ready. And do not think to delay me by dallying, or I'll be forced to bring you down as you are." The glint in his eyes warned her he would tolerate no defiance. He raked her with a glance that left her feeling stripped to the bone, then strode from the chamber.

Though it cost her no small amount of pride, Kathryn was up and dressed in less than ten minutes. She spied Guy alongside his destrier as soon as she entered the bailey. She did not go to him. She remained near the outside stair that led to the great hall.

He did not leave her waiting long. He stopped directly before her, his countenance grim. He spoke without preamble. "Promise me you'll be here when I return."

There was no tenderness, no hint of softness in his manner, nothing but implacable demand. She felt the pain of betrayal as keenly as a knife in her breast—clearly last night meant nothing to him! His hands, his caresses, were naught but a weapon to impose his mastery over her.

She could not hide her bitterness. "Why? My word means little to you."

His hands came out to grip hers. "Tell me you won't run off to Ashbury. I want you here when I return, however long I am gone."

Never had she been so torn, divided in two, sliced cleanly in half. She hated him and yearned desperately to be free of him, yet denial was the furthest thing from her mind! Swamped with confusion, she shook her head. "Ask me anything," she pleaded. "Anything but that!"

She swallowed convulsively, imprisoned in his gaze. Unbelievably his eyes reflected no coldness, no hint of mockery. They held some urgent, nameless appeal she was afraid to acknowledge yet could not ignore.

"Promise me, Kathryn."

His voice was low. To her horror, her throat grew achingly tight. "Aye," she said on a strangled half-sob. "I promise."

Something flickered across his face . . . triumph? Her heart cried out in despair even as an arm slid about her waist, dragging her close.

She surprised them both by twining her arms around his neck. She could deny him nothing, for at that moment, his will mirrored her own. He took her lips in plain view of any onlooker, endlessly long and deep, and she cared not who saw, nor that it was less a kiss than a proclamation of raw male ownership.

She stood rooted to the spot, long after he'd ridden through the gatehouse. Finally, she whirled and ran to her chamber, throwing herself upon the bed where she cried herself to sleep.

It was hours later before she awoke again. She lay very quietly for a moment, feeling dull and lethargic and wanting nothing more than to roll over and go back to sleep. Why was she so exhausted? she wondered. It was probably the strain of the last day, she decided tiredly. There had been so many emotions . . . in so little time.

Gerda entered, offering her a tentative smile. "You missed both the morning and the midday meal, milady. Would you like something to eat?"

Just the thought of food made Kathryn's stomach lurch, though not in hunger. "Not just yet, Gerda." She pressed the back of her hand against her cheeks. She felt strangely hot, but her skin was cool, almost clammy. She pushed aside the furs and rose to her feet, feeling shaky and fluttery inside.

"What is wrong with me?" She put a hand to her forehead. "My stomach heaves, no matter what I do or do not eat. I am constantly weary, no matter how long I sleep. No one else has sickened," she moaned. "Why does this ailment persist?"

Gerda's smile disappeared. She peered at her oddly. "Milady, forgive me for my boldness, but surely you know that 'tis not so much a sickness as . . ." A blush stole into her cheeks as Kathryn stared at her blankly. She bit her lip, "You've had only one course since you've been here, haven't you?"

"Aye." She nodded, beginning to feel dizzy and lightheaded. "But what has that to do with—" She stopped short. Gerda was right—her last monthly flux had come nearly three months ago. With all the turmoil in her life of late, she'd scarcely given it a thought . . . Her eyes grew stricken as a horrible assumption formed in her mind. "No," she whispered tremulously. "Oh, no . . ."

Her heart was pounding heavily. Black specks began to dance before her eyes. Somehow Gerda's voice penetrated the dull buzzing in her ears.

"Milady, 'tis my guess that you're with child." Kathryn slumped to the floor.

Chapter 13

S talemate.

Hugh had long since decided he and Elizabeth were at a stalemate—they could go neither forward nor backward. Though she did not cower away, her reserve was like a wall of stone. Oh, they talked, they chatted, they laughed. But whether she knew it or not, she had set boundaries around her—boundaries he dared not cross for fear of shattering what little they had gained.

They did not speak of that night in her room when he had soothed and held her close. Indeed, it might never have happened—but it was that which stood between them like a towering wall of granite. Hugh sought to gently broach the subject once but she ran off in tears. If Elizabeth had her way, he suspected that they would go on as they were until the end of time.

Hugh could think of only one solution. He prayed it was the right one. Indeed, he thought bitterly, he had nothing to lose by putting it to the test . . . for whether she knew it or not, his heart was already hers.

He approached her one sunny afternoon when she sat in the solar with her sewing. "If it pleases

you," he said pleasantly, "I thought we might walk
outside the walls while it's still warm."

It was on the tip of Elizabeth's tongue to blurt
that it did not please her. While a part of her
longed for just such an opportunity to be with
Hugh, another part feared what might happen if
they were alone. For all that he was charming
and remarkably easy to talk to, at times his eyes
were so piercingly intent she felt he saw clear
inside her.

She gestured at the cloth in her lap. "Mayhap
another time—" she began.

His hands were on the cloth, lifting it aside. To
her horror, in the next instant his hands folded
around hers and he was lifting her to her feet as
well. "You abuse me sorely, Elizabeth. Take pity
on my poor soul and oblige me in this." As he
spoke, he offered a ready smile. Elizabeth thought
frantically that she was wrong—that Hugh was
dangerous indeed. Yet her protest could find no
voice as he led her outside.

Silence prevailed as they began to walk, leaving
the keep behind. While it was not a particularly
comfortable silence, neither was it uncomfortable.
The sun beat warmly on Elizabeth's cheeks; the
scent of tangy salt air teased her nostrils. She had
just begun to relax when it struck her that the
rocky, winding path they trod was vaguely familiar . . . She inhaled sharply, for there, just over the
next rise, was the place where . . . Alarm skittered
through her and she spun abruptly, determined
to flee.

Hugh caught her by the waist and held her fast.
"Let me pass!" she screamed. "Hugh, you must let
me pass!" He glimpsed panic in her eyes and his
resolve nearly waned. He hated himself as never
before. When Elizabeth began to pound his chest

he wrapped his arms around her and subdued her with gentle strength.

He gave a shake of his head, steeling himself and standing firm. "We are almost there, Elizabeth. We cannot stop now."

She railed wildly. "Why are you doing this? My mother died there—you know that, Hugh! Why would you take me back? Oh, how can you be so cruel?"

Hugh felt as though she had landed a blow at the center of his heart. "Believe me when I say this pains me as much as it pains you." The edge in his voice lent truth to the words. "Elizabeth, you are a warm, beautiful woman who deserves to be happy. But I fear this cannot be until you have purged yourself of this horrible memory. There is a place in your mind that only you can set free— and only then will *you* be free. May God strike me from this earth if I am wrong, but I can think of no other way to help you, save this."

Elizabeth began to shake uncontrollably.

He smoothed the flaxen hair from her cheek. "I'd not belittle what happened to your mother." He attempted to explain. "It was tragic, a terrible thing for a child to witness. But you must put it behind you now or it will forever haunt you. I will help you, Elizabeth, if only you'll let me."

"I will have nightmares again if you take me there," she cried piteously. "Hugh, I know I will!"

Nightmares? If she must dream, then let her dreams be of him . . . Even as the fervent prayer echoed through his brain, he bracketed her face with his hands. "Do you trust me, Elizabeth?"

She floundered helplessly. "I did . . . I—I mean I do, only . . . oh, Hugh, must we do this?"

"No harm will come to you, Elizabeth. If you will only come with me, I promise we won't stay long.

We will leave whenever you like."

Elizabeth's mind was whirling. She could not summon the will to argue; she couldn't find the strength to fight him. When he took her by the hand and led her up the path once more, she clung to the soothing tenor of his voice and to him. She kept her eyes downcast, her heart pounding so she feared it would crash through her chest at any moment. At last she stumbled to a halt beside Hugh.

A hard lump of dread coiled in the pit of her stomach. She nearly cried out when he dropped her hand and walked away. It took every ounce of courage she possessed to raise her head and watch him. He stopped some twenty paces distant.

"Elizabeth," he said calmly, "look around you— look well and listen. Then tell me—" He paused. "—if what you see is truly so frightening that you must forever shun this place."

She wrapped her arms about herself as if to ward off a chill, but she did as he asked. Her gaze moved slowly. High above, the sky was a deep, breath-taking blue. Clumps of bracken clustered around an outcropping of boulders near the edge of the bluff. Scraggly blades of grass lay close against the rocky ground, whipped there by the ever-present wind, which rose in a keening wail then fell eerily silent. A nearby shriek gave her a jolt, but it was only the screech of a sea gull. But for the brilliance of the sky, the landscape was stark and barren. And in the midst of it all was Hugh, the wind blowing thick russet-brown hair from his forehead, his shoulders so wide and strong they looked as if they could easily bear the weight of the world.

The terror began to seep from her limbs. She started to smile—but then her gaze chanced to rest on the jutting rock to his left. A shudder racked her body. "It happened there," she whispered brokenly.

"It was there . . . Oh, God, Hugh, it was awful . . . those men! They hit my mother over and over again. And then they . . ." She broke off, swallowing the bile that burned her throat.

Hugh was at her side in an instant, clasping her icy-cold hand in his. "Bloodlust," he said grimly. "I make no excuse—those men deserve to rot in hell for what they did! What you saw was an act of brutality. But not all men are like those bastards— I swear to you by all that is holy—and what happens between a man and a woman is not always ugly. Elizabeth, when a man comes to care about a woman—" He nearly said when a man *loves* a woman. "—there is tenderness and affection. He longs to cherish and protect her. Never—never!— would he hurt or dishonor her."

He paused, his eyes sweeping around them as hers had done. "Evil was done here, aye. But is this place still so evil? I do not ask you to forget what happened here, but mayhap 'tis time to replace that memory with another."

Elizabeth trembled. She longed to believe him— she longed for it with every fiber of her being! "How?" she whispered.

His eyes darkened. "Let me show you," he said softly. He moved close, so close she could feel the warmth of his breath strike her cheek. Oh, she knew what he was about—mayhap she had known all along. But now that the moment was upon her, she was plagued with uncertainty. Her hands came up against his chest, not resisting, but not welcoming either. She ducked her head and closed her eyes in mortal shame.

A strangled cry broke from her lips. "Hugh, I— I'm afraid."

His knuckles slipped beneath her chin. "Nay," he whispered. "Not of me, you're not. And I only mean to kiss you, Elizabeth, the merest touch of your lips against mine."

And before she could draw breath, he was there, his mouth on hers, gentle and wooing and far softer than it looked. Elizabeth's eyes flew open in stunned surprise only to drift shut just as quickly.

Her head began to swim. This was more than just the touching of lips, she thought fuzzily. Her pulse clamored wildly. A bone-deep warmth and sweetness swept through her—it seemed to seep from his body into hers—or was it the other way around? Her hands slowly uncurled against the soft wool covering his chest but she made no effort to break off the kiss. Beneath her fingertips, she could feel the steady throb of his heart. The pressure of his mouth deepened ever so slightly, and then time ceased to exist.

Long moments later, Hugh released her lips reluctantly. The feel of her body soft and plaint against his unraveled a storm of emotion. Her eyes opened slowly, bemused and smoky and dazed. He wanted to shout with triumph but suspected he did not dare.

He nuzzled the velvet skin at her temple. "We should get back to the keep," he murmured.

It pleased him mightily when the slender arms looped around his neck tightened ever so slightly. "Aye," she agreed, her voice very small. She risked a peek at him from beneath her lashes. "But do you think you might kiss me . . . just once more?"

His laugh was shaky. Already his head had begun yet another descent. " 'Twould be no hardship—no hardship at all."

And indeed it was not.

Kathryn tried desperately not to dwell on her pregnancy.

Considering how coldly enraged Guy had been when he discovered she was *not* with child, there was a twinge of dark irony in suddenly finding that she was . . .

Kathryn was not, however, inclined to laugh about it. Indeed, it was something she tried desperately not to dwell on. She wanted to deny what had happened; to cry and rage that it was not so . . . Alas, once again, her body betrayed her. Her breasts grew full and heavy. Her waist thickened, her belly began to round and swell. It would not be long before her condition was blatantly obvious.

The days began to blur, one into another. For the first time in her life, Kathryn found herself floundering, terrified of the future. Guy had warned her not to try to return to Ashbury—the thought of his retribution if she did so made her shiver. Yet he had no feelings for her other than desire—and no doubt that would change once he discovered she was with child!

Even Gerda seemed to share her melancholy mood. From her window one day, Kathryn saw Gerda and Sir Michael in the outer bailey—they spoke in low-voiced whispers. Sir Michael laid a hand on her shoulder, while Gerda shook her head over and over, then suddenly broke away. She hurried away as quickly as her hitched gait allowed. Kathryn could not clearly make out Sir Michael's expression but she sensed he was angry.

It was concern for the girl that made Kathryn tentatively broach the subject a short time later. To her surprise, the mere mention of Sir Michael's name was all it took for Gerda to burst into tears.

Kathryn hurried to her side and slipped her arm around Gerda's shoulders. She gave not a thought to the difference in their stations. This was merely one woman reaching out to comfort another.

"Gerda, tell me what's wrong," she urged. "Has Sir Michael wronged you somehow? Spoken to you harshly perchance?" Secretly Kathryn thought it difficult to picture Sir Michael hurting anyone. For all that he was a knight well versed in the arts of war, Kathryn had come to know him as amicable and seldom without a winsome smile.

Gerda made a choked sound and cried the harder. .

Kathryn's mind searched fleetingly backward. She thought of all the days the three of them—and Peter as well—had spent at the stream, and pictured Gerda handing Sir Michael a slice of cheese, a hunk of bread. Sometimes their hands had brushed—or they had shared a fledgling smile . . . A numbing realization washed over her. How could she have been so blind?

"You're in love with him," she whispered incredulously. "Gerda, you—you love him!"

"Aye, milady." Gerda sat up with a sniff, wiping away her tears with her fingertips.

Kathryn pressed a dainty lace handkerchief into her hands. "Does Sir Michael know?" she asked quietly. Gerda nodded. Kathryn bit her lip. "And how does he feel about it?"

"He—he says he loves me, too." The girl stared at the handkerchief crushed in her hand. "Lady Kathryn," she whispered, "he—he says he would marry me."

Kathryn blinked. "But that's—that's wonderful," she exclaimed. "Gerda, you should be ecstatic, not sitting here in tears!" She frowned suddenly. "He's not a bounder, is he? He certainly doesn't seem that sort."

Gerda shook her head. "Nay, mistress. He is good and kind and honorable. Indeed," she whispered, "no woman could ask for a better man."

Kathryn was utterly bewildered. "So why aren't you dancing for joy?"

" 'Tis not so simple—not simple at all! I love him, but I—I'll not sully myself by being his mistress." She looked ready to cry again. "And I cannot be his wife."

"But why not, Gerda? I'll admit such a marriage is the exception rather than the rule, but marriage between you and Sir Michael would be recognized by the church."

Gerda swallowed. "The Lady Elaine taught me to hold my head high, to be proud of what I am, lame though I am—" She touched her misshapen leg gently. "—and I fear she taught me far too well, for I, too, have my pride and I'll not let Michael discard his so easily."

When Kathryn frowned, she summoned a watery smile. "He comes from good family. He is not the heir, but his father is still a lord." She shook her head and said sadly, "I cannot erase my humble beginnings. I am the daughter of a villein, and will ever be so. Like my father, I am bound to the earl. Michael's family would never accept me as his wife—never! If he were to marry me, he would be an outcast." She paused, her tone very quiet. "I'll not let him stoop so low, milady. That is why I will not marry him."

And there was no dissuading her, though Kathryn tried her best. In the meantime, summer slipped gently into autumn. Fields ripened to harvest and the household set to work filling the granary and replenishing the larder and cellars with food and drink for the long winter. Plowing began in fallow fields in preparation for the next harvest. The sunlit days grew shorter; they blurred, one into the other.

Never had Kathryn been so utterly miserable.

Nor did she understand why. Hadn't she prayed for the day she would be free of the earl? She had what she wanted. She was rid of his hateful presence! Yet no matter whether she hated him or longed for him, he was always on her mind.

One afternoon in late October found the household much more frantic and busy than usual. In the great hall, Kathryn waylaid one of the maids who had just scurried in from the kitchen. "Everyone is rushing about so," she commented. "What is going on?"

The girl's eyes were wide and shining. "A messenger arrived not an hour ago. The earl will be home on the morrow," she announced.

Not until she was alone in her chamber did Kathryn give in to the turmoil inside her. She sank down upon the bed, beset by a flurry of panic. The moment she had dreaded all these weeks— months!—was nearly upon her. Soon Guy would be home. Soon . . .

A helpless despair descended upon her. Like a clamp it squeezed the very breath from her chest. She moaned, remembering that last night when she had lain in Guy's arms—his tenderness, the storm of passion he ignited in her. His desire had known no bounds that night—he had taken her with a yearning hunger that even now stole her breath. Her hand crept to the gentle mound of her belly. Ah, but would he desire her now? He was strong, virile, and handsome. Undoubtedly he had only to crook his finger to have any number of women falling at his feet. Would such a man want a woman who was no longer slim and desirable? Her heart cried out—perhaps he had already taken another to his bed!

Her nails dug into her palms but she did not feel the discomfort. How would Guy react when he saw that she was with child? Would he be angry? Indifferent? Would he even care? A wrenching pain ripped through her, even as a horrible notion uncurled in her brain.

What if Guy cast her aside? Where would she go? Ashbury immediately loomed in her mind. Yet how could she face Elizabeth and all those she had known all her life, knowing she carried their conqueror's child? The thought was unbearable.

An icy shroud of despair encircled her heart. She could not return to Ashbury. She could not remain here at Sedgewick. She was the very thing Gerda feared for Sir Michael . . .

An outcast.

Her eyes squeezed shut in misery. She feared having Guy discover she had fled. But here she was, grown heavy with his child, and she feared facing him in her present condition far more. There was only one way out. She must escape. Flee. Better to do it now, with some small shred of dignity intact, than to have Guy turn her out later . . .

She left at dawn's first light.

For Guy, every day away from Sedgewick was one too many.

But he was not a man to shirk his duty to his king. Like his grandfather, Henry was determined to bring those lawless barons to heel. One way of doing so was by demolishing their fortresses and restricting the building of new ones. Those that escaped the demolition were dependent upon Henry's goodwill to renew the charter—in some cases Henry added to the royal coffers by levying a fee to the holder.

Guy was one of the more fortunate ones. In return for his loyalty Henry had chosen to retain his earldom and had regranted title to all his holdings. Guy had already ascertained the wisdom to be had in backing the new king.

But there were several Welsh marcher lords and a powerful baron in the Midlands who resisted the order of the new government. Guy was among those involved in Henry's effort to deal with the insurgence.

But at last the threat of rebellion had been squelched. Henry had released him since they were so near Sedgewick, but he was to join his king at Ashbury several days hence.

Now, nearly three months later, Guy reined his destrier to a halt, high atop a hill. A feeling of pride welled up in him as he beheld the mammoth walls surrounding Sedgewick. He regretted that he had so little time at home before he must leave again, but he let himself linger a moment, for the noonday sun was brilliant, the endless stretch of the sky above more brilliant still. A fragrant breeze whispered over the hills and fields and meadows, stirring leaves which had deepened to russet and gold. It was very near here, he mused thoughtfully, on that long-ago spring day that he'd given Kathryn her first glimpse of Sedgewick.

Kathryn.

A black scowl darkened his features. He had hoped that these months away from her would resolve his obsession with her. He chafed inside, knowing that time had not erased his need for her—indeed, it had only sharpened it.

He had sworn she would be his—and the deed had been well and truly done. He had claimed her, willing and eager for the touch of his hand. Yet he had somehow thought that once she was his, once he'd sampled the mystery and delights her lithe young body had to offer, the allure that held him enthralled would be no more.

But that was not to be . . . it was not to be, and everything inside him cried out against it.

A brooding mask slipped over his features. Not a single night had passed that he had not fallen asleep thinking of her, dreaming of her. He had tasted those sweet lips bedewed with the wet heat of his; felt the budding crests of her breasts nestled in the crisp furring of his chest as he explored that luscious, satin-and-cream body until he knew it as well as he knew his own. And then he awoke in the morning with her name on his lips, his manhood hard as stone, throbbing like a drum.

His mouth twisted. She was like slow poison, seeping through his blood, clear to his soul. She was a sorceress spawned in hell, with the seductive charms of an angel. If only he could cast off this spell of fever and lust she roused in him—if only he possessed some weapon, some shield against it.

It was a pity he had so little time, he thought again, only now there was a wicked glint in his eye. He was going to satisfy this unbridled craving for Kathryn even if it meant the two of them did not leave his chamber—most assuredly his bed!—the entire length of his stay.

He spurred his destrier and set off again. Aye, he decided with a satisfied smile, he would certainly make the most of what little time he had . . .

Shouts went up when several of his men spotted him. A small crowd gathered to await him as his destrier pranced beneath the gatehouse and into the bailey. A young groom grinning from ear to ear ran up as Guy dismounted. He flashed a brief grin in return and tossed the reins to the boy.

Sir Edward clapped him heartily on the back. "We had little news of King Henry's campaign. It went well?"

"Well enough." Guy smiled dryly. "But I'm not here for long, I'm afraid. I'm to meet up with Henry and his advisors again in a few days' time. There's talk of invading Ireland." They talked for several minutes more before Guy entered the great hall.

Gerda, who had just descended the last step, stopped short. A fleeting panic chased across her face. Some innate sense warned him that all was not well. Gerda rushed over and bobbed a curtsy.

"Welcome home, milord," she said breathlessly. " 'Tis glad we are that you are home safely."

He gave a terse nod, for this was not the homecoming he had envisioned. He'd thought to see Kathryn awaiting him, if not with open arms, at least with yearning dwelling deep in those jade-green eyes. His gaze swept the hall but she was nowhere to be found.

"How goes it here, Gerda? All is well with Peter?"

"He's grown so I vow you'll hardly recognize him." Again that look of anxious distress as she gestured toward the stairs. "He naps just now, milord."

"And Lady Kathryn? Does she nap as well?"

Gerda shook her head. "Nay, my lord," she whispered. "She is . . . gone."

"Gone!" Guy went white about the mouth. His voice boomed like a clap of thunder. "God's blood! Don't tell me she's escaped! How the hell could such a thing happen—this place swarms with my men-at-arms! And everyone knew she was not to leave these walls alone!"

Gerda quailed, wondering if she dared tell him about the babe . . . and decided against it. "My lord," she said shakily, "it happened only this morning. At dawn she told the guard at the gatehouse that she was feeling poorly and needed to gather some healing herbs outside the castle walls. When we realized she was gone, Sir Michael and a dozen others set out after her."

The bitch—the treacherous bitch! He did not realize he swore aloud. She had played him for a fool once again. Not once had he considered Kathryn might not be here. She had said that she would be here when he returned—damn her traitorous soul—and he had believed her! He gnashed his teeth, remembering how he'd gloried in the way she threw her arms around his neck and kissed him so sweetly—all the while promising with lips that ever lied and deceived!

Gerda fell on her knees before him, her eyes shimmering with tears. "Do not blame Sir Michael for this, milord! He was not lax in his guard of her, I swear. If you must punish anyone, punish me, for I did not realize she was gone until well into the morning. And—oh, I know you will find it impossible—but when you find Lady Kathryn, do not judge her so harshly. I beg of you, milord, find it in your heart to be lenient!"

Guy stared down at her bowed head. What magic did Kathryn possess, that she charmed so easily all those within her reach—his son, Sir Michael, even this girl whose loyalty to Elaine had been as fierce as his love for his cherished wife.

But . . . leniency? A brittle determination sealed his heart. Never, he vowed. Never . . . Kathryn had toyed with him for the last time.

He raised Gerda to her feet. "We both know who is to blame," he said flatly, "and 'tis neither you nor Sir Michael. But this I would know, Gerda. Did Kathryn make any other attempt to escape?"

Her answer was swift and unwavering. "Nay, my lord. None at all."

His eyes narrowed. "So it was only after she received word of my return that she made the decision to flee?"

Gerda winced. " 'Twould seem so." She paused, then touched his arm. "Milord, Sir Michael set out to search the road to Ashbury."

"Likelier than not, that's where she's headed." His voice was grim.

Gerda hesitated. "I am not so certain," she said slowly, "for one of the maids—Zelda—just told me that Lady Kathryn questioned her only last night about the convent south of here."

For an instant Guy said nothing. Something elusive tugged at his memory, and all at once Hugh's voice rang through his mind . . . *Why, she was ready last night to scurry off to a nunnery* . . . "Then I will look for her there," he said decisively. "Gerda, see that food and drink are prepared. I'll be going on to Ashbury after I find Kathryn."

Gerda noted rather anxiously he did not say *if* he found her . . . she shivered and prayed that Lady Kathryn would come to no harm from any creatures she might encounter . . . human as well. And she prayed uneasily for Lady Kathryn's safety yet again as she watched Sir Guy gallop away a short time later.

He looked like a man beset with demons.

Darkness dropped its smothering folds about the earth with the suddenness of a candle being snuffed out by invisible fingers. Kathryn huddled closer to the fire, too nervous to sleep, too fitful to try to rest. At least she was on the right road; Zelda had unwittingly told her of several landmarks which she had passed earlier in the day. But knowing Guy had arrived at Sedgewick today left her uneasy. She had no trouble picturing his fury. He would probably set out after her, she thought with a sniff, for he was imperious enough to see her escape as an affront to his manhood.

But he would never find her, she thought, a secret smile tugging at her lips. He would conclude that she had bolted for Ashbury, but by noonday tomorrow she would be safely within the walls of the convent, where she could take refuge until her babe was born . . . and after? There was time enough to consider that later, she reminded herself curtly. Indeed, she had nothing but time . . . She brought her legs to her breast and let her chin drop against her knees.

In the distance the lonely howl of a wolf split the air, then fell eerily silent.

Kathryn tensed, relaxing long minutes later. Soon she began to doze. Unbidden, she remembered a similar night when *he* had lurked in the shadows. As if in a dream, she saw him, legs planted wide apart in that arrogant stance, his shoulders, lean and wide, blotting out the moonlight. His eyes glittered silver, bright and vivid in the firelight as his lips curved in that mocking smile she so hated . . .

This was no dream.

Guy was here—*here!* She was on her feet in an instant, spinning around wildly. She got no further than an arm-length before he caught her elbow and whirled her around. "No!" The sound tore from deep in her throat. *"No!"*

"Oh, yes, Kathryn . . . yes!" His hands descended on her shoulders. His head came closer. In some far distant corner of her mind, she thought vaguely that it was as it had been once before. His mouth plundered the softness of hers, while his hand skimmed her body—breasts, hips, thighs, and belly . . .

They both froze.

He wrenched his mouth from hers at the same instant an expression of incredulous disbelief washed across his features. His gaze slid down her body; had she not been so slender, the rounded swell of her belly would not have been so obvious. His fingers splayed wider, as if to seek confirmation. Stricken, Kathryn could only stare at him while his eyes widened in slow-growing horror. Abruptly, with a suddenness that wrung a startled cry from her, he snatched back his hand with a vile curse, as if he could not stand to touch her.

His reaction was like a physical blow, the ultimate rejection. A giant pair of hands seemed to close about her heart and squeeze. "Damn you," she lashed out furiously. "Why did you have to follow me? Why did you have to find me? I was so close . . . so close!"

His fingers closed around her upper arms. He dragged her to him. "Is this why you ran? Because of the child?"

"God, how can you ask?" she cried out in her anguish and despair. "I fled for the very reason we stand here shouting at each other! Did you think I wanted you to find me like this? I knew you would blame me—I knew it!"

He ignored her railing. "How far gone are you? Four months? Five?" Guy did not doubt that the child was his. She'd been guarded far too well for her to play him false.

"Nearly six," she choked out.

He bit back an oath. "Then you knew you were with child when I left Sedgewick for Henry's side, didn't you? You knew and you refused to tell me!"

She turned her eyes away, unable to meet the angry demand in his.

"Christ, you must have realized . . . you were nearly three months along. Why didn't you tell me?" When she said nothing, his fingers bit into the soft flesh of her arms. He shook her so hard her head fell back. She looked at him, dazed. "Answer me, damn you!"

In his heart he was appalled at his behavior, yet she could not know the pain she inflicted. She had run from him when she learned he was coming home. Perhaps she'd hoped he would not—that he would be killed in battle and never return.

Her lungs burned with the effort it took to hold back her tears. She'd not cry in front of him—she would not!

" 'Twas Gerda who realized . . ." She caught her breath on a dry sob. "I swear I did not know until after you'd gone!"

He stared at her so long and so accusingly she wanted to shrivel up and die. He did not believe her, she realized finally . . . Her heart shattered. A wave of utter desolation swept over her. Against all reason, she suddenly ached for him to take her in his arms. She longed to bury her face against his chest and cling to him, putting aside all their enmity for once.

But he was the cause of all her misery . . . not the cure.

Feeling numb and beaten, she watched as he stalked to his destrier. An instant later he thrust a blanket into her hands. "You might as well sleep while you can," he ordered. "We leave at first light."

In mute acceptance, Kathryn lay down and curled up before the fire. Guy flung himself down beside a tree, propping his back against the rough bark, his mind seething.

He thought of all the lonely nights he'd spent dreaming of her, yearning for her, waking up to find himself hard and throbbing, like an untried lad. Desire flamed within him, as fiery and demanding as ever. The urge to roll her over and take his pleasure was almost overpowering, for he'd lain with no other since the night he'd left Sedgewick. Oh, it wasn't for lack of opportunity. Not three nights past a winsome widow had made it known she would welcome his attentions. But once they were alone in her chamber, he found she stirred him not a whit—her hips were too wide, her breasts too heavy. Feeling like a eunuch, he'd finally excused himself before he humiliated either of them any further.

Kathryn had spoiled him for any other woman, damn her beautiful hide!

And now she lay beside him, as untouchable as ever.

Nay, he dare not lay a hand on her, he decided bitterly. She would fight him and he could not vouch for his behavior right now. Somehow he could never control either his temper or his passions when she was near.

He found no respite in sleep that night.

Kathryn felt she'd barely closed her eyes than he nudged her awake. He said nothing as he helped her to her feet, his expression carefully controlled. But her heart sank once she was on her feet. She gazed fully into his eyes; they were as icy as the frigid waters of the sea.

She sensed his impatience to be off so she quickly tended to her private needs. When she returned he handed her a slab of bread and cheese. By the time she brushed the crumbs from her kirtle, he had their horses ready and waiting.

An hour later they came to a crossroads. Kathryn held back when he guided his destrier down the fork in the dusty road, rather than returning the way she had come. Ever alert, Guy turned and fixed her with a glare.

Her tongue came out to dampen her lips. "Are you certain this is the road to Sedgewick?" She gestured to her right. "I'm sure I came from that way, milord."

"We are not returning to Sedgewick," he informed her curtly. "We go to Ashbury where I am to meet Henry."

A jolt of shock ran through her. For an instant she felt as if everything inside were collapsing. Her face bloodless, she stared at him. "No," she whispered faintly. Her hand moved instinctively to her middle. "You cannot—"

At her look of horror, a blaze ignited within him. He let loose of the storm in his soul. "What!" he mocked. "Does this not please the Lady Kathryn?" He was far too upset to heed his tongue. "For months you've been telling how much you hate Sedgewick, how desperately you long to be back at Ashbury. Well, you finally have your wish, milady, so where is your gratitude now?"

There was no escaping the determined glitter in his eyes. He grabbed her bridle and brought Esmerelda wheeling alongside his destrier. Her heart began to bleed as he slapped her palfrey sharply on the rump. She did not cry, though for once she would have welcomed the release . . .

This was a hurt that went beyond tears.

Chapter 14

Them arrived at Ashbury several days later.
Kathryn's reunion with Elizabeth was all she feared. They were scarcely through the gates than Elizabeth came tearing outside, laughing and crying her name. Kathryn half-turned from Esmerelda, unwittingly providing a side profile of her rounded tummy.

Elizabeth's cries of joy ended on a strangled gasp.

By the time they hugged and embraced, Sir Hugh was there as well. Guy stood next to Kathryn, but it was as if an invisible boundary had been drawn between them. The four of them exchanged greetings, the atmosphere distinctly stilted and awkward.

Now, back in the chamber she had occupied since she was a child, Kathryn released a long sigh of relief. The oaken portal had no sooner creaked shut than Elizabeth threw her arms around her sister and hugged her fiercely once more. "Kathryn," she cried. "Oh, you do not know how I have missed you!"

Tears sprang to Kathryn's eyes. It was difficult to speak around the lump in her throat. "Oh, but I think I do," she said shakily.

Elizabeth squeezed her hands. Her smile faded. "Are you well, sister?" She worriedly noted the pale-purple smudges beneath Kathryn's eyes. "You look so—so wearied."

"The journey was not . . . overly pleasant." Ah, and wasn't that the truth, she reflected bitterly. The discord between herself and Guy had never been greater. They had spoken only when necessary. He could scarcely bring himself to look at her.

Her hand fluttered down to the hard swell of her belly. "I suppose I should explain," she said quietly.

Elizabeth then bit her lip. "I fear I am rather puzzled," she admitted. She hesitated. "You were so certain when you left that you were not—"

"I was not." Kathryn's laugh held no mirth. "At least not then."

Elizabeth was aghast. "Do you mean to say that you . . . I mean the earl . . ." She blushed a fiery red and broke off.

"Aye, Elizabeth. The babe is his." She glimpsed the anxious question in her sister's gaze. "And no, we are neither married nor betrothed. Nor," she stressed shortly, "are we ever likely to be. We may have created a child together, but rest assured that the earl and I have little regard for each other."

As briefly as possible, she told Elizabeth of the earl's mission for King Henry and how he had just learned of her condition. Elizabeth nodded slowly when she'd finished. "Hugh has told me that King Henry is expected any day now." She shivered. "Having the earl here makes me nervous as it is, let alone the king. I—I fear I shall say something wrong."

"You will do fine," Kathryn soothed. But the next instant she studied her sister more closely. She had been concerned for Elizabeth's well-being these many months, afraid she would wilt away from loneliness. But vibrant color bloomed in Elizabeth's cheeks. Her eyes were clear and unwavering. It struck her then that Elizabeth appeared calmer, more confident, despite her words . . . and more at peace with herself.

"You have changed," she said slowly, then smiled slightly. "Tell me, Elizabeth. Is Sir Hugh responsible for the lilt in your voice, the glow in your cheeks?"

Elizabeth's eyes widened with dismay. "It is obvious, then?" She sounded so worried that Kathryn could not help but laugh, her first genuine laugh in days, and soon Elizabeth joined her.

"I—I never thought to feel anything but fear for any man, but Hugh is different," she confided after a moment. "Kathryn, he is ever so kind and thoughtful. He makes me feel very special and—and cherished." She blushed a becoming shade of pink and lowered her voice to a whisper, though there was no one to hear. "Kathryn, I—I love it when he touches me. I love it even more when he kisses me. And oh, it is not frightening as I had feared it might be—indeed, it is the most glorious thing I've ever felt in my life!"

A sharp stab pierced Kathryn's chest. She remembered the searing fusion of Guy's mouth on hers, hot and demanding and fervently exciting . . .

She forced a smile. "You have not been so unhappy then?"

Elizabeth shook her head. "I've missed you sorely, but nay, I've not been unhappy."

Kathryn squeezed her hand. "Then I am glad for you."

There was a tap on the door. It opened and Helga came in, bearing a small tray. She bobbed a curtsy, then placed the tray of honey cakes on the bench between the two sisters. "I thought mayhap Lady Kathryn could use the sustenance—" She straightened, her gaze lingering openly on Kathryn's belly as she gave a trilling laugh. "—being that she's expecting a babe and all."

Kathryn was too stunned to say a word. It was left to Elizabeth to murmur politely, "Thank you, Helga. That will be all now."

Helga swept from the chamber, but not before Kathryn glimpsed her simpering smirk.

Hot shame swept over her. Helga had not acted out of kindness or consideration, or even duty. The girl had merely wished to gape and see the truth for herself . . . Had word spread so quickly then? A feeling of sick dread clutched her insides. She could not eat a single crumb of the tempting honey cakes.

That same moment found Guy striding through the doorway of the chamber he'd occupied previously during his stay here. He'd be damned if he'd sleep in that bastard Richard's bed!

He gestured Hugh inside and closed the door. "There," he muttered. "At least we can speak freely now." He stripped off his leather jerkin and dropped it on the bed. "How goes it here?"

Hugh's mind veered straight to Elizabeth. "Well," he murmured. "Exceedingly well, in fact."

"There's been no insurrection?"

"Only an idle man in the first month or so. Richard was not a man to inspire loyalty among either his tenants or his knights." Hugh's lips tightened. "He was not a man given to compromise or reason—punishment and retaliation were his only methods of keeping those beneath him in line."

"So anyone might have murdered him then," Guy said slowly.

Hugh smothered a smile. "I take it you've decided Kathryn did not kill him." His friend nodded. He had the grace to look slightly ashamed. "Richard is the last man I'd mourn," Hugh added. "But no one has come forward to admit it."

Guy dropped down on the bed, thrusting a booted leg out in front of him. "I dislike not knowing who murdered him."

Hugh grimaced. "I know, Guy. But I've not had any luck in the matter. Frankly, I'm inclined to believe whoever did it may have fled that very night."

When Guy said nothing, Hugh hesitated. "Speaking of Kathryn," he ventured, "I must admit I was startled to see she is with child." A frown puckered his forehead. "Elizabeth confided that she—"

"The child is mine."

Indeed, Hugh thought. He was not about to question his friend's conviction, if Guy's expression was anything to go by—it was sour enough to curdle milk. But as he watched his friend jump up and begin to prowl restlessly around the room, he was unable to still his tongue completely. There were few men who were a match against Guy—and Kathryn was but a woman.

"I see," he said coolly. "And you're angry because your seed found fertile ground in her?"

Guy stopped short. His head swiveled around. "I only lay with her twice." He scowled. "And I most certainly did not take her against her will!"

"Where a man plows the field the harvest will be yielded . . . It takes but a single seed to bear fruit, milord."

"Do not look at me like that," he growled. "I didn't know she was with child when I left Sedgewick and took up Henry's flag." *But you should have,* taunted an inner voice. He was furious with himself for failing to consider the possibility she might be with child, for Hugh was right— it took but once. And then when last he lay with her, he remembered thinking her breasts seemed fuller and riper, her nipples rouged a deeper, darker pink. Aye, he should have at least suspected!

His jaw clamped together. "How was I to know when she chose not to tell me? Why, when she learned I was expected home, she sought to flee to a convent! Only by the grace of God was I able to catch her!"

The sight of his mighty lord scrambling to defend himself was immensely amusing. Hugh bit back a smile. "I take it your time with Kathryn has been rather taxing."

Guy snorted. "That woman would try the patience of a saint."

Hugh sighed. "Did you truly think to tame her? She is much like you, I think. And you've the devil's own temper."

"And she's the devil's mistress!" Guy was rather affronted that his friend was taking Kathryn's side against him.

Hugh sighed. "Guy, you cannot dump the blame for this entirely in her lap."

"I do not intend to." He shoved a hand through his hair and stared broodingly across the room. At length he turned to his friend once more. "Enough of my troubles, Hugh. Let's hear yours instead." He clapped a hand on his shoulder. "When last we saw each other, I swore you were smitten with the Lady Elizabeth."

"And still am." Hugh gave a lopsided smile. "Nor do I expect to be otherwise."

Heavy dark brows shot up. "That's quite a prediction, my friend. Is it so serious then?"

Hugh's smile faded. "I do not know if Kathryn has told you," he said slowly. "But their mother was raped and killed, and Elizabeth saw it done. 'Twas Kathryn who told me how Elizabeth has been fearful and timid around any man since then. I've known almost from the start that I loved her, but for that reason I've had to bide my time and go very slowly with her. My only regret is that I have so little to offer Elizabeth." A light like a thousand suns filled his eyes. "But I think she loves me, Guy. Nay, I *know* she loves me and will take me as I am. So as soon as I'm certain she's ready, I intend to ask her to become my wife."

It was a long time later when Hugh finally left for his own chamber. Sleep did not come easily to Guy, however. Whenever he closed his eyes, images of Kathryn danced behind his eyelids. Over and over he envisioned her expression throughout their journey here. She had looked so lost and hopeless. That expression had haunted him—it haunted him still. And it was with his mind thus occupied that he came to realize . . . there could be but one solution to their dilemma.

Kathryn would fight him. She had fought him on everything else, he reflected bitterly, why not this, too? He knew better than to expect her willing compliance. He stared at the shadows flickering on the ceiling, his mouth tight. Were that the case, she'd have naught but more perfidy in store for him!

But he'd be damned if he'd have her running off at every opportunity that presented itself—and her carrying his child yet! He expelled a long frustrated breath. Somehow, he thought tiredly, they must come to some agreement.

In the morning, he would go to her. Reason and cajole. Demand if need be . . .

But morning came too soon, and with it, Henry's
entourage. For the next four days, Guy scarcely ate
or slept. As was his wont, Henry demanded as
much of his followers as he demanded of himself.
Guy spent the days—and half the night—cloistered with Henry and his advisors. It was well after
midnight before he fell into bed—he dragged himself out before dawn. The privacy he sought with
Kathryn was simply not to be . . . He had no chance
to speak to her, even in passing. He saw her but
once . . .

With Roderick, blast her fickle, faithless hide!

But for Kathryn, too, those days numbered
among the longest—and most painful—of her
life.

King Henry was not what she expected. His
youth took her by surprise, but not for long—the
sheer commanding power of his presence alone
proclaimed that he had taken his place as ruler,
by right as well as might.

She and Elizabeth were summoned to the hall
the morning of his arrival. Kathryn spotted Henry
immediately, for she'd heard tales of his fiery-red
hair—and the temper that matched it. His figure
was lean and spare, his shoulders broad, though
he was not quite as tall as Guy, who stood at his
side, quietly listening and nodding. Though she
could not make out the words, the timbre of his
voice was deep and booming, his manner fierce
and energetic as he gestured and finally threw up
his hands, as if in dismay. Sir Hugh approached the pair and snared their attention, gesturing
over his shoulder toward Kathryn and Elizabeth.
As they awaited introduction, Elizabeth was clearly petrified. She clutched Kathryn's arm so tightly Kathryn knew she'd have bruises on the morrow.

The king stepped up to them, flanked by Guy and Sir Hugh. Guy directed a tiny smile at Elizabeth. "Your Grace, may I present Lady Elizabeth of Ashbury?"

Elizabeth sank into a deep curtsy. When her head came up, it appeared her nervousness had miraculously fled. "Sire—" Her voice betrayed only the merest hint of a quiver. "—you humble us with your presence."

He brought her hand to his lips. "And you humble me with your beauty, Lady Elizabeth, a beauty that rivals my queen's." His ruddy face lit with a grin. " 'Tis glad I am that Eleanor is not with me that I may appreciate such loveliness more fully." While Elizabeth flushed a becoming pink, he turned to Kathryn.

Guy was no longer smiling. "And here, Your Grace, is Lady Elizabeth's elder sister—Lady Kathryn."

Praying her calm would not desert her, Kathryn inhaled deeply and looked up at the king. His face was square and intelligent, his beard as fiery-red as his close-cropped hair. Despite his charm, it gave her a start to see that his eyes were as gray and every bit as keenly piercing as Guy's.

Her curtsy was a bit awkward. "Sire," she murmured, "I hope your stay here is a comfortable one."

Henry raised her to her feet, his eyes on her exquisite features. "God's blood! Not one beauty but two! And sisters, you say?" His gaze bounced between Elizabeth and Kathryn, noting the dramatic contrast in their coloring. "Amazing!" he said with a throaty chuckle.

Guy spared her not a glance as he moved away with the king. Kathryn felt his dismissal like a stinging slap in the face.

Yet despite his indifference, she nursed a half-hearted tendril of hope that Guy would come to her—that he would beg forgiveness and whisper that he was glad of the child. But soon even that frail hope withered and died.

It twisted her heart to see Elizabeth with Hugh, both of them so enamored with each other that when they were together, they had eyes for no one but the other. And when Elizabeth began to speak of love . . .

Kathryn couldn't help it—never in her life had she been so miserable. She was aware she was feeling sorry for herself, but she could not rid herself of this wretched self-pity. She didn't know which was worse, Helga's scornful disdain or the pity she glimpsed on Elizabeth's and Hugh's face whenever their gaze chanced to rest on her thickened waistline.

On her fifth day there, she stood on the parapet, watching the endless procession of carts weave through the gates. It was Hugh who told her King Henry had abandoned his plans to conquer Ireland, at least for the moment. And so the king had departed, on his way to his next destination to carry out the business of running his country.

A bitter despair seeped through her. Henry could go where he chose, whenever he willed—not because he was king, but because he was a man. Her soul cried out at the injustice dealt her by the cruel hand of Providence. Why, even the lowliest villein possessed more choice than she, for if he so desired, he could change his lot in life. He could prosper and buy his freedom from his lord; he might escape and remain free for a year and a day. Or he could enter the Church.

He could aspire to freedom. She, as every other woman of the times, could not . . . She must remain subject to the whim and will of whatever man controlled her destiny, be he father, husband, lord, or king.

From birth until death.

How long she stood there, those bleak and discouraging thoughts her only companion, she did not know. A violent wind whipped her hair and skirts—it did not wipe the chill from her heart.

The sun sank low in the sky before Kathryn finally made her way down the tower stair. She had nearly reached the bottom when guttural male laughter drifted up the narrow enclosure.

" . . . she always did look down her nose at the lot of us—why, even her uncle!"

"She was never like her mouse of a sister, that's for sure," another agreed.

Kathryn froze, one small foot poised on the last step. The men were undoubtedly several of Richard's men-at-arms—and they were talking about *her!*

"Can't say as I blame de Marche for wanting such a fine piece of fluff. Nor did it take him long to dip into her honey pot!" Lewd laughter followed.

"He brought her down a peg or two when he made her his whore. She's not so haughty now he's put his bastard in her belly."

The blood drained from Kathryn's face. There was a horrible constriction in her chest, so painfully acute it hurt to breathe.

Until that moment, she had scarcely let herself think about the child she bore within her; despite the fact that the babe moved within her, it still seemed vague and unreal. But in that mind-splitting instant, the life within her far eclipsed her own.

They called her child bastard. *Bastard.* Oh, God, she thought wildly, she could not even say the word aloud. She couldn't even think it. The pain that blotted her soul was as vivid as a bloodstain.

The rest of the afternoon passed in a blur. She felt listless and drained, unable to summon much feeling for anything. At supper that night she sat at Elizabeth's elbow, pale and withdrawn, saying little, eating even less. As usual, the hall teemed with activity; knights and servants alike swarmed to and fro. Guy was late but Kathryn scarcely noticed. Misery enshrouded her, sealing her off from everything save her own heartache.

The last dish was offered and served; the meal ended. From where he sat on the raised dais, Guy rose to his feet and called for silence.

The rowdy talk and laughter ebbed. Only then did Kathryn rouse herself from her trancelike state. The hall hummed with quiet. Nearly every eye was fixed upon the handsome figure that strode from the dais to the center of the hall, commanding everyone's attention.

Guy raised a hand. "I ask but a moment of your time, and I promise I'll be brief so that you may be off to spend the evening as you will." He smiled slightly and glanced around. "I asked much of you these many months past when first you swore your allegiance to me. It pleases me greatly to know there are none here who have disappointed me. But now it seems I must ask not only for your allegiance once more, but your trust in my judgment as well. There is among us," he went on, "a man you have come to know well—Sir Hugh Bainbridge. Sir Hugh served me well as a boy. He has served me even better as knight, as well as friend."

Kathryn went very still inside. A shiver of uneasiness prickled her skin. She had the sinking feeling some terrible spectacle was about to unfold.

"That is why I've decided 'tis time I rewarded such loyalty and faithfulness." Across the room, Guy's eyes met those of his startled friend. "Sir Hugh, I hereby grant Ashbury Keep and all its holdings to you." He held his cup high in silent salute. "To health, wealth, and happiness, my friend."

A boisterous cheer broke out. Next to Kathryn, Elizabeth threw her arms around Sir Hugh.

Kathryn was beyond hearing, beyond seeing. Her world was splintering all around her. Guy had just granted Ashbury to Sir Hugh . . . *Sir Hugh*. She had thought he could hurt her no more than he already had. Dear God, she was wrong, for Guy spared her nothing. Always, she thought helplessly, always he destroyed her dreams . . . She had just lost all she ever wanted, and to a heart so sorely battered and bruised, it was like a death blow.

There was shouting and laughter all around her— everyone was frivolous and gay. Someone picked up a lute and began to sing a lilting tune of merriment. She could not stay here amidst such revelry . . . she *would* not. She rose and pushed her way forward. Besides, there was no one to see her if she left . . . no one to care . . .

"Kathryn!"

She need not look behind her to realize who called her. Her steps began to quicken, one by one, until she was running.

"Kathryn!"

She was nearly at the top of the stairs. Her breath came in sobbing pants. Guy's heart leaped to his throat when she stumbled on the last step and went sprawling on the narrow landing. Hands on her waist, he tried to help her up.

She wrenched from his hold. "Do not touch me!" she hissed.

She backed toward the corridor, her face white with rage. He stretched out a hand toward her but did not touch her. "Kathryn," he said urgently. "Let me explain."

Her eyes glowed in burning hatred. "What is there to explain?" The ragged breath she drew burned her lungs. "Ashbury was my home—mine and Elizabeth's. Not yours—not Sir Hugh's! Now there is no hope—no hope at all . . ."

Ashbury! Bitter frustration gnawed at him. It always came first with her—it always would! He clenched his jaw, fighting to hold tight to his temper. Didn't she see there was no malice or spite in passing title to Hugh? This was the only way he could think to end her compulsive desire for Ashbury. Indeed, he had hoped it might pacify her.

"Think," he said tightly. "Kathryn, think! Sir Hugh intends to marry Elizabeth. Ashbury will remain her home—always. Possession will still be in your family—"

She clapped her hands over her ears, her eyes wild. "Why should I believe you? You sought to shame me by bringing me here—you trample on my pride and my dignity! You—you take everything from me and leave me nothing!" She whirled and ran toward her chamber.

Guy's hand fell to his side. This time he did not try to stop her. Her heart was closed against him, as surely as a wall of stone. He could only hope that soon she would see reason. Reluctantly he made his way back to the hall.

He did not see the furtive shadow that slipped from the wall behind Kathryn.

Near her chamber, Kathryn reached to snatch open the door. Behind her, a palm splayed wide above hers, thrusting it closed. She spun about with a shriek of rage.

Roderick caught her by the wrists only an instant before she would have clawed his face. Stunned that it was he and not Guy, she gaped at him.

"Shhh, Kathryn. Do not say a word, just hear me out." His hands slipped to her shoulders. "I know how unhappy you are, love. I know it's all because of that arrogant whoreson de Marche. No one knows better than I how he has wronged you! But you need not feel you have no one to turn to, for I am here." With his thumbs he slowly stroked her collarbone. "You have only to say the word and I will always be here."

Her heart began to slow its frantic throb. "I—I do not know what you mean," she whispered.

"We planned to run off and be married once, Kathryn. What's to stop us from doing so now?" He threw back his tawny head and laughed. "Think what sweet revenge it would be on de Marche!"

She searched his face, convinced she'd heard wrong. "You would marry me," she said slowly, "even though I carry another man's child?"

Something hard crossed his handsome features. "You don't love him, Kathryn. I know you don't."

But she did not love him either! Feeling torn and confused, she did not stop him when he pulled her close and smothered her mouth with his. Kathryn submitted passively and let him part her lips, feeling curiously unaffected by the kiss. She felt neither pleasure nor displeasure.

Roderick did not seem to notice. He raised his head and gave a triumphant laugh. "You see, Kathryn? Nothing has changed between us. You cannot refuse to marry me now!"

Kathryn neither agreed nor disagreed. "This is so—so sudden," she said slowly. "Roderick, so much has happened. I must have time to think on this."

His smile vanished, replaced by an ugly sneer. "Judging from the look of you, I'd say time is at a premium. In only a few months your babe will be born a bastard—"

She cried out sharply. "No! Do not say that! My babe is not a bastard!"

"He will be if you don't marry—and quickly. I'll raise the child as my own, I swear." His eyes gleamed. "Kathryn, you must marry me now. Tonight. The monastery is not far. We can leave now and marry there as we once planned."

"Tonight?" A hint of uncertainty dwelled in her tone. "Roderick, that's so soon."

He made a sound of impatience. "It must be tonight. If you do not give the gossip time to die down, it will forever stain your child. Is that what you want?"

Oh, God, she thought starkly. He was right. If she did not act soon, this one single folly would taint the rest of her life—and the life of her child! Guy would never marry her—he hated her too much to bind himself to her for the rest of his life. Unbidden, unwanted, the memory of these past few days crowded her heart. The shame and humiliation, the pity and condemnation—it was more than she could endure. The prospect of bearing her child outside of wedlock made her shudder. She would be forever shunned, forever disgraced.

And her child would have naught but a legacy of shame and degradation.

Roderick was right. She could do little to change her circumstances, but she could not destroy the innocent life within her. At least the child would have a name.

She swallowed. "I—I will marry you, Roderick." Her voice was very low.

He claimed her lips with another long unbroken kiss, then gave her a gentle shove toward her chamber. "Pack a fitting gown," he ordered. "I'll meet you in the stables."

Within minutes they were riding through the gates.

Chapter 15

I t was early yet when Guy excused himself and made his way up the stairs. In the hall, both ale and conversation continued to flow freely. He had rejoined the celebration out of duty and consideration for Hugh. He had even laughed and joked, but it was merely a performance. In truth, after his confrontation with Kathryn, he was scarcely in the mood for festivities.

His footsteps slowed as he neared her door. His gaze bored into the dark oak panel. Within, all was quiet. He wondered if she slept, if her temper had cooled. Did he dare hope she might listen to him now? With a silent sigh, he moved further down the passage.

It seemed he was not in the mood for battle either.

In his chamber, he caught his breath in surprise. The candle in the wall sconce flared brighter, casting flickering shadows on the figure curled beneath the furs. The figure shifted and he caught the rounded flare of a feminine hip, the fleeting glimpse of white limbs.

The breath rushed from his lungs. He drew it in slowly, aware of a drumming pulse beating deep inside him. A slow smile crept across his lips as he moved noiselessly to the bedside. As Kathryn was so often wont to do, this time it appeared he had been the one to judge too hastily . . .

Long dark hair spilled across his pillow. He reached for a trailing strand. Already he could feel it, smooth as silk, clinging to his fingers with a life of its own . . .

Coarse brittle curls chafed his skin. He dropped the hank of hair as if he'd been burned just as the figure in the bed turned and sat up. The sheet fell away, exposing naked, jutting breasts. Helga smiled up at him.

Guy was not amused. "What madness are you about?" he demanded.

She wet her lips. "My lord," she murmured, "you've spent these many nights alone. I seek merely to ease your needs." She arched her back, displaying her breasts in what she perceived to be a seductive endeavor. After Kathryn's small but exquisitely rounded fullness, Helga looked immense and grotesque.

Disgust soured his stomach. "If I wanted a woman in my bed," he said flatly, "she'd be there at my invitation. And as I have no recollection of such an event, kindly remove yourself from my chamber." He grabbed the pile of clothes on the bench behind him and flung them at her.

Helga caught them with a little gasp of rage. "And who would you have? The virtuous Lady Kathryn?" she scoffed. "Why, she'll soon be fat as a sow and then you'll be wishing you had a woman like me to warm your bed."

"I think not." His smile was frigid.

She flounced from the bed. "Think you're too good for me, eh? Well, I've news for you, my fine, fancy lord." She jerked her kirtle over her head.

"Lady Kathryn obviously likes the sport she finds in Roderick's bed far better than yours!"

His smile withered. "What do you imply?" he asked roughly.

"*I* imply nothing. The lady's actions speak for themselves, for she has run off with Sir Roderick!"

"Run off," he repeated. "You mean she is gone?"

"Aye, milord!"

His gut felt as if he'd been rammed broadside with a sword. "Christ . . . how do you know this?" When she said nothing, he grabbed her arm. "Tell me!"

" 'Tis lucky for you I overhead them plotting. They left for the monastery, where they plan to be married."

Guy whirled and grabbed his scabbard from the corner. "This monastery. It is the one outside the village?"

Helga shrugged. "Mayhap you're not so lucky after all," she taunted with a smile. "Why, they're probably wedded and bedded by now!"

If Guy heard, he gave no sign of it. Moments later, the tower watchman scratched his head as yet another horse and rider raced through the gates.

The night was damp and cold and eerily silent. A full moon spilled down in shining splendor, lending an eerie glow to the dense layer of fog that clung to the ground. His mind ran apace with his destrier's flashing hooves. Christ, was Helga right? Did Kathryn truly prefer Roderick over him? He swore a violent oath. If only Henry hadn't demanded his every waking moment! *He* would be the one to whom she'd be wedded and bedded—not Roderick.

A horrible idea clutched at him. He had not considered that Kathryn might not want the child. One thought led to another . . . The possibility she might not want *his* child disturbed him still more.

He spurred his horse faster.

The destrier's sides were heaving and lathered when Guy reined up outside the gray stone walls of the monastery. He quickly tethered his mount and strode through the ivy-drenched archway that marked the entrance. He grabbed the bellpull and tugged insistently, not once but five times. Hollow clanging resounded within the darkened interior.

Guy blew out a breath of frosty air and tried again, this time punctuating the sound with a furious pounding on the door. A restless impatience marked his steps as he paced the muddied cobblestones. Finally a narrow panel on the inside of the door slid back. An owlish countenance framed by a deep cowl peered through the grilled opening. "Tell me, my son," said the monk, "what do you seek?"

"God's mercy and yours—and Father, I need it badly, for I come in search of a woman, Lady Kathryn of Ashbury, who was brought here by a knight named Sir Roderick."

The monk stared at him long and hard, as if to take his measure. Then, apparently satisfied with what he saw, he said slowly, "They have been given rooms for the night. Their marriage vows will be spoken in the morning."

He wasn't too late! He exhaled with vast relief and went on swiftly, "Father, I am Lord Guy de Marche, Earl of Sedgewick. I pledge a generous boon if you can help me. Lady Kathryn is with child—my child, not Sir Roderick's. There has been a grave misunderstanding, a misunderstanding which I intend to rectify . . ."

The monk ushered him down a narrow passage where he pointed out Roderick's room and passed him the rushlight. "Lady Kathryn's is there at the end, milord." The monk quietly retreated.

The room was small and stark, void of any decoration except a wooden crucifix above the narrow bed. A stub of a candle revealed Roderick stretched out there.

His eyes widened as Guy stepped inside. Guy gave him no chance to speak. A fist on the front of his tunic, he hauled him to his feet.

"Mother of Christ!" the other man gasped. "How did you—"

He got no further. "If you value your life," Guy warned flatly, "I suggest you make haste back to Ashbury now—before you make me forget we are in the house of the Lord."

Roderick grabbed his boots and fled.

Down the passageway, Kathryn lay huddled in the narrow bed. She twisted her head around, trying to decide if she'd heard the faint rumble of voices. Or was it merely her imagination . . . ?

The thought progressed no further. The door of her room crashed open. Stark terror brought her upright in the bed.

A powerful figure filled the doorway. In the gloom he appeared dark and faceless—until he stepped forward and she found herself captured in the ruthless hold of glittering silver eyes.

This time there was nowhere to go . . . nowhere to run.

He stripped off his gloves and hurled them aside. "Well, milady—" His expression was as cutting as his tone. "—you've really done it this time."

Kathryn's heart beat like a trapped bird's. She drew the sheet up to her breasts, a pitiable shield against such a peremptory presence. His eyes stabbed at her, piercing her to the quick. "Do not look at me so!" she cried feebly. "What have I done that is so awful?"

All the fires of hell leaped in his eyes. "My God," he said, and his voice was shaking with the force of his anger, "that you can ask that—" Anger exploded into violence. He slammed his fist against the wall. Kathryn had seen Guy angry before, but not like this—never like this! A murderous rage contorted his features into a mask she scarcely recognized.

"Damn you!" he shouted. "How could you marry him when it's my child you carry?" He started toward her, menace apparent in the tightly leashed tension of his body.

Kathryn's eyes cleaved to his, shadowed and frightened. The very air seemed charged with his fury. She scrambled back instinctively until her spine encountered the cold stone wall and pulled her knees to her chest, cowering like a child. Suddenly, without warning, something inside her crumpled. Never had she felt so defeated—so utterly alone. She'd tried so hard to be strong for months now, clinging to a meager thread of hope. But now even that hope was gone and the hurt that descended was unbearable. And in this, her moment of greatest despair, she rested her head in her hands and began to cry. Helplessly. Uncontrollably. With all the tremulous fear hidden deep in her heart.

Shaken and stunned, Guy could only stare, caught wholly off guard and totally unmanned by the sight of this strong, fiery woman in tears. He swallowed. Christ, how many times had he thought her cold and heartless? Never had he considered her vulnerable . . . never, until now.

"Kathryn." His hand hovered just above her head. "I'm sorry. I did not mean to frighten you, I swear." He eased down on the bed and touched her shoulder.

A tremendous shudder wracked her body. At

his touch, a dam seemed to break loose inside her. "Don't be angry," she moaned, over and over. "Oh, please, do not . . . I—I didn't know what else to do . . ."

Her spirit was broken, her bravery and pride in tatters. Seeing her like this was like a knife turning inside him. He wrapped her in his arms with a surge of fierce protectiveness.

"I'm not angry." He sought to reassure her. "But Kathryn, you must understand, I could hardly let you marry Roderick—"

Her head came up. Her face was pale and ashen, her eyes huge and wounded and pleading. "You must!" she cried. Her small hands clutched at him, and suddenly it was all pouring out—the angry hurt she felt in losing Ashbury, her fears and uncertainty about the future . . . and the shame she felt in carrying his child.

"Do not take me back to Ashbury," she begged. "I cannot go back there. Everyone knows that we lay together. They—they think I am your whore."

His anger erupted anew. "The devil take them!" he stormed. "Who would dare to say such a thing!"

"I heard them," she choked. "Two knights . . . they said I was not so haughty now you'd put your bastard in my belly." She began to sob again. "I—I don't want my babe to be a bastard. I don't want this child to be scorned or—or become like my Uncle Richard, selfish and greedy because he must always do battle for what little he has. Peter will have Sedgewick," she wept, "but this child will have nothing. I beg of you, do not stop this wedding—at least let this babe have a name."

Guy closed his eyes, his throat achingly tight. His arms tightened. She was shaking uncontrollably. Scalding tears soaked the front of his tunic; they seeped clear to his heart. Each jagged sob was like the piercing thrust of a blade. She cried until she had no strength left, until he was sure there could not possibly be a drop of emotion left inside her.

He had brought her to this, he realized numbly. He had robbed her of her innocence, stolen her reputation. He had wronged her deeply.

And now he must do what he could to set things aright.

"Kathryn." He nuzzled the baby-soft skin of her temple. "You must cease this weeping—" With his palms he framed her face and tipped it to his. "—for a bride should not cry so the eve before her wedding."

Another time, and he might have smiled at her expression of wide-eyed shock. Instead, he merely awaited her reaction.

Her eyes clung to his. "Do not—toy with me." Her voice caught, still thready with tears. "Please . . . speak plainly."

Staring into her tear-ravaged features, Guy decided she'd never looked more beautiful. He heaved a sigh, for he was feeling rather possessive of her right now—and protective as well. His body, however, was far from immune from those sweetly feminine curves nestled so cozily against him.

But she was so disarmingly vulnerable right now—*too* vulnerable, he reminded himself firmly. He ached with the need to lay her down, strip away her gown, and explore with lips and hands all the fascinating changes that had taken place since the last time he'd touched her. Unfortunately, as he'd so forcibly cued Roderick, this was God's house— hardly the place to make love to a woman, married or otherwise.

With his thumb he sponged the dampness from quivering pink lips. "I can speak no more plainly than this," he whispered. "In the morning you planned to speak your marriage vows—and so it shall be."

Very gently he put her from him and rose. She huddled beneath the covers once more, but her troubled gaze followed his progress toward the door.

"Guy?"

He half-turned.

"I must know . . . you'll truly not prevent this wedding?"

He watched her a moment, his features unusually grave. "This I promise," he said finally. "On the morrow, you will no longer be a maid—" His eyes cleaved directly into hers. "—but a wife."

In the morning, it all seemed like a dream.

She had slept deeply, though she had thought not to sleep at all. She dimly recalled hearing the chapel bell which summoned the monks to morning mass several hours earlier. But she remained where she was, her limbs weighted down with a weariness she suspected was more of the mind than body. With a dispirited sigh, she finally thrust her leg from beneath the covers.

There was a knock on the door. "Kathryn?" called a voice. "Kathryn, are you awake?"

Elizabeth! For a moment Kathryn feared the worst, that Elizabeth was here to dissuade her from her chosen course. Yet when Elizabeth let herself in, her lovely face was wreathed in smiles.

She threw her arms around Kathryn. "Oh, Kathryn, I cannot believe it! You are to be married!" She hugged her fiercely. "You see? I knew things would work out—I just knew it!"

Kathryn was still rather stunned at her arrival. "Elizabeth," she murmured, "I do not understand. How do you come to be here?"

"The earl woke me early this morning and told me the news," she said gaily. "I've come to help you dress and—oh, you could hardly let your wedding take place without your only sister in attendance, could you?"

It was a relief to let Elizabeth take charge. She helped Kathryn dress, then plaited her hair into a shining coronet atop her head. When she'd left Sedgewick, Kathryn had taken none of the gowns she'd fashioned from the cloth Guy had given her, save one—the midnight-blue velvet. In a rare display of vanity, she'd simply been unable to part with it. Now, hearing Elizabeth exclaim delightedly, Kathryn was glad she had not left it behind, if only for Elizabeth's sake.

"Oh, Kathryn." Elizabeth clapped her heads and sighed dreamily. "Your gown is beautiful! You are truly a vision, for I've never seen you look lovelier."

The words made her heart catch. In spite of all that had been between them, she thought of how she had once longed to wear this gown for Guy. But Guy had never seen her in this dress—now he never would.

She summoned a wobbly smile. "Lovely?" she murmured dryly. "Lumpy is more like it, Elizabeth." Her hand moved instinctively to that slight roundness.

"Why, it hardly shows!" Elizabeth replied staunchly. "I only wish there was a glass here in this monk's cell that you might see for yourself."

Kathryn merely shook her head and allowed Elizabeth to lead her from the chamber toward the chapel, feeling numb inside. Where her heart should have dwelled, abrim with joy, there was only a hollow, empty ache that went on and on.

Hugh was there at the entrance, waiting, his smile

broad. Kathryn felt him press her hand. He murmured something, she knew not what. Elizabeth hugged her and drew back. Her beautiful blue eyes glistened with a betraying sheen, but her expression was rapt.

"Oh, Kathryn," she whispered, "this day is just the beginning—your life will be filled with happiness—I feel it with all that I am!"

Her legs leaden, a suffocating heaviness in her chest, Kathryn forced herself to take those first steps that would take her to the man about to become her husband. For the first time that day, Kathryn allowed herself to think of Roderick. An unseen hand seemed to close around her heart and squeeze. If only she could share Elizabeth's elation! This was her wedding day, she realized desperately, but she could not think of it as a blessing. After all, she didn't love Roderick. He wasn't even the father of her child!

Tears pricked her eyelids. She saw everything through a watery blur—the dark-robed priest, the broad back of a tall figure elegantly garbed in rich brown velvet. She cringed inside, not wanting to look at him, yet he drew her gaze with a force more powerful than she.

The tilt of his head was impossibly arrogant . . . impossibly familiar.

Her mouth went dry. Her knees went weak. Her head swam dizzily, and for a mind-splitting instant she thought vaguely that surely this was but a dream. For the man who waited at the altar was not Roderick at all . . .

It was Guy.

Chapter 16

That she could walk was a mystery; her legs were shaking so that she could hardly remain standing. As always, Guy's face was a mask that betrayed nothing of his feelings. She could read nothing in his expression—not dismay or anger, defeat or indifference. Then, all at once, something flickered in his eyes.

He held out his hand.

She never remembered taking that last, fateful step which brought her to his side. Nor did she remember if he reached for her—or she reached for him.

Their fingertips touched. Her heart lurched. Was she elated? Or horrified?

His fingers weaved through hers, warm and tight, reassuring despite the upheaval raging inside her. A gentle tug brought her down on her knees beside him. From then on, Kathryn did not notice the cold of the hard stone floor. Heat and vitality radiated from the man at her side. Swept into the sheer aura of his presence, she found the strength she so sorely needed. She did not stumble and falter as she spoke her vows. And when it was over, a firm hand at her waist guided her to her feet.

As they glided down the aisle, a surge of some powerful, unnamed emotion swelled inside her. This man, she realized dazedly—so tall, so strong and ruggedly handsome—was now her husband. And she was his wife . . . his *wife*.

Outside a tepid sunshine weaved through naked tree branches. Elizabeth had remained inside to help Kathryn gather the rest of her belongings. Hugh turned to Guy. "Will you return to Ashbury?" He chuckled. "You can oversee my first duty as lord there—providing your wedding feast!"

Kathryn's frozen features flashed through Guy's mind—the moment she had realized it was him and not Roderick who stood as her bridegroom. He had held his breath, half-afraid she would run, even when she laid icy-cold fingers within his.

Something hotly primitive surged inside him. The temptation to return to Ashbury was strong. He'd have liked nothing more than to flaunt the morning's deed before Roderick. But, he decided wryly, Kathryn would probably not take kindly to being displayed as a battle prize.

He laid a hand on Hugh's shoulder. "Much as I appreciate the offer, I fear I must refuse. I've been away from Sedgewick too long as it is and I'm anxious to be home again." He paused. "I must ask a boon, though, my friend."

"You have only to name it, Guy."

"I want it known that Kathryn is now my wife." His smile did not reach his eyes. "Roderick may find it to be of particular interest." A silent glimmer of understanding passed between the two men.

Kathryn and Elizabeth emerged then. Kathryn didn't seem surprised when he told her he intended they leave for Sedgewick from here—whether she was relieved or disappointed he couldn't tell, perhaps because he didn't want to. But he couldn't suppress a twinge of guilt when she and Elizabeth said their good-byes. He watched her embrace Elizabeth, who was both laughing and crying. Elizabeth's voice drifted to him.

"Oh, Kathryn, I never thought to see the day . . . you and the earl married! Do you realize you are now his countess?"

Kathryn's reply was lost on him. He scowled when tears sprang to her eyes—tears of happiness? Doubt marched like an invading army inside him. Relief, mayhap? Or tears of despair?

He stepped up and took her elbow. "We must be off, Kathryn. We've a long journey ahead of us." A wounded look sped across her features—too late he realized he spoke more harshly than he intended. But it was just as he'd told Hugh. Perhaps it wasn't the best way to begin a marriage, but he was eager to be back at Sedgewick.

Little did he realize that Kathryn's thoughts followed that same channel. They spent their wedding night lying on cold hard earth, surrounded by a small contingent of men he'd brought with him from Ashbury. There had been reports of several bands of outlaws preying on travelers of late, so Guy took his turn standing watch with his men. Kathryn huddled beneath a pile of furs, cold and miserable and very alone in the meager shelter of their tent. It was very late when he crawled within. He threw an arm around her and brought her close. Within minutes his deep even breathing told her he was asleep.

Her wayward mind gave her no peace. How very different this must have been from his wedding night with Elaine! It might have started out with artless shyness on her part. Sweet persuasive kisses and tender caresses would have followed, and then. . . . She squeezed her eyes shut and willed away the vivid picture in her mind. But if her thoughts were faintly textured with bitterness, she couldn't help it. Elaine had been the bride he loved.

She was only the bride he hated and despised . . . the bride he had not wanted at all.

By the time they arrived at Sedgewick, Kathryn was drained, both physically and mentally.

One of his men rode ahead to announce their arrival. The bailey was filled with knights and servants alike. The crowd let out a cheer and scurried to make way for the horses. Near the entrance to the great hall, Guy dismounted, then lifted her from her palfrey. His hand in hers, he mounted the stairs with long determined strides. Kathryn was gasping when they reached the top. Raising their joined hands high, his voice rang out over the crowd.

"I give you Lady de Marche, Countess of Sedgewick!"

A roaring, deafening cheer went up. Stunned and amazed at such a welcome, a smile appeared from nowhere, wide and radiant. The next thing she knew, a rock-hard arm curled along her waist and pulled her around.

The softness of her form was crushed against unyielding male strength. Even as she drew a startled breath of surprise, his lips boldly captured hers, the contact deep and slow and rousing. Yet even while she clung to him, weak and hot and shivery, her spirits plummeted to a deep despair. For all that his embrace was heady and all-consuming, there was little of tenderness and gentleness, and she wondered at the emotions that prevailed within him. Was this kiss naught but a spectacle to please his people?

When he finally let her go, her radiant smile had

withered. Afraid her face would betray the tumult in her soul, she turned and fled into the hall without a backward glance, struggling for control. The crowd, thinking her embarrassed and shy, roared again.

The evening meal dragged on forever. She sat on the dais beside Guy, her head buzzing from all the laughter and shouting. He was accommodating and solicitous in much the same way he'd been these past days of their journey here . . . was it her imagination or did he seem rather distant? She clasped her fingers tight in her lap to keep them from trembling. Had she done something to displease him—anger him perchance? A sudden notion knotted her stomach. They were but four days wed—did he already feel trapped? Did he regret those sacred vows that bound them husband and wife?

A little moan escaped her. She was simply too worn out right now to seek answers, particularly when she suspected they would scarcely be to her liking.

At the sound, Guy fixed that disturbingly intense gaze on her profile. "What is it?" he asked sharply. "Are you unwell?"

She shook her head and summoned a wan smile. "I am fine. To be sure," she admitted, "I would like nothing more than to seek my bed."

She didn't see the pulse that ticked hard in the leanness of his cheek. "Then you have my leave to do so. I will not be long." Kathryn scarcely heard this last. She needed no further urging to be on her way.

Upstairs in her old chamber, she sat on the edge of the bed and pulled off her wimple. Her braids came tumbling down and she loosed them, running her fingers through the thick strands to free the tangles. There was a knock and Gerda shuffled inside. As fast as her uneven gait allowed, she crossed to her mistress and fell down upon her knees.

"Oh, Lady Kathryn," she burst out. "When I heard the news, I—I cannot tell you how happy I was for you." She drew back, her cheeks flushed with enthusiasm.

Kathryn searched the girl's face, lightly laying a hand on her head. "Gerda," she murmured wonderingly. "Gerda, I must tell you—I was not at all sure you would be pleased."

Gerda tilted her head. "Why would I not be pleased?"

"I know how devoted you were to Lady Elaine," she said slowly. "I know how you loved her. And to be honest, Gerda, I thought it might be hard for you to see another woman take her place—" Her voice caught slightly. "—especially me."

Gerda's eyes darkened. "Milady," she said unevenly, "it shames me to realize that I ever thought ill of you—that I judged you because of who you were, and not by what you are. I wronged you deeply, milady, and I hope you can find it in you to forgive me." She seized Kathryn's hand and kissed it.

Kathryn slowly brought her upright. "Gerda—" She swallowed, her throat achingly tight. "—there is naught to forgive. I don't know what I'd have done these many months without you." She hugged the girl, and they drew back, exchanging watery smiles. Kathryn wiped away a tear, wondering why she was so weepy of late and ever despairing of her ability to control it.

Gerda brushed her hair and helped her undress. Kathryn slipped into bed with a sigh of weary relief. Four nights of sleeping on the cold hard ground made her appreciate such comfort more than ever. She snuggled into the softness more fully and closed her eyes.

Belowstairs, Guy chafed impatiently, eager for the moment he could rise and make his excuses without appearing the overeager bridegroom. In truth, he was exactly that! The thought of Kathryn lying in his bed sent heat singing through his veins. At a lull in the conversation, he rose and gracefully took his leave. His heartbeat quickened apace with his stride. He took the stairs two at a time.

A welcoming fire warmed his chamber, glowing embers casting out their stingy heat. But the room was empty, his bed cold.

Oblivious to the vile oath hurled her way, Kathryn hovered on the fringes of a nebulous dreamworld. True to the day, this was no gentle sleep she had fallen into, but restless and disturbing. Swirling fog stretched before her, as far as the eye could see. A hulking shadow, vaguely resembling a man, shifted and rose from the mists. It glided toward her, slowly at first, and then with racing speed, as if the devil himself had set sail in a sea of fog—maybe it *was* the devil. Terror engulfed her. She saw a vision of herself turn and begin to run, but it was no use. The shadow loomed closer . . . ever closer. Just as it reached her, thunder split the air. Kathryn's eyes flew open. She jolted upright.

Guy towered above her, his features grimly forbidding. No mercy softened that steel-honed gaze that scraped over her. He looked for all the world like a demon bent on destruction—*her* destruction. With a powerful sweep of his arm, he raked the furs from her body and snatched her up high in his arms.

The utter determination she felt in him crammed her protest low in her throat. Dazed and numb, she clung to his neck as he bore her swiftly down the passage to his own chamber. The next thing she knew, she'd been dumped unceremoniously in the middle of his bed.

She lurched to a sitting position while Guy began to storm the length of the room, back and forth like a caged animal. "By all the saints," he fumed, "you try my patience as no other! You are stubborn and willful and acknowledge no authority save your own. You fight me, you defy me at every turn of the hand, woman, but by God, no more . . . no more!" He stomped to a halt and glared at her.

Beneath his blistering regard, Kathryn's heart beat like a captured doe. She stared at him dumbly, wary and uncertain of the violence she sensed in him.

"So soon you forget," he mocked tightly. "You would pretend that nothing has changed, but you are now my wife, Kathryn. And my wife will share my chamber. She will most certainly share my bed— this night and every other night!"

Kathryn clutched a sable fur to her breast. "You think that I sought to anger you by going to my old chamber? Guy, that is not so, I swear." She began to tremble. "You—you gave me leave to retire," she cried wildly. "I—I just was not thinking . . . it never occurred to me you wanted me here . . ."

His condemning silence was unbearable. Her throat worked convulsively as she fought to hold back tears. Her breath tumbled out in a shuddering rush. "I'm sorry," she said brokenly, and then again. "I'm sorry." To her horror, a scalding tear slipped down her cheek, then another and another, for all at once her emotions were a hopeless tangle. She dropped her forehead to her knees and struggled vainly for control.

Guy stared. Her shoulders were shaking; soundless sobs wracked her body. His fury drained as suddenly as it erupted. He swallowed, aware of an odd tightening in his chest.

"Kathryn." He eased down beside her and awkwardly touched her shoulder. He felt her stiffen, then all at once she turned blindly into his chest. His arms encircled her, bringing her shaking body close. With his hand he stroked the midnight cloud of her hair.

"Guy—"

He kissed away the tears spurting from her eyes. "You need not be sorry, Kathryn." He nuzzled the soft skin of her temple and sighed. "Ah, lass, we've had so many battles, you and I. I feared this was but one more."

Her jagged sob tore right into his heart. "I did not mean to fight you. Or even to spite you. It's just that I was so tired . . ."

"I know, sweet. 'Tis my fault and none of yours— none at all." He caught her fingers in his and pressed a kiss on her palm, holding her misty green gaze with his own.

"Please do not cry," he pleaded. "This has not been an easy time for either of us. But now that we are home, I swear it will be better."

Kathryn buried her face in the side of his neck. He was being so kind, so gentle. As always, his gentleness tied her heart in knots. He cradled her against him until her shaking began to subside. Then he eased her back against the pillows. Rising to stand beside the bed, he stripped off his clothes and crawled in beside her, tucking the furs about her shoulders and bringing her flush against his length.

She melted against him like a kitten seeking heat; his warmth was like a benediction straight from heaven. She rubbed her cheek against the sleek hardness of his shoulder, loving the musky male smell of him, the hardness of his arms tight about her back. Why it was so, she did not know, nor did she care. She nestled even closer, for the sheltering protection of his arms offered all she needed in that moment.

Guy savored the way she rested against him, even while he discovered it came with a price. It was impossible not to hold her like this and ignore the soft, womanly shape of her. A hot, familiar ache flooded his loins. But her pride had been sorely battered and bruised these past days. Though his body craved release, she was simply too vulnerable right now.

She twisted slightly, bringing the rounded plumpness of her breast in fleeting contact with his hand. The spiky dampness of her lashes brushed his neck and fluttered closed. Her thready breathing slowly evened out. She seemed so young, he thought with a pang, little more than a child, even though she carried a child. Her very defenselessness spurred his torment further. Did she cling to him because she sought *him*, the man who was now her husband? Or because he was simply there, the only one who offered strength and security?

It was a long, long time before he was able to join her in slumber.

Kathryn woke alone the next morning—and with the certainty that Guy had held her close throughout the night. She shivered, recalling how angry he had been—and then later, how tender and gentle. Her throat swelled just thinking about it. But his abrupt change of mood puzzled her—and troubled her as well, for she never knew what to expect of him.

It was then that she realized . . . They had spent the last four nights together. Guy had yet to consummate their marriage. A nagging fear tugged at her heart. Had time and circumstances managed to erase all desire for her? The thought was devastating. She wanted him to make love to her, she realized. She wanted it with an intensity that left her weak and yearning. But he had scarcely touched her, except for last night when his touch spoke more of comfort than passion. Why, he hadn't even kissed her, save for yesterday in the bailey—and that for the benefit of his people!

Righteously outraged, she pushed off the furs and glanced down, only to confront her swelling belly. She groaned, unsure whether to laugh or cry. Could she really blame Guy if his passion lay dormant, like a fallow field? It seemed she grew rounder with each day.

She spent the day wavering between hurt and indignation.

Guy had ridden out early to catch up on estate affairs, and arrived home late, looking disheveled and rather tired. He ate a hasty meal then excused himself so that he might bathe. Kathryn helped Gerda put Peter to bed, then approached Guy's chamber with a distinct trepidation.

She caught her breath when she discovered he was still soaking in the tub. She paused, wanting to flee yet not certain she dared—she'd not put it past him to come after her, naked or no! She closed the door and cleared her throat nervously, alerting him to her presence.

He merely glanced over his shoulder. "I left the linen on the chest. Could you get it for me?" His manner was easy and nonchalant. He acted as though her presence during his bath were an everyday occurrence.

Swallowing hard, Kathryn passed it into his waiting hand, envying his composure. Her heart beating clear up into her throat, she fled to a stool before the fire, deliberately turning her back to him. Behind her, she heard the slosh of water. It took no stretch of the imagination to picture Guy's bronzed, hair-roughened limbs, sleek and wet, as he climbed from the tub—her traitorous mind did exactly that! An instant later she heard the slap of wet linen against the stone floor then the sound of him climbing into the bed.

Nervously she began the task of unplaiting her hair. Anxious awareness gathered in the pit of her stomach, for she could feel his eyes drilling into her back. She picked up a comb and began to work slowly through the tangles.

Long minutes later, he sighed. "You dally on purpose, Kathryn. I begin to think you find your husband repulsive as a toad."

She had forgotten the night she had riled him with that very taunt. Ah, but he was cruel to remind her so! "Repulsive, nay," she muttered. "Aggravating, of a certainty!"

His laughter grated. "Could it be you need help with your gown then?"

She spun to fix him with a glare—a mistake, that! He was powerful and imposing despite the way he lay indolently sprawled on his side, supporting himself on one elbow. The furs were drawn up no further than the jutting ridge of a narrow hip—he was clearly naked beneath the furs.

The sight of that dark haired chest and belly made her stomach drop clear to the floor. But Kathryn could not be so casual about her own nudity, particularly not in her present condition. Beneath the sheltering protection of her kirtle, she tugged off her hose. Her soft woolen kirtle came next. She pulled it over her head and shook her hair free.

Guy had yet to relieve her of his bold stare. Clad only in her thin linen chemise, she clutched her kirtle to her middle like a shield. "Must you look at me so?"

Her hair spilled over her bare shoulders, sleek and shiny as the wings of a raven, and offering tantalizing glimpses of ivory skin. His gaze lowered slowly from her exquisite features, lingering with avid male interest on the shape of her breasts beneath the sheer linen. One corner of that hard mouth curled upward. "I see no harm in staring," he murmured lazily, "especially when I see much that I like."

She stomped her foot. " 'Tis just like you to—to mock me!"

Guy's smile faded. "Mock you?" he repeated incredulously. "What mockery is there in a man eager to share with his wife the joys of the marriage bed?"

"And I ask you what joy is there? We've been wed for four days—nay, five!—and you've yet to make me truly your wife. Indeed, you've made it very clear that for you it will only be a duty! Well, I hereby relieve you of your duty, milord. No one need ever know our marriage has never been consummated!"

The last was fairly flung at him—in fact, the whole speech was. No longer amused, his jaw clamped shut. "What goes on here?" he demanded. "Do you deny me my rights as a husband?"

"You play the wounded bridegroom well," she said bitterly. "But you need not spare my tender feelings, for I have accepted that you no longer desire me."

"No longer desire you . . . woman, you are mad!"

She shook her head. "Nay," she said unevenly. "That night in the forest before we returned to Ashbury, when you discovered I was with child . . . I saw the way you looked at me, Guy."

"And how—" His voice was dangerously low. "—was that?"

She swallowed, her throat achingly tight. "You looked as if I . . . as if I disgusted you." She didn't hear his impatient exclamation as he swung himself from the bed. Her eyes were swimming so she didn't see him until he'd planted himself directly before her. She gave a tiny shake of her head and went on unsteadily. "Guy, it's all right, really. I understand why you—you no longer want me. I've grown ugly and fat and—"

Lean fingers pressed against her lips stopped the outflow of words. "And since you've been doing far too much thinking and coming to all the wrong conclusions, it seems I must explain after all." He paused, his gaze delving deeply into hers. Kathryn found she couldn't look away.

"I could hardly take you unto me surrounded by my knights," he chided, his voice very low. "And last night, well, you were exhausted." He tugged her kirtle from her grip and tossed it aside. His touch bold and sure, he stretched his fingers wide across the hard mound of her tummy. "Ugly? Fat?" he scolded her gently. "I think not, sweet, for you are enticing and feminine and delightfully round and full. And you are a fool if you believe I find you anything other than desirable."

Her eyes clung to his. She longed to believe him, longed for it with all of her soul. But she was so afraid of being hurt again.

"You do not believe me?" Her uncertainty twisted Guy's heart. "So be it then . . . mayhap I can show you much better . . ."

The abruptness of his movement startled her. Her pulse leaped in protest as his hand closed around hers, flattening her palm and dragging it down across his stomach . . . ever down. She gasped as he brought the plundering journey to a halt, closing her palm around his throbbing member and keeping it there with the insistent pressure of his.

Kathryn was stunned to find him rigid and thick, swollen with arousal. His size made her quiver, yet it was not with fear . . . Her heart pounding wildly, she watched his eyes squeeze shut. A jolt tore through him as she extended her fingertips in an involuntary, tentative caress.

His eyes flicked open, searing hotly into hers. There was a subtle tightening of his hand around hers. "Feel," he said thickly. "Feel what you do to me and never doubt that I want you. Feel how your touch makes me tremble. And know that you alone, Kathryn, hold this power over me. You alone have the power to make me quiver like a stripling lad."

He spoke of power, but the relief that poured through her made her giddy and weak. He wanted her . . . *Guy wanted her*. She gave a strangled little cry and slipped her arms around his neck, melting against him. His hands slid around to cradle her buttocks, pulling her full and tight against him.

He bent his head and sealed her lips with his, a kiss both tender and fierce. His tongue swirled far and deep. She tasted the hunger in his mouth and responded with a wild fervency that made his heart soar.

He tore his mouth from hers, silver eyes aflame. "You make me feel greedy," he muttered, already lowering his head. He feasted on the sweetness of her lips until her legs felt like melted wax; if not for the supporting strength of his arms she'd have fallen into a clumsy heap at his feet. And then she was the one who trembled when strong hands stripped away her chemise. She felt herself lifted and borne upward, lowered gently to the bed a moment later.

He stretched his length beside her, propping himself on an elbow so he could look his fill, his regard slow and unhurried. Kathryn blushed fiercely, her gaze shying away until she finally gathered the courage to glance at him again. A wealth of unexpected tenderness lurked in the depths of his eyes. His expression made her throat ache.

His hand splayed possessively on the naked swell of her belly. "You've naught to be ashamed of," he whispered hoarsely. "I tell you true, sweet, you're beautiful. Everything a man could want . . . everything *I* want."

She clung to the words and to him. Turning her head, she blindly sought his mouth. His kiss was tender and piercingly sweet. Tugging her hands to his chest, he wordlessly invited her touch. Her fingers crept across his chest, tangling in the dense dark fur as she explored his skin, warm and faintly damp. Her touch was shy and untutored but soon grew more daring. The muscles of his stomach clenched as she ventured lower. Her knuckles grazed the ridged plane of his abdomen. Cool fingers curled once again around his straining hardness. Both shy and eager, her small hand shaped and curved, gently stroking with the tips of her fingers, acquainting herself with his satin-and-steel texture, his searing heat and fire. His hand engulfed hers, clamping tight over hers as he showed her the way of it. And then he gritted his teeth against a pleasure so excruciating it bordered on pain.

A groan tore from deep within his chest. Unable to bear her sweet torture any longer, he bore her gently onto her back, hunger wild and rampant in the urgent demand of his mouth on hers. With his thumbs he teased her nipples to aching little buds, over and over until she was nearly delirious with pleasure. Her fingers knotted in his hair.

Heat stormed through her like molten fire. She moaned when at last his mouth encompassed the dark straining center, tugging gently with a rhythm that tipped the world upside down.

But there was more. His fingers stole through the downy nest that shielded the secret folds of her femininity, stroking and parting and teasing, rousing her to the brink of madness. Her heart plunged into a wild frenzy. She thrust up against him, her hips unconsciously circling and seeking those maddeningly elusive fingers, uncaring that he might think her wanton and bold. Her fingers clenched and unclenched against his shoulders. Tiny cries of pleasure burst from deep inside her.

His body was on fire for her. The blood was pounding in his head, roaring through his ears. His shaft was swollen and engorged. The long lonely weeks of emptiness and frustration . . . Need and passion combined, nearly blinding him to all but the compelling urge to plunge deep within her satin heat. It was then that he felt it . . . a slight stirring where her belly pressed his, a reminder of the tiny life sheltered deep within her womb. He raised himself above her, hauling in a stinging lungful of air as he struggled to control his rampaging desire.

Tension strained his arms as he braced himself above her. She touched the rugged hollows of his cheeks, explored the sensuous curve of that beautifully shaped mouth that brought her to the brink of the heavens. She trailed her fingers over his smooth shoulders, explored the tightness of his arms, loving the sleekness of his skin, the resilience of keenly honed muscle. Their eyes met and melded as if a sizzling flame arced between them, and it was in that soul-shattering instant he came inside her.

His entrance was excruciatingly slow and careful, his penetration shallow as he began to move within her. She whimpered, wanting his straining fullness buried full and deep inside her—so deep they were no longer two, but one . . .

Her eyes opened. Her nails dug into his arms. "Please," she gasped. "Oh, Guy, please . . ."

The naked pleading in her tone beat at his resolve. The thrusting, seeking movements of her hips against his wordlessly conveyed her need. A sound of half-frustration, half-surrender escaped his throat.

One powerful thrust took him clear to the heart of her.

Her sob of joy tore at his control. "Kathryn," he groaned. "Oh, God, this is so . . ." He shuddered against a pleasure so acute it was nearly unbearable. When she reached for him, he caught her hands. Their fingers locked together. Entwined. Inseparable. She arched her hips to take all he would give and more . . .

His mouth covered hers. He drank in her mindless cries, each gasping little whimper, each tremor of her quivering flesh clinging tightly to his. The tempo of his thrusts was deep and slow, gradually gaining power and momentum, until the pounding rhythm inside them both reached a fever pitch.

Shivers raced the length of his spine, heralding fulfillment. He cast his head back, the cords of his neck taut, his features twisted into a grimace of pleasure. Amidst the frantic thunder of her heart, Kathryn knew a surge of boundless joy, her pleasure expanding all the more because of his. Then suddenly she was caught in the same explosive rush to completion, hurtled high aloft. His thrusts reached a crescendo. She felt herself swept ever higher, soaring like a falcon on the wind until at last she reached that pinnacle among the clouds. Release claimed her, pulsing through her in wave after delirious wave. She was only dimly aware of crying out his name.

When it was over he eased to his back and tugged the furs over their heated bodies. A sinewed arm swept her tight against his side. Fingers that were incredibly gentle brushed the hair from her flushed cheeks. A long, lingering kiss of infinite sweetness met an eager welcome in lips soft, warm, and willing.

Exhausted, sated, content, they slept.

Chapter 17

Such was not the case a sennight later.

    Kathryn had excused herself early, as she had these last few nights. Oddly enough, marriage to Guy had not yet proved a battleground. Guy had seen to it that her duties as lady of the manor were light, and Kathryn was secretly grateful. Though her pregnancy had not made her pale or wan or sickly, by evening she drooped like a wilted flower, so tired she could scarcely stand—this evening was no exception. Guy had immediately rose to accompany her but she shook her head and waved him back to the game of chess he played with one of his knights.

    Upstairs in their chamber, she shed her kirtle and crawled quickly into bed, shivering a little against the chill. Beyond the shuttered windows, the world lay hushed and still. Early in the day, a dense veil of fog crept across the land. From the tower window she watched trailing fingers of mist stealing through the valley, wrapping like silent tentacles around the trees, until the earth lay cocooned beneath a murky shroud. One of Guy's men had stomped into the hall, complaining that he could scarcely see his hand in front of his face.

It was little wonder that when Kathryn fell asleep, as she had her first night back at Sedgewick, she dreamed she was running through the fog, lost and alone . . . The looming shadow once again raced at her heels. Her heart pounded with terror, for the thing was evil itself. On and on she ran blindly, damp and perspiring, her lungs heaving as she struggled for breath.

But alas, suddenly her way was blocked by a solid wall of stone. Behind her, eerie laughter raised the hair on her neck. With a gasp she spun to face her uncle. Blood poured from the jagged slash on his throat.

"You thought you were so clever, didn't you, girl?" Wet lips pulled into a sneer. "You thought you could be rid of me. You thought you could have Ashbury! You are much like me, girl, more than you know. Like me, 'tis your wont to covet what can never be yours. But now you will have nothing— nothing!—for I will take you with me to the fiery pits of hell!" And he threw back his bloodied head and began to laugh, and laugh . . . and suddenly the shadow fell over her. She was immersed in smothering folds of blackness. Hands snatched at her, clawing her, touching her everywhere, clammy and cold, and all at once she knew . . .

The shadow was death. It was death that stalked her, death that sought to seize her in its grasp and squeeze the life from her.

"Nay! I am not like you, Uncle . . . I am not!" She sobbed wildly, twisting and thrashing, desperate to evade the chilling hands of death. "Oh, please, Guy, you must help me," she screamed. "Guy . . . *Guy!*" But there was nowhere to go, no one to help her, of a certainty not Guy, for he had never wanted her. No doubt he would be heartily glad to find himself rid of her . . .

"Kathryn!" Hard hands curled around her shoulders. She fought wildly. It took a moment before her frantic senses were able to register another presence. Her eyes opened. Her scream turned to a garbled half-sob as she saw Guy hovering above her, and he was not cold and icy, but warm and solid and strong.

"Hush, sweet. 'Tis just a dream, that's all."

She clung to him, shaking, her body damp and perspiring. "I am not like him," she cried desperately. "You must believe me, Guy. I am not like him!"

His arms engulfed her. He tucked her head beneath his chin, his harsh features etched with concern. "Who?" he murmured. "Who do you mean?"

"Richard." Her fingers clenched and unclenched in the front of his tunic. "I—I am not evil and cunning like him, Guy, I am not!"

She lifted her face to his. He could feel her shaking against him. Her cheeks were streaked with tears, her mouth tremulous and vulnerable. The pleading in those misty green eyes speared his heart. "Nay, love. You are not like Richard," he whispered, and knew it for the truth. He gently pushed damp tumbled strands of ebony from her brow. "Were you dreaming of him?"

Resting her cheek against his chest, she nodded slowly, loving the steady throb of his heart beneath her ear, the sheltering protection of his embrace. She gave a breathy little sigh, wishing they could stay like this forever, but Guy was waiting. Her voice halting, she told him of her dream, ending with a shudder. "Guy, I—I do not want to die. I—I do not even like to think about it."

His arms tightened. "It must be the babe," he mused. "Are you afraid of the birth?"

"A little," she admitted, then shivered suddenly. "Richard's wife died in childbed."

With his fingertips he massaged the tightness between her shoulder blades. "There is no reason to think the birth will be anything but normal, Kathryn. If the babe were overly large, you might have a difficult time. But judging from the size of you, the babe must be small—"

"Small! Too small, do you think? Oh, Guy, what if—"

"Kathryn—" He sighed, a rueful smile tugging at his lips. "—I fear I am alarming you when I only thought to reassure you. Do not worry overmuch, for I would guess you'll have an easy time of it."

"Easy!" Her lips parted indignantly. " 'Tis well and good for *you* to say it will be easy," she muttered crossly. "You are not the one who must endure it."

He smiled at her sputtering, sliding his fingers through the silken length of her hair. Kathryn rubbed her cheek against the soft wool covering his shoulder. For a moment each of them were immersed in their own thoughts. Then finally, her troubled gaze sought his.

"Guy," she said quietly, "who murdered Richard?"

She had startled him; she could feel it in the sudden tension that gripped his body. Then, just as suddenly, she felt the tension seep from his limbs. He arched a roguish brow. "I thought you were convinced it was I."

A spurt of guilt shot through her. "Nay," she confided with a shake of her head. "Not for a long time now." A tiny frown appeared between slender dark brows. "You accused me of murdering him," she recalled suddenly. "But it was not I, Guy!"

He smiled crookedly and pressed a fingertip against the indignant pout of her lips. "I'm not sure I ever truly believed you guilty, Kathryn." His smile ebbed. "Likely as not, the secret of Richard's murderer went with him to his grave."

His hands swept down to encircle her waist. He encountered the sticky dampness of the chemise she'd worn to bed. He pulled back with an impatient exclamation. "You're soaked, woman. Come, we'd better get this off you." Even as he spoke, he'd already begun the task. He pulled the linen cloth up and over her head, the tips of his fingers warm and pleasantly rough as they skimmed her thighs and ribs, leaving a trail of fire in their wake. He disposed of his own clothing just as quickly and slid in beside her.

When he cradled her against his length, she pressed against him with a breathy sigh. Her terror had subsided, but not her desperate need to be held. Her fingers crept up to tangle in the furry darkness on his chest. She burrowed her face into the musky hollow of his shoulder, needing the reassurance only his nearness could give.

His thumb slipped beneath the fall of her hair, caressing the tender skin of her nape and sending tiny pulses of pleasure winging through her. "It occurs to me," she heard him say, "that I've yet to give you a wedding gift."

All at once Kathryn felt she'd been plunged into a vat of frigid cold. "There is no need," she faltered. "Indeed, I—I would not feel right in accepting such a gift."

"And why not?"

"Because you gained no marriage portion. Need I remind you that my uncle sold my dower lands?" She swallowed miserably. "Guy, I've brought nothing to this marriage."

His eyes darkened as he glimpsed her distress. "Ah, but you are wrong," he said huskily. Deliberately he splayed his hand on the hard curve of her belly. "You bring the gift of life, a gift beyond price—mayhap the greatest gift of all."

His tenderness wrenched at her chest. Her throat clogged with some powerful, unnamed emotion, she wound her arms around his neck and blindly sought his mouth. Guy took full advantage and leisurely sampled the honeyed sweetness of those tempting lips. When at last he released her mouth, he trailed a fingertip down her nose. "Now tell me, wench. Give me some hint of the gift you would have, not something you have need of, but something you desire very dearly."

Unbidden—unwanted—a maelstrom of longing rose within her. Mayhap it was this strange mood that had sprung up between them—his gentleness was wholly disarming. But in that moment, all she yearned for was that he truly care for her—nay, not out of duty or obligation, but straight from the heart. Perchance even to love her . . .

She quickly relinquished the thought, just a little appalled at the direction her mind had taken. Someday mayhap, Guy might come to hold her in some affection, if only because of the child they would share. But he would never, ever love her . . .

"Well?" His crooked smile made her heart catch.

She bit her lip, her manner hesitant. "I could have anything I wanted?"

"Aye, anything within my power to give."

"Then I would have you grant Gerda her freedom."

"Gerda! Kathryn, this is the gift you would seek?"

She laid her fingers against his jaw. "It is the only thing I wish," she whispered.

His hand lifted to cover hers. His eyes snared hers as he pressed a kiss to her fingers. " 'Tis good as done, milady."

That rare, sweet smile just before she ducked her head and snuggled against him told him she was well pleased with herself. But inside Guy was still stunned that she asked nothing for herself—a new gown or some bauble perhaps. At times he was certain he knew her mind as well as his own ... at times like this he felt he knew her not at all.

She fell asleep quickly, but Guy made no move to put her from him. Instead he held her, unmindful of the way her hair tickled his chin. He enjoyed feeling the rise and fall of her breasts against his side, the warm womanly softness of her. A rueful smile tugged at his lips as he thought of all their tempestuous encounters. It seemed nothing less than a miracle that she lay so trusting and pliant in his arms.

But she had come to him willingly—nay, eagerly!—every night since their marriage. And every night he had held her thus, his body physically satiated beyond anything he'd ever known before. It should have been enough—if only it were! Yet he felt oddly out of step, as if something vitally important—and damnably elusive—were missing.

Kathryn belonged to him. She was now his wife. She would share his life, bear his children. Even as he knew the greatest of pride, a bitter ache swelled his chest. What mystery, what madness was this, that this one small slip of a girl was able to rouse such hunger, such longing in him? But he had long since acknowledged he could not break this web of need and desire she spun so easily about him.

He thought of Elaine. His life. His love. He braced himself inwardly, waiting for the familiar, stabbing pain to strike his soul.

It did not come.

Shame pricked him deeply, for he had held fast to her memory for so long now. He'd thought his heart taken for all eternity. But that was before a dark-haired enchantress had swept into his life . . .

Kathryn . . . He dared to breathe her name . . . And then he dared even more . . . Did he love her?

Elaine's image spun through his mind: eyes like a summer sky, flaxen hair floating about her like a halo of gold, so delicate and sweet. With Elaine, love had been a gentle wind to ease the spirit, a soothing balm to heal and comfort.

And then there was Kathryn. With her he felt passion and fire, a blaze that flamed his senses to white-hot coals and scorched his soul. Even now, it took but a fleeting glance down the length of her and the dormant flames of desire flared hot and bright within him.

Her hair tumbled over his bare chest, as black and shiny as a raven's wing. She was strong, he acknowledged, fierce and defiant, with a temper to match his own. Though she possessed no sword or shield, she had fought Richard. She had fought for Ashbury. And she had fought him . . . Yet now she lay curled against him, as trustingly as a child, and he was filled with an aching tenderness.

Did he love her? He knew only that Kathryn made him feel things he'd never thought he could feel for any woman again. But he could not deny that his love for Elaine was vastly different than whatever it was that he felt for Kathryn.

Yet she had only to ask, and he would gladly move heaven and earth itself . . .

A weary bleakness slipped over him. It was said that he was a great warrior, for he'd fought and won many battles in his day. But he'd never fought one quite so fierce as the one before him now. It was then that he realized . . . the greatest battle was fought alone.

The greatest battle of all was with the heart.

The next afternoon Gerda burst into Kathryn's chamber. "Lady Kathryn," she cried. "You will not believe this but I—I am free! Sir Guy no longer holds me bound to my father's oath."

Kathryn set aside her sewing. "Aha," she teased. "And how did Sir Michael take this news?"

The girl blushed and clapped her hands together. "He returned only this morning from a visit with his father—and—oh, Lady Kathryn, this is almost like a dream come true! His father has granted Michael a small manor in Dorset. Michael says the manor house is in poor condition and will take many months to repair. But he said this time he will not take no for an answer—we are to be married as soon as the manor house is finished, mayhap as soon as late spring!" Kathryn laughed, for Gerda's elation was something to behold. Her liquid brown eyes shone as brightly as a summer morn.

The next moment, though, she tipped her head to the side. "Milady," she said softly, "why do I sense that you are not surprised?"

"Oh, but I am," Kathryn retorted gaily. "Though I did not know about Sir Michael and the manor."

Dawning realization crept into Gerda's expression. "Wait," she said slowly. "Was this your doing?"

"The choice was Guy's," Kathryn reminded her. A tiny smile twitched at her lips. "Although I did drop a hint as to my feelings in the matter."

"Granting my freedom—" Gerda shook her head. " 'Tis no small thing, to be sure." She knelt before Kathryn, her expression soft and dreamy. "He must love you very much," she murmured.

The happiness in Kathryn's heart wilted. Love was the one thing she could never even *hope* to expect from Guy. Yet Gerda's features contained such shining certainty that Kathryn could not find it in her to object.

Instead she said softly, "You and Sir Michael love each other. 'Tis only right that the two of you should be together."

"Milady, you have just changed my whole life." Tears sprang to Gerda's eyes. "How can I ever thank you?"

Kathryn laid a hand on her shoulder. "You just have."

Gerda clasped her hand, her gaze fixed searchingly on Kathryn's face. "I—I cannot tell you the joy this day has brought me. And I long for nothing more than for you to be happy, too."

"Then set your mind at ease, Gerda, for I am happy." She told herself it was not an out-and-out lie, for she was not unhappy. Indeed, she was as happy as she could possibly be . . . for a woman whose husband did not love her.

November was wet and rainy, interspersed with brief periods of warmth and sunshine. Early December found winter dropping its chill upon the land. The stream froze solid and a glittering veil of snow softened the contours of the hills and valleys, but the bitter freeze cut to the bone. Those who ventured without did not do so for long; they soon returned to huddle around the roaring fire in the hall.

Throughout those long weeks, Kathryn found herself besieged by fear and doubt. She shared Guy's chamber and his bed—and the pleasure therein as well. But though her nights were spent in the warmth and comfort of his arms, her days were fraught with worry. She was well aware he hadn't

married her because of any tender regard for her . . .
mayhap he only meant to make certain he had his
heir and spare. After all, he had already fathered a
son by Elaine, the woman he had loved.

And what of *their* child, the child whose life
burgeoned within her? If their child was a girl,
would Guy love her less than he loved Peter? Or
because the babe's mother was her—Kathryn—and
not Elaine . . .

All these thoughts and more disturbed her. Her
restless soul found little ease from its torment. Yet
she could not banish the frail seed of hope that took
root within her, for Guy was so tender and sweet
she could almost believe he *did* love her . . . or was
she only seeing what she wished to see?

She did not know. Heaven help her, but she
did not.

She and Gerda spent much of their time sewing for Gerda and the babe, but there were times
Kathryn chafed at the enforced confinement. When
Gerda asked her to come along with her and Peter
to the stream one afternoon, that was all the encour-
agement Kathryn needed.

They dressed warmly, layer upon layer. Just
as they departed the gates, a sudden whirlwind
slapped icy crystals of snow against her cheeks,
making her gasp and inhale a stinging mouthful
of air. But although the temperature was frigid,
the sun shone glorious and bright, and the sky
was a brilliant vivid blue. All at once Kathryn felt
free and unfettered as she had not felt in months.
Catching Peter's eye, she blew a huge puff of frosty
air that sailed away with the breeze. Peter giggled
delightedly.

At the stream Gerda tied horses' shinbones to her
boots and Peter's; holding his hand, she gingerly
led the boy onto the frozen surface of the stream.

Kathryn watched in fascination as she showed Peter
how to skim the ice, pushing himself along with a
stick. She began to glide faster and faster, her braid
flying out behind her, her expression alive with
excitement. Kathryn sighed wistfully, wishing she
could join them, but she knew a fall might prove
disastrous. With Gerda's help, Peter did quite well,
but when he tried on his own he went sprawling
across the ice on his belly. He ran crying into
Kathryn's waiting embrace. She tenderly hugged
and soothed him, then coaxed him back onto the
ice with Gerda.

The brisk air tired Peter, though Kathryn needed
no such excuse when she retired later that night.
Guy had been gone for several days and had only
just returned that evening—she readily admitted,
at least to herself, that she had missed him sorely!
She rose from the trestle table with her regrets, then
laid her fingertips on Guy's shoulder. "Will you be
long, milord?" she murmured.

He gave a slight shake of his head, twisting slightly and carrying her hand to his lips. His gaze spoke
much more eloquently—and intimately, for within
those silver eyes was a heated glow that promised
much.

In their chamber she left but a single candle burning. She thought to disrobe quickly and slip into
bed to await him, for she was still shy about Guy
seeing her bare when she was so misshapen. Were
she slim she was sure she'd not have felt her embarrassment so keenly, but alas, slim she was not!
She felt the weight of her pregnancy more with
each day.

But she had scarcely loosened her hair and shook
it free about her shoulders than Guy made his
appearance. Standing before the blazing fire in
the hearth, Kathryn recognized the exact instant

he stepped within. Though she could not see him, nor hear him move, her senses clamored an alert. A melting heat fanned low in her middle. His sheer presence made her quiver inside. Then she felt the sweep of powerful arms coming around her from behind, cradling her, cradling her womb.

His hands moved boldly, fingers exploring, tracing the swelling curve lightly. "Guy!" Her objection was feeble indeed. " 'Tis not decent that a man should want to touch a woman so!"

He closed his hands with deliberate possessiveness over the mounds of her breasts, grown delightfully full and ripe. His smile was utterly wicked. "It is when the woman is his wife."

The warmth of his breath rushing past her ear made her weak inside. But when his hands descended once more over her middle she moaned. "Not when she is with child and looks like a cow," she grumbled. With that she turned to face him.

Knowing she carried his child filled him with masculine pride. In his mind, the swell of her middle did not detract from her beauty in the least. With her hair tumbling like tousled black silk about her shoulders and hips, she looked young and appealing and incredibly lovely, a veritable feast for his eyes.

Husky laughter rumbled from his chest. "Despite this precious burden you carry, you are as comely as ever and well you know it."

Before she could protest he plucked her kirtle up and over her head, leaving her clad in only her thin linen chemise. Pulling her to the bed, he settled her on his lap, chuckling at the lovely tide of color that rushed to her cheeks. He'd have bared her completely were it not for the faint anxiety he glimpsed in her eyes. But he was not to be dissuaded, so he splayed his fingers wide against the tautness of her belly, slowly stroking, chuckling again as he felt an unmistakable kick beneath his palm.

His fingers lightly traced a tiny protrusion as he mused aloud. "What is this, I wonder? A foot? An elbow, do you think?" The jab came again, even stronger this time. His crooked grin was irreverent. "Ah, and this prodding here . . . mayhap this proves the babe is a lad—his father's son, indeed!"

Crimson and mortified, Kathryn didn't know whether to laugh or cry. She settled for burying her face in his shoulder.

He gently brushed the hair from her cheek, then slipped his fingers beneath her chin, commanding her attention. Though he was smiling, he was no longer teasing. "I have no wish to embarrass you, sweet. But this is my child, too, and all of this is as new to me as it is to you." His tone grew husky. "I would feel him grow before he is born, as you do."

She spoke unthinkingly. "But—how can this be new to you when you already have a son? Surely before Peter was born you—" She broke off, stunned to find all expression wiped clean from Guy's features.

She heard his voice, hard and brittle. "I was bound for the Holy Land when Peter was born, Kathryn. And I learned of his existence while sitting in a bloody dungeon in Toulouse more than a year later."

Kathryn stared at him, half-afraid to even speak. "You were never with Elaine while she carried Peter?"

His silence was never-ending, the thrust of his jaw taut and unyielding . . . condemning? Staring into his carefully controlled features, she sensed she had done something wrong, but what? When at last he shook his head, all at once she realized . . .

this was the first time Elaine's name had passed between them.

Too late she realized her mistake. He put her gently from him and though his manner was not harsh, his tenderness was gone. An elusive hurt twisted her insides. She nearly cried out in anguish, for his pain . . . and hers.

Elaine was dead and gone. Kathryn did not pretend to misunderstand Guy's reaction to the mention of his dead wife's name. She tried convincing herself it did not matter that he cared so deeply after all this time. But it did. God help her, it did.

A hollow emptiness welled up inside her. She crawled beneath the furs and curled into a tight miserable ball. Guy had moved to stand before the fire. How long he remained there, she did not know. She tossed and turned in a vain attempt to sleep, but a nagging ache persisted in the small of her back. Her hand crept around to massage it.

She had scarcely begun than she felt Guy's weight settle beside her. His fingers brushed hers aside and pressed gently, kneading and stroking. Though no words passed between them, a feeling akin to relief seeped through her; she soon fell into a deep, dreamless sleep.

She woke in the middle of the night to find herself alone in the bed. Guy stood near the window. An errant glimmer of moonlight threw his features into stark relief. She sensed his distance and did not know how to breach it; it was as if he had retreated to a realm where she could never belong. Tears stung her eyelids, hot and burning. Stark yearning rose within her. She wanted his arms around her, not only in the heat of passion, but protecting her, soothing her, cherishing her . . . She longed to plead for him to sweep her in his embrace as he had done earlier. Pride alone crammed the entreaty back in her throat.

She must have made some small sound, for he turned his gaze toward the bed. In an instant he was beside her. His knuckles grazed the smoothness of her cheek. "I'm sorry," he murmured. "Did I wake you?"

Kathryn shook her head. Her throat was clogged so that speech was impossible. She caught at his hands. "Please," she whispered, despising the betraying little quiver in her voice. "Come back to bed."

He slipped in beside her. Drawing her against his side, he ran his fingers idly over the curve of her shoulder, but his touch seemed absentminded, hardly the caress she craved. There had been other nights they had not come together in passion, yet somehow Kathryn had always thought he refrained in deference to her condition. Tonight, however, she felt the loss keenly.

Though the chamber was rife with shadowed darkness, she need not see him to visualize that splendid frame, lean and hard. Heart-stoppingly aware of his nudity, she drew a deep sharp breath.

His arm anchored her close, yet it was not nearly close enough. The need to touch him was overwhelming. She curled her nails into her palms but it was no use. She craved his nearness. Her fingers crept up to tangle in the hair on his chest. She pressed her naked breasts against him, uncaring if he thought her bold or wanton.

"Kathryn—" There was a deep, rough catch in his voice. He twisted his head upon the pillow, and she felt his eyes upon her, dark and questioning.

She made no answer. Instead she eased up over him so that she could reach his mouth. Her lips grazed his, the merest butterfly caress. When she met no resistance, she deepened the kiss further, letting her tongue limn the seam of his lips. A curious sort of power filled her, for she could feel his tension, the shudder that shook him as her tongue danced evocatively against his.

Courage bloomed within her, even as she grew heavy and feverish with need. With reckless abandon, she coasted her fingers down his chest, to lower regions, a tentative exploration that began with shy clumsiness. Feeling the ridged muscles of his stomach clench, she hovered uncertainly, her heart beating high in her throat. Her fingers uncurled slowly—straining heat surged bold and hard against her palm.

Guy inhaled sharply. "Sweet—" His hand clamped almost convulsively over her smaller one. He gave a shaky laugh, his heart about to burst through the wall of his chest. "You are nearing your eighth month now. As much as I want you, this may not be wise—"

He wanted her. *He wanted her*. His words thrummed through her mind, flooding her being like warm, sweet wine. A dark torrent of longing rushed through her, overriding all but the deep, driving need for him to make love to her.

She slipped her arms around his neck. "It will be weeks yet," she whispered. "And I am fine, Guy, truly."

Her lips hovered temptingly . . . ah, so temptingly, over his. Her hair swirled all around him like a dark cloud of midnight, trapping him in silken enticement. The cushioned fullness of her breasts was crushed against his chest, burning him like twin peaks of fire. Her unexpected offering was more temptation than Guy could withstand, the promise of ecstasy too much to withhold.

"Please, Guy," she whispered huskily. "Please . . ." She turned her head so that their lips just barely met.

He was lost. With a groan he pressed her back into the softness of the bed. His fingers wound into her hair. He took her mouth in a soul-blistering kiss, sliding his palms beneath her hips, lifting . . . lowering . . . plunging into the hot velvet of her sheath, stroking and seeking, harder and faster . . .

Ah, such sweet, piercing pleasure! Kathryn cried out softly. His stretching fullness inside her unleashed a storm of passion and splendor. She clung to his muscled shoulders. His skin was hot and sleek like sun-warmed satin. Again and again he bound their hips together, a ritual dance of pagan glory, the muscles of his buttocks churning and flexing. A tempest brewed inside her, whipping into a frenzy of pure sensation. Her blood pounded in a scalding rush along her veins. Release came in a blinding explosion of thunder and lightning, so torrid and tempestuous she was left quaking in the aftermath.

A long time later she felt the rigidness slowly seep from his body. He eased slightly away, relieving her of the pressure of his weight. His lips feathered over her neck, the fragile line of her jaw, the delicate sweep of her cheeks in an unhurried quest for her mouth. And it was there he tasted the salty warmth of a tear trapped between their lips.

A low exclamation broke from him. "Kathryn!" He raised his head to stare at her in stunned confusion. "What is it? Did I hurt you?"

She pressed her hot face into the pillow. "Nay," she said on a strangled breath. "You did not hurt me."

He cursed softly, slipping his knuckles beneath her chin and lifting her face to his, refusing to let her hide. "Kathryn, tell me! What is wrong?"

Kathryn swallowed. Through sheer effort of will she offered a tremulous smile. " 'Tis nothing," she managed. "I just . . . oh, Guy, I just need you to . . . to hold me."

Powerful arms wrapped her close and tight. The flutter of whispered words grazed her temple. He held her tenderly. Sweetly. With such gentle concern that she clung to him all the harder.

Her hair was a wild tangle spread across the breadth of his chest. His fingers combed idly through the silken strands, sifting lightly, letting errant tendrils trail over his hand until at last he twined it over and over around his palm. Through the silvered darkness, she thought she detected a smile.

All at once Kathryn could no longer control the dictates of her mind—it wandered where it would and she could not stop it.

That smile . . . Did Guy pretend the hair wrapped so possessively round his fist was as pale and gold as summer wheat? Did he even now compare dark to fair, past wife to present? The pain that ripped through her was agony. It was like a knife slicing into her, plunging deeper and deeper. She wished she could forget the anguish this night had wrought—if only she could! Oh, she knew she had pleased him . . . but had Elaine pleased him more?

She drew a sharp, painful breath. It was her own name she wanted on his lips, his mind so filled with her that thoughts of no other dared intrude. But Kathryn was suddenly terrified, for although she was the one he held and touched and caressed . . .

Did his heart still dwell with another?

Chapter 18

S everal days later a missive arrived from Elizabeth. Kathryn was resting when a page delivered it to her chamber. She quickly hurried to the bench below the window and broke the seal eagerly. She had just finished skimming the contents when Guy entered.

"I hear you've a letter from Elizabeth."

Kathryn nodded, her eyes shining. "She and Hugh are going to be married!"

Guy smiled indulgently, but his casual air was deceiving. Inwardly his nerves were humming. He crossed to her, his keen, watchful gaze roving her delicate features. Fingers beneath her chin, he brought her eyes to his. "And does this please you?"

"Aye," Kathryn admitted, then smiled. "Elizabeth is ecstatic about the wedding. She loves Hugh and Hugh loves her. How could I begrudge my sister her happiness?"

Perhaps a better question was whether she begrudged Hugh his possession of Ashbury . . . Guy curbed the thought. He did not know—he had no desire to know. The subject of Ashbury was one both he and Kathryn mentioned but seldom.

He was quick to note the faint shadow which crept into her eyes. Tenderly imprisoning both her hands in his, he pulled her to her feet. "What fickleness is this that you frown so already?" he teased. "As Elizabeth's elder sister, have you decided that Hugh is not good enough for her after all?"

She shook her head. "Of course not. Hugh is an honorable and worthy man," she said quietly, startling Guy just a little with such a ready admission. She hesitated. "In her letter Elizabeth said she would understand if we could not attend, but . . . oh, Guy, I do so wish that I could be there!" Her tone was imploring.

Guy went very still inside. "When is the wedding to be?"

She did not notice his sudden tension. "Several days before Epiphany."

"Epiphany! Kathryn, the babe is due not long after that. Why, you cannot travel then."

"The babe is not due until the end of January," she pointed out. "I should not think that I would deliver much before then."

"You have no way of knowing for certain. I'm sorry, Kathryn, but we cannot attend Elizabeth's wedding."

His thin-lipped stare caught her off guard. "You refuse to even consider it?"

Guy's jaw clamped shut. He dropped her hands, his expression as black as a thundercloud. He could not control the bitterness that abruptly seeped inside him. The darker side of reason made him wonder . . . Did Kathryn truly care so little about her life and the life of their child? His mind raced on. Mayhap she didn't care if the babe died—mayhap she did not want *his* child.

"Aye," he said, an edge of steel in his tone. "I'll not consider it, for I'll not have you delivering my child on some rutted, frozen road between here and Ashbury."

His sharpness stabbed at her, but she tipped her chin, determined not to show her hurt. Even as a part of her acknowledged he was right, something deep within her would not let her give in so easily. "I'd not be alone," she was compelled to argue. "Guy, please! Elizabeth is my only sister! I—I would be with her on the day of her wedding if only I could!"

"You plead so prettily, sweet. But I wonder— why are you so determined?" Some devil inside took him in thrall and refused to release him. His lip curled. "Mayhap it's not Elizabeth you wish to be with at all, milady. Mayhap you cannot wait to see your Roderick!"

Kathryn did not stop to think. She simply reacted with all the rebellious fury that leaped within her, drawing back her hand and dealing a stinging, open-handed slap to the bronzed hardness of his cheek.

His response was instantaneous and relentless. His hands closed about her wrists like iron manacles. Anger kindled in his eyes. They blazed like molten silver. "By God," he bit out from between clenched teeth, "I'll allow you that once, but do not think to ever—ever!—strike me again."

"Then do not insult me so!" she cried. She twisted against him but his grip was merciless.

"I see no insult here, milady." Soft though his tone was, the words were fairly flung at her. "Indeed, I see naught but truth. You cannot deny it was Roderick you sought to marry—nay, not once, but twice!"

His pitiless condemnation tore her to shreds. "Guy," she choked out. "You forget that—"

"I forget nothing, Kathryn, nothing! Not once have you run to me. Nay, you must always run *from* me. Ah, and we both know who you seek as your savior!"

A flicker of fear ran through her when he dragged her as close as her swollen belly would allow. Her heart thudding wildly, she strained against his hold, stunned at the barely restrained violence that seethed within him.

He lowered his head so that his hot breath rushed past her cheek. "I may have been the first to lay with you," he said tightly. "But tell me this, milady. That night at the monastery . . . did I find you and Roderick too early—" His lips twisted. "—or too late?"

He did not wait for an answer, merely thrust her away and spun about as if he could no longer stand the sight of her. He strode from the room, slamming the door so hard the rafters shook. Kathryn gave an impotent little cry of rage, but imbedded in her fury was anguish, a world of it. What he accused her of was unspeakable . . . unforgivable! Did he truly believe she had lain with Roderick?

Her lungs burned from the effort it took not to cry. Raw pain spilled through her, and she stumbled to the bed numbly. And then the tears began to come, slow and scalding. She had fought long and hard against Guy—and against herself. But in that mind-splitting instant, Kathryn could no longer hide from her feelings any more than she could hide the torment in her soul.

She loved him. *She loved him.*
Helplessly.
Hopelessly.
Endlessly.

Her stormy heart knew no peace.

There was no comfort in the truth, no sweet joy of fulfillment to be gained from loving Guy. He had touched her and held her, while the winds of passion blew fierce and tempestuous. And he had held her close, his sinewed arms a sheltering haven of comfort and strength . . .

Never had he claimed to love her.

It pained her greatly to admit that she was afraid. Afraid of the future. Afraid Guy would never grow to love her . . .

Yield to me, Kathryn. Yield . . .

Time and again she remembered his fervent demand that long-ago night. She *had* yielded, body and soul . . .

But she dared not let him know it.

Never would she willingly confess her love to him—not when he neither wanted or needed it. Indeed, he had enough power over her already! Even in this mockery they called a marriage, he snatched her will from her. He'd not even asked if she would marry him—he had simply gone ahead and done the deed . . . and she had let him! Didn't that make her a fool? A pawn?

Nay, she decided over and over again, she did not love Guy. She *would* not love him. She must not weaken, for then he would truly be master of her heart.

And her heart was the one thing he could never force her to surrender, the one thing she could bestow freely, the one thing that was truly her own.

Yet despite all her resolve, all her determination, Kathryn sorely missed all that had gone before . . .

For a time, a curious kind of peace had existed between her and Guy. She had come to know him as the man she had refused to see before—fair and principled and honest, unwavering in his beliefs. Aye, he was fierce and warlike when provoked to anger, yet he was also sensitive and caring and so very, very gentle. He was a man greatly respected and admired, and the people of Sedgewick loved him dearly.

Kathryn did not broach the subject of attending Elizabeth's wedding again. She was convinced their argument that day had little to do with whether or not she should travel—Kathryn would not soon forget Guy's veiled accusation that she lay with Roderick. Not for an instant did she consider he might be jealous—he did not care enough to be jealous. Guy was a man who guarded his own closely. His arrogant high-handedness was spawned of possessiveness, no more, no less.

Their bitter exchange that fateful day had changed everything. The measure of closeness that reigned so briefly had been shattered by all they dared to speak . . . by all they dared *not* speak.

And so they shared their meals together, shared the warmth of their bodies in the chill of long winter nights. But there were no tender kisses, no heated caresses, no passionate joinings that left them weak and gasping for breath.

They were strangers, strangers who were together . . . yet ever distant.

Kathryn did not delude herself. In all this time, they had done naught but come full circle.

One evening she crooned softly to Peter, who was so tired he was about to drop on his feet, yet still fought sleep. She lay down beside him in his bed and let him press his chubby hand against the life in her womb. He was intensely curious, and she spoke to him often about his soon-to-be brother or sister, so that he would be prepared when the babe finally came.

After a while his lashes began to flutter. Soon he slept. But Kathryn remained where she was, content to feel his warmth curled close to her side.

She pressed a kiss to his forehead and hugged him tight, for she had come to love Peter even before she had loved his father. As if not to be outdone, the babe thumped and moved within her, a great rolling motion that made her stomach ripple.

A smile curved her lips. Would she bear a lad or a lass? She trailed a fingertip along the downy curve of Peter's cheek, her eyes tracing the miniature features so like his father's. If the babe were a boy, would he look like Peter? He was a beautiful child, tall for his age, his build sturdy, his shoulders wide despite his youth. Peter would grow to be strong and handsome, every bit as handsome as Guy. Nay, she'd not mind at all if their child resembled Peter.

One morning in mid-January she woke with a dull ache in the small of her back. She eased to her side and lay for a while, but the nagging ache persisted no matter what her position. At last she rose with a grimace twisting her lovely features. But her bare feet had no sooner touched the cold floor than a torrent of liquid gushed down her legs.

That was how Guy found her—staring in dumbfounded amazement at the puddle around her feet. Her gaze slowly lifted and she shook her head. "Guy," she began in bemusement, "I do not know—"

He had already rushed to her side. "It's the birth waters," he said urgently. "Christ, your time has come!" He bent and lifted her carefully in his arms, easing her onto the bed.

He bent over her. "When did it start?"

"I—I do not know," she said faintly. "I've had naught but a terrible ache in my back." But just then there was a subtle drawing and tightening of her womb. It lasted only a few seconds then was gone.

Guy, who had laid a hand on her belly, felt the tightening as well. Kathryn's wide, frightened gaze met his. Her hand lay icy-cold in his. "I'd better find Gerda," he muttered, "and fetch the midwife."

Kathryn clutched at him when he would have straightened. "Wait!" she cried feebly.

"What is it, sweet? Do you hurt again?" He smoothed a feathery tendril of black hair from her cheek.

Kathryn shook her head, unable to speak for the painful ache that swelled her throat. Guy's gentleness—his concern as he bent over her—was suddenly too much. It had been so long since he had looked at her thus . . . Her heart bleeding, she bit back foolish, bitter tears. She didn't want him to leave. She wanted him to reach out and wrap her hard and tight against him, for she was suddenly terrified of the ordeal ahead of her.

But pride would not let her admit to such weakness. " 'Tis nothing," she managed at last, summoning a watery smile.

He squeezed her fingers. "You'll be all right, love. Just hold tight and I'll send Gerda to you," he promised.

Gerda burst into the chamber a few minutes later, scurrying to Kathryn's side. "Milady," she cried. "My lord said that the babe is coming!"

Kathryn sat up with Gerda's assistance. "Mayhap this is a false alarm," she said with a shaky laugh. "I feel different, but I've yet to suffer any real pains."

But it wasn't long before the strange tautness spread around and gripped her middle again—and with growing intensity. Kathryn was too restless, both excited and fearful, to stay abed for long. Instead she paced the length of the chamber, catching her breath and bending slightly whenever the pain caught her unawares.

It was well past noonday when the midwife arrived, having tended to another birth in the village that morning. Elsa was a hulking woman with a thin thatch of iron-gray hair. Guy, who had chafed all morning at the delay, followed her up the stairs but at the chamber door, she turned him away, chastening him soundly.

"Ach, my lord, a man attending the birth of a wee one?" She clucked disapprovingly. "Why, I've never heard of such a thing! You men have the stomach for battle but I'll wager there's not a man alive who has the stomach for childbirth! Wife or no, son or no, I'll not have ye gettin' in the way. No doubt it'll be hours yet since this is yer lady's firstborn. Aye, down the stairs with ye now! You'll see your son when the time is right, that I promise."

Guy glared at her, prepared to argue, yet he couldn't deny the woman undoubtedly knew far better than he. He scowled blackly, then turned away and lumbered down the stairs.

The pains were not unbearable, but by late afternoon Kathryn had retreated once again to the bed to rest when she was able. She gasped whenever her womb was seized with another spasm, constricting her muscles and holding her breath until it passed.

By the time night cast its shroud about the earth, the pain was like daggers slicing through her. Both Gerda and Elsa urged her to pant and breathe, but by then Kathryn was lost in an endless sea of agony. Buried deep in her brain was the notion that if she held it inside, it would make it easier to bear. And so she made not a sound, not a cry or even a whimper, for she did not want Guy to hear. He would be like Uncle, she decided fuzzily, he would laugh and think her cowardly and spineless. She was scarcely aware of Gerda and Elsa hovering around her, wiping her face and rubbing her belly between pains.

Belowstairs in the great hall, Guy paced like a caged animal. He'd been up and down the stairs a dozen times, but Elsa's warning always clanged through his mind at the last instant, stopping him cold. He knew the dangers of childbirth—there were women who did not always survive . . . and Kathryn was so small and fragile. The thought of anything happening to her made him break out in a cold sweat—and there was no sound from above, none at all! What was going on up there?

By the time the frigid winter moon climbed high in the sky, Guy could stand it no longer. "Blast that midwife's hide," he growled to Sir Michael. "This is my home and I'll enter where I will!" He took the stairs two at a time and burst into the chamber with a frenzied rush.

Whatever he'd expected, it wasn't the two worried faces which swiveled to regard him. The chamber was oddly quiet—a chill ran down his spine. Four long strides took him to where his wife lay in the center of the bed. Kathryn's eyes were closed, her skin as white as the linen beneath her. Her hair was spread in dark, tangled skeins across the pillow. Guy's pulse leaped to his throat; chilling tendrils of dread clutched at his insides. She lay so still and unmoving that for the space of a heartbeat he feared she'd left this world for another.

But then she stirred. Her fists clenched at her sides. Guy noted in horror that her lower lip was raw and bleeding from biting it the way she did now. Her back bowed and her head thrashed back and forth on the pillow until abruptly all the tension—indeed, it seemed her life's breath itself—left her body.

He turned shocked eyes toward the midwife. "Christ!" he said hoarsely. "What's wrong? Why is it taking so long?"

"Milord," the woman said shakily, "the babe would have been here long since were your lady to allow nature to take its course."

Guy's face went ashen. "What do you mean?"

It was Gerda who replied, chokingly. "She holds all the pain locked tight inside her." Tears ran unchecked down her face. "Milord, she has not cried out even once . . . if she were to just let go, I believe it would speed the birth along, but she does not make a sound, not even a whimper. We have tried and tried to tell her, but I—I do not think she hears us any longer!"

Just then another great shudder shook Kathryn's body, wrenching the breath from her. She clamped her legs together, twisting and turning until the contraction ebbed. Comprehension washed over Guy in a flash.

He dropped down beside her, grabbing her shoulders and giving her a slight shake. Her eyes fluttered open, glazed and unfocused. "Kathryn," he said firmly, "sweet, listen to me. When the pain comes, you must not tense up so, for you only make it worse. I know 'tis hard, but do not fight it. Yell. Shout. Scream if it makes it easier."

She stared at him vaguely. "Nay," she said faintly. "I cannot scream . . . I must not, for he will think me weak . . . weak and helpless . . . he will taunt me . . . that his will must ever triumph over mine . . ."

Numbly he realized she was talking about *him*. He groaned and framed her face with his hands. "Kathryn," he said raggedly, "I do not think you weak at all. You are strong and brave and fiercely proud and I would have you no other way . . . oh, sweet, I love you . . . do you hear me? . . . I love you . . ."

Another contraction knotted her body. Feeling it, Guy spoke sharply. "Nay, Kathryn! Bear with it, do you hear? Do not fight it, Kathryn, do not!"

Kathryn winced, surfacing slowly through foggy layers of pain, aware of his sharpness but not his words. She opened her eyes and Guy's face swam before her, grim and unsmiling. She tried to push him away, despairing, thinking he was angry with her again. He was always angry with her . . .

God, she was so tired. So tired she just wanted to close her eyes and sleep forever. But within her the clawing pressure was mounting again—she wanted to cry and sob in despair, but she didn't have the strength. She sank back against the pillows, limp and only half-conscious, while the pain undulated over her, wave after wave.

Guy's face was ashen. His hands were shaking as he reached out helplessly. "Kathryn!" he ground out in sheer desperation. "You did not give in to your uncle so easily—you never give in to me! How can you give up now? Are you a coward after all?"

Somehow his words penetrated the haze in her mind. She opened her eyes in mute outrage just as another contraction seized her. This time she could not stop the anguished moan that escaped. And then suddenly the pains were coming faster, almost constant, and very, very hard. Indeed, nature seemed to have taken over her body in its task to expel the child from her womb. Kathryn did not scream or cry but she was no longer fighting it.

Gentle fingers smoothed the tangled hair from her cheek. "That's the way, sweet. It'll be over soon, I promise. Here, take my hands and squeeze . . ." Kathryn was hazily aware of his presence; she clung to his soothing voice and to him, her nails digging into his palm.

From the foot of the bed Gerda gave a half-sob. "Oh, milord, milady! I can see the head—I can see it!"

Elsa's frantic cry joined hers. "With the next pain you must push, milady! You must bear down and push!"

A racking pain gripped her entire body. Kathryn groaned and felt a tremendous gush from her body, and then a thin, mewling cry filled the air. Guy leaned over and kissed her lingeringly on the mouth, smiling crookedly at her dazed look when he drew away.

The thin, wavering wail from the corner had begun to gain strength and volume. It was several moments before Kathryn fully registered the import of that cry.

She raised her head from the pillow. "My baby—"

"A little girl, milady!" Gerda laughed, busy cleaning the slippery little body. "She's tiny, but, oh, she's a beauty!"

Kathryn turned her head but all she could see was swaddling being wrapped around the babe. "Let me hold her," she said weakly. Tears seeped from her eyes when she tried to sit up and failed.

Her exhaustion grabbed hold of Guy's heart. Deep mauve circles shadowed her eyes; her skin was almost colorless. He twisted around on the bed and lifted her gently so that her back rested flush against his chest, then beckoned to Gerda.

Gerda settled the swaddled bundle into the curve of Kathryn's arm, while Guy supported them both. A deep sigh of contentment shook her body; she stared raptly at the babe, too choked up to speak, silent tears running down her cheeks. But she was smiling, a brilliant smile that sailed straight to his heart.

A powerful surge of emotion swelled his chest. But the thrill that shot through him was purely male, purely possessive. His arms tightened around his daughter and his wife—his wife . . .

He would never let her go, he thought fiercely . . . never!

And if it took him until the end of time, he would make her love him.

Chapter 19

Sunlight gilded the chamber a pale yellow-gold when Kathryn next awoke. She had slept deeply, unable to remember when she'd felt so exhausted. From across the chamber came a woeful little cry. Though she was tired and sore, Kathryn turned eagerly toward the sound, in time to see Gerda lift a tiny bundle to her shoulder.

"Ah, you're awake! And just in time, too!"

Gerda laid the babe on the foot of the bed, changing her swaddling while Kathryn propped herself on an elbow and looked on, anxiously counting ten tiny fingers and toes and breathing a sigh of relief that the child was whole and perfect. When at last Gerda laid the babe in her arms, Kathryn smiled weakly, feeling a trifle unsure of herself, suddenly both terrified and awed by the baby's tiny size. Yet when the babe was settled into the crook of her elbow, her slight weight felt perfect.

Gerda helped Kathryn ease her gown off her shoulder to offer her breast to the fretting infant. Quite by accident her nipple brushed the babe's cheek. The babe rooted frantically. Like a dainty flowering bud, the tiny little mouth opened and latched onto her nipple with a ferocity that wid-

331

ened her mother's eyes. "Oh, my." She laughed shakily. "It seems she knows better than I what to do."

Gerda merely chuckled and left mother and daughter alone.

Kathryn cradled her hand around the infant's head which was covered with fine dark fuzz. Love, pure and sweet, poured through her, filling her like golden shafts of sunshine. She bent her head low and pressed her lips to the softness of the babe's scalp. Tears stung her eyes, but they were tears of joy and wonder.

Near the door, a tall figure lingered. Guy stared at those two dark heads nestled so closely together, at the tiny fist curled on the swell of an ivory, blue-veined breast. A surge of emotion tore through him, so strong it rendered him powerless. For a timeless moment, he could not move.

Kathryn had just switched the babe to her other breast when he approached the bed. She glanced up, coloring prettily when she spied his eyes feasting boldly on her pink bareness. Sensing her shyness, Guy's hard mouth curled in a faint half-smile. But she made no move to cover herself; instead she wordlessly extended her free hand in silent invitation.

It was an invitation no sane man could resist. He took her hand and carried it to his lips. "How are you feeling?" he murmured.

Though she was still tired and her body ached, the heat of his mouth went through her like a bolt of lightning. Kathryn smiled, a willing captive of warm silver eyes. "I am fine," she whispered. The tip of her tongue crept out to moisten her lips. "What of you, milord? What do you think of your daughter?"

"*Our* daughter," he corrected. Kathryn felt a rush

of tenderness. He eased down beside her and ran a callused fingertip across the infant's cheek. The rosebud mouth stopped working her nipple; dark brows drew together over a tiny nubbin nose as if in puzzlement.

They both laughed.

"What shall we name her?" Guy asked.

Kathryn had been so convinced she would bear him another son, she'd scarce considered names for a girl. Now, she bit her lip and considered. "I can think of only one," she admitted. "What think you of Brenna?"

"Brenna," he repeated, testing it upon his tongue. He grinned suddenly. " 'Tis a fitting name, for indeed she'll grow to be a maiden with hair as black as a raven . . . what about Brenna Elizabeth?"

Kathryn's face lit up. "Aye," she breathed. "That would please me—" It was her turn to laugh. "—and I know it will please Elizabeth!"

"Then Brenna Elizabeth it shall be."

Kathryn beamed her satisfaction, smiling directly into her husband's eyes. Guy stared into the sparkling beauty of her upturned features. She was a trifle pale, but there was a radiant glow about her. Lord knew he'd have handed heaven and earth to her just to see such undisguised pleasure in her eyes once again.

After a moment Kathryn lowered her gaze. "Has Peter seen her?"

Guy nodded. "Her cries last night woke him, so I brought him in to see her." There was a slight pause. "You were already sleeping," he said softly. Then, softer still, "You gave me a fright last night, Kathryn." He could not bear to say his greatest fear was that he would lose her—he could not bear to even think it.

Kathryn ducked her head. Her long labor was

hazy and fuzzy in her mind, but she knew Guy had been with her at the moment of Brenna's birth. She'd have known the touch of those lean, dark hands anywhere, so strong and yet so gentle. And afterward, she remembered him cradling her close—both her and Brenna.

Not knowing what else to say, she murmured, " 'Tis glad I am that it is over." She hesitated, not daring to look at him. The words slipped out before she could halt them. "Guy, I would know . . . Are you . . . terribly displeased?"

"Displeased! Why on earth should I be displeased?" His tone reflected his astonishment.

The shining curtain of her hair fell forward, shielding her expression from him. "Because I gave you a daughter instead of another son," she whispered, her voice little more than a wisp of air.

The next thing she was aware of was the touch of his fingertips upon her jaw. With the pressure of his thumb, he urged her face to his. Kathryn swallowed, fearful of what she would see . . . just as fearful what she might not see . . . But his expression reflected only warmth and gentleness, his hold upon her wholly tender.

With his thumb he grazed the pouting fullness of her lips. "Listen to me, sweet. My only concern was that you and the child, be it daughter or son, be healthy and well. I thank God that He has seen fit to bless me with such a wondrous gift."

His quiet intensity made her tremble inside. She wanted desperately to believe him, yet wondered if she dared . . . A blunted fingertip reached out to trace the arch of one tiny dark brow, his hand big and dark against the babe's tiny form.

"She's very precious," he said softly. "I've no doubt she'll rival her mother in beauty." He bent and kissed the soft downy head.

Kathryn's hand came out to twine in the thick black hair that grew low on his nape, an unconscious caress. He raised his head to smile at her.

Kathryn's eyes slipped to Brenna, now asleep at her breast. She marveled anew. Long dark lashes lay fanned against the infant's cheeks, her skin so fair and delicate it was almost translucent.

"She is beautiful, isn't she?" There was a breathless catch in Kathryn's voice as she laughed. "She's not at all wrinkled and red, and her features are dainty and fine . . . !"

"That she is," Guy agreed. But this time his gaze was locked not on his daughter, but his wife . . .

A hard arm locked around her and brought her close. His kiss was magic and bliss, long and unbearably sweet, spinning her away to the gates of heaven and beyond.

And when at long last he released her mouth she buried her face against the corded column of his neck, breathing deeply of his musky male scent. Her fingertips were splayed against his chest—beneath she could feel the drumming rhythm of his heart. Happiness blossomed within her, for this was a moment to treasure—a moment she would horde in her soul for all eternity . . . and therein lay the bittersweet hurt that wilted her joy. It would have been so very, very perfect . . .

If only he loved her.

A month later, Kathryn sat nursing Brenna in the great hall. Most of the men were scattered about the day's work so the hall was deserted except for the occasional servant.

Brenna's small size did not hinder her appetite—nor her growth, as her mother could attest to. She was thriving and healthy—her little belly grew hard and round, her cheeks plump and pink. It was little wonder that Kathryn was enraptured of this tiny creature who was her daughter. Since Gerda would soon be marrying Sir Michael, they'd brought in a young village girl named Norah to tend to Peter and the babe. Kathryn refused to bring in a wet-nurse; she was nearly as loath to give over any of Brenna's care to either Gerda or Norah, for she derived no greater pleasure than when she cradled and cuddled the wee form of her child.

Despite Guy's assurances, she was half-afraid that he would care very little about the child. Didn't all men desire sons? Yet she could not count the times Guy had appeared in her chamber in the middle of the night, easing Brenna from her breast after her frequent night feedings and lulling the infant back to sleep.

But he no longer shared their bed—*his* bed—and he had not done so since the night of Brenna's birth. Instead, he slept in the chamber across the hall.

With a sigh Kathryn rose, climbing the steps to her chamber where she laid Brenna in the wooden cradle at the foot of the bed. The infant released a long, bubbly breath. Kathryn smiled slightly and wiped away a frothy drop of milk from the corner of her mouth. As she knelt beside the cradle, she did not understand the sudden shadow that crept over her. At times, like now, her happiness was tinged with pain.

Guy was just as preoccupied as he entered the great hall, his mind beset by images of his lovely wife—aye, and wasn't it always? He treasured these days since Brenna's birth—they had been marked by a peaceful contentment he'd once thought could never exist between himself and the beauty he now called wife. He dared to hope that they could put the past behind them and begin anew. Oh, she was

still as fiery and fervent as ever! But she had gained
a mature strength, a calm serenity and confidence
that lured him ever deeper into her spell. He had
only to gaze at her and feel himself possessed for
all time.

And still she turned him inside out! He'd been
chafing inside for days already, searching for some
sign that she wanted him back in their chamber.
Oh, he knew it was too soon after the birth to seek
the pleasures of the flesh with her. But it would
have been enough to hold her, to feel her softness
clinging to his hardness in the chill of the night.
Oh, she smiled that bewitching smile that sent his
pulse to pounding like a pagan drum; she dropped
an idle hand upon his shoulder from time to time;
she leaned against him when he helped her up the
stairs after a long, exhausting day. And there at the
door of their chamber, she wished him the sweetest
of good nights with lips that ever enchanted . . .
ever beckoned.

Joy had gladdened his heart when Brenna was
born—their daughter provided a link that Kathryn
could neither deny nor break. By now Guy was
desperate enough to use whatever means he could
to bind her to him. But he'd not swear undying love
where it was not wanted!

A self-derisive smile twisted his lips as he climbed
the stairs. How, he thought with a stab of dark
humor, did one woo and win a woman he'd already
taken to wife . . . a woman who shared his name and
his home . . . a woman who claimed his very bed—
and shunned the husband that rightly should have
lain alongside her in it!

Yet the sight of her pulled him up short. She knelt
beside the cradle, the delicate mauve of her skirts
pooled about her knees. The waning trickle of the
wintry sun through the shutters etched her profile

in palest gold. But what set him back was the air of melancholy sadness that clung to her.

Kathryn did not hear his silent entrance. Even as he approached, she gently brushed her fingers against the babe's cheek. "Oh, Brenna," she murmured, and she could not hide the ache in her heart. "I love you dearly, but how much better had you been a boy! I wish for you so very much, yet I pity you, child, for you will have so little."

Guy froze. Her tone, as much as the words themselves, went through him like the tip of a lance. At precisely that instant, Kathryn realized she was no longer alone . . .

Darting a glance over her shoulder, she beheld the aloof regard of her husband. His very lack of expression left her in no doubt that he'd heard every word she spoke to the babe.

"Mayhap you'd like to explain that statement, mistress. Especially since you know as well as I that Brenna will lack for nothing."

His smile was chilling, his tone glacial. A slow burn began to simmer along Kathryn's veins. It was just like a man to think that food in her belly, a roof over her head, and a little affection was all it took to make a woman happy! She rose to her feet, meeting his stare with a challenge of her own.

"I mean only this, milord earl. From now until the time Brenna grows to womanhood, her choices will not be her own. Were she a boy, she could choose her own path, whether it be landowner, knighthood, or the Church—no man, her father included, could force his will on her. But by simple virtue of her sex, Brenna will neither go where she pleases, nor when. She will be naught but a possession, a pawn. First you will control her life, and then her husband will control it— a husband, no doubt, chosen by you. Indeed,

I fear she is doomed to a life no better than mine!"

His eyes were glittering. "Ah, so now the truth comes out. Tell me, sweet. Is this truly how you feel? As if I hold you prisoner here?"

Curse her bloody tongue! Too late Kathryn realized where her recklessness had taken her. Yet it wasn't solely her fault. If Guy did not goad her so, she'd not be so tempted to retaliate!

"I did not say that—" she began.

"Nay, you need not say it at all," he bit out tightly. "You make yourself very plain, Kathryn. You'd rather be free of me." He gave a short harsh laugh. "Well, in this you are right, sweet, for you'll not have your way. We are married in the eyes of God and man, and by all the saints, so we shall remain!" He spun about and started for the door, only to stop halfway there. "I came to tell you I have received an urgent summons from Henry to join him in London. I thought perchance you might find it in your heart to cheer a lonely man's spirit on the eve before his departure. But since you find my presence so distasteful, I see no point in waiting till dawn to take my leave."

Stricken, she made no effort to stop him when he strode from the room. An hour later, she stood near the entrance to the bailey, watching as he prepared to depart.

At last he stopped before her, his helm tucked under his arm, so tall and handsome he took her breath away. Brenna was tucked into the crook of her arm; Peter stood at her side. Try though she might, Kathryn could not find the courage to meet his eyes.

He bent and kissed the soft down of the babe's head. Peter was next, lifted high in his arms for a hug. "You must be a brave lad and watch over your sister for me," he whispered to the boy.

Peter beamed.

Not once did he look at her. Something inside Kathryn seemed to wither and die—she felt as if she did not even exist.

Do not do this, she longed to cry. *Oh, don't you see that I love you!* All at once she wanted desperately to heal this breach between them. But what was the use? She thought despairingly. His heart was set against it—his heart was set against her! And so in the end, she dared not speak the words that welled in her throat.

It seemed the pride that had long been her staunchest ally was now her fiercest enemy.

A sennight passed, and then another. The month of March was upon them, bringing glorious skies and the promise of warmer days to come. For the people of Sedgewick—and all across the breadth of England—spring was a time that heralded growth and revival and prosperity. There were fields to be plowed, crops to be sown. Spirits were merry and jovial for all but the lady of the manor.

She could not help but remember her nightmare— how her uncle had taunted her . . . *'Tis your wont to covet what can never be yours.*

Her heart cried out in anguish. Mayhap it was true—for the one thing she wanted most was the one thing she could never have . . .

Her husband's love.

She was sitting in the hall early one evening when the sound of shouting in the bailey reached her ears. One of the maids moved to peer outside.

Kathryn frowned. "What is it, Meg?"

Meg's eyes were round as saucers. "A small troop of men, milady—methinks they are not the earl's."

Just then Sir Edward appeared. "Milady, there is a knight without who wishes to see you."

"He asks to see me?" Puzzled, she put aside her sewing and rose.

"He says he is from Ashbury, milady."

Her lips parted. Ashbury! Why, she could think of no one except . . .

"Roderick!" she cried out in surprise as he limped through the entrance, supported on each side by two men she recognized as Richard's former men-at-arms.

She rushed forward. The men lowered him slowly onto one of the benches stacked against the far wall. He favored his left leg, grimacing as he eased it ahead of him. She gasped when she saw that his chausses was soaked through with blood.

"My God, Roderick! What has happened?"

"Ah, Lady Kathryn! I and my friends were on our way to a tournament in Warwickshire when we were attacked by a band of cutthroats less than a day's ride from here. We managed to defeat the rogues, but I was not so lucky as my comrades." He managed a sickly smile. "I fear I must humbly ask you and your lord's generosity in seeking shelter for the night."

"Guy is in London," she said. "And of course you may stay—indeed, you are welcome to remain until your leg is healed and you are able to ride again." She turned and briskly asked Meg to fetch bandages and hot water.

"You are truly too kind, Kathryn." His eyes roved over her lovely features. Kathryn flushed, for she did not miss the intensity of his gaze.

She summoned Gerda to tend to his wound, relieved to see that it was not so bad as she'd first believed. Though the slash had bled profusely, it showed no signs of infection. Gerda sprinkled a healing powder on it, then deftly bound it tightly with strips of clean linen.

Kathryn was anxious for news of Elizabeth, so she plied him eagerly during the evening meal. "How is Elizabeth? Oh, I miss her so! And the wedding—were you there?"

Roderick laughed. "Aye, I was there. And Elizabeth was truly radiant. Indeed, marriage seems to agree with her, for I've never seen her look better."

Kathryn breathed a sigh of relief. "If Sir Hugh makes her happy, then I can ask no more."

"Enough of Elizabeth," he said lightly. "What of you, Kathryn?" His voice lowered; his tawny head dipped nearer. "Does the earl make *you* happy?"

Kathryn inhaled sharply, caught off guard by the hungry look in his eyes.

He mistook her silence. Emboldened, he reached out and caught her hand where it lay on her knee. "Kathryn, you have only to say the word. If he has mistreated you—" His fingers tightened around hers.

Kathryn rose, tugging in earnest on her hand. He merely pulled her closer, refusing to free her. She made a sound of distress, uncomfortable with his familiarity—and mindful of what the servants might think. Lord, all she needed was for someone to carry tales to Guy . . . Guy! Too late she wondered what Guy might think were he to return home and find Roderick here.

She turned wide pleading eyes his way. "Roderick!" she whispered, "you must not touch me so! Do you forget that I am a married woman now?"

He released her so abruptly she stumbled and nearly lost her balance. "You are right, milady. 'Tis not my place to interfere." His gaze flickered past her shoulder at the same instant a trickle of foreboding raised the hairs on the back of her neck.

She didn't need to turn to know her husband had finally arrived. But turn she did, as if commanded from afar.

He was coming toward her, she noted with a pang in her heart. He was travel-stained and dusty, and lines of weariness scored his cheeks, but he was as wickedly handsome as ever.

Fear and yearning and an agony of longing swept through her. Her nails dug into her palms so hard they were sure to leave marks. The need to touch and be touched was overwhelming—she ached with the need to run to him, to cling to his shoulders and lift her mouth to his. But no hint of a smile softened the grim line of his lips, and the wistful throb of her heartbeat faltered. By the look of him, naught had changed since the day he'd left. Nay, she'd not play the eager wife while he was so obviously the reluctant husband!

Her delicate chin tilted. "My lord," she greeted him coolly. "We did not expect you home so soon."

His smile was frigid. "So I see." A lean hand dropped heavily on her shoulder; he drew her to his side. Kathryn's color mounted, along with her temper, for there was naught of affection in his touch—it was more a show of possessiveness.

His icy gray eyes were pinned on Roderick, who had risen to his feet and stood a bit stiffly. "I wonder that you dare to show your face at Sedgewick." Though Guy's tone was easy, there was a note of danger that did not go unnoticed by either his wife or the other man.

"A case of needs must, my lord. I and the rest of my party were on our way to a joust in Warwickshire when we met up with a band of cutthroats late last eve." Roderick touched his injured leg lightly. "I fear I did not fare so well. We stopped here for assistance and Lady Kathryn was gracious enough to bid us stay until my injury heals."

"Motherhood has made my lady generous indeed." Guy's lips still smiled; his eyes did not. His fingers tightened on Kathryn's waist. He started to turn away, but the other man's voice halted him.

"My lord?"

A dark brow arched in silent inquiry.

"My lord, I see that you look upon me with disfavor. This I understand—truly I do. But I would remind you that I swore my loyalty to you at Ashbury, and I would ask that you hold no malice toward me, for in truth, I bear you no grudge."

Ah, but he was so glib, so facile, always ready with a winsome smile! Was that how he had won Kathryn? Mayhap he spoke the truth—mayhap he did not. Either way, Guy was not prepared to let down his guard.

"Then I would remind *you* of this, Sir Roderick. You were invited to stay at my wife's pleasure—you remain at mine."

He walked away, making certain Kathryn was firmly anchored to his side. But once they were in the passage at the top of the stairs, she twisted away from him. He made no move to reclaim her but instead followed in her wake.

Brenna was fussing as Kathryn walked through the door. Norah was bent over her cradle, preparing to pick her up. She straightened at Kathryn's entrance. "Milady! I was just about to fetch you." She chuckled. "It seems the babe has decided she's waited long enough for her supper."

Kathryn smiled. "Thank you, Norah. I won't be needing you any more tonight, but would you check on Peter for me, please?"

The girl dropped a curtsy to her lord and lady. Kathryn's smile vanished when she saw Guy had followed her inside. She whirled and reached for the babe, but strong dark hands peremptorily pushed hers aside.

He raised Brenna high, letting the swaddling drop to the floor. The babe had quieted the instant she was picked up. Her legs kicking idly, she crammed a tiny fist in her mouth and gazed curiously at her father. Guy's eyes swept the length of that small naked body. "Lord." He gave an incredulous laugh, his expression incredibly tender. "I cannot believe how she's grown!"

Seeing the pair thus, Kathryn felt a painful tug on her heart. Guy's attachment to his daughter was unquestionable . . . if only she could command the same warmth and devotion!

He replaced Brenna's swaddling and cradled her in the crook of his elbow. He laughed softly when she instinctively began to root against his tunic, her little mouth open, avidly searching.

He glanced at Kathryn. "She's hungry." He said it as if he were less than pleased.

Whatever softness had dwelled in his expression had vanished. He was once again stark and remote. Her heart twisted in mute despair . . . Was it because of Roderick? Or because he did not care? Inside she was shattered, but by God, she'd not let him know it!

She took Brenna from his arms and settled herself on the bench beneath the window. Guy stood his ground, making no move to grant her privacy though she knew by the glint in his eyes that he knew she wished it.

Pride alone dictated her objection. She raised her chin and matched his bold stare. "Must you watch?" Her tone was curt.

Something flickered in his eyes—anger? It was gone so quickly she couldn't be certain. "She's my daughter, too, I would remind you. And this is hardly the first time I've watched you nurse her."

True, Kathryn admitted silently. All at once she felt chastened and subdued, perilously close to tears and hating both herself and Guy for it. She clutched the babe tighter, for this was somehow different from all those other times, because he was angry . . . and she was resentful . . . and oh, why were they acting as if they were strangers!

But Brenna was squalling in earnest now, squirming and questing frantically, her wrenching cries spiraling in frustration. Unable to stand it any longer, Kathryn fumbled with her gown and bared her breast.

The babe's wails ceased abruptly; the tension in the room grew ever more strident.

Brenna suckled noisily, making tiny sounds of contented gratification, unaware of the tumult raging in the heart and minds of both her mother and father.

Guy moved to stand directly above his wife. Her head was bowed low, her attention confined to their daughter. His gaze journeyed slowly over the curve of her cheek, down the slender grace of her neck to linger on the swelling mound of her exposed breast.

Desire knotted his gut. He longed to clamp his strong brown fingers across the milky whiteness of her breasts and stare his fill, knowing he would find the contrast riveting and mesmerizing; he could almost feel the velvety smoothness of her skin, the supple weight of her flesh filling his palms. He nearly groaned when she switched the babe to the other breast—her nipple was ripe and glistening, bedewed with milk. Blood pooled thickly in his loins, hot and potent.

The child slept far sooner than Kathryn would

have wished. Guy bent, sliding his hands beneath the infant, his knuckles grazing her belly. Kathryn stiffened, scarcely daring to breathe. But she instinctively started to protest as he began to lift the child away. One glance from searing gray eyes crammed the impulse back in her throat. Kathryn, primly covered once again, looked on as he laid Brenna in her cradle, wary of his next move. To her horror, her pulse was thudding wildly. Would he leave her now? Or would he stay? And what did *she* want? When the babe was covered to his satisfaction, he straightened and turned.

For a frozen moment in time, neither one moved— neither one spoke. Gray eyes clashed fiercely with green.

Once again, the battle raged anew.

Guy smiled at her suspicious regard. "What!" he mocked. "Have you no proper greeting now that we are finally alone?" He went on coolly, "Indeed, I wonder at your attitude, mistress. I had thought you would miss me after my absence." His smile turned ugly. "Or could it be that the welcome which should have gone to your husband has gone to another?"

"I suppose you mean Roderick," she snapped.

"Roderick! Well, now that you mention it, sweet, I must confess I was hardly prepared to find him so snugly ensconced in my home—and with my wife hovering over him ready to see to his every need!"

"He only just arrived, for heaven's sake!" she replied heatedly. "I merely offered the same hospitality and consideration I'd have offered to any wounded man."

So fiery. So righteous and indignant. So very *convincing*. But was her outrage real or feigned? Now there was a question . . .

"Indeed? And what solace do you offer your husband, whose heart is wounded that you ignore him for another?"

"Ignore you . . . Wounded! . . . Why, your heart wears a shield of iron!" she challenged. "Need I remind you that 'twas you who took yourself from this chamber, milord—you who chose not to return!"

"And need I remind you that you are my wife? I have every right to claim what is mine—and I would do so now."

Anger brought her surging to her feet. He had not changed—he was still as arrogant as ever! She tried to march past him but he seized her by the waist and brought her up hard against him so their hips were bound together, and then all she could feel was the turgid strength of his manhood rigid and taut against her belly.

A shiver of longing raced through her, even as everything within her decried her body's traitorous response. It seemed so long since she had seen him—since he had held her thus! But she yearned for the warmth she knew he was capable of, some sign that he cared, even a little . . . But there was no tenderness in his eyes, nothing but the brilliant hard sheen of passion.

"Take your lust elsewhere, my lord earl—mayhap back to London and the last bed you lay in. I daresay there's a woman in court who is not so particular as I am!"

His grip on her arms tightened. He stared down at her. For the space of a heartbeat, it was as if she saw clear inside him, and his soul was as tortured and anguished as her own.

"I've lain with no other since I first laid eyes on you that long-ago day at Ashbury," he said harshly. "Does that please you, sweet?"

Kathryn could not answer. Stunned by the revelation, she could only gape at him.

"You are the one who haunts my dreams, who lights the fire in my loins, who creates a passion in me that knows no bounds—you, Kathryn, who are forever on my mind, whether I will it or no. And aye, it seems that you are the only one who can ease this burning hunger in my soul, for no one can satisfy me as you do, sweet witch."

His admission swept her from the heights of heaven . . . to the dregs of hell . . . in but the blink of an eye. He spoke of passion and fire and hunger, but not love . . . nay, never love.

And yet a treacherous warmth seeped through her limbs, for his nearness rocked her senses. *Where is your pride?* a voice within her berated her furiously. He had only to touch her and she would melt in his arms, yield him anything—everything—he wished! She wanted more than just some small scrap of affection.

She wanted his heart, for she'd already given her own.

Suddenly she was trembling so that she could hardly stand, confused and frightened by all he made her feel. She swallowed miserably. "What would you have me say?" she whispered. " 'Tis the same for me—you know that, for I have known the touch of no man but you, despite what you think!" When he said nothing, merely continued watching her in that disturbingly piercing way he had, she cried out in weary despair, "Damn you, Guy, I—I do not know what you want from me!"

His expression seemed to tighten. "What do I want? All that you have to give—all that you refuse to give!"

His eyes tangled with hers, seeming to possess her, inside and out. The temptation was strong to give up the struggle within her and cry out that she loved him. But he took all from her—and still he demanded more. Nay! She could not surrender all to him, for she was desperately afraid of losing some vital part of herself, of being wholly in his power.

But when his lips captured hers, she could fight him no longer—she could no longer fight herself. She clung to him blindly as he lifted her and carried her to the bed.

Her gown was swept to the floor, swiftly followed by his tunic, braies, and chausses. To deny him was to deny her very self, for in spite of her fear and anger, she wanted him . . . She wanted him with a yearning desperation that seared her blood and a tempest that stormed the heart. Firelight played over the muscles of his shoulders, gleaming and bronzed, and in him, she discovered all that she sought. He was muscled and sinewed; he was beauty and strength, sleek and naked and gloriously hard as he lowered himself beside her.

He kissed her, his hands wandering at will, his tongue dueling with hers in a wild prelude of what was to come. He played with the tips of her breasts, tantalizing and arousing. A dark heavy warmth unfurled within her, centered low in her belly. Lightning sizzled through her when at last his mouth encompassed first one straining peak and then the other. Her teeth dug into her lower lip as she bit back a cry of pleasure. And still he was not content.

He shifted suddenly; the heel of his hand grazed the fleecy apex of her thighs. The muscles of her stomach quivered as that brazen mouth charted a forbidden pathway down over the newly concave hollow of her belly. His hands caught at her hips and her heart leaped to her throat. The heated trickle of his breath fanned lower still . . . Her eyes flew wide. She gazed in stricken horror at that dark head poised between the cradle of her thighs.

"No," she whispered. "Oh, no . . ."

Slowly he raised his head, his eyes fever-bright. "You are mine, Kathryn," he said thickly. "And before this night is over you will know it, too."

A dry sob escaped. She pushed frantically at his shoulders, but it was no use. He was as immovable as stone.

His breath caressed her first, warm and damp, like the first faint whispery wings of night. Her heart raced madly. Her entire body jerked when at last he found her heated core. He discovered the dark, tangy taste of her, the rasp of his tongue a divine torment. She shuddered, her fists twisting into the sheet as a piercing wave of pleasure crashed over her. The blood pounded in her ears so that she could scarcely think, and then she wasn't thinking at all. All she could do was *feel* . . . With lips and tongue he lured her into a whirlwind of pure sensation. Little whimpers of wanton splendor tore from her throat as he brought her to the brink of rapture.

She nearly cried out when he left her. But suddenly he was there above her, the velvet tip of his manhood poised at the heart of her. Her breasts rose and fell with each frenzied breath. She dug her fingers into his shoulders, trying to clutch him to her but he braced himself above her, his arms bulging.

"Christ, you're beautiful." His voice rushed past her ear, hoarse and strained, his eyes nearly black with the passion that seared his veins.

The look in his eyes robbed her of breath. Hot and possessive, it thrilled her to the tips of her toes. "Please," she whispered. "Oh, please . . ." The sound was no more than a wisp of air; it was a marvel she could speak at all. Her senses clamoring, she thrust up against him, seeking desperately to show him what she wanted.

He gave an odd little laugh and kissed her nose, her cheeks, her lips. "Easy, sweet," he muttered. "Or you will make me forget this is your first time since the babe."

Even as he spoke, he began to fuse their bodies. His penetration was slow, so agonizingly careful she thought she would go mad before his rigid length lay fully sheathed within her. But then there was only the glorious wonder of being filled with him again.

Shivers played along her spine as he began to move. His breath rushed past her ear, harsh and ragged. The tempo of his thrusts was at first slow and rhythmic, but the velvet clasp of her body around his splintered his self-control. He plunged deep, over and over, driving and lunging and mindlessly hungry. And when the spasms of release spun her away on a cloud of ecstasy, he gripped her hips and followed her to heaven's gate. With a guttural cry, he gave one final soul-shattering plunge, his seed flooding hot and honeyed within her.

Long moments passed before the throb of their heartbeats grew deep and even. Guy combed his fingers gently through the wild web of black silky hair tangled about them both. Easing to his side, he pressed Kathryn's face against his shoulder. His hand lay just beneath her breast, the hollow of her belly flush against the jutting ridge of his hip. She lay curled against him as if they had lain just so for the span of a lifetime.

Though the winds of passion brought the sweet satisfaction he craved, he could not stop the weary bleakness that slipped over him like a shroud. The peace his tormented mind sought was simply not to be, for he realized with stark painful clarity that while Kathryn's body had accepted him long, long ago, her heart was another matter.

Chapter 20

The day was unseasonably warm for spring. The sun shone high and brilliant, bathing the valley in a glorious golden haze. A faint breeze carried with it the sweet scent of wildflowers.

Guy and Sir Michael had spent the afternoon hawking, though the enjoyment Guy usually gained from such sport was sorely lacking. He was restless, and even brooding.

He need not wonder why.

Two days. Two days had gone by since his return home from London. Egad, it seemed like a lifetime! And to think how he had driven himself and his destrier to a point near exhaustion, eager to hold his wife in his arms again, anxious to make amends to her, so very determined to set aright all that had gone wrong between them.

But he'd be damned if he'd give her his heart when she gave hers elsewhere!

"Michael." He spoke abruptly. "I would know what you think of Sir Roderick.

Michael's eyes flickered. Somehow Guy's question did not surprise him, since he was well aware of the dissension between his lord and lady. Nor was it difficult to attribute such to the presence of a young and handsome outsider. Michael surveyed his lady and the knight in question when he thought they did not see; Lady Kathryn eyed her husband with longing and distress, her heart plainly writ upon her sleeve. Michael heaved a silent sigh. Unfortunately, the earl had always been rather blind where his lady was concerned . . .

"To be sure," Michael said finally, "I can find little fault with Sir Roderick's behavior. He certainly seems an agreeable fellow."

Aye, Guy thought blackly, Sir Roderick was the perfect guest . . . his wife the perfect hostess. Roderick was charming and engagingly humorous despite his injury, Kathryn attentive and considerate of his every need.

Guy said nothing, merely stared moodily off into the distance.

Michael eyed him with a frown. "I have the feeling, milord," he said slowly, "you do not trust Sir Roderick."

"I cannot," Guy replied bluntly, "if for no other reason than that he was one of Richard's most trusted men."

"He pledged his oath to you," Michael reminded him. "And now Sir Hugh as well."

Guy's laugh was short and harsh. "A man will swear most anything when he fears death is his only other choice. And methinks Roderick's first loyalty is to himself—"

He broke off, suddenly twisting in his saddle, his gaze intent as he scanned the surrounding forest. The woodland animals went on about their chatter as if naught was amiss. Someone, he thought, was watching them . . .

The thought advanced no further. Nearby there was a whoosh of sound. Vaguely aware of Michael shouting, Guy threw himself low in his saddle, and only just in time, for an arrow whizzed by his head, so close he felt a hiss of air sting his cheek.

The thunder of hooves shook the earth. There was the sound of someone crashing through the underbrush.

Michael had already ripped his sword from his scabbard, his spurs digging into his mount as he took off toward a copse of trees. Guy whirled his destrier and quickly followed; the light of battle leaped in his eyes.

But it was no use. The assailant had plotted his retreat well; the two knights could not catch even a glimpse of him before he was lost amidst the shadowed woodland.

Back in the clearing, Sir Michael dismounted and strode to where the arrow had lodged in the trunk of a black oak tree. He heaved it free, spinning the narrow shaft between thumb and forefinger as he turned to Guy.

"This arrow," he said grimly, "was meant for you."

Murder. Someone had tried to murder him. The realization chilled Guy's blood, but he cautioned Michael to silence when they returned to Sedgewick.

He did not question the loyalty of any of his men. But Roderick . . . now there was a possibility, a very good possibility indeed . . .

Guy's mood was guarded, his expression granite-hard as the evening progressed. His gaze followed Kathryn as she moved about the great hall. The sheen of firelight gilded the arch of her throat as she tilted her head and smiled at something Gerda said. Her form, clad in crimson velvet, was soft and lush and newly slim.

His mouth compressed. It was little wonder that

Roderick—indeed, every man in the hall tonight, including himself—could scarce take his eyes off her. She was all that a man could desire—fierce yet gentle, vibrant and spirited, alive and alluring.

With a scowl he turned aside, and still her picture rose high in his mind. He envisioned the flawless perfection of her skin, her elegantly sculpted features, winged black brows and lips as tempting and dewy as succulent summer berries. And he remembered the feel of her slim hands entwined with his own, the way her hips churned wildly beneath his in the heat of midnight fires.

A surge of possessiveness shot through him. He had wed her, made her his lady in name and in deed. He had gained all that he sought—he had bound her to him in every way possible.

And then he heard her laugh, the sound lilting and musical. But that sweet sound did not bring solace to the bleakness etched in his soul. For she did not laugh for him . . . but for another.

Someone pressed ale into his hand. He accepted it blindly, all the while simmering inside, jealous and furious. He despised himself as weak for the pain that so controlled him, yet he was unable to banish it.

He felt like an intruder—and in his own home yet!

He turned burning eyes to Roderick, who had settled himself on the bench across from Kathryn. *The blackguard!* Guy thought fiercely. *He eats my food. He drinks my wine. And does he also help himself to my wife?* He watched Kathryn throw back her head and laugh again. She was cool and reserved and distant tonight—but there was a spark within her she chose not to reveal to him.

Guy could not prevent the bitterness that seeped inside him, nor the sudden doubts that crowded his mind. Did she still long for Ashbury? Did she regret the circumstances which had brought her into his arms—and his bed? Of a certainty she found passion there—but she had never claimed to love him . . . Mayhap because she still loved Roderick. Had the two of them hatched the plan to kill him—did they even now plot his downfall?

She turned suddenly—and caught his eye. Her smile continued to dally about her lips . . . lips that ever lied and deceived.

With a lift of that dainty chin, she turned back to Roderick.

To Guy, it was like a slap in the face. His ire burst into flames. He swore furiously. By all the saints! He'd not stand by and watch her make a fool of him!

He rose and moved to the end of the table where the pair that so tormented him still sat. At his approach, all conversation ceased. Two pair of eyes fixed upon him, polite but questioning.

Again he felt the outsider.

"Sir Roderick," he said coolly, "how fares your wound this eve?"

"My leg fares well, indeed, thanks to Gerda's ministrations." His eyes warmed as he glanced at Kathryn. "And Kathryn, of course."

"How fortunate it heals so well and so quickly," Guy murmured with an easy smile. He laid a hand on Kathryn's shoulder. "Especially since I'm sure you and your men are anxious to be on your way with all due haste."

Beneath his fingers, Kathryn stiffened. Roderick appeared first startled, then rather uncertain.

"And now," Guy went on lightly, "I fear I must rob you of the pleasure of my wife's company." He lifted Kathryn from the bench and pulled her back against his chest, letting his fingers splay possessively across her belly.

Her color heightened, along with her temper. Guy was well aware of the storm building inside her but paid no heed.

"As you can see, the duties of a wife are many. Kathryn must see to the needs of our daughter—" He gave a low, husky laugh and pressed a kiss on the scented hollow in front of her ear. "—and her husband."

With that he spun her away, his fingers digging unmercifully into the soft flesh of her arm. Once they were out of sight, she wrenched herself free and glided up the stairs before him, her head held regally high.

A savage stare tracked their progress; neither one noticed Roderick's tight-lipped regard.

Guy said nothing while Kathryn dismissed Norah for the night, nor did he miss the way her lovely mouth tightened in disapproval as he bolted the door.

"I take it," he said mildly, "you have something to say."

"That I do," she snapped, and wasted no time in heaping her displeasure on his head. "Your behavior was rude and inexcusable, milord. Need I remind you that we have guests? 'Tis not right that we leave them unattended at such an early hour. Nor was it right for you to suggest that we . . . that you . . ." Color stained her cheeks as she struggled to find the right words.

Guy had no such problem. "That I had every intention of dragging you off to my bed? As if I could not wait to lay my hands on that luscious body of yours?" He tugged off his tunic and dropped it on the bed. "Why pretend otherwise when it's true?"

Such arrogant self-confidence! And no wonder, she thought in bitter frustration. His arms were roped with muscle, his shoulders bronzed and sleek. The sight of his naked torso made her middle tingle. With a ragged inhalation, she tore her gaze from his chest. "You're drunk," she snapped. "Well, you can go below and drown yourself in ale for all I care. I'll not have you in my bed in such a sorry state."

A dangerous smile curled his lips. He advanced closer, his aura distinctly predatory. "Ah, but you will have me in your bed, sweet. This night and every other night."

She placed her fingertips upon his chest, not resisting, yet not yielding either. Yet she could not help the way her chest grew heavy and tight. With every breath, with every heartbeat, she wanted him more—she loved him more! If she cast her heart before him, he would stomp on it, cast it aside, and then where would she be? She had to have something for herself—no matter how little!

"It's not me you want," she said shakily. "You only do this because of Roderick—because I married you and not him! You wish only to flaunt me in his face." Her dignity was lost in an angry cry. "You—you do this only as punishment!"

His features were shadowed and tense. His fingers tangled in her hair. He brought her head back so that her face was tipped to his. "Then tell me this," he said roughly. "Who do I punish, Kathryn—you or me?"

His mouth came down on hers, hard and demanding, and all at once her heart beat wild and reckless. Lean fingers swept away her kirtle, and her feeble resistance along with it. Heat rose inside her, like a raging fever. And when he lay her back upon the bed, imprinting her body with the weight of his own, she surrendered her lips with a low sobbing moan.

Her nails dug into the sleek flesh of his shoulders. Their union was heated and driving, breath-stealing and desperate. Her legs clamped about his hips, as if she would keep him inside her for all eternity. She found her pleasure in his, and he in hers. With one final groan he collapsed against her, spent and sated.

The tempest within them grew still and silent. Kathryn slid her fingers through the midnight darkness of his hair; only then did she feel the scalding tears slipping down her cheeks. She cried because she loved him and dared not let him know it.

Guy was certain she cried because she did not.

The eastern sky was awash with a pale-violet haze when Guy slipped from the bed the next morning. He rose and quickly donned his tunic, chausses, and boots. Near the foot of the bed he paused, glancing down at the wooden cradle. The unflagging determination on his face eased slightly. His daughter, angel that she was, had obliged her father greatly—she'd slept the night through and not awakened her mother for her nightly feeding. Her legs were drawn up beneath her tummy so that her little rump protruded into the air. One small fist lay near her cheek; even as he watched, her little mouth opened and made small sucking movements. He laughed softly and laid a hand on the soft down of her scalp, aware of a slight tug at his heart as he noted how his big hand engulfed the babe's dark head. Pride swelled his chest, for she would someday be as beautiful as her mother.

It was inevitable that his gaze return to Kathryn. His footsteps carried him to the bedside. There he stared down where Kathryn lay curled on her side, sleeping as sweetly and innocently as their child. His gaze lingered on the smooth ivory flesh of one bare shoulder, peeping out from beneath the tumbled darkness of her hair. Her features were fragile and dainty, her cheeks the creamiest of pink, her lips as moist as fragrant summer rain. He felt his loins tighten and swell. The urge to explore the warm, sleep-scented hollows of her body swept over him, weakening his resolve, eroding his will.

But sweet and innocent she was not, a harsh voice inside reminded him caustically. She plied the arts of feminine bewitchment with the hand of a master, weaving him ever more deeply into her spell.

The smile deserted his heart. He turned away with a black scowl.

He had a purpose for rising so early—and he'd not be swayed from it, no matter how strong the temptation.

But the great hall was already stirring to life when he arrived belowstairs. Most of Roderick's entourage was breaking the morning fast, dressed in boots and hauberk, clearly ready for travel. Guy stopped short, for this was an unexpected pleasure. He'd thought to prod Roderick on his way, but apparently there was no need.

"Milord!"

The subject of his thoughts hailed him. Guy remained where he was, his relaxed manner giving the lie to the seething tension that roiled within him.

"Sir Roderick," he said coolly. "You leave us today for Warwickshire?"

"Aye, milord." Roderick hesitated, appearing as if he wanted to say more.

Guy waited, his jaw tense, his expression remote—his dislike of Roderick had long ago hardened into hatred.

"Milord, if I have done something to incur your displeasure I am heartily sorry."

"Are you now?" Guy's tone was aloof and detached. It was plain that he tolerated the other man, but only barely.

Roderick shifted uneasily. "Milord, I tell you true. Whatever was once between Lady Kathryn and me is no more. I have accepted that she is your wife and I've no wish to make trouble between you and your lady."

Hah! No doubt that was his *only* wish.

"Sir Roderick," he murmured, "had you openly shown some sign that you covet my wife, you'd not be here in the flesh before me right now." His voice was so pleasant—he was even smiling—so that it took an instant before Roderick perceived it for the threat it was.

His eyes flickered, but he stood his ground. Guy decided idly that he was either very courageous— or very, very foolish.

"I value my life," Roderick said stiffly, "as you should value yours."

In the back of his mind, it struck Guy that there was something vaguely disturbing about that statement. But before either of them could say more, one of Roderick's men called for his assistance outside in the bailey.

Minutes later he watched Roderick and his men parade through the gatehouse. A smile of satisfaction curved his hard mouth, the first genuine one that day. He did not regret Roderick leaving . . . Then his smile withered.

He suspected Kathryn would not feel the same.

Neither Guy nor Roderick was anywhere around when Kathryn found her way to the hall several hours later. After the furor of the past few days, it seemed abnormally quiet. Kathryn questioned the first maid she came upon, who told her Roderick had left early that morning.

"I see. And the earl? Is he about this morning?" Kathryn was half-afraid Guy had driven Roderick from Sedgewick with the point of his sword at his back.

"No, milady. I heard him tell Sir Edward he planned to be out hunting this morn."

It was not a good way to start the day. Kathryn was hurt that Guy hadn't seen fit to tell her his whereabouts. And she was also rather miffed that Roderick had left without saying good-bye—it took no stretch of the imagination to know that Guy had something to do with that.

The noonday meal passed with no sign of Guy. Kathryn stewed silently and retreated to her chamber. She was stabbing her needle in and out of a length of cloth when he made an appearance early that afternoon. She ignored him completely.

Guy discovered the coolness of her mood the minute he entered their chamber. He knew she was aware of his presence, for her lovely mouth tightened. But she neither raised her eyes nor spoke. At any other time, perhaps, Guy might have been amused. Today he was not so inclined.

Three long strides brought him before her. Undaunted by her aloofness, he dragged her sewing from her hands and tossed it aside. Her head shot up with a muted sound of fury. She clamped her lips together, green eyes afire.

He smiled slowly. "Your haughtiness does not escape me, milady. Are you so angry then that your wounded knight has gone?"

The charge was so ridiculous she'd be damned if she'd dignify it with an answer. But she didn't bother to hide her impatient disgust. "You ordered

Roderick from Sedgewick, didn't you, Guy?"

"Aye, I'd have put him from here. But there was no need—Roderick made the choice himself."

"No doubt with a great deal of persuasion on your part!"

A hand at her elbow, he dragged her to her feet. "Do you call me a liar, sweet?"

The dangerous glint in his eye did not go unnoticed by Kathryn. "If I am angry," she said, determined to set him straight once and for all, "it is because you showed so little compassion—"

"Compassion?" He sneered openly. "I think not, milady. Indeed, I wonder just how far your noble Roderick would go to be rid of me. What would you say if I told you I very nearly met with an untimely death?" He surveyed her closely, hating the wary suspicion which leaped inside him but unable to still it so easily.

A hand at her throat, Kathryn stared at him, stunned and confused. "What are you saying? That Roderick tried to—" She could hardly bring herself to speak the word aloud. "—to murder you?"

"Yesterday in the forest someone sought to pierce my heart with an arrow. Considering I've had no other attempts on my life of late—" His tone was mocking. "—I think even you can see why Roderick immediately comes to mind, love."

"But Guy, while you and Sir Michael were out hawking, he was here—"

"With you?"

Too late she realized the path she trod. She nodded miserably.

"That hardly absolves him of guilt, Kathryn." His eyes cut into her, like daggers of silver. "No doubt you sought a discreet liaison, safe from the prying eyes of any who might have seen you."

It was a moment before she gleaned his meaning—and then she went cold to the tips of her fingers.

He made a sound of disgust and would have left, but she caught his arm. Beneath her fingers his muscles were rigid and taut, but she doggedly kept her hand in place. "Guy, it was not what you think! We only talked—of Ashbury and Elizabeth, I swear!"

Hard fingers caught at her chin, jerking her face to his. "Be that as it may," he said harshly. "But I ask you this, Kathryn. Did you plot with him against me?"

The words sliced through her like the jagged edge of a knife. She struggled for air, every breath burning like fire. She was well aware Guy didn't love her . . . but did they have so little that Guy could actually believe she would betray him?

Stricken, she stared at him through eyes that stung painfully. The torment in her soul brought agony to her voice. "Is that what you think?"

Her vulnerability stabbed at him. His fingers tightened so that she feared her jaw might snap. Then abruptly, he dropped his hand, wrenching away and plowing a hand through his hair. "I don't know what to think anymore!" he exploded. "By all that is holy, you've had me twisted and tied in knots for months already! And Roderick has never stopped wanting you, Kathryn!"

Kathryn flinched, remembering the day Roderick had arrived—the way he had touched her so boldly. There was a heartbeat of silence—and then another. A weary bleakness descended, like an oppressive cloud of doom. Why did she bother? she wondered achingly. His frigid regard was all-consuming . . . but most of all damning.

"I do not pretend to know his mind!" She pleaded with him mutely, begging him to understand,

to make him see that he was the one she loved—
the only one she had ever loved. "You are my husband," she cried. "I spoke our vows before God and
I would never forsake them, no matter what!"

Every muscle in Guy's body was tense and rigid—he felt as if he were being torn apart inside.
He wanted Kathryn's loyalty—aye, even her love,
especially her love!—yet he knew not if he would
ever have either! And he hated both himself—and
her—for not knowing if he could trust her even if
she swore it were true.

He stared at her, his countenance stark and
unyielding. "You turned to Roderick before,
Kathryn, you cannot deny it! He was the one
you sought, not I! So tell me, Kathryn. Why should
I believe you?"

"Why, indeed," she said bitterly. Suddenly she
was crying, laughing, sobbing, beating her fists
against his chest. "You asked me before if I was
angry . . . aye, I am angry! Angry that you are so
blind. Angry that I must hide all that I feel—"

"And what do you feel, Kathryn?" He trapped
her flailing hands within his, catching her wrists
and dragging her close to stare into her face with
the steely probe of his eyes.

With her hands thus imprisoned, she could not
dash away the salty trickle of tears which seeped
down her cheeks; the taste of despair was bitter
upon her tongue. Even in this he defeated her . . .

All the fight drained from her abruptly. She
longed to shut out the relentless glitter of his
eyes, but she could not. Her breath wavered,
and when she was able to find her voice again,
it emerged as a trembling, broken whisper. "Don't
you know?"

He stared down into eyes as green as the hills of
Wales, misty-bright and suspiciously moist. For an

instant, it was as if he reached clear inside her, all the way into her heart . . .

His own stopped beating, then resumed with thick uneven strokes.

His expression was taut. "Tell me, Kathryn. Tell me what you feel . . . and why you must hide it."

Tears brimmed anew. "Because it's been you all along! You accuse me of dallying with another, when there has been none but you . . . All along it has been you," she cried wildly. Her voice caught painfully, thick with tears both shed and unshed. "I did not want to, but I . . . oh, God! Don't you know that I love you—"

From without came a thunderous pounding on the chamber door. "Milord!" someone shouted.

Guy swore hotly, torn between the trembling woman in his arms and the man at the door. He was sorely tempted to ignore him but the pounding came again.

"Milord! I must speak with you on a matter most urgent!"

Guy spun about, muttering under his breath as he wrenched open the door. Sir Edward and two other knights stood in the hall. Sir Edward stepped forward. "Milord, we've just received a message that Ramsay Keep is under attack!"

"Under attack!" Guy's gaze encompassed the three. "Who are these raiders? Whose pennon do they carry?"

Sir Edward shook his head. "We do not know," he said. "The messenger says he fled under cover of darkness when the siege first began, and thus did not see them." He paused. "Your men-at-arms even now ready themselves in the stable. Will you ride with them, milord?"

Guy's nod was terse. He bitterly cursed the fates for such an untimely intervention. He had no desire to leave his wife's side . . . now or ever again. "Have my destrier saddled," he told Sir Edward. "I'll be down shortly."

The three hurried away. Guy turned to Kathryn, who hovered just a pace behind him. "I have no choice but to go with them," he said grimly.

"I know." A horrible ache gripped her heart, but she masked it with a tremulous smile.

Hands at her waist, he caught her to him almost roughly. "I'll be back as soon as I can, Kathryn. I swear it." There was barely time to nod her assent before his mouth crushed hers. His kiss was fervent and consuming, passionate and tender. Her arms twined about his neck. She clung to him helplessly, wishing desperately that it could go on and on forever, that never again would he have to leave her.

But it was over far too soon . . . and then he was gone.

Moments later she watched him thunder through the gates along with his troops; it was then that an eerie tingle sneaked its way up her spine. She felt suddenly cold as death, despite the cozy warmth of the fire. Try as she might, she could not banish the terrifying sensation that something awful was about to happen . . .

In that, she was right.

Chapter 21

⌒‿⌒

Try as she might, Kathryn could not dispel the notion that something was wrong. Though she sought to reassure herself that all was well—that Guy would soon return home safe and unharmed— the feeling of apprehension remained. She retired to the solar to feed Brenna, while Peter played at her feet. Scarcely an hour had passed since Guy's departure than Kathryn heard the watchman shout—the thunder of hooves followed. She rose and eased Brenna into the cradle, then peered toward the bailey. A groom was leading a dark stallion she didn't recognize into the stable. The rider had already disappeared.

A moment later there was a knock on the door. Gerda opened it and peered within. "Milady, you have a visitor."

Roderick stepped around the girl and across the threshold. Kathryn inhaled sharply, stunned at his appearance. "Roderick! Guy told me you'd gone on to Warwickshire."

Gerda had already quietly withdrawn. A smile twisting his full lips, Roderick raised his brows. "I must speak with you, Kathryn." He glanced at Peter. "Alone," he added pointedly.

Kathryn hesitated. His stance was almost arrogant, his manner overbearing. She paused, then lifted Peter to his feet. "Peter, love, can you be a good lad and go find Gerda?" His lower lip trembled; he was clearly unhappy. Kathryn smiled and tweaked his cheek. "The two of you can ask Cook for one of those fruited honey cakes you liked so well last eve." The boy's face brightened. Kathryn gave him a quick kiss on the forehead and he ran off.

The heavy door closed for the second time. Slowly Kathryn straightened. She did not like the way Roderick eyed her. His regard was avid and bold.

She wet her lips nervously. "I must confess I am surprised you have returned. Why do you not join your men in Warwickshire?"

He shook his head. "I've changed my mind. Instead I return to Ashbury."

His smile sent a prickle of unease winging down the back of her neck. She wished fervently that Gerda had remained, for she had no desire to be alone with Roderick.

She started toward the door. "I'll have someone prepare food and drink," she said stiffly, "but then you must be on your way—"

Ruthless fingers dug into the flesh of her arm. He whirled her around so abruptly that she fell against him. But he did not release her—nay, his arms encircled her. He clamped her tight against his chest, his expression rife with triumph as one hand trespassed over the roundness of her buttocks.

"Roderick!" Kathryn screamed her outrage and slammed her fists against his chest. "I am a married woman! I demand that you cease handling me in this manner and release me at once!"

Unmoved by her struggles, he threw back his

tawny head and laughed. "Ah, love, that's rich, for you will be a widow this very day!" A strange light seemed to burn in his eyes. "But fear not, Kathryn, for I promise I'll not let you remain a widow for long. We'll be wed as soon as I can arrange it."

Kathryn's heart froze. Her hands became as still as her mind. She stared at him blankly. A vague assumption uncurled in her brain—she tried to thrust it away, for it was too horrible to even consider, but there was no help for it.

"What have you done, damn you? Where is Guy?"

His laugh sent a prickle of warning rippling over her skin. "Even now he rides toward death, Kathryn."

Her mouth had gone dry. "Nay!" she cried. "He rides to Ramsay Keep—"

"Ah, but he'll not reach it! He will be attacked most unexpectedly, Kathryn. He and his men will not expect it so soon, you see, and so they will be at their most vulnerable . . . He was lucky the other day in the forest. But this time my men will make certain he does not survive."

A jolt of raw pain ripped through her; her breath came jerkily. "It's a trap—you tricked him!"

"Aye, and so easy it was, too! He did not even suspect that the messenger was one of my own!" Roderick laughed in evil delight.

Guy . . . dead. *Dead.* Nay! Her heart cried out the injustice, even while fury flooded her veins.

She went wild, wrenching from Roderick's hold, pummeling his chest and clawing him. Roderick cursed lewdly when her nails found their mark, tearing into the flesh of his cheek. He shoved her back against the wall with a force that slammed the breath from her lungs.

Huddled against the wall, she struggled for

breath, all the while staring at Roderick furiously, hating him with her glare, damning him with all her soul.

"Why?" she cried bitterly. "Why should you seek to kill him? You have nothing to gain from Guy's death."

"But *you* do, my love." His eyes gleamed when dawning realization widened her own. "Ah, yes, I see you take my meaning. As Guy's widow, you are entitled to one-third of his estates. You'll be one of the wealthiest widows in all of England— and it will all be mine once we are wed!"

"You are mad if you think I will wed my husband's murderer!"

A tawny brow rose high. "You were not so angry when I disposed of your uncle."

Her blood ran cold. The world seemed to blacken and tilt. "Dear God," she said faintly. "It was you—you murdered Uncle!" She shook her head dazedly—this was too much to take in. "I do not understand . . . Guy had already taken possession of Ashbury . . . why would you kill Richard instead?"

"Because I'd not take the chance Richard would interfere later." His expression had turned ugly. "You see, Kathryn, Guy would have been the next to die. With Richard *and* Guy out of the way, Ashbury would have been mine . . . ours! But Guy left before I could execute my plan—and he took you with him. I must admit, for a time I thought there was little hope . . . Ah, but I could have gladly killed the bastard when he married you and granted Ashbury's title to Sir Hugh!" The searing hatred in his eyes frightened her, as did the slow smile he gave her. "But as you can see, it's all turned out so much better than I ever dreamed, for now I'll have so much more than just Ashbury."

Kathryn pressed her back against the wall. "The

night you came here—" She had to force her lips to do her bidding. "—you and your men were not attacked by cutthroats, were you? Your wound . . . it was naught but a ploy."

"I had to gain entrance to Sedgewick somehow. And I could hardly be certain of a hearty welcome by de Marche." His laughter taunted her cruelly. "So little pain," he whispered, "for so much gain."

She tilted her head, fiercely defiant. "And I say again, I'll never marry you, Roderick."

He shrugged. "You loved me once. You'll love me again."

"I never loved you, Roderick—never! I merely sought to use you to gain Ashbury, even as you now seek to use me to gain Guy's lands!"

"Then we are a well-matched pair, are we not?" His look hardened. He crossed to her. "Pack what you need for yourself and your babe. We leave for Ashbury at once, for I dare not be found here lest someone connect me with the earl's slaying. If you are on your way to Ashbury with me when word of his death is received, no one will ever suspect me."

Her dainty chin tipped high. "I'll go nowhere with you," she said clearly. "Not now, nor ever."

His fingers bit into the soft flesh of her arm so brutally she bit back a gasp of pain. Roderick towered over her, his expression tight, his lip curled into a snarl. Menace raged across his features and for an instant Kathryn feared he would strike her. She braced herself, but the dreaded blow was never to fall.

He dropped her arm and spun around. Before she knew what he was about, he had snatched Brenna from her cradle. "Were I you, Kathryn, I'd reconsider." The softness of his voice belied the savage intent on his face. He lowered his gaze;

his bland smile sent chills the length of her. "Your daughter is so tiny and fragile, my love. 'Twould be so easy to snap her neck—to crush the breath from her in but an instant."

Kathryn stared at him in stricken horror. Would he truly rob an innocent child of life? His features bore a look of shuttered indifference—before her was a cold and ruthless killer. She shuddered, no longer doubting that Roderick would do exactly as he said. She had no choice, she realized—no choice but to do as he demanded.

She turned and stuffed clothing into a bundle—she scarce knew what she was doing. A curtain of numbness descended over her when they descended into the great hall. Roderick refused to relinquish Brenna. The infant slept on in his arms, unaware of the turmoil all around her.

Gerda was just coming in from the kitchens. She stopped short, her smooth brow knit in puzzlement as she spied the bundle of clothing Kathryn carried.

"Lady Kathryn," the girl said with concern, "surely you are not leaving!"

Roderick's voice rang out over Kathryn's head. "Aye, but she is," he said coolly. "It has been a long time since Lady Kathryn has seen her sister. She has decided to return with me to Ashbury."

Kathryn could feel Gerda looking at her. She opened her mouth, seeking desperately to convey some sign of her plight that Roderick would overlook—but alas, his grip tightened to a point just short of pain. Her heart beat with pounding fury, yet she dared not say a word.

"But Lady Kathryn—" Gerda was wringing her hands. "—what am I to tell the earl when he returns?"

It was Roderick who answered, a smile dallying

about his lips. "You may tell the earl he need not worry. I will guard his lady's safety as well as my own."

Kathryn's gaze swung sharply to his. Oh, how she longed to smack the insolent smirk from his handsome face! But already he was ushering her from the hall. Outside the stable, Esmerelda and Roderick's horse were already saddled and waiting. A groom assisted her in mounting. Kathryn's lips compressed and she turned to Roderick, holding out her arms for Brenna. For a moment she feared he would refuse; at last he laid the babe in her arms, but his eyes stabbed into hers. Kathryn did not delude herself—he was warning her not to raise the alarm.

The afternoon sun glittered brilliant and golden as they left Sedgewick behind them, but fear enveloped Kathryn's heart like a shroud. Where was Guy now? Did he yet live? Or had the steely tip of some warrior's sword wrenched from him his last gasping breath of life?

Nay! a voice inside her cried. *He yet lives . . .* For she could not bear to think otherwise. She clung to that meager hope, and it was that alone which kept her from plummeting to the depths of despair.

Wordlessly she began to pray for Guy's safety, for the safety of their child . . . She prayed as never before.

"Hold!" Guy flung up his arm and reined his destrier to an abrupt stop. Behind him, the crashing thunder of hooves dwindled as the long column of men and horses behind him came to a standstill.

Sir Michael trotted his horse forward, casting a wary eye beyond his lord toward the encroaching woodland. "Milord?" he queried, drawing up beside Guy. "What is amiss that we halt so soon?"

For a moment Guy said nothing. He could not explain the nagging restlessness within him. He knew only that it grew apace with every step that took him further from Sedgewick . . . and Kathryn.

"I cannot say for certain," Guy said uneasily, "but I am unable to rid myself of the feeling that something is not right."

"How so, milord?"

Something Roderick had said earlier tolled through Guy's mind. *I value my life . . . as you should value yours.* Only now did he perceive it for the threat it may have well been . . .

"Roderick left only this morning," he told Michael. "In but a matter of hours we received a message that Ramsay Keep is under siege. I know that is the way of raiders—to attack with the element of surprise in their favor. Yet now that I think on it, it seems almost a little too . . . convenient."

Sir Michael rubbed his chin, his expression now as troubled as his lord's. "You think this summons was meant to lure you away from Sedgewick?"

Only now did Guy fervently wish he'd left more troops in place at Sedgewick. The thought of Kathryn alone there with only a skeleton force to defend her kindled a tingling of unease deep in his gut.

"I do not know," he said grimly. "But I mean to find out."

"You mean to return to Sedgewick, milord?"

"Aye. And Michael, I wish for you to escort these men the rest of the way to Ramsay Keep. If all is well there, we have lost nothing. If not, my troops are in your hands to lead in battle as you see fit. Guard yourself well against a trap, my friend."

Michael drew himself up very straight. He was aware of the responsibility Guy had placed on his shoulders; false alarm or no, Guy was not a man to entrust another with so great a task. He felt oddly humbled, knowing the earl trusted him as he had trusted few others. "I'll not fail you, milord," he promised.

Guy left a billowing cloud of dust in his wake.

It was his most fervent prayer that when at last he arrived back at Sedgewick, all would be as before. Kathryn would be presiding over the evening meal in his absence—or mayhap tending to Brenna in their chamber. He pictured the tender scene that might greet him—Kathryn enthralled and smiling at the babe, while Brenna supped at her mother's breast, kneading the ivory fullness with a tiny fist.

But he found the great hall at Sedgewick nearly deserted. Guy strode toward the stairs, taking them two at a time.

Nor was Kathryn in her chamber—*their* chamber. He advanced within, idly picking up the gauzy folds of a wimple and bringing it to his lips, inhaling deeply. The scent of Kathryn's hair still clung to it, flowery and sweet and fragrant. He imagined he could feel it flowing through his fingers, thick and lustrous and silky . . . *Where was she?* A flicker of disquiet took root inside him, for it was then that he noted Brenna did not sleep peacefully in her cradle either. Indeed, it was quiet as a tomb . . .

He whirled, a slight rustle at the door catching his attention. Gerda stood there, her hands gathered tightly at her waist. Guy's eyes narrowed, for he did not imagine her wide-eyed dismay.

"Where is Lady Kathryn?"

Gerda hesitated. The leap of fear in her eyes gave her away—Guy knew then the answer to his question. There was a sharp, dagger-like twinge in his chest that he refused to acknowledge as pain. A stab of anger pierced through the hurt, and then a violent rage erupted inside him. The delicate material of her wimple rent in two beneath the pressure of his powerful hands. He flung it aside and turned to Gerda.

"By all the saints!" he ground out furiously. "She's gone, isn't she? And taken Brenna along with her!"

Gerda opened her mouth but he gave her no chance to speak.

"I suppose I need not ask if she's gone to Ashbury!"

Gerda winced, for his anger was a terrible sight to behold. "Milord," she began shakily, "not long after you and your troops departed, Roderick returned here alone and—"

"Roderick, that bloody bastard! She left with him?" When Gerda nodded miserably, he swore vilely from between clenched teeth. He would have spun and stalked from the room but Gerda latched onto his arm.

"Milord!" she cried. "Will you not go after her?"

"Aye!" he thundered, while Gerda quailed beneath a glare of fearsome intensity. "I'll have my daughter back but I'll be damned if I'll take the mother. I do not know if it's Roderick she wants or Ashbury—but either way she has made her choice for the last time, and by God, she shall live with it!"

Gerda began to weep. "But it is not what you think, milord! Aye, she left for Ashbury because of Sir Roderick, but I cannot believe she left willingly! Oh, milord, she cares naught for Roderick. This I know with all my heart and—and you should, too!"

Gerda could not have known the pain she wrought, for within Guy's breast a fierce and tumultuous battle was being waged. He shut his eyes, feeling as if he were being ripped apart inside. How, he wondered bitterly, with his heart so full of pain and distrust, could he still love Kathryn?

Fool! taunted a voice inside. Was it any wonder that she harbored no tenderness toward him? He had wrested her away from all she held dear. He had toyed with her, stolen her innocence and taken her to him, heedless of her wishes. He had not cherished her tenderly, as a wife deserved to be cherished and adored. Instead, he was ever suspicious, ever wary. There had been so much bitterness between them, so much distrust, he thought bleakly . . . Everything within him cried out in anguish. Mother of Christ! Did his own wife truly wish him dead?

Gerda tugged frantically on his arm. "Oh, milord, you judge her too harshly and far too quickly! God forgive me for speaking so to you, but how can you not see all that you are to her? She would never willingly seek another man—not Roderick or any other!"

His eyes opened. He stared at her mutely. In the far reaches of his mind he recalled how Kathryn, too, had accused him of being blind . . . Her image danced before him, her eyes huge and pleading, silently beseeching, all that she felt nakedly exposed. And again he heard her desperate cry.

Oh, God . . . Don't you know that I love you!

He despised the voice inside that reminded him she had deceived him before—still another refuted it. But his heart remembered. His heart knew . . . Kathryn was strong and fiery, so rebellious and mutinous. She would curse and battle him to the ends of the earth before she would ever yield or surrender. And never—never!—would she swear love so lightly . . . A fierce exultation shot through him. Suddenly, despite his doubts and fears, Guy was very very certain he would have known had she lied . . .

She loved him. *She loved him.*

Gerda wept openly. "Oh, please, you must go after her and bring her and the babe home again, for I say again, milord, something was not right! She said nary a word before they left. She was pale and subdued and . . . oh, it was almost as if she were afraid. And Lady Kathryn is never afraid, milord, never!"

No, Guy thought slowly. Or if she were, she was not one to show it . . . All at once he went pale as linen. Was it true then? Had Roderick coerced Kathryn into leaving with him? For all that she was fierce and defiant, she did not possess the physical strength of a man.

In that moment, Guy knew fear as he'd never known fear before.

He spoke quickly. "How long ago did they leave, Gerda?"

"Several hours ago. If you hurry, milord, mayhap you can catch them before nightfall." Gerda choked back a sob, her voice frantic. "Oh, I will never forgive myself if anything happens to them! I wanted to send someone after them but I feared what Sir Roderick might do if he realized he was being followed!"

"You did the right thing, Gerda." He patted her shoulder awkwardly, then strode down the hallway, his mind racing. Roderick was several hours ahead of him. But he could hardly set a breakneck pace for Ashbury. Having Brenna along, he thought, would slow Roderick's speed considerably . . .

His bellow for his destrier shook the rafters.

No sound could have been more dear to Gerda's ears.

Roderick was in no particular hurry; he was convinced the time for haste had passed. Indeed, he was feeling immensely proud of himself. By now his plans had been launched and executed—the trap had been well and truly sprung! His men would not fail him—they did not dare for fear of forfeiting their own lives. The Earl of Sedgewick could not have survived the fray.

His enemy was dead and no longer posed a threat.

So it was that when Kathryn pleaded to stop for the night he did not argue. He led them to a sheltered clearing behind a bluff which shielded them from the night breeze. Roderick dismounted and reached for her. Kathryn stiffened and suffered his touch while he lifted her down, but the instant her slippers touched the ground she jerked away.

Roderick laughed, a sound that set her teeth on edge. "You'll come to me soon enough, I vow."

She gritted her teeth and presented him with her back, marching toward a tall oak tree. She lowered herself to the damp earth and settled herself against the rough bark to watch while Roderick built a fire and set out a meal of bread and cheese. Though she had no stomach for it, she forced herself to eat and drink, knowing she would need her strength. Her arms ached from holding Brenna for so long but she'd not give her babe over to Roderick no matter what! She had barely finished her crust of bread than Brenna began to squirm and cry fretfully. Kathryn tried to soothe her but it was no use.

Roderick's lips pulled over his teeth in a nasty smile. "What ails her, milady?"

Kathryn's lips tightened—as if he did not know! "She's hungry!" she snapped.

He leered openly, refusing to grant her the privacy he knew she craved. Brenna's cries had turned to screams which reached an ear-shattering pitch. Directing a scathing glance at Roderick, Kathryn turned aside and fumbled with her kirtle. Brenna's wails ceased abruptly as she latched onto her mother's nipple. The babe was bundled well to guard against the cold. Kathryn tugged on a corner of a woolen blanket in an effort to shield herself, but even then she felt invaded by Roderick's hated regard.

Her hand cradled the soft dark fuzz that covered Brenna's head. A painful tightness crept around her chest, threatening to choke her. Guy, she thought piercingly. Did he yet live? Or did he lay sprawled upon the damp, bare earth, his heart still and silent? She inhaled sharply, for the thought pained her. She could not bear to think him dead and so she must believe that he still lived.

She raged inwardly, torn between helpless despair and a bittersweet hope. She loved him, but she knew not if he had believed her! Oh, if only she had told him days ago—weeks ago! What would happen when he returned to Sedgewick and discovered her gone? She trembled to think of it. What if he were convinced she had deserted him—that she had gone willingly with Roderick? He would hate her—despise her as never before. Mayhap he would not even come after her . . .

Yet all that mattered was that he be spared. A silent litany poured through her, over and over, as she beseeched and pleaded with her maker. She would gladly forfeit her own life—if only Guy was alive, if only he could somehow escape Roderick's treachery.

Darkness fell while she nursed Brenna, and with it an air of impending doom. Roderick drank freely from a skin of ale. Kathryn watched uneasily, dreading the moment when Brenna slept again.

Suddenly he threw back his head and laughed. The guttural sound sent a jolt through her. She raised her chin and met his brazen stare. "You appear well satisfied with yourself," she observed tightly.

"Mayhap because I am, for soon I will have all I ever wanted and more," he boasted. "Sedgewick is grand indeed, don't you agree, love? Aye, and mayhap someday we'll even have Ashbury back. You'd like that, wouldn't you?"

"Marrying me may gain you lands, but it will not gain you Sedgewick Hall. You forget Guy already has an heir!"

"Aye," he agreed mildly. "But for how long?"

He laughed again, a sound that sent eerie tingles along her skin. At first Kathryn could not fathom why . . . Then icy fingers of dread plied their way the length of her spine. Stricken, she stared at him numbly. Dear God, it wasn't enough that he had murdered Richard and sought to murder Guy—he intended to kill Peter, too! And for what? Her stomach heaved and churned. For land and power and wealth. He cared naught about her—she was but a tool to help him attain his goal. It sickened her to realize that, in her own way, she was nearly as guilty as he. All those months before her marriage, she had thought of nothing but reclaiming Ashbury for herself and Elizabeth—it mattered not that it was for love of home and family. Like Roderick, her motives had been selfish . . . but no more. *No more.*

Her heart pounded a rampant rhythm. She lowered her head so he would not glimpse her intent. She had to stop him, but how? Her beleaguered mind could form no clear-cut plan.

Roderick spoke, his tone cold. "Put her down, milady—" He nodded at Brenna, who had fallen asleep. "—for if you do not, I will. And in my haste to claim you, I cannot promise I will be gentle with her."

Just the thought of him touching her made her skin crawl. But she did as he demanded, laying Brenna on a small pile of furs between two trees.

She rose slowly, delaying the inevitable as long as possible. She knew he meant to bed her—his desire was plainly writ in the glitter of his eyes. Never had she decried her womanhood more than at this moment. She feared there was little she could do to stop him, for her strength was as nothing compared to his—and there was Brenna to think of. The thought of his possessing her disgusted her, but she dared to hope she could flee afterward in the dead of night, while he slept. If she were to escape, she could rally Guy's men . . . if there were any left after Roderick's butchery.

He strode to where she stood, yanking her hard against his chest. He bent his head to seek the sweetness of her mouth but she flung her head back, straining from him in a futile attempt to escape his hold.

"What is this?" he sneered. "You met my kisses eagerly enough once before, Kathryn."

"That was before I had known the touch of my husband. You can take my body—I can do little to stop you. But know this, Roderick. My heart belongs to Guy! And only he can stir me, Roderick—not you, never you!"

"He was never half the man I am!"

Kathryn taunted him with a soft laugh. "Surely you jest! Why, you are naught but a coward! You murdered Richard while he slept! And you feared facing Guy in battle. You left him to your men because you feared defeat."

His arms tightened so that she was half-afraid he would snap her spine in half. Anger transformed his features into an ugly mask. His voice deepened to a raging snarl. "By God, woman, you've the

tongue of a shrew. I wonder that Guy has not cast
you off long ago!" he jeered. "Mayhap I shall be the
one to cast you off, eh? If you are wise, Kathryn,
you'll try hard to please me, lest I decide you and
your brat are not worth the trouble."

His mouth came down on hers, searing and wet.
His breath, sour and hot, nearly made her gag. With
a twist of his body, he tumbled her hard to the
ground. She fought wildly, arms and legs flailing,
seeking to pummel him with her fists. He caught
her wrists and clamped them above her head, his
grip savage and merciless. His weight was like a
pile of stone atop her chest so that she could scarcely breathe. She gasped for much-needed air and he
pounced. The pressure of his mouth parted her lips
cruelly. He violated the silken interior of her mouth
with rapacious strokes of his tongue. Kathryn gave
a choked little scream and bit down hard.

He jerked away, falling back upon his knees
though he continued to straddle her. The blazing
fury of his gaze fell full upon her as he touched a
hand to his lip; it came away bloody.

"You vicious little bitch!" His lips flattened
against his teeth in a feral snarl. His bloodied
hand raised high, balling into a huge fist. Kathryn
braced herself. Mayhap it was better this way, she
thought dimly. If he beat her senseless, perchance
she'd be lucky enough to remember little of his
assault . . .

The blow never fell.

His weight was plucked from her, like a bird
from its nest. Hauled to his feet, Roderick's jaw
sagged in bewildered astonishment. Kathryn jolted
upright with a cry of joy—Guy was here! He was
not dead!

But in the instant between one breath and the
next, her cry became one of horror. Roderick leaped

across the fire and snatched up his sword, whirling to face Guy.

"You claim what is mine for the last time, Roderick. And I have no need of a weapon to kill you." Guy's words were a silken taunt. "You will meet your death with naught but my bare hands." He ripped his sword from its scabbard and tossed it aside.

But Roderick did not meet his challenge. He merely retained his grip on his sword and smiled, an evil, cunning smile.

Kathryn began to tremble; panic raced through her. Mother of Christ! Was Guy mad? Unarmed, with no weapon, how could he defend himself?

But she had forgotten . . . Guy was a warrior, all power and grace, his muscles splendidly atuned to his every need, his reflexes quick and instinctive. When Roderick barreled forward, blade upraised, Guy had only to step neatly aside. His laughter only enraged Roderick all the more.

"What, Roderick! Have you consumed too much ale this night?"

"You bastard!" Roderick bellowed. "Ale or no, I'll see you dead at my feet!"

Kathryn snatched up Brenna and ran to the edge of the clearing. Sheltering her babe in her arms, she looked on, her heart beating high in her throat. Roderick's rage made him reckless. His face contorted and ugly, he stomped and weaved back and forth, slashing and slicing while Guy continued to spin and elude him, taking him further from the firelight and into the shadowed woodland. Only then did she guess Guy's ploy—if Roderick could not see he could not strike out.

The moon slid out from behind a cloud, casting an eerie halo of light all around. Kathryn cried out sharply as Roderick rushed savagely forward.

Kathryn thought surely she would faint when Guy stood his ground, as though he welcomed the blow that would strike him dead. But at the last instant he leaped aside. His boot lashed up and out, knocking the sword from Roderick's grip. It flew high and away, end over end until it landed far distant.

A bloodcurdling howl erupted from Roderick's chest. Fingers curled and outstretched, like the claws of some hideous demon, he lunged for Guy's throat.

Guy's fist hit him in his gut and felled him to his knees. Guy half-turned, his chest heaving, searching frantically for Kathryn. He did not see Roderick lurch to his feet and reach inside his boot.

But Kathryn did. She gave a strangled scream. "Guy! Behind you!"

Guy whirled and flung up an arm to ward off the attack; the dagger sliced a bloody furrow in his shoulder. He lost his balance and fell backward. Roderick followed him down and she heard the thud of bodies upon the ground. Then suddenly they were both rolling and twisting in the dirt, grappling for control of the dagger. Kathryn had one terrifying glimpse of Roderick atop Guy, the dagger raised high, and then the veil of darkness was no longer friend but foe as the moon slipped behind a cloud once more.

Terror clogged her throat as she strained to see. There was a heaving grunt, followed by a horrible gurgling sound . . .

Then all was quiet.

Chapter 22

The silence was more terrifying than all that had gone before.

Through the darkness, the shadowed outline of a man staggered upright. The body of the other lay sprawled on the ground. Kathryn's heart seemed to stop beating. Her worst fear took hold and blotted out all else. She imagined she could see the stain on Guy's breast spreading like a crimson river.

"Guy!" It was a cry of anguish, a scream of pain. Brenna awoke and began to wail piteously. Kathryn's eyes closed as she clutched the babe tighter to her breast. Jagged sobs tore from deep inside her.

Strong hands closed about her shoulders. Exhausted, his breathing heavy and belabored, Guy dragged her against him, burying his face in the fragrant cloud of her hair. A low, tortured whisper rushed past her ear.

"Hush, sweet. Do not cry so. 'Tis over and done."

He was alive—Guy was alive!

She began to tremble. "I thought you were dead," she choked out, over and over. "Oh, Guy, I thought you were dead!"

His heart twisted. She was shaking, he realized, and suddenly so was he. "I assure you, love, I am alive and well—and heartily glad to be so."

"He murdered Richard—Guy, it was Roderick who murdered Richard. And you were right all along! He sought to have you killed that day in the forest. And the messenger from Ramsay was one of his own men—there were no raiders! It was a trap to lure you from Sedgewick—he had a party of men lying in wait to kill you!"

"I suspected as much," Guy said grimly. "That's why I returned to Sedgewick."

Her breath caught at the tension that gripped his rugged features. Tears streamed down her cheeks as she raised her face to his. "He forced me to leave with him," she cried. "He said he would kill Brenna if I did not. Guy, I—I did not aid him in this treachery, I swear!" She wept brokenly. "I did not betray you—I *would* not! Oh, Guy, I beg of you, you must believe me. I would never leave you . . . never . . . I love you far too much . . ."

Her desperation gouged at him, even as a rush of emotion crowded his chest. He could feel her against him, quivering as if she were weak and frail. But weak and frail she was not, he thought achingly. She was strong and so very, very proud— yet here she was, casting heart and soul before him . . .

With his muscular arms, he tugged her closer still, smiling a little at Brenna's indignant mewl. But he was not satisfied until Kathryn's heart beat hard against his . . . and his against hers. With his mouth he stifled her halting entreaty.

"Nay, wench," he said against lips gone slack in surprise and wonder, "you'll not leave me again . . . for you are right where you belong."

Kathryn was not sure she dared speculate on his meaning . . . But throughout the long ride home, hope beat in Kathryn's heart like the fluttering wings of a butterfly. They spoke but little, both anxious to be safely within the walls of Sedgewick once again.

They had scarcely passed through the gates than Sir Michael and the rest of Guy's men returned as well. It seemed that shortly after Guy had departed for Sedgewick, they had ridden straight into an ambush. Luckily, they were on guard and prepared for such an attack. Only two of Guy's men had been wounded, neither mortally.

Kathryn shuddered to think how close Guy had come to death—not once this night, but twice. Thankfully the gash on his shoulder was only a flesh wound.

While Guy heard further news of the battle in the great hall, Kathryn nursed Brenna back to sleep upstairs. Easing the infant into her cradle, she moved silently down the passage to check on Peter. The boy was asleep, one small hand tucked under his chin. Her expression soft, she bent low and pressed a kiss on his cheek. As she returned to her chamber and settled down to await Guy, her thoughts strayed inevitably to the woman who had been Peter's mother . . .

Elaine. Her heart filled with sad yearning. She could feel no envy, if indeed she ever had, for poor Elaine would never again stand at her husband's side; she would not see her son grow sturdy and tall as the oak trees which grew by the stream . . . The door swung open.

It was Guy. Hazy firelight flickered over the striking symmetry of face and form. For the span of a heartbeat, he was bathed in golden silhouette, a presence so commanding and handsome he robbed her of breath.

He paused several paces distant. "You look so

troubled," he murmured. "The danger is over, Kathryn. You need not worry any longer."

Her courage was elusive at best; she spoke quickly before she lost what little she had. "I was thinking about Elaine." She swallowed bravely and went on, her voice scarcely audible. "You loved her very much, didn't you?"

She saw him go very still. She remained poised on the edge of the bench, afraid to look at him, just as afraid not to.

It was love of Elaine that had driven Guy to Ashbury to seek vengeance for her death. Kathryn did not begrudge him the love they had shared— she truly did not! But all at once she wondered . . . Had time healed the wound in his heart, the bitter emptiness in his soul? She prayed that it had, for she could not bear it were it not so!

Yet still he said nothing, and the silence scraped her nerves. Just when she was certain she could stand it no longer, he held out a hand.

"Come here," he said simply.

Kathryn rose, her legs so unsteady she feared they would crumple beneath her. His fingers closed about hers, hard and warm and strong. He tugged her to stand directly before him.

"Aye," he said slowly. "I loved Elaine very much."

Raw pain throbbed in her breast. All at once Kathryn was unprepared to deal with such honesty. "Nay, love, do not turn from me," he said quickly, dragging her against him when she would have twisted away.

"Please, Guy—" She gave a choked little cry and would have buried her face in the hair-roughened hollow of his throat but he would not let her. A lean hand splayed against the small of her back, molding her close against his hips. With the other he threaded his fingers in her hair and pulled her head back so that she had no choice but to face him.

"Listen to me, sweet. Aye, I loved Elaine." His voice was very low. He bestowed on her a gaze of scorching intensity, his own eyes lighting to a smoldering flame. "But 'tis you, Kathryn, you who command my heart as no woman ever has—" His voice went lower still. "—as no other ever will."

The words washed through her. Kathryn stared. Tears stung her eyes but she scarcely noticed. Her lips moved but no sound came out. Guy arched a brow in utterly wicked amusement. "What are you saying?" She drew a shaky breath, her lips trembling. "That you . . . that you love me?"

He bent so that his lips just grazed hers. "Aye," he whispered. "I love you, Kathryn."

A rush of emotion swept through her, rendering her dizzy and weak from the force of it. Everything inside her came all undone. Her cry of joy quickly became a watery sob. She could do naught but cling to him, overwhelmed and awed.

Words poured forth unbidden, her voice husky and shaky. "Oh, Guy, I—I love you, too," she cried. "I loved you long ago . . . even when I hated you for making me love you . . . I did not want to, but I could not stop it . . . and then I was terrified you could never come to love me in return . . ."

Her eyes were huge and glistening. She sought to blink back the betraying moisture but it was no use. Her eyes brimmed and overflowed. Guy skimmed the salty heat from her cheeks with the pads of his thumbs; he had not expected tears. With infinite gentleness, he lowered his head and kissed them away, one by one.

"Never doubt that I love you," he whispered. "Before you came into my life, I feared winter's cold would forever reign within me. But you have brought fire and the warmth of summer and driven away the wintry chill in my heart, sweet." The intensity of his tone shook her anew. "By all that is holy, I swear I love you more with every beat of my heart."

Kathryn smiled through her tears, a brilliantly sweet smile. "At times," she teased, "the only thing I fire is your temper."

"True," he conceded with a crooked grin. "You are obstinate and defiant and prickly as a rose." His laughter faded; he was suddenly intent.

" 'Tis not in spite of those things that I love you," he said quietly. " 'Tis because of them, for I love you as you are, Kathryn, no matter how stubborn and willful you are—" His eyes darkened. "—and I would have you no other way."

Both his look and his tone rocked her to her core. There were no ghosts between them now, she thought wonderingly—not Elaine, not Roderick, not even Richard. They were both free to love as they would . . . She twined her arms about his neck with a low moan and offered the tempting sweetness of her lips. Guy fed greedily, his kiss hungry and tender, gentle and fierce.

With a groan he lifted her and carried her to their bed, where passion's fury wrapped them in splendor.

It was only when Kathryn lay peaceful and replete in the shelter of Guy's arms that she realized . . . Nearly a twelvemonth had passed since Guy had brought her to Sedgewick. She remembered how heartbroken she had been that he had forced her to leave Elizabeth and Ashbury.

But Elizabeth and Hugh were happy—she knew it with all her heart. And Ashbury . . . well, she had once been certain that Ashbury was her whole world—that without it, she had nothing.

A secret smile curved her lips. How wrong she had been—and how foolish.

Because here in Guy's arms, she had discovered something far more precious, far more lasting than a jutting pile of stone and timber. Guy loved her— and she loved him. And in loving him she hadn't lost a part of herself at all . . .

She'd found the other half.

Avon Romances—
the best in exceptional authors and unforgettable novels!